TALES OF THE MYSTERIOUS
AND MACABRE

TALES OF THE MYSTERIOUS

AND MACABRE

by

ALGERNON BLACKWOOD

SPRING BOOKS
LONDON · NEW YORK · SYDNEY · TORONTO

This edition first published 1967 by
The Hamlyn Publishing Group Limited
London · New York · Sydney · Toronto
Hamlyn House, Feltham, Middlesex, England

5th Impression 1972

Printed in Czechoslovakia by Tisk Brno

ISBN 0 600 03867 X

51620/5

CONTENTS

CHINESE MAGIC

Dr. Owen Francis felt a sudden wave of pleasure and admiration sweep over him as he saw her enter the room. He was in the act of going out; in fact, he had already said good-bye to his hostess, glad to make his escape from the chattering throng, when the tall and graceful young woman glided past him. Her carriage was superb; she had black eyes with a twinkling happiness in them; her mouth was exquisite. Round her neck, in spite of the warm afternoon, she wore a soft thing of fur or feathers; and as she brushed by to shake the hand he had just shaken himself, the tail of this touched his very cheek. Their eyes met fair and square. He felt as though her eyes also touched him.

Changing his mind, he lingered another ten minutes, chatting with various ladies he did not in the least remember, but who remembered him. He did not, of course, desire to exchange banalities with these other ladies, yet did so gallantly enough. If they found him absent-minded, they excused him since he was the famous mental specialist whom everybody was proud to know. And all the time his eyes never left the tall graceful figure that allured him almost to the point of casting a spell upon him.

His first impression deepened as he watched. He was aware of excitement, curiosity, longing; there was a touch even of exaltation in him; yet he took no steps to seek the introduction which was easily enough procurable. He checked himself, if with an effort. Several times their eyes met across the crowded room; he dared to believe—he felt instinctively—that his interest was returned. Indeed, it was more than instinct, for she was certainly aware of his presence, and he even caught her indicating him to a woman she spoke with, and evidently asking who he was. Once he half bowed, and once, in spite of himself, he went so far as to smile, and there came, he was sure, a faint, delicious brightening of the eyes in answer.

7

CHINESE MAGIC

There was he fancied, a look of yearning in the face. The young woman charmed him inexpressibly; the very way she moved delighted him. Yet at last he slipped out the room without a word, without an introduction, without even knowing her name. He chose his moment when her back was turned. It was characteristic of him.

For Owen Francis had ever regarded marriage, for himself at least, as a disaster that could be avoided. He was in love with his work, and his work was necessary to humanity. Others might perpetuate the race, but he must heal it. He had come to regard love as the bait wherewith Nature lays her trap to fulfil her own ends. A man in love was a man enjoying a delusion, a deluded man. In his case, and he was nearing forty-five, the theory had worked admirably, and the dangerous exception that proved it had as yet not troubled him.

'It's come at last—I do believe,' he thought to himself, as he walked home, a new tumultuous emotion in his blood; 'the exception, quite possibly, has come at last. I wonder....'

And it seemed he said it to the tall graceful figure by his side, who turned up dark eyes smilingly to meet his own, and whose lips repeated softly his last two words 'I wonder....'

The experience, being new to him, was baffling. A part of his nature, long dormant, received the authentic thrill that pertains actually to youth. He was a man of chaste, abstemious custom. The reaction was vehement. That dormant part of him became obstreperous. He thought of his age, his appearance, his prospects; he looked thirty-eight, he was not unhandsome, his position was secure, even remarkable. That gorgeous young woman—he called her gorgeous—haunted him. Never could he forget that face, those eyes. It was extraordinary—he had left her there unspoken to, unknown, when an introduction would have been the simplest thing in the world.

'But it still is,' he reflected. And the reflection filled his being with a flood of joy.

He checked himself again. Not so easily is established habit routed. He felt instinctively that, at last, he had met his mate; if he followed it up, he was a man in love, a lost man enjoying a delusion, a deluded man. But the way she had looked at him! That air of intuitive invitation which not even the sweetest modesty could conceal! He felt an immense confidence in himself; also he felt oddly sure of her.

The presence of that following figure, already precious, came with him into his house, even into his study at the back where he sat over a number of letters by the open window. The pathetic little London garden showed its pitiful patch. The lilac had faded, but a smell of roses entered. The sun was just behind the buildings opposite, and the garden lay soft and warm in summer shadows.

He read and tossed aside the letters; one only interested him, from Edward Farque, whose journey to China had interrupted a friendship of long standing. Edward Farque's work on Eastern art and philosophy, on Chinese painting and Chinese thought in particular, had made its mark. He was an authority. He was to be back about this time, and his friend smiled with pleasure. ' "Dear old unpractical dreamer," as I used to call him,' he mused. 'He's a success, anyhow!' And as he mused the presence that sat beside him came a little closer, yet at the same time faded. Not that he forgot her—that was impossible— but that just before opening the letter from his friend he had come to a decision. He had definitely made up his mind to seek acquaintance. The reality replaced the remembered substitute.

'As the newspapers may have warned you' [ran the familiar and kinky writing], 'I am back in England after what the scribes term my ten years of exile in Cathay. I have taken a little house in Hampstead for six months, and am just settling in. Come to us to-morrow night and let me prove it to you. Come to dinner. We shall have much to say; we both are ten years wiser. You know how glad I shall be to see my old-time critic and disparager, but let me add frankly that I want to ask you a few professional, or, rather, technical, questions. So prepare yourself to come as doctor and as friend. I am writing, as the papers said truthfully, a treatise on Chinese thought. But—don't shy!—it is about Chinese Magic that I want your technical advice' [the last two words were substituted for "professional wisdom", which had been crossed out] 'and the benefit of your vast experience. So come, old friend, come quickly, and come hungry! I'll feed your body as you shall feed my mind.

YOURS,

EDWARD FARQUE

'P.S.—The coming of a friend from a far-off land—is not this true joy?'

Dr. Francis laid down the letter with a pleased anticipatory chuckle, and it was the touch in the final sentence that amused him. In spite of being an authority, Farque was clearly the same fanciful, poetic dreamer as of old. He quoted Confucius as in other days. The firm but kinky writing had not altered either. The only sign of novelty he noticed was the use of scented paper, for a faint and pungent aroma clung to the big quarto sheet.

'A Chinese habit, doubtless,' he decided, sniffing it with a puzzled air of disapproval. Yet it had nothing in common with the scented sachets some ladies use too lavishly, so that even the air of the street is polluted by their passing for a dozen yards. He was familiar with every kind of perfumed note-paper used in London, Paris, and Constantinople. This one was different. It was delicate and penetrating for all its faintness, pleasurable too. He rather liked it, and while annoyed that he could not name it, he sniffed at the letter several times, as though it were a flower.

'I'll go,' he decided at once, and wrote an acceptance then and there. He went out and posted it. He meant to prolong his walk into the Park, taking his chief preoccupation, the face, the eyes, the figure, with him. Already he was composing the note of inquiry to Mrs. Malleson, his hostess of the tea-party, the note whose willing answer should give him the name, the address, the means of introduction he had now deteremined to

10

secure. He visualized that note of inquiry, seeing it in his mind's eye; only, for some odd reason, he saw the kinky writing of Farque instead of his own more elegant script. Association of ideas and emotions readily explained this. Two new and unexpected interests had entered his life on the same day, and within half an hour of each other. What he could not so readily explain, however, was that two words in his friend's ridiculous letter, and in that kinky writing, stood out sharply from the rest. As he slipped his envelope into the mouth of the red pillar-box they shone vividly in his mind. These two words were 'Chinese Magic.'

II

It was the warmth of his friend's invitation as much as his own state of inward excitement that decided him suddenly to anticipate his visit by twenty-four hours. It would clear his judgment and help his mind if he spent the evening at Hampstead rather than alone with his own thoughts. 'A dose of China,' he thought, with a smile, 'will do me good. Edward won't mind. I'll telephone.'

He left the Park soon after six o'clock and acted upon his impulse. The connexion was bad, the wire buzzed and popped and crackled; talk was difficult; he did not hear properly. The Professor had not yet come in, apparently. Francis said he would come up anyhow on the chance.

'Velly pleased,' said the voice in his ear, as he rang off.

Going into his study, he drafted the note that should result in the introduction that was now, it appeared, the chief object of his life. The way this woman with the black, twinkling eyes obsessed him was—he admitted it with joy—extraordinary. The draft he put in his pocket, intending to rewrite it next morning, and all the way up to Hampstead Heath the gracious figure glided silently beside him, the eyes were ever present, his cheek still glowed where the feather boa had touched his skin. Edward Farque remained in the background. In fact, it was on the very door-step, having rung the bell, that Francis

11

realised he must pull himself together. 'I've come to see old Farque,' he reminded himself, with a smile. 'I've got to be interested in him and his, and, probably, for an hour or two, to talk Chinese——' when the door opened noiselessly, and he saw facing him, with a grin of celestial welcome on his yellow face, a Chinaman.

'Oh!' he said, with a start. He had not expected a Chinese servant.

'Velly pleased,' the man bowed him in.

Dr Francis stared round him with astonishment he could not conceal. A great golden idol faced him in the hall, its gleaming visage blazing out of a sort of miniature golden palanquin, with a grin, half dignified, half cruel. Fully double human size, it blocked the way, looking so life-like that it might have moved to meet him without too great a shock to what seemed possible. It rested on a throne with four massive legs, carved, the doctor saw, with serpents, dragons, and mythical monsters generally. Round it on every side were other things in keeping. Name them he could not, describe them he did not try. He summed them up in one word—China: pictures, weapons, cloths and tapestries, bells, gongs, and figures of every sort and kind imaginable.

Being ignorant of Chinese matters, Dr. Francis stood and looked about him in a mental state of some confusion. He had the feeling that he had entered a Chinese temple, for there was a faint smell of incense hanging about the house that was, to say the least, un-English. Nothing English, in fact, was visible at all. The matting on the floor, the swinging curtains of bamboo beads that replaced the customary doors, the silk draperies and pictured cushions, the bronze and ivory, the screens hung with fantastic embroideries, everything was Chinese. Hampstead vanished from his thoughts. The very lamps were in keeping, the ancient lacquered furniture as well. The value of what he saw, an expert could have told him, was considerable.

'You likee?' queried the voice at his side.

He had forgotten the servant. He turned sharply.

'Very much; it's wonderfully done,' he said. 'Makes you feel at home, John, eh?' he added tactfully, with a smile, and was going to ask how long all this preparation had taken, when a voice sounded on the stairs beyond. It was a voice he knew, a note of hearty welcome in its deep tones.

'The coming of a friend from a far-off land, even from Harley Street—is not this true joy?' he heard, and the next minute was shaking the hand of his old and valued friend. The intimacy between them had always been of the truest.

'I almost expected a pigtail,' observed Francis, looking him affectionately up and down, 'but, really—why, you've hardly changed at all!'

'Outwardly, not as much, perhaps, as Time expects,' was the happy reply, 'but inwardly——!' He scanned appreciatively the burly figure of the doctor in his turn. 'And I can say the same of you,' he declared, still holding his hand tight. 'This is a real pleasure, Owen,' he went on in his deep voice; 'to see you again is a joy to me. Old friends meeting again—there's nothing like it in life, I believe, nothing.' He gave the hand another squeeze before he let it go. 'And we,' he added, leading the way into a room across the hall, 'neither of us is a fugitive from life. We take what we can, I mean.'

The doctor smiled as he noted the un-English turn of language, and together they entered a sitting-room that was, again, more like some inner chamber of a Chinese temple than a back room in a rented Hampstead house.

'I only knew ten minutes ago that you were coming, my dear fellow,' the scholar was saying, as his friend gazed round him with increased astonishment, 'or I would have prepared more suitably for your reception. I was out till late. All this' —he waved his hand— 'surprises you, of course, but the fact is I have been home some days already, and most of what you see was arranged for me in advance of my arrival. Hence its apparent completion. I say "apparent," because, actually, it is far from faithfully carried out. Yet to exceed,' he added, 'is as bad as to fall short.'

The doctor watched him while he listened to a somewhat

13

lengthy explanation of the various articles surrounding them. The speaker—he confirmed his first impression—had changed little during the long interval; the same enthusiasm was in him as before, the same fire and dreaminess alternately in the fine grey eyes, the same humour and passion about the mouth, the same free gestures, and the same big voice. Only the lines had deepened on the forehead, and on the fine face the air of thoughtfulness was also deeper. It was Edward Farque as of old, scholar, poet, dreamer and enthusiast, despiser of Western civilisation, contemptuous of money, generous and upright, a type of value, an individual.

'You've done well, done splendidly, Edward, old man,' said his friend presently, after hearing of Chinese wonders that took him somewhat beyond his depth perhaps. 'No one is more pleased than I. I've watched your books. You haven't regretted England, I'll be bound?' he asked.

'The philosopher has no country, in any case,' was the reply, steadily given. 'But out there I confess I've found my home.' He leaned forward, a deeper earnestness in his tone and expression. And into his face, as he spoke, came a glow of happiness. 'My heart,' he said softly, 'is in China.'

'I see it is, I see it is,' put in the other, conscious that he could not honestly share his friend's enthusiasm. 'And you're fortunate to be free to live where your treasure is,' he added after a moment's pause. 'You must be a happy man. Your passion amounts to nostalgia, I suspect. Already yearning to get back there, probably?'

Farque gazed at him for some seconds with shining eyes. 'You remember the Persian saying, I'm sure,' he said. ' "You see a man drink, but you do not see his thirst." Well,' he added, laughing happily, 'you may see me off in six months' time, but you will not see my happiness.'

While he went on talking the doctor glanced round the room, marvelling still at the exquisite taste of everything, the neat arrangement, the perfect matching of form and colour. A woman might have done this thing, occurred to him, as the haunting figure shifted deliciously into the foreground of his mind again. The thought of her had been momentarily replaced by all he heard and saw. She now returned, filling him with joy, anticipation, and enthusiasm. Presently, when it was his turn to talk, he would tell his friend about this new, unimagined happiness that had burst upon him like a sunrise. Presently, but not just yet. He remembered, too, with a passing twinge of possible boredom to come, that there must be some delay before his own heart could unburden itself in its turn. Farque wanted to ask some professional questions, of course. He had for the moment forgotten that part of the letter in his general interest and astonishment.

'Happiness, yes...' he murmured, aware that his thoughts had wandered and catching at the last word he remembered hearing. 'As you said just now in your own queer way—you haven't changed a bit, let me tell you, in your picturesqueness of quotation, Edward!—one must not be fugitive from life; one must seize happiness when and where it offers'.

He said it lightly enough, hugging internally his own sweet secret; but he was a little surprised at the earnestness of his friend's rejoinder: 'Both of us, I see,' came the deep voice, backed by the flash of the far-seeing grey eyes, 'have made some progress in the doctrine of life and death.' He paused, gazing at the other with sight that was obviously turned inwards upon his own thoughts. 'Beauty,' he went on presently, his tone even more serious, 'has been my lure; yours, Reality....'

'You don't flatter either of us, Edward. That's too exclusive a statement,' put in the doctor. He was becoming every minute more and more interested in the workings of his friend's mind. Something about the signs offered eluded his understanding. 'Explain yourself, old scholar-poet. I'm a dull, practical mind, remember, and can't keep pace with Chinese subtleties.'

'*You've* left out Beauty,' was the quiet rejoinder, 'while *I* left out Reality. That's neither Chinese nor subtle. It's simply true.'

'A bit wholesale, isn't it?' laughed Francis. 'A big genera-

15

lisation, rather.'

A bright light seemed to illuminate the scholar's face. It was as though an inner lamp was suddenly lit. At the same moment the sound of a soft gong floated in from the hall outside, so soft that the actual strokes were not distinguishable in the wave of musical vibration that reached the ear.

Farque rose to lead the way in to dinner.

'What if I—' he whispered, 'have combined the two?' And upon his face was a look of joy that reached down into the other's own full heart with its unexpectedness and wonder. It was the last remark in the world he had looked for. He wondered for a moment whether he interpreted it correctly.

'By Jove...!' he exclaimed. 'Edward, what d'you mean?'

'You shall hear—after dinner,' said Farque, his voice mysterious, his eyes still shining with his inner joy. 'I told you I have some questions to ask you—professionally.' And they took their seats round an ancient, marvellous table, lit by two swinging lamps of soft green jade, while the Chinese servant waited on them with the silent movements and deft neatness of his imperturbable celestial race.

III

To say that he was bored during the meal were an over-statement of Dr. Francis's mental condition, but to say that he was half-bored seemed the literal truth; for one half of him, while he ate his steak and savoury and watched Farque manipulating *chou chop suey* and *chou om dong* most cleverly with chop-sticks, was too preoccupied with his own new romance to allow the other half to give its full attention to the conversation.

He had entered the room, however, with a distinct quickening of what may be termed his instinctive and infallible sense of diagnosis. That last remark of his friend's had stimulated him. He was aware of surprise, curiosity, and impatience. Willy-nilly, he began automatically to study him with a profounder interest. Something, he gathered, was not quite as it should be in

Edward Farque's mental composition. There was what might be called an elusive emotional disturbance. He began to wonder and to watch.

They talked, naturally, of China and of things Chinese, for the scholar responded to little else, and Francis listened with what sympathy and patience he could muster. Of art and beauty he had hitherto known little, his mind was practical and utilitarian. He now learned that all art was derived from China, where a high, fine, subtle culture had reigned since time immemorial. Older than Egypt was their wisdom. When the Western races were eating one another, before Greece was even heard of, the Chinese had reached a level of knowledge and achievement that few realised. Never had they, even in earliest times, been deluded by anthropomorphic conceptions of the Deity, but perceived in everything the expressions of a single whole whose vast activities they reverently worshipped. Their contempt for the Western scurry after knowledge, wealth, machinery, was justified, if Farque was worthy of belief. He seemed saturated with Chinese thought, art, philosophy, and his natural bias toward the celestial race had hardened into an attitude to life that had now become ineradicable.

'They deal, as it were, in essences,' he declared, 'they discern the essence of everything, leaving out the superfluous, the unessential, the trivial. Their pictures alone prove it. Come with me,' he concluded, 'and see the *Earthly Paradise,* now in the British Museum. It is like Botticelli, but better than anything Botticelli ever did. It was painted'—he paused for emphasis—'600 years B. C.'

The wonder of this quiet, ancient civilization, a sense of its depth, its wisdom, grew upon his listener as the enthusiastic poet described its charm and influence upon himself. He willingly allowed the enchantment of the other's Paradise to steal upon his own awakened heart. There was a good deal Francis might have offered by way of criticism and objection, but he preferred on the whole to keep his own views to himself, and to let his friend wander unhindered through the mazes of his passionate evocation. All men, he well knew, needed

17

a dream to carry them through life's disappointments, a dream that they could enter at will and find peace, contentment, happiness. Farque's dream was China. Why not? It was as good as another, and a man like Farque was entitled to what dream he pleased.

'And their women?' he inquired at last, letting both halves of his mind speak together for the first time.

But he was not prepared for the expression that leaped upon his friend's face at the simple question. Nor for his method of reply. It was no reply, in point of fact. It was simply an attack upon all other types of woman, and upon the white, the English, in particular—their emptiness, their triviality, their want of intuitive imagination, of spiritual grace, of everything, in a word, that should constitute woman a meet companion for man, and a little higher than the angels into the bargain. The doctor listened spellbound. Too humorous to be shocked, he was, at any rate, disturbed by what he heard, displeased a little, too. It threatened too directly his own new tender dream.

Only with the utmost self-restraint did he keep his temper under, and prevent hot words he would have regretted later from tearing his friend's absurd claim into ragged shreds. He was wounded personally as well. Never now could he bring himself to tell his own secret to him. The outburst chilled and disappointed him. But it had another effect—it cooled his judgment. His sense of diagnosis quickened. He divined an *idée fixe,* a mania possibly. His interest deepened abruptly. He watched. He began to look about him with more wary eyes, and a sense of uneasiness, once the anger passed, stirred in his friendly and affectionate heart.

They had been sitting alone over their port for some considerable time, the servant having long since left the room. The doctor had sought to change the subject many times without much success, when suddenly Farque changed it for him.

'Now,' he announced, 'I'll tell you something,' and Francis guessed that the professional questions were on the way at last.

'We must pity the living, remember, and part with the dead. Have you forgotten old Shan-Yu?'

The forgotten name came back to him, the picturesque East End dealer of many years ago. 'The old merchant who taught you your first Chinese? I do recall him dimly, now you mention it. You made quite a friend of him, didn't you? He thought very highly of you—ah, it comes back to me now— he offered something or other very wonderful in his gratitude, unless my memory fails me.'

'His most valuable possession,' Farque went on, a strange look deepening on his face, an expression of mysterious rapture, as it were, and one that Francis recognised and swiftly pigeonholed in his now attentive mind.

'Which was?' he asked sympathetically. 'You told me once, but so long ago that really it's slipped my mind. Something magical, wasn't it?' He watched closely for his friend's reply.

Farque lowered his voice to a whisper almost devotional:

'The Perfume of the Garden of Happiness,' he murmured, with an expression in his eyes as though the mere recollection gave him joy. ' "Burn it," he told me, "in a brazier; then inhale. You will enter the Valley of a Thousand Temples wherein lies the Garden of Happiness, and there you will meet your Love. You will have seven years of happiness with your Love before the Waters of Separation flow between you. I give this to you who alone of men here have appreciated the wisdom of my land. Follow my body toward the Sunrise. You, an Eastern soul in a barbarian body, will meet your Destiny." '

The doctor's attention, such is the power of self-interest, quickened amazingly as he heard. His own romance flamed up with power. His friend—it dawned upon him suddenly— loved a woman.

'Come,' said Farque, rising quietly, 'we will go into the other room, and I will show you what I have shown to but one other in the world before. You are a doctor,' he continued, as he led the way to the silk-covered divan where golden dragons swallowed crimson suns, and wonderful jade horses

19

hovered near. 'You understand the mind and nerves. States of consciousness you also can explain, and the effect of drugs is, doubtless, known to you.' He swung to the heavy curtains that took the place of a door, handed a lacquered box of cigarettes to his friend, and lit one himself. 'Perfumes, too,' he added, 'you probably have studied, with their extraordinary evocative power.' He stood in the middle of the room, the green light falling on his interesting and thoughtful face, and for a passing second Francis, watching keenly, observed a change flit over it and vanish. The eyes grew narrow and slid tilted upward, the skin wore a shade of yellow underneath the green from the lamp of jade, the nose slipped back a little, the cheek-bones forward.

'Perfumes,' said the doctor, 'no. Of perfumes I know nothing, beyond their interesting effect upon the memory. I cannot help you there. But you, I suspect,' and he looked up with an inviting sympathy that concealed the close observation underneath, 'you yourself, I feel sure, can tell me something of value about them?'

'Perhaps,' was the calm reply, 'perhaps, for I have smelt the Perfume of the Garden of Happiness, and I have been in the Valley of a Thousand Temples.' He spoke with a glow of joy and reverence almost devotional.

The doctor waited in some suspense, while his friend moved toward an inlaid cabinet across the room. More than broad-minded, he was that much rarer thing, an open-minded man, ready at a moment's notice to discard all preconceived ideas, provided new knowledge that necessitated the holocaust were shown to him. At present, none the less, he held very definite views of his own. 'Please ask me any questions you like,' he added. 'All I know is entirely yours, as always.' He was aware of suppressed excitement in his friend that betrayed itself in every word and look and gesture, an excitement intense, and not as yet explained by anything he had seen or heard.

The scholar, meanwhile, had opened a drawer in the cabinet and taken from it a neat little packet tied up with purple silk.

He held it with tender, almost loving care, as he came and sat down on the divan beside his friend.

'This,' he said, in a tone, again, of something between reverence and worship, 'contains what I have to show you first.' He slowly unrolled it, disclosing a yet smaller silken bag within, coloured a deep rich orange. There were two vertical columns of writing on it, painted in Chinese characters. The doctor leaned forward to examine them. His friend translated:

'The Perfume of the Garden of Happiness,' he read aloud, tracing the letters of the first column with his finger. 'The Destroyer of Honourable Homes,' he finished, passing to the second, and then proceeded to unwrap the little silken bag. Befory it was actually open, however, and the pale shredded material resembling coloured chaff visible to the eyes, the doctor's nostrils had recognised the strange aroma he had first noticed about his friend's letter received earlier in the day. The same soft, penetrating odour, sharply piercing, sweet and delicate, rose to his brain. It stirred at once a deep emotional pleasure in him. Having come to him first when he was aglow with his own unexpected romance, his mind and heart full of the woman he had just left, that delicious, torturing state revived in him quite naturally. The evocative power of perfume with regard to memory is compelling. A livelier sympathy toward his friend, and toward what he was about to hear, awoke in him spontaneously.

He did not mention the letter, however. He merely leaned over to smell the fragrant perfume more easily.

Farque drew back the open packet instantly, at the same time holding out a warning hand. 'Careful,' he said gravely, 'be careful, my old friend—unless you desire to share the rapture and the risk that have been mine. To enjoy its full effect, true, this dust must be burned in a brazier and its smoke inhaled; but even sniffed, as you now would sniff it, and you are in danger——'

'Of what?' asked Francis, impressed by the other's extraordinary intensity of voice and manner.

'Of Heaven; but, possibly, of Heaven before your time.'

IV

The tale that Farque unfolded then had certainly a strange celestial flavour, a glory not of this dull world; and as his friend listened, his interest deepened with every minute, while his bewilderment increased. He watched closely, expert that he was, for clues that might guide his deductions aright, but for all his keen observation and experience he could detect no inconsistency, no weakness, nothing that betrayed the smallest mental aberration. The origin and nature of what he already decided was an *idée fixe,* a mania, evaded him entirely. This evasion piqued and vexed him; he had heard a thousand tales of similar type before; that this one in particular should baffle his unusual skill touched his pride. Yet he faced the position honestly; he confessed himself baffled until the end of the evening. When he went away, however, he went away satisfied, even forgetful—because a new problem of yet more poignant interest had replaced the first.

'It was after three years out there,' said Farque, 'that a sense of my loneliness first came upon me. It came upon me bitterly. My work had not then been recognised; obstacles and difficulties had increased; I felt a failure; I had accomplished nothing. And it seemed to me I had misjudged my capacities, taken a wrong direction, and wasted my life accordingly. For my move to China, remember, was a radical move, and my boats were burnt behind me. This sense of loneliness was really devastating.'

Francis, already fidgeting, put up his hand.

'One question, if I may,' he said, 'and I'll not interrupt again.'

'By all means,' said the other patiently. 'What is it?'

'Were you—we are such old friend's—he apologised—'were you still celibate as ever?'

Farque looked surprised, then smiled. 'My habits had not changed,' he replied. 'I was, as always, celibate.'

'Ah!' murmured the doctor, and settled down to listen.

'And I think now,' his friend went on, 'that it was the lack of companionship that first turned my thoughts toward conscious disappointment. However that may be, it was one evening, as I walked homeward to my little house, that I caught my imagination lingering upon English memories, though chiefly, I admit, upon my old Chinese tutor, the dead Shan-Yu.

'It was dusk, the stars were coming out in the pale evening air, and the orchards, as I passed them, stood like wavering ghosts of unbelievable beauty. The effect of thousands upon thousands of these trees, flooding the twilight of a spring evening with their sea of blossom, is almost unearthly. They seem transparencies, their colour hangs sheets upon the very sky. I crossed a small wooden bridge that joined two of these orchards above a stream, and in the dark water I watched a moment the mingled reflection of stars and flowering branches on the quiet surface. It seemed too exquisite to belong to earth, this fairy garden of stars and blossoms, shining faintly in the crystal depths, and my thought, as I gazed, dived suddenly down the little avenue that memory opened into former days. I remembered Shan-Yu's present, given to me when he died. His very words came back to me: The Garden of Happiness in the Valley of the Thousand Temples, with its promise of love, of seven years of happiness, and the prophecy that I should follow his body toward the Sunrise and meet my destiny.

'This memory I took home with me into my lonely little one-story house upon the hill. My servants did not sleep there. There was no one near. I sat by the open window with my thoughts, and you may easily guess that before very long I had unearthed the long-forgotten packet from among my things, spread a portion of its contents on a metal tray above a lighted brazier, and was comfortably seated before it, inhaling the light blue smoke with its exquisite and fragrant perfume.

'A light air entered through the window, the distant orchards below me trembled, rose, and floated through the dusk, and I found myself, almost at once, in a pavilion of flowers; a blue river lay shining in the sun before me, as it wandered through a lovely valley where I saw groves of flowering trees among a thousand scattered temples. Drenched in light and colour, the Valley lay dreaming amid a peaceful loveliness that woke what seemed impossible, unrealisable, longings in my heart. I yearned toward its groves and temples; I would bathe my soul in that flood of tender light and my body in the blue coolness of that winding river. In a thousand temples must I worship. Yet these impossible yearnings instantly were satisfied. I found myself there at once... and the time that passed over my head you may reckon in centuries, if not in ages. I was in the Garden of Happiness, and its marvellous perfume banished time and sorrow; there was no end to chill the soul, nor any beginning, which is its foolish counterpart.

'Nor was there loneliness.' The speaker clasped his thin hands, and closed his eyes a moment in what was evidently an ecstasy of the sweetest memory man may ever know. A slight trembling ran through his frame, communicating itself to his friend upon the divan beside him—this understanding, listening, sympathetic friend, whose eyes had never once yet withdrawn their attentive gaze from the narator's face.

'I was not alone,' the scholar resumed, opening his eyes again, and smiling out of some deep inner joy. 'Shan-Yu came down the steps of the first temple and took my hand, while the great golden figures in the dim interior turned their splendid shining heads to watch. Then, breathing the soul of his ancient wisdom in my ear, he led me through all the perfumed ways of that enchanted Garden, worshipping with me at a hundred deathless shrines; led me, I tell you, to the sound of soft gongs and gentle bells, by fragrant groves and sparkling streams, mid a million gorgeous flowers, until beneath that unsetting sun, we reached the heart of the Valley, where the source of the river gushed forth beneath the lighted mountains. He stopped and pointed across the narrow waters. I saw the woman—'

'*The* woman,' his listener murmured beneath his breath, though Farque seemed unaware of interruption.

'She smiled at me and held her hands out, and while she did so, even before I could express my joy and wonder in response, Shan-Yu, I saw, had crossed the narrow stream and stood beside her. I made to follow them, my heart burning with inexpressible delight. But Shan-Yu held up his hand, as they began to move down the flowered bank together, making a sign that I should keep pace with them, though on my own side.

'Thus, side by side, yet with the blue, sparkling stream between us, we followed back along its winding course, through the heart of that enchanted Valley, my hands stretched out toward the radiant figure of my Love, and hers stretched out toward me. They did not touch, but our eyes, our smiles, our thoughts, these met and mingled in a sweet union of unimagined bliss, so that the absence of physical contact was unnoticed and laid no injury on our marvellous joy. It was a spirit union, and our kiss a spirit kiss. Therein lay the subtlety and glory of the Chinese wonder, for it was our *essences* that met, and for such union there is no satiety and, equally, no possible end. The Perfume of the Garden of Happiness is an essence. We were in Eternity.

'The stream, meanwhile, widened between us, and as it widened, my Love grew farther from me in space, smaller, less visibly defined, yet ever essentially more perfect, and never once with a sense of distance that made our union less divinely close. Across the widening reaches of blue, sunlit water I still knew her smile, her eyes, the gestures of her radiant being; I saw her exquisite reflection in the stream; and, mid the music of those soft gongs and gentle bells, the voice of Shan-Yu came like a melody to my ears:

' "You have followed me into the Sunrise, and have found your Destiny. Behold now your Love. In this Valley of a Thousand Temples you have known the Garden of Happiness, and its Perfume your soul now inhales."

' "I am bathed," I answered, "in a happiness divine. It is for ever."

' "The Waters of Separation," his answer floated like a bell, "lie widening between you."

'I moved nearer to the bank, impelled by the pain in his words to take my Love and hold her to my breast.

' "But I would cross to her," I cried, and saw that, as I moved, Shan-Yu and my Love came likewise closer to the water's edge across the widening river. They both obeyed, I was aware, my slightest wish.

' "Seven years of happiness you may know," sang his gentle tones across the brimming flood, "if you would cross to her. Yet the Destroyer of Honourable Homes lies in the shadows that you must cast outside."

'I heard his words, I noticed for the first time that in the blaze of this radiant sunshine we cast no shadows on the sea of flowers at our feet, and—I stretched out my arms toward my Love across the river.

' "I accept my destiny," I cried, "I will have my seven years of bliss," and stepped forward into the running flood. As the cool water took my feet, my Love's hands stretched out both to hold me and to bid me stay. There was acceptance in her gesture, but there was warning too.

'I did not falter. I advanced until the water bathed my knees, and my Love, too, came to meet me, the stream already to her waist, while our arms stretched forth above the running flood toward each other.

'The change came suddenly. Shan-Yu first faded behind her advancing figure into air; there stole a chill upon the sunlight; a cool mist rose from the water, hiding the Garden and the hills beyond; our fingers touched, I gazed into her eyes, our lips lay level with the water—and the room was dark and cold about me. The brazier stood extinguished at my side. The dust had burnt out, and no smoke rose. I slowly left my chair and closed the window, for the air was chill.'

V

It was difficult at first to return to Hampstead and the details of ordinary life about him. Francis looked round him slowly, freeing himself gradually from the spell his friend's words had laid even upon his analytical temperament. The transition was helped, however, by the details that everywhere met his eye. The Chinese atmosphere remained. More, its effect had gained, if anything. The embroideries of yellow gold, the pictures, the lacquered stools and inlaid cabinets—above all, the exquisite figures in green jade upon the shelf beside him— all this, in the shimmering pale olive light the lamps shed everywhere, helped his puzzled mind to bridge the gulf from the Garden of Happiness into the decorated villa upon Hampstead Heath.

There was silence between the two men for several minutes. Far was it from the doctor's desire to injure his old friend's delightful fantasy. For he called it fantasy, although something in him doubted. He remained, therefore, silent. Truth to tell, perhaps, he knew not exactly what to say.

Farque broke the silence himself. He had not moved since the story ended; he sat motionless, his hands tightly clasped, his eyes alight with the memory of his strange imagined joy, his face rapt and almost luminous, as though he still wandered through the groves of the enchanted Garden and inhaled the perfume of its perfect happiness in the Valley of the Thousand Temples.

'It was two days later,' he went on suddenly in his quiet voice, 'only two days afterwards, that I met her.'

'You met her? You met the woman of your dream?' Francis's eyes opened very wide.

'In that little harbour town,' repeated Farque calmly, 'I met her in the flesh. She had just landed in a steamer from up the coast. The details are of no particular interest. She knew me, of course, at once. And, naturally, I knew her.'

The doctor's tongue refused to act as he heard. It dawned upon him suddenly that his friend was married. He remembered the woman's touch about the house; he recalled, too, for the first time that the letter of invitation to dinner had said 'come to *us*'. He was full of a bewildered astonishment.

The reaction upon himself was odd, perhaps, yet wholly natural. His heart warmed toward his imaginative friend. He could now tell him his own new strange romance. The woman who haunted him crept back into the room and sat between them. He found his tongue.

'You married her, Edward?' he exclaimed.

'She is my wife,' was the reply, in a gentle, happy voice.

'A Ch——' he could not bring himself to say the word. 'A foreigner?'

'My wife is a Chinese woman,' Farque helped him easily, with a delighted smile.

So great was the other's absorption in the actual moment that he had not heard the step in the passage that his host had heard. The latter stood up suddenly.

'I hear her now,' he said. 'I'm glad she's come back before you left.' He stepped toward the door.

But before he reached it, the door was opened and in came the woman herself. Francis tried to rise, but something had happened to him. His heart missed a beat. Something, it seemed, broke in him. He faced a tall, graceful young English-woman with black eyes of sparkling happiness, the woman of his own romance. She still wore the feather boa round her neck. She was no more Chinese than he was.

'My wife,' he heard Farque introducing them, as he struggled to his feet, searching feverishly for words of congratulation, normal, everyday words he ought to use. 'I'm so pleased, oh, so pleased,' Farque was saying—he heard the sound from a distance, his sight was blurred as well—'my two best friends in the world, my English comrade and my Chinese wife.' His voice was absolutely sincere with conviction and belief.

'But we have already met,' came the woman's delightful voice, her eyes full upon his face with smiling pleasure. 'I saw yout at Mrs. Malleson's tea only this afternoon.'

And Francis remembered suddenly that the Mallesons were old acquaintances of Farque's as well as of himself. 'And I even dared to ask who you were,' the voice went on, floating from some other space, it seemed, to his ears. 'I had you pointed out to me. I had heard of you from Edward, of course. But you vanished before I could be introduced.'

The doctor mumbled something or other polite and, he hoped, adequate. But the truth had flashed upon him with remorseless suddenness. She had 'heard of' him—the famous mental specialist. Her interest in him was cruelly explained, cruelly both for himself and for his friend. Farque's delusion lay clear before his eyes. An awakening to reality might involve dislocation of the mind. *She*, too moreover, knew the truth. She was involved as well. And her interest in himself was—consultation.

'Seven years we've been married, just seven years to-day,' Farque was saying thoughtfully, as he looked at them. 'Curius, rather, isn't it?'

'Very,' said Francis, turning his regard from the black eyes to the grey.

Thus it was that Owen Francis left the house a little later with a mind in a measure satisfied, yet in a measure forgetful too—forgetful of his own deep problem, because another of even greater interest had replaced it.

'Why undeceive him?' ran his thought. 'He need never know. It's harmless, anyhow—I can tell her that.'

But side by side with this reflection ran another that was oddly haunting, considering his type of mind: 'Destroyer of Honourable Homes,' was the form of words it took. And with a sigh he added, 'Chinese Magic.'

FIRST HATE

THEY had been shooting all day; the weather had been perfect and the powder straight, so that when they assembled in the smoking-room after dinner they were well-pleased with themselves. From discussing the day's sport and the weather outlook, the conversation drifted to other, though still cognate, fields. Lawson, the crack shot of the party, mentioned the instinctive recognition all animals feel for their natural enemies, and gave several instances in which he had tested it—tame rats with a ferret, birds with a snake, and so forth.

'Even after being domesticated for generations,' he said, 'they recognise their natural enemy at once by instinct, an enemy they can never even have seen before. It's infallible. They know instantly.'

'Undoubtedly,' said a voice from the corner chair; 'and so do we.'

The speaker was Ericssen, their host, a great hunter before the Lord, generally uncommunicative but a good listener, leaving the talk to others. For this latter reason, as well as for a certain note of challenge in his voice, his abrupt statement gained attention.

'What do you mean exactly by "so do we"?' asked three men together, after waiting some seconds to see whether he meant to elaborate, which he evidently did not.

'We belong to the animal kingdom, of course,' put in a fourth, for behind the challenge there obviously lay a story, though a story that might be difficult to drag out of him. It was.

Ericssen, who had leaned forward a moment so that his strong, humorous face was in clear light, now sank back again into his chair, his expression concealed by the red lampshade at his side. The light played tricks, obliterating the humorous, almost tender, lines, while emphasising the stength of the jaw and nose. The red glare lent to the whole a rather grim expression.

Lawson, man of authority among them, broke the little pause.

'You're dead right,' he observed; 'but how do you know it?'—for John Ericssen never made a positive statement without a good reason for it. That good reason, he felt sure, involved a personal proof, but a story Ericssen would never tell before a general audience. He would tell it later, however when the others had left. 'There's such a thing as instinctive antipathy, of course,' he added, with a laugh, looking round him. 'That's what you mean, probably.'

'I meant exactly what I said,' replied the host bluntly. 'There's first love. There's first hate, too.'

'Hate's a strong word,' remarked Lawson.

'So is love,' put in another.

'Hate's strongest,' said Ericssen grimly. 'In the animal kingdom, at least,' he added suggestively, and then kept his lips closed, except to sip his liquor, for the rest of the evening —until the party at length broke up, leaving Lawson and one other man, both old trusted friends of many years' standing.

'It's not a tale I'd tell to everybody,' he began, when they were alone. 'It's true, for one thing; for another, you see, some of those good fellows' —he indicated the empty chairs with an expressive nod of his great head—'some of 'em knew him. You both knew him too, probably.'

'The man you hated,' said the understanding Lawson.

'And who hated me,' came the quiet confirmation. 'My other reason,' he went on, 'for keeping quiet was that the tale involves my wife.'

The two listeners said nothing, but each remembered the curiously long courtship that had been the prelude to his marriage. No engagement had been announced, the pair were devoted to one another, there was no known rival on either side, yet the courtship continued without coming to its expected conclusion. Many stories were afloat in consequence. It was a social mystery that intrigued the gossips.

'I may tell you two,' Ericssen continued, 'the reason my wife refused for so long to marry me. It is hard to believe, perhaps, but it is true. Another man wished to make her his wife, and she would not consent to marry me until that other man was dead. Quixotic, absurd, unreasonable? If you like. I'll tell you what she said.' He looked up with a significant expression in his face which proved that he, at least, did not now judge her reason foolish. ' "Because it would be murder," she told me. "Another man who wants to marry me would kill you." '

'She had some proof for the assertion, no doubt?' suggested Lawson.

'None whatever,' was the reply. 'Merely her woman's instinct. Moreover, *I* did not know who the other man was, nor would she ever tell me.'

'Otherwise you might have murdered him instead?' said Baynes, the second listener.

'I did', said Ericssen grimly. 'But without knowing he was the man.' He sipped his whisky and relit his pipe. The others waited.

'Our marriage took place two months later—just after Hazel's disappearance.'

'Hazel?' exclaimed Lawson and Baynes in a single breath. 'Hazel! Member of the Hunters!' His mysterious disappearance had been a nine days' wonder some ten years ago. It had never been explained. They had all been members of the Hunters' Club together.

'That's the chap,' Ericssen said. 'Now I'll tell you the tale, if you care to hear it.' They settled back in their chairs to listen. and Ericssen, who had evidently never told the affair to another living soul except his own wife, doubtless, seemed glad this time to tell it to two men.

'It began some dozen years ago when my brother Jack and I came home from a shooting trip in China. I've often told you about our adventures there, and you see the heads hanging up here in the smoking-room—some of 'em'. He glanced round proudly at the walls. 'We were glad to be in town again after two years' roughing it, and we looked forward to our first good dinner at the Club, to make up for the rotten cooking we had endured so long. We had ordered that dinner in anticipatory detail many a time together. Well, we had it and enjoyed it up to a point—the point of the *entrée*, to be exact.

'Up to that point it was delicious, and we let ourselves go, I can tell you. We had ordered the very wine we had planned months before when we were snow-bound and half starving in the mountains.' He smacked his lips as he mentioned it. 'I was just starting on a beautifully cooked grouse,' he went on, 'when a figure went by our table, and Jack looked up and nodded. The two exchanged a brief word of greeting and explanation, and the other man passed on. Evidently they knew each other just enough to make a word or two necessary, but enough.

' "Who's that?" I asked.

' "A new member, named Hazel," Jack told me. "A great shot." He knew him slightly, he explained; he had once been a client of his—Jack was a barrister, you remember—and had defended him in some financial case or other. Rather an unpleasant case, he added. Jack did not 'care about' the fellow, he told me, as he went on with his tender wing of grouse.'

Ericssen paused to relight his pipe a moment.

'Not care about him!' he continued. 'It didn't surprise me, for my own feeling, the instant I set eyes on the fellow, was one of violent, instinctive dislike that amounted to loathing. Loathing! No. I'll give it the right word—hatred. I simpy couldn't help myself; I hated the man from the very first go off. A wave of repulsion swept over me as I followed him down the room a moment with my eyes, till he took his seat at a distant table and was out of sight. Ugh! He was a big, fat-faced man, with an eyeglass glued into one of his pale-blue cod-like eyes—out of condition, ugly as a toad, with a smug expression of intense self-satisfaction on his jowl that made me long to————

'I leave it to you to guess what I would have liked to do to him. But the instinctive loathing he inspired in me had another aspect, too. Jack had not introduced us during the momentary pause beside our table, but as I looked up I caught the fellow's

33

eye on mine—he was glaring at me instead of at Jack, to whom he was talking—with an expression of malignant dislike, as keen evidently as my own. That's the other aspect I meant. He hated me as violently as I hated him. We were instinctive enemies, just as the rat and ferret are instinctive enemies. Each recognised a mortal foe. It was a case—I swear it—of whoever got first chance.'

'Bad as that!' exclaimed Baynes. 'I knew him by sight. He wasn't pretty, I'll admit.'

'I knew him to nod to,' Lawson mentioned. 'I never heard anything particular against him.' He shrugged his shoulders.

Ericssen went on. 'It was not his character or qualities I hated,' he said. 'I didn't even know them. That's the whole point. There's no reason you fellows should have disliked him. *My* hatred—our mutual hatred—was instinctive, as instinctive as first love. A man knows his natural mate; also he knows his natural enemy. I did, at any rate, both with him and with my wife. Given the chance, Hazel would have done me in; just as surely, given the chance, I would have done him in. No blame to either of us, what's more, in my opinion.'

'I've felt dislike, but never hatred like that,' Baynes mentioned. 'I came across it in a book once, though. The writer did not mention the instinctive fear of the human animal for its natural enemy, or anything of that sort. He thought it was a continuance of a bitter feud begun in an earlier existence. He called it memory.'

'Possibly,' said Ericssen briefly. 'My mind is not speculative. But I'm glad you spoke of fear. I left that out. The truth is, I feared the fellow, too, in a way; and had we ever met face to face in some wild country without witnesses I should have felt justified in drawing on him at sight, and he would have felt the same. Murder? If you like. I should call it self-defence. Anyhow, the fellow polluted the room for me. He spoilt the enjoyment of that dinner we had ordered months before in China.'

'But you saw him again, of course, later?'

'Lots of times. Not that night, because we went on to a the-

34

atre. But in the Club we were always running across one another—in the houses of friends at lunch or dinner; at race-meetings; all over the place; in fact, I even had some trouble to avoid being introduced to him. And every time we met, our eyes betrayed us. He felt in his heart what I felt in mine. Ugh! He was as loathsome to me as leprosy, and as dangerous. Odd, isn't it? The most intense feeling, except love, I've ever known. I remember'—he laughed gruffly—'I used to feel quite sorry for him. If he felt what I felt, and I'm convinced he did, he must have suffered. His one object—to get me out of the way for good—was so impossible. Then Fate played a hand in the game. I'll tell you how.

'My brother died a year or two later, and I went abroad to try and forget it. I went salmon fishing in Canada. But, though the sport was good, it was not like the old times with Jack. The camp never felt the same without him. I missed him badly. But I forgot Hazel for the time; hating did not seem worth while, somehow.

'When the best of the fishing was over on the Atlantic side I took a run back to Vancouver and fished there for a bit. I went up the Campbell River, which was not so crowded then as it is now, and had some rattling sport. Then I grew tired of the rod and decided to go after wapiti for a change. I came back to Victoria and learned what I could about the best places, and decided finally to go up the west coast of the island. By luck I happened to pick up a good guide, who was in the town at the moment on business, and we started off together in one of the little Canadian Pacific Railway boats that ply along that coast.

'Outfitting two days later at a small place the steamer stopped at, the guide said we needed another man to help pack our kit over portages, and so forth, but the only fellow available was a Siwash of whom he disapproved. My guide would not have him at any price; he was lazy, a drunkard, a liar, and even worse, for on one occasion he came back without the sportsman he had taken up country on a shooting trio, and his story was not convincing, to say the least. These disappearances are always awkward, of course, as you both know. We preferred, anyhow, to go without the Siwash, and off we started.

'At first our luck was bad. I saw many wapiti, but no good heads; only after a fortnight's hunting did I manage to get a decent head, though even that was not so good as I should have liked.

'We were then near the head waters of a little river that ran down into the Inlet; heavy rains had made the river rise; running downstream was a risky job, what with old log-jams shifting and new ones forming; and, after many narrow escapes, we upset one afternoon and had the misfortune to lose a lot of our kit, amongst it most of our cartridges. We could only muster a few between us. The guide had a dozen; I had two—just enough, we considered, to take us out all right. Still, it was an infernal nuisance. We camped at once to dry out our soaked things in front of a big fire, and while this laundry work was going on the guide suggested my filling in the time by taking a look at the next little valley, which ran parallel to ours. He had seen some good heads over there a few weeks ago. Possibly I might come upon the herd. I started at once, taking my two cartridges with me.

'It was the devil of a job getting over the divide, for it was a badly bushed-up place, and where there were no bushes there were boulders and fallen trees, and the going was slow and tiring. But I got across at last and came out upon another stream at the bottom of the new valley. Signs of wapiti were plentiful, though I never came up with a single beast all the afternoon. Blacktail deer were everywhere, but the wapiti remained invisible. Providence, or whatever you like to call that fate which there is no escaping in our lives, made me save my two cartridges.'

Ericssen stopped a minute then, It was not to light his pipe or sip his whisky. Nor was it because the remainder of his story failed in the recollection of any vivid detail. He paused a moment to think.

'Tell us the lot,' pleaded Lawson. 'Don't leave out anything.'

Ericssen looked up. His friend's remark had helped him to

make up his mind apparently. He *had* hesitated about something or other, but the hesitation passed. He glanced at both his listeners.

'Right,' he said. 'I'll tell you everything. I'm not imaginative, as you know, and my amount of superstition, I should judge, is microscopic.' He took a longer breath, then lowered his voice a trifle. 'Anyhow,' he went on, 'it's true, so I don't see why I should feel shy about admitting it—but as I stood there, in that lonely valley, where only the noises of wind and water were audible, and no human being, except my guide, some miles away, was within reach, a curious feeling came over me I find difficult to describe. I felt'—obviously he made an effort to get the word out—'I felt creepy.'

'You,' murmured Lawson, with an incredulous smile— 'you creepy?' he repeated under his breath.

'I felt creepy and afraid,' continued the other, with conviction. 'I had the sensation of being seen by someone—as if someone, I mean, was watching me. It was so unlikely that anyone was near me in that God-forsaken bit of wilderness that I simply couldn't believe it at first. But the feeling persisted. I felt absolutely positive somebody was not far away among the red maples, behind a boulder, across the little stream, perhaps —somewhere, at any rate, so near that I was plainly visible to him. It was not an animal. It was human. Also, it was hostile.

'I was in danger.

'You may laugh, both of you, but I assure you the feeling was so positive that I crouched down instinctively to hide myself behind a rock. My first thought, that the guide had followed me for some reason or other, I at once discarded. It was not the guide. It was an enemy.

'No, no, I thought of no one in particular. No name, no face occurred to me. Merely that an enemy was on my trail, that he saw me, and I did not see him, and that he was near enough to me to—well, to take instant action. This deep instinctive feeling of danger, of fear, of anything you like to call it, was simply overwhelming.

'Another curious detail I must also mention. About half an hour before, having given up all hope of seeing wapiti, I had decided to kill a blacktail deer for meat. A good shot offered itself, not thirty yards away. I aimed. But just as I was going to pull the trigger a queer emotion touched me, and I lowered the rifle. It was exactly as though a voice said, "Don't!" I heard no voice, mind you; it was an emotion only, a feeling, a sudden inexplicable change of mind—a warning, if you like. I didn't fire, anyhow.

'But now, as I crouched behind that rock, I remembered this curious little incident, and was glad I had not used up my last two cartridges. More than that I cannot tell you. Things of that kind are new to me. They're difficult enough to tell let alone to explain. But they were *real*.

'I crouched there, wondering what on earth was happening to me, and feeling a bit of a fool, if you want to know, when suddenly, over the top of the boulder, I saw something moving. It was a man's hat. I peered cautiously. Some sixty yards away the bushes parted, and two men came out on to the river's bank, and I knew them both. One was the Siwash I had seen at the store. The other was Hazel. Before I had time to think I cocked my rifle.'

'Hazel. Good Lord!' exclaimed the listeners.

'For a moment I was too surprised to do anything but cock that rifle. I waited, for what puzzled me was that, after all, Hazel had *not* seen me. It was only the feeling of his beastly proximity that had made me feel I was seen and watched by him. There was something else, too, that made me pause before—er—doing anything. Two other things, in fact. One was that I was so intensely interested in watching the fellow's actions. Obviously he had the same uneasy sensation that I had. He shared with me the nasty feeling that danger was about. His rifle, I saw, was cocked and ready; he kept looking behind him, over his shoulder, peering this way and that, and sometimes addressing a remark to the Siwash at his side. I caught the laughter of the latter. The Siwash evidently did not think there was danger anywhere. It was, of course, unlikely enough——'

'And the other thing that stopped you?' urged Lawson, impatiently interrupting.

Ericssen turned with a look of grim humour on his face.

'Some confounded or perverted sense of chivalry in me, I suppose,' he said, 'that made it impossible to shoot him down in cold blood, or, rather, without letting him have a chance. Fo my blood, as a matter of fact, was far from cold at the moment. Perhaps, too, I wanted the added satisfaction of letting him know who fired the shot that was to end his vile existence.'

He laughed again. 'It was rat and ferret in the human kingdom,' he went on, 'but I wanted my rat to have a chance, I suppose. Anyhow, though I had a perfect shot in front of me at easy distance, I did not fire. Instead I got up, holding my cocked rifle ready, finger on trigger, and came out of my hiding-place. I called to him. "Hazel, you beast! So there you are—at last!"

'He turned, but turned away from me, offering his horrid back. The direction of the voice he misjudged. He pointed down-stream, and the Siwash turned to look. Neither of them had seen me yet. There was a big log-jam below them. The roar of the water in their ears concealed my footsteps. I was, perhaps, twenty paces from them when Hazel, with a jerk of his whole body, abruptly turned clean round and faced me. We stared into each other's eyes.

'The amazement on his face changed instantly to hatred and resolve. He acted with incredible rapidity. I think the unexpected suddenness of his turn made me lose a precious second or two. Anyhow he was ahead of me. He flung his rifle to his shoulder. 'You devil!' I heard his voice. 'I've got you at last!' His rifle cracked, for he let drive the same instant. The hair stirred just above my ear.

'He had missed!

'Before he could draw back his bolt for another shot I had acted.

' "You're not fit to live!" I shouted, as my bullet crashed

into his temple. I had the satisfaction, too, of knowing that he heard my words. I saw the swift expression of frustrated loathing in his eyes.

'He fell like an ox, his face splashing in the stream. I shoved the body out. I saw it sucked beneath the log-jam instantly. It disappeared. There could be no inquest on him, I reflected comfortably. Hazel was gone—gone from this earth, from my life, our mutual hatred over at last.'

The speaker paused a moment. 'Odd,' he continued presently—'very odd indeed.' He turned to the others. 'I felt quite sorry for him suddenly. I suppose,' he added,' the philosophers are right when they gas about hate being very close to love.'

His friends contributed no remark.

'Then I came away,' he resumed shortly. 'My wife—well, you know the rest, don't you? I told her the whole thing. She—she said nothing. But she married me, you see.'

There was a moment's silence. Baynes was the first to break it. 'But—the Siwash?' he asked. 'The witness?'

Lawson turned upon him with something of contemptuous impatience.

'He told you he had *two* cartridges.'

Ericssen, smiling grimly, said nothing at all.

THE OLIVE

HE laughed involuntarily as the olive rolled toward his chair across the shiny parquet floor of the hotel dining-room.

His table in the cavernous *salle à manger* was apart: he sat alone, a solitary guest; the table from which the olive fell and rolled toward him was some distance away. The angle, however, made him an unlikely objective. Yet the lob-sided, juicy thing, after hesitating once or twice *en route* as it plopped along, came to rest finally against his feet.

It settled with an inviting, almost an aggressive, air. And he stooped and picked it up, putting it rather self-consciously, because of the girl from whose table it had come, on the white tablecloth beside his plate.

Then, looking up, he caught her eye, and saw that she, too, was laughing, though not a bit self-consciously. As she helped herself to the *hors-d'oeuvre* a false move had sent it flying. She watched him pick the olive up and set it beside his plate. Her eyes then suddenly looked away again—at her mother—questioningly.

The incident was closed. But the little oblong, succulent olive lay beside his plate, so that his fingers played with it. He fingered it automatically from time to time until his lonely meal was finished.

When no one was looking he slipped it into his pocket, as though, having taken the trouble to pick it up, this was the very least he could do with it. Heaven alone knows why, but he then took it upstairs with him, setting it on the marble mantelpiece among his field-glasses, tobacco tins, ink-bottles, pipes, and candlestick. At any rate, he kept it—the moist, shiny, lob-sided, juicy little oblong olive. The hotel lounge wearied him; he came to his room after dinner to smoke at his ease, his coat off and his feet on a chair; to read another chapter of Freud, to write a letter or two he didn't in the least want to write, and then to go to bed at ten o'clock. But this

41

evening the olive kept rolling between him and the thing he read; it rolled between the paragraphs, between the lines; the olive was more vital than the interest of these eternal 'complexes' and 'suppressed desires.'

The truth was that he kept seeing the eyes of the laughing girl beyond the bouncing olive. She had smiled at him in such a natural, spontaneous, friendly way before her mother's glance had checked her—a smile, he felt, that might lead to acquaintance on the morrow.

He wondered! A thrill of possible adventure ran through him.

She was a merry-looking sort of girl, with a happy, half-roguish face that seemed on the look-out for somebody to play with. Her mother, like most of the people in the big hotel, was an invalid; the girl, a dutiful and patient daughter. They had arrived that very day, apparently.

A laugh is a revealing thing, he thought as he fell asleep to dream of a lob-sided olive rolling consciously toward him, and of a girl's eyes that watched its awkward movements, then looked up into his own and laughed. In his dream the olive had been deliberately and cleverly dispatched upon its uncertain journey. It was a message.

He did not know, of course, that the mother, chiding her daughter's awkwardness, had muttered:

'There you are again, child! True to your name, you never see an olive without doing something queer and odd with it!'

A youngish man, whose knowledge of chemistry, including invisible inks and suchlike mysteries, had proved so valuable to the Censor's Department that for five years he had overworked without a holiday, the Italian Riviera had attracted him, and he had come out for a two months' rest. It was his first visit. Sun, mimosa, blue seas and brilliant skies had tempted him; exchange made a pound worth forty, fifty, sixty, and seventy shillings. He found the place lovely, but somewhat untenanted.

He stayed on, however, caught by the sunshine and the good exchange, also without the physical energy to discover a better, livelier place. He went for walks among the olive-groves; he sat beside the sea and palms; he visited shops and bought things he did not want because the exchange made them seem cheap; he paid immense 'extras' in his weekly bill, then chuckled as he reduced them to shillings and found that a few pence covered them; he lay with a book for hours among the olive-groves.

The olive-groves! His daily life could not escape the olive-groves; to olive-groves, sooner or later, his walks, his expeditions, his meanderings by the sea, his shopping—all led him to these ubiquitous olive-groves.

If he bought a picture postcard to send home, there was sure to be an olive-grove in one corner of it. The whole place was smothered with olive groves, the people owed their incomes and existence to these irrepressible trees. The villages among the hills swam roof-deep in them. They swarmed even in the hotel gardens.

The guide-books praised them as persistently as the residents brought them, sooner or later, into every conversation. They grew lyrical over them:

'And how do you like our olive-trees? Ah, you think them pretty. At first, most people are disappointed. They grow on one.'

'They do,' he agreed.

'I'm glad you appreciate them. I find them the embodiment of grace. And when the wind lifts the underleaves across a whole mountain slope—why, it's wonderful, isn't it? One realises the meaning of "olive-green." '

'One does.' He sighed. 'But, all the same, I should like to get one to eat—an olive, I mean.'

'Ah, to eat, yes. That's not so easy. You see, the crop is...'

'Exactly,' he interrupted impatiently, weary of the habitual and evasive explanations. 'But I should like to taste the *fruit*. I should like to enjoy one.'

For, after a stay of six weeks, he had never once seen an olive on the table, in the shops, nor even on the street barrows at the market-place. He had never tasted one. No one sold olives, though olive-trees were a drug in the place; no one bought them, no one asked for them; it seemed that no one wanted them. The trees, when he looked closely, were thick with a dark little berry that seemed more like a sour sloe than the succulent, delicious, spicy fruit associated with its name.

Men climbed the trunks, everywhere shaking the laden branches and hitting them with long bamboo poles to knock the fruit off, while women and children, squatting on their haunches, spent laborious hours filling baskets underneath, then loading mules and donkeys with their daily 'catch.' But an olive to eat was unobtainable. He had never cared for olives, but now he craved with all his soul to feel his teeth in one.

'Ach! But it is the Spanish olive that you *eat*,' explained the head waiter, a German 'from Basel'. 'These are for oil only.' After which he disliked the olive more than ever—until that night when he saw the first eatable specimen rolling across the shiny parquet floor, propelled toward him by the careless hand of a pretty girl, who then looked up into his eyes and smiled.

He was convinced that Eve, similarly, had rolled the apple toward Adam across the emerald sward of the first garden in the world. The dull, accumulated resentment he had come to feel, subconsciously perhaps, against an elusive fruit was changed in the twinkling of an eye into a source of joy, a symbol of romance.

.   .   .   .   .

He slept usually like the dead. It must have been something very real that made him open his eyes and sit up in bed alertly. There was a noise against his door. He listened. The room was still quite dark. It was early morning. The noise was not repeated.

'Who's there?' he asked in a sleepy whisper. 'What is it?'

The noise came again. Someone was scratching on the door. No, it was somebody tapping.

'What d'you want?' he demanded in a louder voice. 'Come in,' he added, wondering sleepily whether he was presentable. Either the hotel was on fire or the porter was waking the wrong person for some sunrise expedition.

Nothing happened. Wide awake now, he turned the switch on, but no light flooded the room. The electricians, he remembered with a curse, were out on strike. He fumbled for the matches, and as he did so a voice in the corridor became distincly audible. It was just outside his door.

'Aren't you ready?' he heard. 'You sleep for ever.'

And the voice, although, never having heard it before, he could not have recognised, belonged, he knew suddenly, to the girl who had let the olive fall. In an instant he was out of bed. He lit a candle.

'I'm coming,' he called softly, as he slipped rapidly into some clothes. 'I'm sorry I've kept you. I shan't be a minute.'

'Be quick then!' he heard, while the candle-flame slowly grew, and he found his garments. Less than three minutes later he openecd the door and, candle in hand, peered into the dark passage.

'Blow it out!' came a peremptory whisper. He obeyed, but not quick enough. A pair of red lips emerged from the shadows. There was a puff, and the candle was extinguished. 'I've got my reputation to consider. We mustn't be seen, of course!'

The face vanished in the darkness, but he had recognised it—the shining skin, the bright, glancing eyes. The sweet breath touched his cheek. The candlestick was taken from him by a swift, deft movement. He heard it knock the wainscoting as it was set down. He went out into a pitch-black corridor, where a soft hand seized his own and led him—by a back-door, it seemed—out into the open air of the hillside immediately behind the hotel.

He saw the stars. The morning was cool and fragrant, the sharp air waked him, and the last vestiges of sleep went flying. He had been drowsy and confused, had obeyed the summons without thinking. He now realised suddenly that he was engaged in an act of madness.

45

The girl, dressed in some flimsy material thrown loosely about her head and body, stood a few feet away, looking, he thought, like some figure called out of dreams and slumber of a forgotten world, out of legend almost. He saw her evening shoes peep out; he divined an evening dress beneath the gauzy covering. The light wind blew it close against her figure. He thought of a nymph.

'I say—but haven't you been to bed?' he asked stupidly.

He had meant to expostulate, to apologize for his foolish rashness, to scold and say they must go back at once. Instead, this sentence came. He guessed she had been sitting up all night. He stood still a second, staring in mute admiration, his eyes full of bewildered question.

'Watching the stars,' she met his thought with a happy laugh. 'Orion has touched the horizon. I came for you at once. We've got just four hours!' The voice, the smile, the eyes, the reference to Orion, swept him off his feet. Something in him broke loose and flew wildly, recklessly to the stars.

'Let us be off!' he cried, 'before the Bear tilts down. Already Alcyone begins to fade. I'm ready. Come!'

She laughed. The wind blew the gauze aside to show two ivory-white limbs. She caught his hand again, and they scampered together up the steep hillside toward the woods. Soon the big hotel, the villas, the white houses of the little town where natives and visitors still lay soundly sleeping, were out of sight. The farther sky came down to meet them. The stars were paling, but no sign of actual dawn was yet visible. The freshness stung their cheeks. Slowly, the heavens grew lighter, the east turned rose, the outline of the trees defined themselves, there was a stirring of the silvery-green leaves. They were among olive-groves—but the spirits of the trees were dancing. Far below them, a pool of deep colour, they saw the ancient sea. They saw the tiny specks of distant fishing-boats. The sailors were singing to the dawn, and birds among the mimosa of the hanging gardens answered them.

Pausing a moment at length beneath a gaunt old tree, whose struggle to leave the clinging earth had tortured its great

46

writhing arms and trunk, they took their breath, gazing at one another with eyes full of happy dreams.

'You understood so quickly,' said the girl, 'my little message. I knew by your eyes and ears you would.' And she first tweaked his ears with two slender fingers mischievously, then laid her soft palm with a momentary light pressure on both eyes.

'You're half-and-half, at any rate,' she went on looking him up and down for a swift instant of appraisement, 'if you're not altogether.' The laughter showed her white, even little teeth.

'You know how to play, and that's something,' she added. Then, as if to herself, 'You'll be altogether before I've done with you.'

'Shall I?' he stammered, afraid to look at her.

Puzzled, some spirit of compromise still lingering in him, he knew not what she meant; he knew only that the current of life flowed increasingly through his veins, but that her eyes confused him.

'I'm longing for it,' he added. 'How wonderfully you did it! They roll so awkwardly——'

'Oh, that!' She peered at him through a wisp of hair. 'You've kept it, I hope.'

'Rather. It's on my mantelpiece——'

'You're sure you haven't eaten it?' and she made a delicious mimicry with her red lips, so that he saw the tip of a small, pointed tongue.

'I shall keep it,' he swore, 'as long as these arms have life in them,' and he seized her just as she was crouching to escape, and covered her with kisses.

'I knew you longed to play,' she panted, when he released her. 'Still, it was sweet of you to pick it up before another got it.'

'Another!' he exclaimed.

'The gods decide. It's a lob-sided thing, remember. It can't roll straight.' She looked oddly mischievous, elusive.

He stared at her.

'If it had rolled elsewhere—and another had picked it up——?'

he began.

'I should be with that other now!' And this time she was off and away before he could prevent her, and the sound of her silvery laughter mocked him among the olive-trees beyond. He was up and after her in a second, following her slim whiteness in and out of the old-world grove, as she flitted lightly, her hair flying in the wind, her figure flashing like a ray of sunlight or the race of foaming water—till at last he caught her and drew her down upon his knees, and kissed her wildly, forgetting who and where and what he was.

'Hark!' she whispered breathlessly, one arm close about his neck. 'I hear their footsteps. Listen! It is the pipe!'

'The pipe——!' he repeated, conscious of a tiny but delicious shudder.

For a sudden chill ran through him as she said it. He gazed at her. Her hair fell loose about her cheeks, flushed and rosy with his hot kisses. Her eyes were bright and wild for all their softness. Her face, turned sideways to him as she listened, wore an extraordinary look that for an instant made his blood run cold. He saw the parted lips, the small white teeth, the slim neck of ivory, the young bosom panting from his tempestuous embrace. Of an unearthly loveliness and brightness she seemed to him, yet with this strange, remote expression that touched his soul with sudden terror.

Her face turned slowly.

'Who *are* you?' he whispered. He sprang to his feet without waiting for her answer.

He was young and agile; strong, too, with that quick response of muscle they have who keep their bodies well; but he was no match for her. Her speed and agility outclassed his own with ease. She leaped. Before he had moved one leg forward toward escape, she was clinging with soft, supple arms and limbs about him, so that he could not free himself, and as her weight bore him downward to the ground her lips found his own and kissed them into silence. She lay buried again in his embrace, her hair across his eyes, her heart against his heart, and he forgot his question, forgot his little fear, forgot the very world he knew....

'They come, they come,' she cried gaily. 'The Dawn is here. Are you ready?'

'I've been ready for five thousand years,' he answered, leaping to his feet beside her.

'Altogether!' came upon a sparkling laugh that was like wind among the olive-leaves.

Shaking her last gauzy covering from her, she snatched his hand, and they ran forward together to join the dancing throng now crowding up the slope beneath the tress. Their happy singing filled the sky, Decked with vine and ivy, and trailing silvery-green branches, they poured in a flood of radiant life along the mountain-side. Slowly they melted away into the blue distance of the breaking dawn, and, as the last figure disappeared, the sun came up slowly out of a purple sea....

They came to the place he knew—the deserted earthquake village—and a faint memory stirred in him. He did not actually recall that he had visited it already, had eaten his sandwiches with 'hotel friends' beneath its crumbling walls; but there was a dim troubling sense of familiarity—nothing more. The houses still stood, but pigeons lived in them, and weasels, stoats, and snakes had their uncertain homes in ancient bedrooms. Not twenty years ago the peasants thronged its narrow streets, through which the dawn now peered and cool wind breathed among dew-laden brambles.

'I know the house,' she cried, 'the house where we would live!' and raced, a flying form of air and sunlight, into a tumbled cottage that had no roof, no floor or windows. Wild bees had hung a nest against the broken wall.

He followed her. There was sunlight in the room, and there were flowers. Upon a rude, simple table lay a bowl of cream, with eggs, and honey and butter close against a homemade loaf. They sank into each orher's arms upon a couch of fragrant grass and boughs against the window where wild roses bloomed ... and the bees flew in and out.

It was Bussana, the so-called earthquake village, because a sudden earthquake had fallen on it one summer morning when all the inhabitants were at church. The crashing roof killed sixty, the tumbling walls another hundred, and the rest had left it where it stood.

'The church,' he said, vaguely remembering the story. 'They were at prayer——'

The girl laughed carelessly in his ear, setting his blood in a rush and quiver of delicious joy. He felt himself untamed, wild as the wind and animals. 'The true God claimed His own,' she whispered. 'He came back. Ah, they were not ready— —the old priests had seen to that. But He came. They heard His music. Then His tread shook the olive-groves, the old ground danced, the hills leapt for joy——'

'They called it earthquake! And the houses crumbled,' he laughed as he pressed her closer to his heart.

'And now we've come back!' she cried merrily. 'We've come back to worship and be glad!' She nestled into him, while the sun rose higher. 'I hear them—hark!' she cried, and again leapt, dancing, from his side. Again he followed her like wind. Through the broken window they saw the naked fauns and nymphs and satyrs rolling, dancing, shaking their soft hoofs amid the ferns and brambles. Toward the ruptured church they sped with feet of light and air. A roar of happy song and laughter rose.

'Come!' he cried. 'We must go too.'

Hand in hand they raced to join the tumbling, dancing throng. She was in his arms and on his back and flung across his shoulders as he ran. They reached the broken building, its whole roof gone sliding years ago, its walls atremble still, its shattered shrines alive with nestling birds.

'Hush!' she whispered, in a tone of awe, yet pleasure. '*He* is there!' She pointed, her bare arm outstretched, above the bending heads.

There, in the empty space, where once stood sacred Host and cup, He sat, filling the niche sublimely and with awful power. His shaggy form, benign yet terrible, rose through the broken stone. The great eyes shone and smiled. The feet were lost in brambles....

'God!' cried a wild, frightened voice, yet with deep worship in it—and the old familiar panic came with portentous swiftness. The great Figure rose.

The birds flew screaming, the animals sought holes, the worshippers, laughing and glad a moment ago, rushed tumbling over one another for the doors.

'He goes again! Who called? Who called like that? His feet shake the ground!'

'It is the earthquake!' screamed a woman's shrill accents in ghastly terror.

'Kiss me—one kiss before we forget again!...' sighed a laughing, passionate voice against his ear. 'Once more your arms, your heart beating on my lips...! You recognised His power. You are now *altogether!* We shall remember!'

But he woke, with the heavy bedclothes stuffed against his mouth and the wind of early morning sighing mournfully about the hotel walls.

.   .   .   .   .

'Have they left again—those ladies?' he inquired casually of the head waiter, pointing to the table. 'They were here last night at dinner.'

'Who do you mean?' replied the man stupidly, gazing at the spot indicated with a face quite blank. 'Last night—at dinner?' He tried to think.

'An English lady, elderly, with—ner daughter——' at which moment precisely the girl came in alone. Lunch was over, the room empty.

There was a second's difficult pause. It seemed ridiculous not to speak. Their eyes met. The girl blushed furiously.

He was very quick for an Englishman. 'I was allowing, myself to ask after your mother,' he began. 'I was afraid' —he glanced at the table laid for one— 'she was not well, perhaps?'

'Oh, but that's very kind of you, I'm sure.' She smiled. He saw the small white even teeth....

51

And before three days had passed he was so deeply in love that he simply couldn't help himself.

'I believe,' he said lamely, 'this is yours. You dropped it, you know. Er—may I keep it? It's only an olive.'

They were, of course, in an olive-grove when he asked it, and the sun was setting.

She looked at him, looked him up and down, looked at his ears, his eyes. He felt that in another second her little fingers would slip up and tweak the first or close the second with a soft pressure——

'Tell me,' he begged: 'did you dream anything—that first night I saw you?'

She took a quick step backward. 'No,' she said, as he followed her more quickly still, 'I don't think I did. But,' she went on breathlessly as he caught her up, 'I knew—from the way you picked it up——'

'Knew what?' he demanded, holding her tightly so that she could not ge away again.

'That you were already half and half, but would soon be altogether.'

And, as he kissed her, he felt her soft fingers tweak his ears.

THE SACRIFICE

I

LIMASSON was a religious man, though of what depth and quality were unknown, since no trial of ultimate severity had yet tested him. An adherent of no particular creed, he yet had his gods; and his self-discipline was probably more rigorous than his friends conjectured. He was so reserved. Few guessed, perhaps, the desires conquered, the passions regulated, the inner tendencies trained and schooled—not by denying their expression, but by transmuting them alchemically into nobler channels. He had in him the makings of an enthusiastic devotee, and might have become such but for two limitations that prevented. He loved his wealth, labouring to increase it to the neglect of other interests; and, secondly, instead of following up one steady line of search, he scattered himself upon many picturesque theories, like an actor who wants to play all parts rather than concentrate on one. And the more picturesque the part, the more he was attracted. Thus, though he did his duty unshrinkingly and with a touch of love, he accused himself sometimes of merely gratifying a sensuous taste in spiritual sensations. There was this unbalance in him that argued want of depth.

As for his gods—in the end he discovered their reality by first doubting, then denying their existence.

It was this denial and doubt that restored them to their thrones, converting his dilettante skirmishes into genuine, deep belief; and the proof came to him one summer in early June when he was making ready to leave town for his annual month among the mountains.

With Limasson mountains, in some inexplicable sense, were a passion almost, and climbing so deep a pleasure that the ordinary scrambler hardly understood it. Grave as a kind of worship it was to him; the preparations for an ascent, the ascent

53

itself in particular, involved a concentration that seemed symbolical as of a ritual. He not only loved the heights, the massive grandeur, the splendour of vast proportions blocked in space, but loved them with a respect that held a touch of awe. The emotion mountains stirred in him, one might say, was of that profound, incalculable kind that held kinship with his religious feelings, half realised though these were. His gods had their invisible thrones somewhere among the grim, forbidding heights. He prepared himself for this annual mountaineering with the same earnestness that a holy man might approach a solemn festival of his church.

And the impetus of his mind was running with big momentum in this direction, when there fell upon him, almost on the eve of starting, a swift series of disasters that shook his being to its last foundations, and left him stunned among the ruins. To describe these is unnecessary. People said, 'One thing after another like that! What appalling luck! Poor wretch!' then wondered, with the curiosity of children, how in the world he would take it. Due to no apparent fault of his own, these disasters were so sudden that life seemed in a moment shattered, and his interest in existence almost ceased. People shook their heads and thought of the emergency exit. But Limasson was too vital a man to dream of annihilation. Upon him it had a different effect—he turned and questioned what he called his gods. They did not answer or explain. For the first time in his life he doubted. A hair's breadth beyond lay definite denial.

The ruin in which he sat, however, was not material; no man of his age, possessed of courage and a working scheme of life, would permit disaster of a material order to overwhelm him. It was collapse of a mental, spiritual kind, an assault upon the roots of character and temperament. Moral duties laid suddenly upon him threatened to crush. His *personal* existence was assailed, and apparently must end. He must spend the remainder of his life caring for others who were nothing to him. No outlet showed, no way of escape, so diabolically complete was the combination of events that rushed his inner trenches. His faith was shaken. A man can but endure so much, and remain human. For him the saturation point seemed reached. He experienced the spiritual equivalent of that physical numbness which supervenes when pain has touched the limit of endurance. He laughed, grew callous, then mocked his silent gods.

It is said that upon this state of blank negation there follows sometimes a condition of lucidity which mirrors with crystal clearness the forces driving behind life at a given moment, a kind of clairvoyance that brings explanation and therefore peace. Limasson looked for this in vain. There was the doubt that questioned, there was the sneer that mocked the silence into which his questions fell; but there was neither answer nor explanation, and certainly not peace. There was no relief. In this tumult of revolt he did none of the things his friends suggested or expected; he merely followed the line of least resistance. He yielded to the impetus that was upon him when the catastrophe came. To their indignant amazement he went out to his mountains.

All marvelled that at such a time he could adopt so trivial a line of action, neglecting duties that seemed paramount; they disapproved. Yet in reality he was taking no definite action at all, but merely drifting, with the momentum that had been acquired just before. He was bewildered with so much pain, confused with suffering, stunned with the crash that flung him helpless amid undeserved calamity. He turned to the mountains as a child to its mother, instinctively. Mountains had never failed to bring him consolation, comfort, peace. Their grandeur restored proportion whenever disorder threatened life. No calculation, properly speaking, was in his move at all; but a blind desire for a violent physical reaction such as climbing brings. And the instinct was more wholesome than he knew.

In the high upland valley among lonely peaks whither Limasson then went, he found in some measure the proportion he had lost. He studiously avoided thinking; he lived in his muscles recklessly. The region with its little Inn was familiar to him; peak after peak he attacked, sometimes with, but more often without a guide, until his reputation as a sane climber, a laurelled member of all the foreign Alpine Clubs, was seriously in danger. That he overdid it physically is beyond question, but that the mountains breathed into him some portion of their enormous calm and deep endurance is also true. His gods, meanwhile, he neglected utterly for the first time in his life. If he thought of them at all, it was as tinsel figures imagination had created, figures upon a stage that merely decorated life for those whom pretty pictures pleased. Only—he had left the theatre and their make-believe no longer hypnotised his mind. He realised their impotence and disowned them. This attitude, however, was subconscious; he lent to it no substance, either of thought or speech. He ignored rather than challenged their existence.

And it was somewhat in this frame of mind—thinking little, feeling even less—that he came out into the hotel vestibule after dinner one evening, and took mechanically the bundle of letters the porter handed to him. They had no possible interest for him; in a corner where the big steam-heater mitigated the chilliness of the hall, he idly sorted them. The score or so of other guests, chiefly expert climbing men, were trailing out in twos and threes from the dining-room; but he felt as little interest in them as in his letters: no conversation could alter facts, no written phrases change his circumstances. At random, then, he opened a business letter with a typewritten address—it would probably be impersonal, less of a mockery, therefore, than the others with their tiresome sham condolences. And, in a sense, it was impersonal; sympathy from a solicitor's office is mere formula, a few extra ticks upon the universal keyboard of a Remington. But as he read it, Limasson made a discovery that startled him into acute and bitter sensation. He had imagined the limit of bearable suffering and disaster already reached. Now, in a few dozen words, his error was proved convincingly. The fresh blow was dislocating.

This culminating news of additional catastrophe disclosed within him entirely new reaches of pain, of biting, resentful fury. Limasson experienced a momentary stopping of the heart as he took it in, a dizziness, a violent sensation of revolt whose impotence induced almost physical nausea. He felt like—death.

'Must I suffer all things?' flashed through his arrested intelligence in letters of fire.

There was a sullen rage in him, a dazed bewilderment, but no positive suffering as yet. His emotion was too sickening to include the smaller pains of disappointment; it was primitive, blind anger that he knew. He read the letter calmly, even to the neat paragraph of machine-made sympathy at the last, then placed it in his inner pocket. No outward sign of disturbance was upon him; his breath came slowly; he reached over to the table for a match, holding it at arm's length lest the sulphur fumes should sting his nostrils.

And in that moment he made his second discovery. The fact that further suffering was still possible included also the fact that some touch of resignation had been left in him, and therefore some vestige of belief as well. Now, as he felt the crackling sheet of stiff paper in his pocket, watched the sulphur die, and saw the wood ignite, this remnant faded utterly away. Like the blackened end of the match, it shrivelled and dropped off. It vanished. Savagely, yet with an external calmness that enabled him to light his pipe with untrembling hand, he addressed his futile deities. And once more in fiery letters there flashed across the darkness of his passionate thought:

'Even this you demand of me—this cruel, ultimate sacrifice?'

And he rejected them, bag and baggage; for they were a mockery and a lie. With contempt he repudiated them for ever. The stage of doubt had passed. He denied his gods. Yet, with a smile upon his lips; for what were they after all but the puppets his religious fancy had imagined? They never had existed. Was it, then merely the picturesque, sensational aspect of his devotional temperament that had created them? That side of his nature, in any case, was dead now, killed by a single devastating blow. The gods went with it.

57

Surveying what remained of his life, it seemed to him like a city that an earthquake has reduced to ruins. The inhabitants think no worse thing could happen. Then comes the fire.

Two lines of thought, it seems, then developed parallel in him and simultaneously, for while underneath he stormed against this culminating blow, his upper mind dealt calmly with the project of a great expedition he would make at dawn. He had engaged no guide. As an experienced mountaineer, he knew the district well; his name was tolerably familiar, and in half an hour he could have settled all details, and retired to bed with instructions to be called at two. But, instead, he sat there waiting, unable to stir, a human volcano that any moment might break forth into violence. He smoked his pipe as quietly as though nothing had happened, while through the blazing depths of him ran ever this one self-repeating statement: 'Even this you demand of me, this cruel, ultimate sacrifice!...' His self-control, dynamically estimated, just then must have been very great and, thus repressed, the store of potential energy accumulated enormously.

With thought concentrated largely upon this final blow, Limasson had not noticed the people who streamed out of the *salle à manger* and scattered themselves in groups about the hall. Some individual, now and again, approached his chair with the idea of conversation, then, seeing his absorption, turned away. Even when a climber whom he slightly knew reached across him with a word of apology for the matches, Limasson made no response, for he did not see him. He noticed nothing. In particular he did not notice two men, who, from an opposite corner, had for some time been observing him. He now looked up—by chance?—and was vaguely aware that they were discussing him. He met their eyes across the hall, and started.

For at first he thought he knew them. Possibly he had seen them about in the hotel—they seemed familiar—yet he certainly had never spoken with them. Aware of his mistake, he turned his glance elsewhere, though still vividly conscious of their attention. One was a clergyman or a priest; his face wore an air of gravity touched by sadness, a sternness about the lips counteracted by a kindling beauty in the eyes that betrayed enthusiasm nobly regulated. There was a suggestion of stateliness in the man that made the impression very sharp. His clothing emphasised it. He wore a dark tweed suit that was strict in its simplicity. There was austerity in him somewhere.

His companion, perhaps by contrast, seemed inconsiderable in his conventional evening dress. A good deal younger than his friend, his hair, always a tell-tale detail, was a trifle long; the thin fingers that flourished a cigarette wore rings; the face, though picturesque, was flippant, and his entire attitude conveyed a certain insignificance. Gesture, that faultless language which challenges counterfeit, betrayed unbalance somewhere. The impression he produced, however, was shadowy compared to the sharpness of the other. 'Theatrical' was the word in Limasson's mind, as he turned his glance elsewhere. But as he looked away he fidgeted. The interior darkness caused by the dreadful letter rose about him. It engulfed him. Dizziness came with it....

Far away the blackness was fringed with light, and through this light, stepping with speed and carelessness as from gigantic distance, the two men, suddenly grown large, came at him. Limasson, in self-protection, turned to meet them. Conversation he did not desire. Somehow he had expected this attack.

Yet the instant they began to speak—it was the priest who opened fire—it was all so natural and easy that he almost welcomed the diversion. A phrase by way of introduction—and he was speaking of the summits. Something in Limasson's mind turned over. The man was a serious climber, one of his own species. The sufferer felt a certain relief as he heard the invitation, and realised, though dully, the compliment involved.

'If you felt inclined to join us—if you would honour us with your company,' the man was saying quietly, adding something then about 'your great experience' and 'invaluable advice and judgment.'

Limasson looked up, trying hard to concentrate and understand.

'The Tour du Néant?' he repeated, mentioning the peak proposed. Rarely attempted, never conquered, and with an ominous record of disaster, it happened to be the very summit he had meant to attack himself next day.

'You have engaged guides?' He knew the question foolish.

'No guide will try it,' the priest answered, smiling, while his companion added with a flourish, 'but we—we need no guide—if *you* will come.'

'You are unattached, I believe? You are alone?' the priest enquired, moving a little in front of his friend, as though to keep him in the background.

'Yes,' replied Limasson. 'I am quite alone.'

He was listening attentively, but with only part of his mind. He realised the flattery of the invitation. Yet it was like flattery addressed to some one else. He felt himself so indifferent, so—dead. These men wanted his skilful body, his experienced mind; and it was his body and mind that talked with them, and finally agreed to go. Many a time expeditions had been planned in just this way, but to-night he felt there was a difference. Mind and body signed the agreement, but his soul, listening elsewhere and looking on, was silent. With his rejected gods it had left him, though hovering close still. It did not interfere; it did not warn; it even approved; it sang to him from great distance that this expedition cloaked another. He was bewildered by the clashing of his higher and his lower mind.

'At one in the morning then, if that will suit you...' the older man concluded.

'I'll see to the provisions,' exclaimed the younger enthusiastically, 'and I shall take my telephoto for the summit. The porters can come as far as the Great Tower. We're over six thousand feet here already, you see, so...' and his voice died away in the distance as his companion led him off.

Limasson saw him go with relief. But for the other man he would have declined the invitation. At heart he was indifferent enough. What decided him really was the coincidence

60

that the Tour du Néant was the very peak he had intended to attack himself *alone,* and the curious feeling that this expedition cloaked another somehow—almost that these men had a hidden motive. But he dismissed the idea—it was not worth thinking about. A moment later he followed them to bed. So careless was he of the affairs of the world, so dead to mundane interests, that he tore up his other letters and tossed them into a corner of the room—unread.

II

Once in his chilly bedroom he realised that his upper mind had permitted him to do a foolish thing; he had drifted like a schoolboy into an unwise situation. He had pledged himself to an expedition with two strangers, an expedition for which normally he would have chosen his companions with the utmost caution. Moreover, he was guide; they looked to him for safety, while yet it was they had arranged and planned it. But who were these men with whom he proposed to run grave bodily risks? He knew them as little as they knew him. Whence came, he wondered, the curious idea that this climb was really planned by another who was no one of them?

The thought slipped idly across his mind; going out by one door, it came back, however, quickly by another. He did not think about it more than to note its passage through the disorder that passed with him just then for thinking. Indeed, there was nothing in the whole world for which he cared a single brass farthing. As he undressed for bed, he said to himself: 'I shall be called at one... but why am I going with these two on this wild plan?... And who made the plan?'...

It seemed to have settled itself. It came about so naturally and easily, so quickly. He probed no deeper. He didn't care. And for the first time he omitted the little ritual, half prayer, half adoration, it had always been his custom to offer to his deities upon retiring to rest. He no longer recognised them.

How utterly broken his life was! How blank and terrible and lonely! He felt cold, and piled his overcoats upon the bed, as though his mental isolation involved a physical effect as well. Switching off the light by the door, he was in the act of crossing the floor in the darkness when a sound beneath the window caught his ear. Outside there were voices talking. The roar of falling water made them indistinct, yet he was sure they were voices, and that one of them he knew. He stopped still to listen. He heard his own name uttered—'John Limasson.' They ceased. He stood a moment shivering on the boards, then crawled into bed beneath the heavy clothing. But in the act of settling down, they began again. He raised himself again hurriedly to listen. What little wind there was passed in that moment down the valley, carrying off the roar of falling water; and into the moment's space of silence dropped fragments of definite sentences:

'They are close, you say—close down upon the world?' It was the voice of the priest surely.

'For days they have been passing,' was the answer—a rough, deep tone that might have been a peasant's, and a kind of fear in it, 'for all my flocks are scattered.'

'The signs are sure? You know them?'

'Tumult,' was the answer in much lower tones. 'There has been tumult in the mountains...'

There was a break then as though the voices sank too low to be heard. Two broken fragments came next, end of a question—beginning of an answer.

'...the opportunity of a lifetime?'

'...if he goes of his own free will, success is sure. For acceptance is...'

And the wind, returning, bore back the sound of the falling water, so that Limasson heard no more...

An indefinable emotion stirred in him as he turned over to sleep. He stuffed his ears lest he should hear more. He was aware of a sinking of the heart that was inexplicable. What in the world were they talking about, these two? What was the meaning of these disjointed phrases? There lay behind them a grave significance almost solemn. That 'tumult in the mountains' was somehow ominous, its suggestion terrible

62

and mighty. He felt disturbed, uncomfortable, the first emotion that had stirred in him for days. The numbness melted before its faint awakening. Conscience was in it—he felt vague prickings —but it was deeper far than conscience. Somewhere out of sight, in a region life had as yet not plumbed, the words sank down and vibrated like pedal notes. They rumbled away into the night of undecipherable things. And, though explanation failed him, he felt they had reference somehow to the morrow's expedition: how, what, wherefore, he knew not; his name had been spoken—then these curious sentences; that was all. Yet to-morrow's expedition, what was it but an expedition of impersonal kind, not even planned by himself? Merely his own plan taken and altered by others—made over? His personal business, his personal life, were not really in it at all.

The thought startled him a moment. He had no personal life...!

Struggling with sleep, his brain played the endless game of disentanglement without winning a single point, while the under-mind in him looked on and smiled—because it *knew*. Then, suddenly, a great peace fell over him. Exhaustion brought it perhaps. He fell asleep; and next moment, it seemed, he was aware of a thundering at the door and an unwelcome growling voice, ' *'s ist bald ein Uhr, Herr! Aufstehen!*'

Rising at such an hour, unless the heart be in it, is a sordid and depressing business; Limasson dressed without enthusiasm, conscious that thought and feeling were exactly where he had left them on going to sleep. The same confusion and bewilderment were in him; also the same deep solemn emotion stirred by the whispering voices. Only long habit enabled him to attend to detail, and ensured that nothing was forgotten. He felt heavy and oppressed, a kind of anxiety about him; the routine of preparation he followed gravely, utterly untouched by the customary joy; it was mechanical. Yet through it ran the old familiar sense of ritual, due to the practice of so many years, that cleansing of mind and body for a big Ascent—like initiatory rites that once had been as important

63

to him as those of some priest who approached the worship of his deity in the temples of ancient time. He performed the ceremony with the same care as though no ghost of vanished faith still watched him, beckoning from the air as formerly.... His knapsack carefully packed, he took his ice-axe from beside the bed, turned out the light, and went down the creaking wooden stairs in stockinged feed, lest his heavy boots should waken the other sleepers. And in his head still rang the phrase he had fallen asleep on—as though just uttered:

'The signs are sure; for days they have been passing—close down upon the world. The flocks are scattered. There has been tumult—tumult in the mountains.' The other fragments he had forgotten. But who were 'they'? And why did the word bring a chill of awe into his blood?

And as the words rolled through him Limasson felt tumult in his thoughts and feelings too. There had been tumult in his life, and all his joys were scattered—joys that hitherto had fed his days. The signs were sure. Something was close down upon his little world—passing—sweeping. He felt a touch of terror.

Outside in the fresh darkness of very early morning the strangers stood waiting for him. Rather, they seemed to arrive in the same instant as himself, equally punctual. The clock in the church tower sounded one. They exchanged low greetings, remarked that the weather promised to hold good, and started off in single file over soaking meadows towards the first belt of forest. The porter—mere peasant, unfamiliar of face and not connected with the hotel led the way with a hurricane lantern. The air was marvellously sweet and fragrant. In the sky overhead the stars shone in their thousands. Only the noise of falling water from the heights, and the regular thud of their heavy boots broke the stillness. And, black against the sky, towered the enormous pyramid of the Tour du Néant they meant to conquer.

Perhaps the most delightful portion of a big ascent is the beginning in the scented darkness while the thrill of possible conquest lies still far off. The hours stretch themselves queerly;

64

last night's sunset might be days ago; sunrise and the brilliance coming seem in another week, part of dim futurity like children's holidays. It is difficult to realise that this biting cold before the dawn, and the blazing heat to come, both belong to the same to-day.

There were no sounds as they toiled slowly up the zigzag path through the first fifteen hundred feet of pine-woods; no one spoke; the clink of nails and ice-axe points against the stones was all they heard. For the roar of water was felt rather than heard; it beat against the ears and the skin of the whole body at once. The deeper notes were below them now in the sleeping valley; the shriller ones sounded far above, where streams just born out of ponderous snow-beds tinkled sharply....

The change came delicately. The stars turned a shade less brilliant, a softness in them as of human eyes that say farewell. Between the highest branches the sky grew visible. A sighing air smoothed all their crests one way; moss, earth, and open spaces brought keen perfumes; and the little human procession, leaving the forest, stepped out into the vastness of the world above the tree-line. They paused while the porter stooped to put his lantern out. In the eastern sky was colour. The peaks and crags rushed closer.

Was it the Dawn? Limasson turned his eyes from the height of sky where the summits pierced a path for the coming day, to the faces of his companions, pale and wan in the early twilight. How small, how insignificant they seemed amid this hungry emptiness of desolation. The stupendous cliffs fled past them, led by headstrong peaks crowned with eternal snows. Thin lines of cloud, trailing half way up precipice and ridge, seemed like the swish of movement—as though he caught the earth turning as she raced through space. The four of them, timid riders on the gigantic saddle, clung for their lives against her titan ribs, while currents of some majestic life swept up at them from every side. He drew deep draughts of the rarefied air into his lungs. It was very cold. Avoiding the pallid, insignificant faces of his companions, he pretended interest in the porter's operations; he stared fixedly on the ground. It seemed twenty minutes before the flame was extinguished, and the lantern fastened to the pack behind. This Dawn was unlike any he had seen before.

For, in reality, all the while Limasson was trying to bring order out of the extraordinary thoughts and feelings that had possessed him during the slow forest ascent, and the task was not crowned with much success. The Plan, made by others, had taken charge of him, he felt; and he had thrown the reins of personal will and interest loosely upon its steady gait. He had abandoned himself carelessly to what might come. Knowing that he was leader of the expedition, he yet had suffered the porter to go first, taking his own place as it was appointed to him, behind the younger man, but before the priest. In this order, they had plodded, as only experienced climbers plod, for hours without a rest, until half way up a change had taken place. He had wished it, and instantly it was effected. The priest moved past him, while his companion dropped to the rear—the companion who forever stumbled in his speed, whereas the older man climbed surely, confidently. And thereafter Limasson walked more easily—as though the relative positions of the three were of importance somehow. The steep ascent of smothering darkness through the woods became less arduous. He was glad to have the younger man behind him.

For the impression had strengthened as they climbed in silence that this ascent pertained to some significant Ceremony, and the idea had grown insistently, almost stealthily, upon him. The movements of himself and his companions, especially the positions each occupied relatively to the other, established some kind of intimacy that resembled speech, suggesting even question and answer. And the entire performance, while occupying hours by his watch, it seemed to him more than once, had been in reality briefer than the flash of a passing thought, so that he saw it within himself—pictorially. He thought of a picture worked in colours upon a strip of elastic. Some one pulled the strip, and the picture stretched. Or some one released it again, and the picture flew back, reduced to a mere stationary speck. All happened in a single speck of time.

And the little change of position, apparently so trivial, gave point to this singular notion working in his under-mind—that this ascent was a ritual and a ceremony as in older days, its significance approaching revelation, however, for the first time—now. Without language, this stole over him; no words could quite describe it. For it came to him that these three formed a unit, himself being in some fashion yet the acknowledged principal, the leader. The labouring porter had no place in it, for this first toiling through the darkness was a preparation, and when the actual climb began, he would disappear, while Limasson himself went first. This idea that they took part together in a Ceremony established itself firmly in him, with the added wonder that, though so often done, he performed it now for the first time with full comprehension, knowledge, truth. Empty of personal desire, indifferent to an ascent that formerly would have thrilled his heart with ambition and delight, he understood that climbing had ever been a ritual for his soul and of his soul, and that power must result from its sincere accomplishment. It was a symbolical ascent.

In words this did not come to him. He felt it, never criticising. That is, he neither rejected nor accepted. It stole most sweetly, grandly, over him. It floated into him while he climbed, yet so convincingly that he had felt his relative position must be changed. The younger man held too prominent a post, or at least a wrong one—in advance. Then, after the change, effected mysteriously as though all recognised it, this line of certainty increased, and there came upon him the big, strange knowledge that all of life is a Ceremony on a giant scale, and that by performing the movements accurately, with sincere fidelity, there may come—knowledge. There was gravity in him from that moment.

This ran in his mind with certainty. Though his thought assumed no form of little phrases, his brain yet furnished detailed statements that clinched the marvellous thing with simile and incident which daily life might apprehend: that knowledge arises from action; that to do the thing invites the teaching and explains it. Action, moreover, is symbolical; a group of men, a family, an entire nation, engaged in those daily movements which are the working out of their destiny, perform a Ceremony which is in direct relation somewhere to the pattern of greater happenings which are the teachings of the Gods. Let the body imitate, reproduce—in a bedroom, in a wood—anywhere—the movements of the stars, and the meaning of those stars shall sink down into the heart. The movements constitute a script, a language. To mimic the gestures of a stranger is to understand his mood, his point of view—to establish a grave and solemn intimacy. Temples are everywhere, for the entire earth is a temple, and the body, House of Royalty, is the biggest temple of them all. To ascertain the pattern its movements trace in daily life, *could* be to determine the relation of that particular ceremony to the Cosmos, and so learn power. The entire system of Pythagoras, he realised, could be taught without a single word—by movements; and in everyday life even the commonest act and vulgarest movement are part of some big Ceremony—a message from the Gods. Ceremony, in a word, is three-dimensional language, and action, therefore, is the language of the Gods. The Gods he had denied were speaking to him... passing with tumult close across his broken life.... Their passage it was, indeed, that had caused the breaking!

In this cryptic, condensed fashion the great fact came over him—that he and these other two, here and now, took part in some great Ceremony of whose ultimate object as yet he was in ignorance. The impact with which it dropped upon his mind was tremendous. He realised it most fully when he stepped from the darkness of the forest and entered the expanse of glimmering, early light; up till this moment his mind was being prepared only, whereas now he knew. The innate desire to worship which all along had been his, the momentum his religious temperament had acquired during forty years, the yearning to have proof, in a word, that the Gods he once

acknowledged were really true, swept back upon him wih
that violent reaction which denial had aroused.

He wavered where he stood....

Looking about him, then, while the others rearranged
burdens the returning porter now discarded, he perceived the
astonishing beauty of the time and place, feeling it soak into
him as by the very pores of his skin. From all sides this beauty
rushed upon him. Some radiant, winged sense of wonder
sped past him through the silent air. A thrill of ecstasy ran
down every nerve. The hair of his head stood up. It was far
from unfamiliar to him, this sight of the upper mountain
world awakening from its sleep of the summer night, but
never before had he stood shuddering thus at its exquisite
cold glory, nor felt its significance as now, so mysteriously
within himself. Some transcendent power that held sublimity
was passing across this huge desolate plateau, far more majestic
than the mere sunrise among mountains he had so often
witnessed. There was Movement. He understood why he
had seen his companions insignificant. Again he shivered
and looked about him, touched by a solemnity that held deep
awe.

Personal life, indeed, was wrecked, destroyed, but something
greater was on the way. His fragile alliance with a spiritual
world was strengthened. He realised his own past insolence.
He became afraid.

III

The treeless plateau, littered with enormous boulders,
stretched for miles to right and left, grey in the dusk of very
early morning. Behind him dropped thick guardian pine-
woods into the sleeping valley that still detained the darkness
of the night. Here and there lay patches of deep snow, gleaming
faintly through thin rising mist; singing streams of icy water
spread everywhere among the stones, soaking the coarse
rough grass that was the only sign of vegetation. No life
was visible; nothing stirred; nor anywhere was movement,

but of the quiet trailing mist and of his own breath that drifted past his face like smoke. Yet through the splendid stillness there *was* movement; that sense of absolute movement which results in stillness—it was owing to the stillness that he became aware of it—so vast, indeed, that only immobility could express it. Thus, on the calmest day in summer, may the headlong rushing of the earth through space seem more real than when the tempest shakes the trees and water on its surface; or great machinery turn with such vertiginous velocity that it appears steady to the deceived function of the eye. For it was not through the eye that this solemn Movement made itself known, but rather through a massive sensation that owned his entire body as its organ. Within the league-long amphitheatre of enormous peaks and precipices that enclosed the plateau, piling themselves upon the horizon, Limasson felt the outline of a Ceremony extended. The pulses of its grandeur poured into him where he stood. Its vast design was knowable because they themselves had traced—were even then tracing—its earthly counterpart in little. And the awe in him increased.

'This light is false. We have an hour yet before the true dawn,' he heard the younger man say lightly. 'The summits still are ghostly. Let us enjoy the sensation, and see what we can make of it.'

And Limasson, looking up startled from his reverie, saw that the far-away heights and towers indeed were heavy with shadow, faint still with the light of stars. It seemed to him they bowed their awful heads and that their stupendous shoulders lowered. They drew together, shutting out the world.

'True,' said his companion, 'and the upper snows still wear the spectral shine of night. But let us now move faster, for we travel very light. The sensations you propose will but delay and weaken us.'

He handed a share of the burdens to his companion and to Limasson. Slowly they all moved forward, and the mountains shut them in.

And two things Limasson noted then, as he shouldered his heavier pack and led the way: first, that he suddenly knew their destination though its purpose still lay hidden; and, secondly, that the porter's leaving before the ascent proper began signified finally that ordinary climbing was not their real objective. Also—the dawn was a lifting of inner veils from off his mind, rather than a brightening of the visible earth due to the nearing sun. Thick darkness, indeed, draped this enormous, lonely amphitheatre where they moved.

'You lead us well,' said the priest a few feet behind him, as he picked his way unfalteringly among the boulders and the streams.

'Strange that I do so,' replied Limasson in a low tone, 'for the way is new to me, and the darkness grows instead of lessening.' The language seemed hardly of his choosing. He spoke and walked as in a dream.

Far in the rear the voice of the younger man called plaintively after them:

'You go so fast, I can't keep up with you,' and again he stumbled and dropped his ice-axe among the rocks. He seemed for ever stooping to drink the icy water, or clambering off the trail to test the patches of snow as to quality and depth. 'You're missing all the excitement,' he cried repeatedly. 'There are a hundred pleasures and sensations by the way.'

They paused a moment for him to overtake them; he came up panting and exhausted, making remarks about the fading stars, the wind upon the heights, new routes he longed to try up dangerous couloirs, about everything, it seemed, except the work in hand. There was eagerness in him, the kind of excitement that saps energy and wastes the nervous force, threatening a probable collapse before the arduous object is attained.

'Keep to the thing in hand,' replied the priest sternly. 'We are not really going fast; it is you who are scattering yourself to no purpose. It wears us all. We must husband out resources,' and he pointed significantly to the pyramid of the Tour du Néant that gleamed above them at an incredible altitude.

'We are here to amuse ourselves; life is a pleasure, a sensation, or it is nothing,' grumbled his companion; but there was

71

a gravity in the tone of the older man that discouraged argument and made resistance difficult. The other arranged his pack for the tenth time, twisting his axe through an ingenious scheme of straps and string, and fell silently into line behind his leaders. Limasson moved on again... and the darkness at length began to lift. Far overhead, at first, the snowy summits shone with a hue less spectral; a delicate pink spread softly from the east; there was a freshening of the chilly wind; then suddenly the highest peak that topped the others by a thousand feet of soaring rock, stepped sharply into sight, half golden and half rose. At the same instant, the vast Movement of the entire scene slowed down; there came one or two terrific gusts of wind in quick succession; a roar like an avalanche of falling stones boomed distantly—and Limasson stopped dead and held his breath.

For something blocked the way before him, something he knew he could not pass. Gigantic and unformed, it seemed part of the architecture of the desolate waste about him, while yet it bulked there, enormous in the trembling dawn, as belonging neither to plain nor mountain. Suddenly it was there, where a moment before had been mere emptiness of air. Its massive outline shifted into visibility as though it had risen from the ground. He stood stock still. A cold that was not of this world turned him rigid in his tracks. A few yards behind him the priest had halted too. Farther in the rear they heard the stumbling tread of the younger man, and the faint calling of his voice—a feeble broken sound as of a man whom sudden fear distressed to helplessness.

'We're off the track, and I've lost my way,' the words came on the still air. 'My axe is gone... let us put on the rope!... Hark! Do you hear that roar?' And then a sound as though he came slowly groping on his hands and kness.

'You have exhausted yourself too soon,' the priest answered sternly. 'Stay where you are and rest, for we go no farther. This is the place we sought.'

There was in his tone a kind of ultimate solemnity that for a moment turned Limasson's attention from the great

obstacle that blocked his farther way. The darkness lifted
veil by veil, not gradually, but by a series of leaps as when
some one inexpertly turns a wick. He perceived then that
not a single Grandeur loomed in front, but that others of
similar kind, some huger than the first, stood all about him,
forming an enclosing circle that hemmed him in.

Then, with a start, he recovered himself. Equilibrium
and common sense returned. The trick that sight had played
upon him, assisted by the rarefied atmosphere of the heights
and by the witchery of dawn, was no uncommon one, after
all. The long straining of the eyes to pick the way in a uncertain
light so easily deceives perspective. Delusion ever follows
abrupt change of focus. These shadowy encircling forms were
but the rampart of still distant precipices whose giant walls
framed the tremendous amphitheatre to the sky.

Their closeness was a mere gesture of the dusk and distance.

The shock of the discovery produced an instant's unsteadiness
in him that brought bewilderment. He straightened up,
raised his head, and looked about him. The cliffs, it seemed,
to him, shifted back instantly to their accustomed places;
as though after all they *had* been close; there was a reeling
among the topmost crags; they balanced fearfully, then stood
still against a sky already faintly crimson. The roar he heard,
that might well have seemed the tumult of their hurrying
speed, was in reality but the wind of dawn that rushed against
their ribs, beating the echoes out with angry wings. And
the lines of trailing mist, streaking the air like proofs of rapid
motion, merely coiled and floated in the empty spaces.

He turned to the priest, who had moved up beside him.
'How strange,' he said, 'is this beginning of new light.
My sight went all astray for a passing moment. I thought
the mountains stood right across my path. And when I looked
up just now it seemed they all ran back.' His voice was small
and lost in the great listening air.

The man looked fixedly at him. He had removed his slouch
hat, hot with the long ascent, and as he answered, a long thin
shadow flitted across his features. A breadth of darkness

dropped about them. It was as though a mask were forming. The face that now was covered had been—naked. He was so long in answering that Limasson heard his mind sharpening the sentence like a pencil.

He spoke very slowly. '*They* move perhaps even as Their powers move, and Their minutes are our years. Their passage ever is in tumult. There is disorder then among the affairs of men; there is confusion in their minds. There may be ruin and disaster, but out of the wreckage shall issue strong, fresh growth. For like a sea, They pass.'

There was in his mien a grandeur that seemed borrowed marvellously from the mountains. His voice was grave and deep; he made no sign or gesture; and in his manner was a curious steadiness that breathed through the language a kind of sacred prophecy.

Long, thundering gusts of wind passed distantly across the precipices as he spoke. The same moment, expecting apparently no rejoinder to his strange utterance, he stooped and began to unpack his knapsack. The change from the sacerdotal language to this commonplace and practical detail was singulary bewildering.

'It is the time to rest,' he added, 'and the time to eat. Let us prepare.' And he drew out several small packets and laid them in a row upon the ground. Awe deepened over Limasson as he watched, and with it a great wonder too. For the words seemed ominous, as though this man, upon the floor of some vast Temple, said: 'Let us prepare a sacrifice...!' There flashed into him, out of depths that had hitherto concealed it, a lightning clue that hinted at explanation of the entire strange proceeding—of the abrupt meeting with the strangers, the impulsive acceptance of their project for the great ascent, their grave behaviour as though it were a Ceremonial of immense design, his change of position, the bewildering tricks of sight, and the solemn language, finally, of the older man that corroborated what he himself had deemed at first illusion. In a flying second of time this all swept through him—and with it the sharp desire to turn aside, retreat, to run away.

Noting the movement, or perhaps divining the emotion prompting it the priest looked up quickly. In his tone was a coldness that seemed as though this scene of wintry desolation uttered words:

'You have come too far to think of turning back. It is not possible. You stand now at the gates of birth—and death. All that might hinder, you have so bravely cast aside. Be brave now to the end.'

And, as Limasson heard the words, there dropped suddenly into him a new and awful insight into humanity, a power that unerringly discovered the spiritual necessities of others, and therefore of himself. With a shock he realised that the younger man who had accompanied them with increasing difficulty as they climbed higher and higher—was but a shadow of reality. Like the porter, he was but an encumbrance who impeded progress. And he turned his eyes to search the desolate landscape.

'You will not find him,' said his companion, 'for he is gone, Never, unless you weakly call, shall you see him again, nor desire to hear his voice.' And Limasson realised that in his heart he had all the while disapproved of the man, disliked him for his theatrical fondness of sensation and effect, more, that he had even hated and despised him. Starvation might crawl upon him where he had fallen and eat his life away before he would stir a finger to save him. It was with the older man he now had dreadful business in hand.

'I am glad,' he answered, 'for in the end he must have proved my death—our death!'

And they drew closer round the little circle of food the priest had laid upon the rocky ground, an intimate understanding linking them together in a sympathy that completed Limasson's bewilderment. There was bread, he saw, and there was salt; there was also a little flask of deep red wine. In the centre of the circle was a miniature fire of sticks the priest had collected from the bushes of wild rhododendron. The smoke rose upwards in a thin blue line. It did not even quiver, so profound was the surrounding stillness of the mountain air, but far away among the precipices ran the boom of falling water, and behind it again, the muffled roar as of peaks and snow-fields that swept with a rolling thunder through the heavens.

'They are passing,' the priest said in a low voice, 'and They know that you are here. You have now the opportunity of a lifetime; for, if you yield acceptance of your own free will, success is sure. You stand before the gates of birth and death. They offer you life.'

'Yet... I denied Them!' He murmured it below his breath.

'Denial is evocation. You called to them, and They have come. The sacrifice of your little personal life is all They ask. Be brave—and yield it.'

He took the bread as he spoke, and, breaking it in three pieces, he placed one before Limasson, one before himself, and the third he laid upon the flame which first blackened and then consumed it.

'Eat it and understand,' he said, 'for it is the nourishment that shall revive your fading life.'

Next, with the salt, he did the same. Then, raising the flask of wine, he put it to his lips, offering it afterwards to his companion. When both had drunk there still remained the greater part of the contents. He lifted the vessel with both hands reverently towards the sky. He stood upright.

'The blood of your personal life I offer to Them in your name. By the renunciation which seems to you as death shall you pass through the gates of birth to the life of freedom beyond. For the ultimate sacrifice that They ask of you is—this.'

And bending low before the distant heights, he poured the wine upon the rocky ground.

For a period of time Limasson found no means of measuring, so terrible were the emotions in his heart, the priest remained in this attitude of worship and obeisance. The tumult in the mountains ceased. An absolute hush dropped down upon the world. There seemed a pause in the inner history of the universe itself. All waited—till he rose again. And, when he did so, the mask that had for hours now been spreading across his features, was accomplished. The eyes gazed sternly down into his own. Limasson looked—and recognised. He stood face to face with the man whom he knew best of all others in the world... himself.

There had been death. There had also been that recovery of splendour which is birth and resurrection.

And the sun that moment, with the sudden surprise that mountains only know, rushed clear above the heights, bathing the landscape and the standing figure with a stainless glory. Into the vast Temple where he knelt, as into that greater inner Temple which is mankind's true House of Royalty, there poured the completing Presence which is—Light.

'For in this way, and in this way only, shall you pass from death to life,' sang a chanting voice he recognised also now for the first time as indubitably his own.

It was marvellous. But the birth of light is ever marvellous. It was anguish; but the pangs of resurrection since time began have been accomplished by the sweetness of fierce pain. For the majority still lie in the pre-natal stage, unborn, unconscious of a definite spiritual existence. In the womb they grope and stifle, depending ever upon another. Denial is ever the call to life, a protest against continued darkness for deliverance. Yet birth is the ruin of all that has hitherto been depended on. There comes then that standing alone which at first seems desolate isolation. The tumult of destruction precedes release.

Limasson rose to his feet, stood with difficulty upright, looked about him from the figure so close now at his side to the snowy summit of that Tour du Néant he would never climb. The roar and thunder of *Their* passage was resumed. It seemed the mountains reeled.

'They are passing,' sang the voice that was beside him and within him too, 'but They have known you, and your offering is accepted. When They come close upon the world there is ever wreckage and disaster in the affairs of men. They bring disorder and confusion into the mind, a confusion that seems final, a disorder that seems to threaten death. For there is tumult in Their Presence, and apparent chaos that seems the abandonment of order. Out of this vast ruin, then, there issues life in new design. The dislocation is its entrance, the dishevelment its strength. There has been birth....'

The sunlight dazzled his eyes. That distant roar, like a wind, came close and swept his face. An icy air, as from a passing star, breathed over him.

'Are you prepared?' he heard.

He knelt again. Without a sign of hesitation or reluctance, he bared his chest to the sun and wind. The flash came swiftly, instantly, descending into his heart with unerring aim. He saw the gleam in the air, he felt the fiery impact of the blow, he even saw the stream gush forth and sink into the rocky ground, far redder than the wine....

He gasped for breath a moment, staggered, reeled, collapsed... and within the moment, so quickly did all happen, he was aware of hands that supported him and helped him to his feet. But he was too weak to stand. They carried him up to bed. The porter, and the man who had reached across him for the matches five minutes before, intending conversation, stood, one at his feet and the other at his head. As he passed through the vestibule of the hotel, he saw the people staring, and in his hand he crumpled up the unopened letters he had received so short a time ago.

'I really think—I can manage alone,' he thanked them. 'If you will set me down I can walk. I felt dizzy for a moment.'

'The heat in the hall——' the gentleman began in a quiet, sympathetic voice.

They left him standing on the stairs, watching a moment to see that he had quite recovered. Limasson walked up the two flights to his room without faltering. The momentary dizziness had passed. He felt quite himself again, strong, confident, able to stand alone, able to move forward, able to *climb*.

THE DAMNED

I

'I'm over forty, Frances, and rather set in my ways,' I said good-naturedly, ready to yield if she insisted that our going together on the visit involved her happiness. 'My work is rather heavy just now too, as you know. The question is, *could* I work there—with a lot of unassorted people in the house?'

'Mabel doesn't mention any other people, Bill,' was my sister's rejoinder. 'I gather she's alone—as well as lonely.'

By the way she looked sideways out of the window at nothing, it was obvious she was disappointed, but to my surprise she did not urge the point; and as I glanced at Mrs. Franklyn's invitation lying upon her sloping lap, the neat, childish handwriting conjured up a mental picture of the banker's widow, with her timid, insignificant personality, her pale grey eyes and her expression as of a backward child. I thought, too, of the roomy country mansion her late husband had altered to suit his particular needs, and of my visit to it a few years ago when its barren spaciousness suggested a wing of Kensington Museum fitted up temporarily as a place to eat and sleep in. Comparing it mentally with the poky Chelsea flat where I and my sister kept impecunious house, I realised other points as well. Unworthy details flashed across me to entice: the fine library, the organ, the quiet work-room I should have, perfect service, the delicious cup of early tea, and hot baths at any moment of the day—without a geyser!

'It's a longish visit, a month—isn't it?' I hedged, smiling at the details that seduced me, and ashamed of my man's selfishness, yet knowing that Frances expected it of me. 'There *are* points about it, I admit. If you're set on my going with you, I could manage it all right.'

I spoke at length in this way because my sister made no

answer. I saw her tired eyes gazing into the dreariness of Oakley Street and felt a pang strike through me. After a pause, in which again she said no word, I added: 'So, when you write the letter, you might hint, perhaps, that I usually work all the morning, and—er—am not a very lively visitor! Then she'll understand, you see.' And I half-rose to return to my diminutive study, where I was slaving, just then, at an absorbing article on Comparative Aesthetic Values in the Blind and Deaf.

But Frances did not move. She kept her grey eyes upon Oakley Street where the evening mist from the river drew mournful perspectives into view. It was late October. We heard the omnibuses thundering across the bridge. The monotony of that broad, characterless street seemed more than usually depressing. Even in June sunshine it was dead, but with autumn its melancholy soaked into every house between King's Road and the Embankment. It washed thought into the past, instead of inviting it hopefully towards the future. For me, its easy width was an avenue through which nameless slums across the river sent creeping messages of depression, and I always regarded it as Winter's main entrance into London —fog, slush, gloom trooped down it every November, waving their forbidding banners till March came to rout them. Its one claim upon my love was that the south wind swept sometimes unobstructed up it, soft with suggestions of the sea. These lugubrious thoughts I naturally kept to myself, though I never ceased to regret the little flat whose cheapness had seduced us. Now, as I watched my sister's impassive face, I realised that perhaps she, too, felt as I felt, yet, brave woman, without betraying it.

'And, look here, Fanny,' I said, putting a hand upon her shoulder as I crossed the room, 'it would be the very thing for you. You're worn out with catering and housekeeping. Mabel is your oldest friend, besides, and you've hardly seen her since *he* died———'

'She's been abroad for a year, Bill, and only just came back,' my sister interposed. 'She came back rather unexpectedly, though I never thought she would go *there* to live——' She stopped abruptly. Clearly, she was only speaking half her mind. 'Probably,' she went on, 'Mabel wants to pick up old links again.'

'Naturally,' I put in, 'yourself chief among them.' The veiled reference to the house I let pass. It involved discussing the dead man for one thing.

'I feel *I* ought to go anyhow,' she resumed, 'and of course it would be jollier if you came too. You'd get in such a muddle here by yourself, and eat wrong things, and forget to air the rooms, and—oh, everything!' She looked up laughing. 'Only,' she added, 'there's the British Museum——?'

'But there's a big library there', I answered, 'and all the books of reference I could possibly want. It was of you I was thinking. You could take up your painting again; you always sell half of what you paint. It would be a splendid rest too, and Sussex is a jolly country to walk in. By all means, Fanny, I advise——'

Our eyes met, as I stammered in my attempts to avoid expressing the thought that hid in both our minds. My sister had a weakness for dabbling in the various 'new' theories of the day, and Mabel, who before her marriage had belonged to foolish societes for investigating the future life to the neglect of the present one, had fostered this undersirable tendency. Her amiable, impressionable temperament was open to every psychic wind that blew. I deplored, detested the whole business. But even more than this I abhorred the later influence that Mr. Franklyn had steeped his wife in, capturing her body and soul in his sombre doctrines. I had dreaded lest my sister also might be caught.

'Now that she is alone again——'

I stopped short. Our eyes now made pretence impossible, for the truth had slipped out inevitably, stupidly, although unexpressed in definite language. We laughed, turning our faces a moment to look at other things in the room. Frances picked up a book and examined its cover as though she had made an important discovery, while I took my case out and lit a cigarette I did not want to smoke. We left the matter there. I went out of the room before further explanation could cause tension. Disagreements grow into discord from such tiny things—wrong adjectives, or a chance inflection of the voice. Frances had a right to her views of life as much as I had. At least, I reflected comfortably, we had separated upon an agreement this time, recognised mutually, though not actually stated.

And this point of meeting was, oddly enough, our way of regarding some one who was dead. For we had both disliked the husband with a great dislike, and during his three years' married life had only been to the house once—for a week-end visit; arriving late on Saturday, we had left after an early breakfast on Monday morning. Ascribing my sister's dislike to a natural jealousy at losing her old friend, I said merely that he displeased me. Yet we both knew that the real emotion lay much deeper. Frances, loyal, honourable creature, had kept silence; and beyond saying that house and grounds—he altered one and laid out the other—distressed her as an expression of his personality somehow ("distressed" was the word she used), no further explanation had passed her lips.

Our dislike of his personality was easily accounted for—up to a point, since both of us shared the artist's point of view that a creed, cut to measure and carefully dried, was an ugly thing, and that a dogma to which believers must subscribe or perish everlastingly was a barbarism resting upon cruelty. But while my own dislike was purely due to an abstract worship of Beauty, my sister's had another twist in it, for with her 'new' tendencies, she believed that all religions were an aspect of truth and that no one, even the lowest wretch, could escape 'heaven' in the long run.

Samuel Franklyn, the rich banker, was a man universally respected and admired, and the marriage, though Mabel was fifteen years his junior, won general applause; his bride was an heiress in her own right—breweries—and the story of her conversion at a revivalist meeting where Samuel Franklyn had spoken fervidly of heaven, and terrifyingly of sin, hell and damnation, even contained a touch of genuine romance. She was a brand snatched from the burning; his detailed eloquence had frightened her into heaven; salvation came in the nick of time; his words had plucked her from the edge of that lake of fire and brimstone where their worm dieth not and the fire is not quenched. She regarded him as a hero, sighed her relief upon his saintly shoulder, and accepted the peace he offered her with a grateful resignation.

For her husband was a 'religious man' who successfully combined great riches with the glamour of winning souls. He was a portly figure, though tall, with masterful, big hands, the fingers rather thick and red; and his dignity, that just escaped being pompous, held in it something that was implacable. A convinced assurance, almost remorseless, gleamed in his eyes when he preached especially, and his threats of hell fire must have scared souls stronger than the timid, receptive Mabel whom he married. He clad himself in long frock-coats that buttoned unevenly, big square boots, and trousers that invariably bagged at the knee and were a little short; he wore low collars, spats occasionally, and a tall black hat that was not of silk. His voice was alternately hard and unctuous; and he regarded theatres, ball-rooms and race-courses as the vestibule of that brimstone lake of whose geography he was as positive as of his great banking offices in the City. A philanthropist up to the hilt, however, no one ever doubted his complete sincerity; his convictions were ingrained, his faith borne out by his life—as witness his name upon so many admirable Societes, as treasurer, patron, or heading the donation list. He bulked large in the world of doing good, a broad and stately stone in the rampart against evil. And his heart was genuinely king and soft for others—who believed as he did.

Yet, in spite of this true sympathy with suffering and his desire to help, he was narrow as a telegraph wire and unbending as a church pillar; he was intensely selfish; intolerant as an officer of the Inquisition, his bourgeois soul constructed a revolting scheme of heaven that was reproduced in miniature in all he did and planned. Faith was the *sine qua non* of salvation, and by 'faith' he meant belief in his own particular view of things—'which faith, except every one do keep whole and undefiled, without doubt he shall perish everlastingly.' All the world but his own small, exclusive sect must be damned eternally—a pity, but alas, inevitable. *He* was right.

Yet he prayed without ceasing, and gave heavily to the poor—the only thing he could not give being big ideas to his provincial and suburban deity. Pettier than an insect, and more obstinate than a mule, he had also the superior, sleek humility of a 'chosen one'. He was churchwarden too. He read the Lesson in a 'place of worship', either chilly or over-heated, where neither organ, vestments, nor lighted candles were permitted, but where the odour of hair-wash on the boys' heads in the back rows pervaded the entire building.

This portrait of the banker, who accumulated riches both on earth and in heaven, may possibly be overdrawn, however, because Frances and I were 'artistic temperaments' that viewed the type with a dislike and distrust amounting to contempt. The majority considered Samuel Franklyn a worthy man and a good citizen. The majority, doubtless, held the saner view. A few years more, and he certainly would have been made a baronet. He relieved much suffering in the world, as assuredly as he caused many souls the agonies of torturing fear by his emphasis upon damnation. Had there been one point of beauty in him, we might have been more lenient; only we found it not, and, I admit, took little pains to search. I shall never forget the look of dour forgiveness with which he heard our excuses for missing Morning Prayers that Sunday morning of our single visit to The Towers. My sister learned that a change was made soon afterwards, prayers being 'conducted' after breakfast instead of before.

The Towers stood solemnly upon a Sussex hill amid park-like modern grounds, but the house cannot better be described—it would be so wearisome for one thing—than by saying that it was a cross between an overgrown, pretentious Norwood villa and one of those saturnine Institutes for cripples the train passes as it slinks ashamed through South London into

Surrey. It was 'wealthily' furnished and at first sight imposing, but on closer acquaintance revealed a meagre personality, barren and austere. One looked for Rules and Regulations on the walls, all signed By Order. The place was a prison that shut out 'the world.' There was, of course, no billiard-room, no smoking-room, no room for play of any kind, and the great hall at the back, once a chapel, which might have been used for dancing, theatricals, or other innocent amusements, was consecrated in his day to meetings of various kinds, chiefly brigades, temperance or missionary societies. There was a harmonium at one end—on the level floor—a raised dais or platform at the other, and a gallery above for the servants, gardeners and coachmen. It was heated with hot-water pipes, and hung with Doré's pictures, though these latter were soon removed and stored out of sight in the attics as being too unspiritual. In polished, shiny wood, it was a representation in miniature of that poky exclusive Heaven he took about with him, externalising it in all he did and planned, even in the grounds about the house.

Changes in The Towers, Frances told me, had been made during Mabel's year of widowhood abroad—an organ put into the big hall, the library made liveable and recatalogued—when it was permissible to suppose she had found her soul again and returned to her normal, healthy views of life, which included enjoyment and play, literature, music and the arts, without, however, a touch of that trivial thoughtlessness usually termed worldliness. Mrs. Franklyn, as I remembered her, was a quiet little woman, shallow, perhaps, and easily influenced, but sincere as a dog and thorough in her faithful friendship. Her tastes at heart were catholic, and that heart was simple and unimaginative. That she took up with the various movements of the day was sign merely that she was searching in her limited way for a belief that should bring her peace. She was, in fact, a very ordinary woman, her calibre a little less than that of Frances. I knew they used to discuss all kinds of theories together, but as these discussions never resulted in action, I had come to regard her as harmless. Still,

I was not sorry when she married, and I did not welcome now a renewal of the former intimacy. The philanthropist she had given no children, or she would have made a good and sensible mother. No doubt she would marry again.

'Mabel mentions that she's been alone at The Towers since the end of August,' Frances told me at tea-time; 'and I'm sure she feels out of it and lonely. It would be a kindness to go. Besides, I always liked her.'

I agreed. I had recovered from my attack of selfishness. I expressed my pleasure.

'You've written to accept,' I said, half statement and half question.

Frances nodded. 'I thanked for you,' she added quietly, 'explaining that you were not free at the moment, but that later, if not inconvenient, you might come down for a bit and join me.'

I stared. Frances sometimes had this independent way of deciding things. I was convicted, and punished into the bargain.

Of course there followed argument and explanation, as between brother and sister who were affectionate, but the recording of our talk could be of little interest. It was arranged thus, Frances and I both satisfied. Two days later she departed for The Towers, leaving me alone in the flat with everything planned for my comfort and good behaviour—she was rather a tyrant in her quiet way—and her last words as I saw her off from Charing Cross rang in my head for a long time after she was gone:

'I'll write and let you know, Bill. Eat properly, mind, and let me know if anything goes wrong.'

She waved her small gloved hand, nodded her head till the feather brushed the window, and was gone.

II

After the note announcing her safe arrival a week of silence passed, and then a letter came; there were various suggestions

86

for my welfare, and the rest was the usual rambling information and description Frances loved, generously italicised.

'... and we are quite alone,' she went on in her enormous handwriting that seemed such a waste of space and labour, 'though some others are coming presently, I believe. You could work here to your heart's content. Mabel *quite* understands, and says she would love to have you when you feel free to come. She has changed a bit—back to her old natural self: she never mentions *him*. The place has changed too in certain ways: it has more cheerfulness, I think. *She* has put it in, this cheerfulness, spaded it in, if you know what I mean; but it lies about uneasily and is not natural—quite. The organ is a beauty. She must be very rich now, but she's as gentle and sweet as ever. Do you know, Bill, I think he must have *frightened* her into marrying him. I get the impression she was afraid of him.' This last sentence was inked out, but I read it through the scratching; the letters being too big to hide. 'He had an inflexible will beneath all that oily kindness which passed for spiritual. He was a real personality, I mean. I'm sure he'd have sent you and me cheerfully to the stake in another century—*for our own good*. Isn't it odd she never speaks of him, even to me?' This, again, was stroked through, though without the intention to obliterate— merely because it was repetition, probably. 'The only reminder of him in the house now is a big copy of the presentation portrait that stands on the stairs of the Multitechnic Institute at Peckham—you know—that life-size one with his fat hand sprinkled with rings resting on a thick Bible and the other slipped between the buttons of a tight frock-coat. It hangs in the dining-room and rather dominates our meals. I wish Mabel would take it down. I think she'd like to, if she *dared*. There's not a single photograph of him anywhere, even in her own room. Mrs. Marsh is here—you remember her, *his* housekeeper, the wife of the man who got penal servitude for killing a baby or something—*you* said she robbed him and justified her stealing because the story of the unjust steward was in the Bible! How we laughed over that! *She's* just the same too, gliding about all over the house and turning up when least expected.'

Other reminiscences filled the next two sides of the letter, and ran, without a trace of punctuation, into instructions about a Salamander stove for heating my work-room in the flat; these were followed by things I was to tell the cook, and by requests for several articles she had forgotten and would like sent after her, two of them blouses, with descriptions so lengthy and contradictory that I sighed as I read them—'unless you come down soon, in which case perhaps you wouldn't mind bringing them; *not* the mauve one I wear in the evening some-times, but the pale blue one with lace round the collar and the crinkly front. They're in the cupboard—or the drawer, I'm not sure which—of my bedroom. *Ask Annie* if you're in doubt. Thanks most *awfully*. Send a telegram, remember, and we'll meet you in the motor *any time*. I don't quite know if I shall stay the whole month—*alone*. It all depends....' And she closed the letter, the italicised words increasing recklessly towards the end, with a repetition that Mabel would love to have me 'for myself,' as also to have a 'man in the house', and that I only had to telegraph the day and the train.... This letter, coming by the second post, interrupted me in a moment of absorbing work, and, having read it through to make sure there was nothing requiring instant attention, I threw it aside and went on with my notes and reading. Within five minutes, however, it was back at me again. That restless thing called 'between the lines' fluttered about my mind. My interest in the Balkan States—political article that had been 'ordered'—faded. Somewhere, somehow I felt disquieted, disturbed. At first I persisted in my work, forcing myself to concentrate, but soon found that a layer of new impressions floated between the article and my attention. It was like a shadow, though a shadow that dissolved upon inspection. Once or twice I glanced up, expecting to find some one in the room, that the door had opened unobserved and Annie was waiting for instructions. I heard the 'buses thundering across the bridge. I was aware of Oakley Street. Montenegro and the

blue Adriatic melted into the October haze along that depressing Embankment that aped a river bank, and sentences from
the letter flashed before my eyes and stung me. Picking it up
and reading it through more carefully, I rang the bell and told
Annie to find the blouses and pack them for the post, showing
her finally the written description, and resenting the superior
smile with which she at once interrupted. '*I* know them, sir,'
and disappeared.

But it was not the blouses: it was that exasperating thing
'between the lines' that put an end to my work with its elusive
teasing nuisance. The first sharp impression is alone of value
in such a case, for once analysis begins the imagination con-
structs all kinds of false interpretation. The more I thought,
the more I grew fuddled. The letter, it seemed to me, wanted
to say another thing; instead the eight sheets *conveyed* it merely.
It came to the edge of disclosure, then halted. There was
something on the writer's mind, and I felt uneasy. Studying
the sentences brought, however, no revelation, but increased
confusion only; for while the uneasiness reamined, the first
clear hint had vanished. In the end I closed my books and
went out to look up another matter at the British Museum
Library. Perhaps I should discover it that way—by turning
the mind in a totally new direction. I lunched at the Express
Dairy in Oxford Street close by, and telephoned to Annie
that I would be home to tea at five.

And at tea, tired physically and mentally after breathing the
exhausted air of the Rotunda for five hours, my mind suddenly
delivered up its original impression, vivid and clear-cut; no
proof accompanied the revelation; it was mere presentiment,
but convincing. Frances was disturbed in her mind, her orderly,
sensible, housekeeping mind; she was uneasy, even perhaps
afraid; something in the house distressed her, and she had need
of me. Unless I went down, her time of rest and change, her
quite necessary holiday, in fact, would be spoilt. She was too
unselfish to say this, but it ran everywhere between the lines.
I saw it clearly now. Mrs. Franklyn, moreover—and that
meant Frances too—would like a 'man in the house.' It was

a disagreeable phrase, a suggestive way of hinting something she dared not state definitely. The two women in that great, lonely barrack of a house were afraid.

My sense of duty, affection, unselfishness, whatever the composite emotion may be termed, was stirred; also my vanity. I acted quickly, lest reflection should warp clear, decent judgment. 'Annie,' I said, when she answered the bell, 'you need not send those blouses by the post. I'll take them down tomorrow when I go. I shall be away a week or two, possibly longer.' And, having looked up a train, I hastened out to telegraph before I could change my fickle mind.

But no desire came that night to change my mind. I was doing the right, the necessary thing. I was even in something of a hurry to get down to The Towers as soon as possible. I chose an early afternoon train.

III

A telegram had told me to come to a town ten miles from the house, so I was saved the crawling train to the local station, and travelled down by an express. As soon as we left London the fog cleared off, and an autumn sun, though without heat in it, painted the landscape with golden browns and yellows. My spirits rose as I lay back in the luxurious motor and sped between the woods and hedges. Oddly enough, my anxiety of overnight had disappeared. It was due, no doubt, to that exaggeration of detail which reflection in loneliness brings. Frances and I had not been separated for over a year, and her letters from The Towers told so little. It had seemed unnatural to be deprived of those intimate particulars of mood and feeling I was accustomed to. We had such confidence in one another, and our affection was so deep. Though she was but five years younger than myself, I regarded her as a child. My attitude was fatherly. In return, she certainly mothered me with a solicitude that never cloyed. I felt no desire to marry while she was still alive. She painted in water-colours with a reasonable success, and kept house for me; I wrote, reviewed books and lectured on aesthetics; we were a humdrum couple of quasi-artists, well satisfied with life, and all I feared for her was that she might become a suffragette or be taken captive by one of these wild theories that caught her imagination sometimes, and that Mabel, for one, had fostered. As for myself, no doubt she deemed me a trifle solid or stolid—I forget which word she preferred—but on the whole there was just sufficient difference of opinion to make intercourse suggestive without monotony, and certainly without quarrelling. Drawing in deep draughts of the stinging autumu air, I felt happy and exhilarated. It was like going for a holiday, with comfort at the end of the journey instead of bargaining for centimes.

But my heart sank noticeably the moment the house came into view. The long drive, lined with hostile monkey trees and formal wellingtonias that were solemn and sedate, was mere extension of the miniature approach to a thousand semi-detached suburban 'residences'; and the appearance of The Towers, as we turned the corner with a rush, suggested a commonplace climax to a story that had begun interestingly, almost thrillingly. A villa had escaped from the shadow of the Crystal Palace, thumped its way down by night, grown suddenly monstrous in a shower of rich rain, and settled itself insolently to stay. Ivy climbed about the opulent red-brick walls, but climbed neatly and with disfiguring effect, sham as on a prison or—the simile made me smile—an orphan asylum. There was no hint of the comely roughness of untidy ivy on a ruin. Clipped, trained and precise it was, as on a brand-new protestant church. I swear there was not a bird's nest nor a single earwig in it anywhere. About the porch it was particularly thick, smothering a seventeenth-century lamp with a contrast that was quite horrible. Extensive glass-houses spread away on the farther side of the house; the numerous towers to which the building owed its name seemed made to hold school bells; and the window-sills, thick with potted flowers, made me think of the desolate suburbs of Brighton or Bexhill. In a commanding position upon the crest of a hill, it overlooked miles of undulating, wooded country southwards to the Downs, but behind it, to the north, thick banks of ilex, holly and privet protected it from the cleaner and more stimulating winds. Hence, though highly placed, it was shut in. Three years had passed since I last set eyes upon, it, but the unsightly memory I had retained was justified by the reality. The place was deplorable.

It is my habit to express my opinions audibly sometimes, when impressions are strong enough to warrant it; but now I only sighed 'Oh, dear,' as I extricated my legs from many rugs and went into the house. A tall parlour-maid, with the bearing of a grenadier, received me, and standing behind her was Mrs. Marsh, the housekeeper, whom I remembered because her untidy back hair had suggested to me that it had been burnt. I went at once to my room, my hostess already dressing for dinner, but Frances came in to see me just as I was struggling with my black tie that had got tangled like a bootlace. She fastened it for me in a neat, effective bow, and while I held my chin up for the operation, staring blankly at the ceiling, the impression came—I wondered, was it her touch that caused it?—that something in her trembled. Shrinking perhaps is the truer word. Nothing in her face or manner betrayed it, nor in her pleasant, easy talk while she tidied my things and scolded my slovenly packing, as her habit was, questioning me about the servants at the flat. The blouses, though right, were crumpled, and my scolding was deserved. There was no impatience even. Yet somehow or other the suggestion of a shrinking reserve and holding back reached my mind. She had been lonely, of course, but it was more than that; she was glad that I had come, yet for some reason unstated she could have wished that I had stayed away. We discussed the news that had accumulated during our brief separation, and in doing so the impression, at best exceedingly slight, was forgotten. My chamber was large and beautifully furnished; the hall and dining-room of our flat would have gone into it with a good remainder; yet it was not a place I could settle down in for work. It conveyed the idea of impermanence, making me feel transient as in a hotel bedroom. This, of course,

was the fact. But some rooms convey a settled, lasting hospi-
tality even in a hotel; this one did not; and as I was accustomed
to work in the room I slept in, at least when visiting, a slight
frown must have crept between my eyes.

'Mabel has fitted a work-room for you just out of the library,'
said the clairvoyant Frances. 'No one will disturb you there,
and you'll have fifteen thousand books all catalogued within
easy reach. There's a private staircase too. You can breakfast
in your room and slip down in your dressing-gown if you
want to.' She laughed. My spirits took a turn upwards as
adsurdly as they had gone down.

'And how are *you?*' I asked, giving her a belated kiss. 'It's
jolly to be together again. I did feel rather lost without you,
I'll admit.'

'That's natural,' she laughed. 'I'm so glad.'

She looked well and had country colour in her cheeks.
She informed me that she was eating and sleeping well, going
out for little walks with Mabel, painting bits of scenery again,
and enjoying a complete change and rest; and yet, for all her
brave description, the word somehow did not quite ring
true. Those last words in particular did not ring true. There
lay in her manner, just out of sight, I felt, this suggestion
of the exact reverse—of unrest, shrinking, almost of anxiety.
Certain small strings in her seemed over-tight. 'Keyed-up'
was the slang expression that crossed my mind. I looked
rather searchingly into her face as she was telling me this.

'Only—the evenings,' she added, noticing my query, yet
rather avoiding my eyes, 'the evenings are—well, rather heavy
sometimes, and I find it difficult to keep awake.'

'The strong air after London makes you drowsy,' I suggested,
'and you like to get early to bed.'

Frances turned and looked at me for a moment steadily.
'On the contrary, Bill, I dislike going to bed—here. And
Mabel goes so early.' She said it lightly enough, fingering the
disorder upon my dressing-table in such a stupid way that
I saw her mind was working in another direction altogether.
She looked up suddenly with a kind of nervousness from the

brush and scissors. 'Billy,' she said abruptly, lowering her voice, 'isn't it odd, but I *hate* sleeping alone here? I can't make it out quite; I've never felt such a thing before in my life. Do you—think it's all nonsense?' And she laughed, with her lips but not with her eyes; there was a note of defiance in her I failed to understand.

'Nothing a nature like yours feels strongly is nonsense, Frances,' I replied soothingly.

But I, too, answered with my lips only, for another part of my mind was working elsewhere, and among uncomfortable things. A touch of bewilderment passed over me. I was not certain how best to continue. If I laughed she would tell me no more, yet if I took her too seriously the strings would tighten further. Instinctively, then, this flashed rapidly across me: that something of what she felt, I had also felt, though interpreting it differently. Vague it was, as the coming of rain or storm that announce themselves hours in advance with their hint of faint, unsettling excitement in the air. I had been but a short hour in the house—big, comfortable, luxurious house—but had experienced this sense of being unsettled, unfixed, fluctuating—a kind of impermanence that transient lodgers in hotels must feel, but that a guest in a friend's home ought not to feel, be the visit short or long. To Frances, an impressionable woman, the feeling had come in the terms of alarm. She disliked sleeping alone, while yet she longed to sleep. The precise idea in my mind evaded capture, merely brushing through me, three-quarters out of sight; I realised only that we both felt the same thing, and that neither of us could get at it clearly. Degrees of unrest we felt, but the actual thing did not disclose itself. It did not happen.

I felt strangely at sea for a moment. Frances would interpret hesitation as endorsement, and encouragement might be the last thing that could help her.

'Sleeping in a strange house,' I answered at length, 'is often difficult at first, and one feels lonely. After fifteen months in our tiny flat one feels lost and uncared-for in a big house. It's an uncomfortable feeling—I know it well. And this *is* a barrack, isn't it? The masses of furniture only make it worse. One feels in storage somewhere underground—the furniture doesn't furnish. One must never yield to fancies, though——'

Frances looked away towards the windows; she seemed disappointed a little.

'After our thickly-populated Chelsea,' I went on quickly, 'it seems isolated here.'

But she did not turn back, and clearly I was saying the wrong thing. A wave of pity rushed suddenly over me. Was she really frightened, perhaps? She was imaginative, I knew, but never moody; common sense was strong in her, though she had her times of hypersensitiveness. I caught the echo of some unreasoning, big alarm in her. She stood there, gazing across my balcony towards the sea of wooded country that spread dim and vague in the obscurity of the dusk. The deepening shadows entered the room, I fancied, from the grounds below. Following her abstracted gaze a moment, I experienced a curious sharp desire to leave, to escape. Out yonder was wind and space and freedom. This enormous building was oppressive, silent, still. Great catacombs occured to me, things beneath the ground, imprisonment and capture. I believe I even shuddered a little.

I touched her shoulder. She turned round slowly, and we looked with a certain deliberation into each other's eyes.

'Fanny,' I asked, more gravely than I intended, 'you are not frightened, are you? Nothing has happened, has it?'

She replied with emphasis, 'Of course not! How could it—I mean, why should I?' She stammered, as though the wrong sentence flustered her a second. 'I'ts simply—that I have this ter—this dislike of sleeping alone.'

Naturally, my first thought was how easy it would be to cut our visit short. But I did not say this. Had it been a true solution, Frances would have said it for me long ago.

'Wouldn't Mabel double-up with you?' I said instead, 'or give you an adjoining room, so that you could leave the door between you open? There's space enough, heaven knows.'

And then, as the gong sounded in the hall below for dinner, she said, as with an effort, this thing:

'Mabel did ask me—on the third night—after I had told her. But I declined.'

'You'd rather be alone than with her?' I asked, with a certain relief.

Her reply was so gravely given, a child would have known there was more behind it: 'Not that; but that she did not really want it.'

I had a moment's intuition and acted on it impulsively. 'She feels it too, perhaps, but wishes to face it by herself—and get over it?'

My sister bowed her head, and the gesture made me realise of a sudden how grave and solemn our talk had grown, as though some portentous thing were under discussion. It had come of itself—indefinite as a gradual change of temperature. Yet neither of us knew its nature, for apparently neither of us could state it plainly. Nothing happened, even in our words.

'That *was* my impression,' she said, '—that if she yields to it she encourages it. And a habit forms so easily. Just think,' she added with a faint smile that was the first sign of lightness she had yet betrayed, 'what a nuisance it would be—everywhere —if everybody was afraid of being alone—like that.'

I snatched readily at the chance. We laughed a little, though it was a quiet kind of laughter that seemed wrong. I took her arm and led her towards the door.

'Disastrous, in fact,' I agreed.

She raised her voice to its normal pitch again, as I had done. 'No doubt it will pass,' she said, 'now that you have come. Of course, it's chiefly my imagination.' Her tone was lighter, though nothing could convince me that the matter itself was light—just then. 'And in any case,' tightening her grip on my arm as we passed into the bright enormous corridor and caught sight of Mrs. Franklyn waiting in the cheerless hall below, 'I'm *very* glad you're here, Bill, and Mabel, I know, is too.'

'If it doesn't pass,' I just had time to whisper with a feeble attempt at jollity, 'I'll come at night and snore outside your

96

door. After that you'll be so glad to get rid of me that you won't mind being alone.'

'That's a bargain,' said Frances.

I shook my hostess by the hand, made a banal remark about the long interval since last we met, and walked behind them into the great dining-room, dimly lit by candles, wondering in my heart how long my sister and I should stay, and why in the world we had ever left our cosy little flat to enter this desolation of riches and false luxury at all. The unsightly picture of the late Samuel Franklyn, Esq., stared down upon me from the farther end of the room above the mighty mantel-piece. He looked, I thought, like some pompous Heavenly Butler who denied to all the world, and to us in particular, the right of entry without presentation cards signed by his hand as proof that we belonged to his own exclusive set. The majority, to his deep grief, and in spite of all his prayers on their behalf, must burn and 'perish everlastingly.'

IV

With the instinct of the healthy bachelor I always try to make myself a nest in the place I live in, be it for long or short. Whether visiting, in lodging-house, or in hotel, the first essential is this nest—one's own things built into the walls as a bird builds in its feathers. It may look desolate and uncomfortable enough to others, because the central detail is neither bed nor wardrobe, sofa nor arm-chair, but a good solid writing-table that does not wriggle, and that has wide elbow-room. And The Towers is vividly described for me by the single fact that I could not 'nest' there. I took several days to discover this, but the first impression of impermanence was truer than I knew. The feathers of the mind refused here to lie one way. They ruffled, pointed and grew wild.

Luxurious furniture does not mean comfort; I might as well have tried to settle down in the sofa and arm-chair department of a big shop. My bedroom was easily managed; it was the private workroom, prepared especially for my reception, that made me feel alien and outcast. Externally, it was all one could desire: an ante-chamber to the great library, with not one, but two generous oak tables, to say nothing of smaller ones against the walls with capacious drawers. There were reading-desks, mechanical devices for holding books, perfect light, quiet as in a church, and no approach but across the huge adjoining room. Yet it did not invite.

'I hope you'll be able to work here,' said my little hostess the next morning, as she took me in—her only visit to it while I stayed in the house—and showed me the ten-volume Catalogue. 'It's absolutely quiet and no one will disturb you.'

'If you can't, Bill, you're not much good,' laughed Frances, who was on her arm. 'Even I could write in a study like this!'

I glanced with pleasure at the ample tables, the sheets of thick blotting-paper, the rulers, sealing-wax, paper-knives, and all the other immaculate paraphernalia. 'It's perfect,' I answered with a secret thrill, yet feeling a little foolish. This was for Gibbon or Carlyle, rather than for my pot-boiling insignificancies. 'If I can't write masterpieces here, it's certainly not *your* fault,' and I turned with gratitude to Mrs. Franklyn. She was looking straight at me, and there was a question in her small pale eyes I did not understand. Was she noting the effect upon me, I wondered?

'You'll write here—perhaps a story about the house,' she said, 'Thompson will bring you anything you want; you only have to ring.' She pointed to the electric bell on the central table, the wire running neatly down the leg. 'No one has ever worked here before, and the library has been hardly used since it was put in. So there's no previous atmosphere to affect your imagination—er—adversely.'

We laughed. 'Bill isn't that sort,' said my sister; while I wished they would go out and leave me to arrange my little nest and set to work.

I thought, of course, it was the huge listening library that made me feel so inconsiderable—the fifteen thousand silent, staring books, the solemn aisles, the deep, eloquent shelves. But when the women had gone and I was alone, the beginning of the truth crept over me, and I felt that first hint of disconsolateness which later became an imperative No. The mind shut down, images ceased to rise and flow. I read, made copious notes, but I wrote no single line at The Towers. Nothing completed itself there. Nothing happened.

The morning sunshine poured into the library through ten long narrow windows; birds were singing; the autumn air, rich with a faint aroma of November melancholy that stung the imagination pleasantly, filled my ante-chamber. I looked out upon the undulating wooded landscape, hemmed in by the sweep of distant Downs, and I tasted a whiff of the sea. Rooks cawed as they floated above the elms, and there were lazy cows in the nearer meadows. A dozen times I tried to make my nest and settle down to work, and a dozen times, like a turning fastidious dog upon a hearth-rug, I rearranged my chair and books and papers. The temptation of the Catalogue and shelves, of course, was accountable for much, yet not, I felt, for all. That was a manageable seduction. My work, moreover, was not of the creative kind that requires absolute absorption; it was the mere readable presentation of data I had accumulated. My note-books were charged with facts ready to tabulate— facts, too, that interested me keenly. A mere effort of the will was necessary, and concentration of no difficult kind. Yet, somehow, it seemed beyond me: something for ever pushed the facts into disorder... and in the end I sat in the sunshine, dipping into a dozen books selected from the shelves outside, vexed with myself and only half-enjoying it. I felt restless. I wanted to be elsewhere.

And even while I read, attention wandered. Frances, Mabel, her late husband, the house and grounds, each in turn and sometimes all together, rose uninvited into the stream of thought, hindering any consecutive flow of work. In disconnected fashion came these pictures that interrupted concentration, yet presenting themselves as broken fragments of a bigger thing my mind already groped for unconsciously. They fluttered round this hidden thing of which they were aspects, fugitive interpretations, no one of them bringing complete

99

revelation. There was no adjective, such as pleasant or unpleasant, that I could attach to what I felt, beyond that the
result was unsettling. Vague as the atmosphere of a dream,
it yet persisted, and I could not dissipate it. Isolated words
or phrases in the lines I read sent questions scouring across
my mind, sure sign that the deeper part of me was restless
and ill at ease.

Rather trivial questions too—half-foolish interrogations,
as of a puzzled or curious child: Why was my sister afraid to
sleep alone, and why did her friend feel a similar repugnance,
yet seek to conquer it? Why was the solid luxury of the house
without comfort, its shelter without the sense of permanence?
Why had Mrs. Franklyn asked *us* to come, artists, unbelieving
vagabonds, types at the farthest possible remove from the
saved sheep of her husband's household? Had a reaction set
in against the hysteria of her conversion? I had seen no signs
of religious fervour in her; her atmosphere was that of an
ordinary, high-minded woman, yet a woman of the world.
Lifeless, though, a little, perhaps, now that I came to think
about it: she had made no definite impression upon me of
any kind. And my thoughts ran vaguely after this fragile clue.

Closing my book, I let them run. For, with this chance
reflection came the discovery that I could not *see* her clearly
—could not feel her soul, her personality. Her face, her small
pale eyes, her dress and body and walk, all these stood before
me like a photograph; but her Self evaded me. She seemed
not there, lifeless, empty, a shadow—nothing. The picture
was disagreeable, and I put it by. Instantly she melted out,
as though light thought had conjured up a phantom that had
no real existence. And at that very moment, singularly enough,
my eye caught sight of her moving past the window, going
silently along the gravel path. I watched her, a sudden new
sensation gripping me. 'There goes a prisoner,' my thought
instantly ran, 'one who wishes to escape, but cannot.'

What brought the outlandish notion, heaven only knows.
The house was of her own choice, she was twice an heiress,
and the world lay open at her feet. Yet she stayed—unhappy,

frightened, caught. All this flashed over me, and made a sharp impression even before I had time to dismiss it as absurd. But a moment later explanation offered itself, though it seemed as far-fetched as the original impression. My mind, being logical, was obliged to provide something, apparently. For Mrs. Franklyn, while dressed to go out, with thick walking-boots, a pointed stick, and a motor-cap tied on with a veil as for the windy lanes, was obviously content to go no farther than the little garden paths. The costume was a sham and a pretence. It was this, and her lithe, quick movements that suggested a caged creature—a creature tamed by fear and cruelty that cloaked themselves in kindness—pacing up and down, unable to realise why it got no farther, but always met the same bars in exactly the same place. The mind in her was barred.

I watched her go along the paths and down the steps from one terrace to another, until the laurels hid her altogether; and into this mere imagining of a moment came a hint of something slightly disagreeable, for which my mind, search as it would, found no explanation at all. I remembered then certain other little things. They dropped into the picture of their own accord. In a mind not deliberately hunting for clues, pieces of a puzzle sometimes come together in this way, bringing revelation, so that for a second there flashed across me, vanishing instantly again before I could consider it, a large, distressing thought. I can only describe vaguely as a Shadow. Dark and ugly, oppressive certainly it might be described, with something torn and dreadful about the edges that suggested pain and strife and terror. The interior of a prison with two rows of occupied condemned cells, seen years ago in New York, sprang to memory after it—the connection between the two impossible to surmise even. But the 'certain other little things' mentioned above were these: that Mrs. Franklyn, in last night's dinner talk, had always referred to 'this house', but never called it 'home'; and had emphasised unnecessarily, for a well-bred woman, our 'great kindness' in coming down to stay so long with her. Another time, in answer to my futile compliment about the 'stately rooms', she said quietly, 'It is an enormous house for so small a party; but I stay here very little, and only till I get it straight again.' The three of us were going up the great staircase to bed as this was said, and, not knowing quite her meaning, I dropped the subject. It edged delicate ground, I felt. Frances added no word of her own. It now occurred to me abruptly that 'stay' was the word made use of, when 'live' would have been more natural. How insignificant to recall! Yet why did they suggest themselves just at this moment?... And, on going to Frances's room to make sure she was not nervous or lonely, I realised abruptly, that Mrs. Franklyn, of course, had talked with *her* in a confidential sense that I, as a mere visiting brother, could not share. Frances had told me nothing. I might easily have wormed it out of her, had I not felt that for us to discuss further our hostess and her house merely because we were under the roof together, was not quite nice or loyal.

'I'll call you, Bill, if I'm scared,' she had laughed as we parted, my room being just across the big corridor from her own. I had fallen asleep, thinking what in the world was meant by 'getting it straight again'.

And now in my ante-chamber to the library, on the second morning, sitting among piles of foolscap and sheets of spotless blotting-paper, all useless to me, these slight hints came back and helped to frame the big, vague Shadow I have mentioned. Up to the neck in this Shadow, almost drowned, yet just treading water, stood the figure of my hostess in her walking costume. Frances and I seemed swimming to her aid. The Shadow was large enough to include both house and grounds, but farther than that I could not see.... Dismissing it, I fell to reading my purloined book again. Before I turned another page, however, another startling detail leaped out at me: the figure of Mrs. Franklyn in the Shadow was not living. It floated helplessly, like a doll or puppet that has no life in it. It was both pathetic and dreadful.

Any one who sits in reverie thus, of course, may see similar ridiculous pictures when the will no longer guides construction. The incongruities of dreams are thus explained. I merely record the picture as it came. That it remained by me for several days, just as vivid dreams do, is neither here nor there. I did not allow myself to dwell upon it. The curious thing, perhaps, is that from this moment I date my inclination, though not yet my desire, to leave. I purposely say 'to leave.' I cannot quite remember when the word changed to that aggressive, frantic thing which is escape.

V

We were left delightfully to ourselves in this pretentious country mansion with the soul of a villa. Frances took up her painting again, and, the weather being propitious, spent hours out of doors, sketching flowers, trees and nooks of woodland, garden, even the house itself where bits of it peered suggestively across the orchards. Mrs. Franklyn seemed always busy about something or other, and never interfered with us except to propose motoring, tea in another part of the lawn, and so forth. She flitted everywhere, preoccupied, yet apparently doing nothing. The house engulfed her rather. No visitor called. For one thing, she was not supposed to be back from abroad yet; and for another, I think, the neighbourhood—her husband's neighbourhood—was puzzled by her sudden cessation from good works. Brigades and temperance societies did not ask to hold their meetings in the big hall, and the vicar arranged the school-treats in another's field without explanation. The full-length portrait in the dining-room, and the presence of the housekeeper with the 'burnt' backhair, indeed, were the only reminders of the man who once had lived here. Mrs. Marsh retained her place in silence, well-paid sinecure as it doubtless was, yet with no hint of that suppressed disapproval one might have expected from her. Indeed there was nothing positive to disapprove, since nothing 'worldly' entered grounds or building. In her master's lifetime she had been another 'brand snatched from the burning', and it had then been her custom to give vociferous 'testimony' at the revival meetings where he adorned the platform and led in

103

streams of prayer. I saw her sometimes on the stairs, hovering, wandering, half-watching and half-listening, and the idea came to me once that this woman somehow formed a link with the departed influence of her bigoted employer. She, alone among us, *belonged* to the house, and looked at home there. When I saw her talking—oh, with such correct and respectful mien—to Mrs. Franklyn, I had the feeling that for all her unaggressive attitude, she yet exerted some influence that sought to make her mistress stay in the building for ever —live there. She would prevent her escape, prevent 'getting it straight again,' thwart somehow her will to freedom, if she could. The idea in me was of the most fleeting kind. But another time, when I came down late at night to get a book from the library ante-chamber, and found her sitting in the hall—alone—the impression left upon me was the reverse of fleeting. I can never forget the vivid, disagreeable effect it produced upon me. What was she doing there at half-past eleven at night, all alone in the darkness? She was sitting upright, stiff, in a big chair below the clock. It gave me a turn. It was so incongruous and odd. She rose quietly as I turned the corner of the stairs, and asked me respectfully, her eyes cast down as usual, whether I had finished with the library, so that she might lock up. There was no more to it than that; but the picture stayed with me—unpleasantly.

These various impressions came to me at odd moments, of course, and not in a single sequence as I now relate them. I was hard at work before three days were past, not writing, as explained, but reading, making notes, and gathering material from the library for future use. It was in chance moments that these curious flashes came, catching me unawares with a touch of surprise that sometimes made me start. For they proved that my under-mind was still conscious of the Shadow, and that far away out of sight lay the cause of it that left me with a vague unrest, unsettled, seeking to 'nest' in a place that did not want me. Only when this deeper part knows harmony, perhaps, can good brain work result, and my inability to write was thus explained. Certainly, I was always seeking for something here I could not find—an explanation that continually evaded me. Nothing but these trivial hints offered themselves. Lumped together, however, they had the effect of defining the Shadow a little. I became more and more aware of its very real existence. And, if I have made little mention of Frances and my hostess in this connection, it is because they contributed at first little or nothing towards the discovery of what this story tries to tell. Our life was wholly external, normal, quiet, and uneventful; conversation banal—Mrs. Franklyn's conversation in particular. They said nothing that suggested revelation. Both were in this Shadow, and both knew that they were in it, but neither betrayed by word or act a hint of interpretation. They talked privately, no doubt, but of that I can report no details.

And so it was that, after ten days of a very commonplace visit, I found myself looking straight into the face of a Strangeness that defied capture at close quarters. 'There's something here that never happens,' were the words that rose in my mind, 'and that's why none of us can speak of it.' And as I looked out of the window and watched the vulgar blackbirds, with toes turned in, boring out their worms, I realised sharply that even they, as indeed everything large and small in the house and grounds, shared this strangeness, and were twisted out of normal appearance because of it. Life, as expressed in the entire place, was crumpled, dwarfed, emasculated. God's meanings here were crippled, His love of joy was stunted. Nothing in the garden danced or sang. There was hate in it. 'The Shadow,' my thought hurried on to completion, 'is a manifestation of hate; and hate is the Devil.' And then I sat back frightened in my chair, for I knew that I had partly found the truth.

Leaving my books I went out into the open. The sky was overcast, yet the day by no means gloomy, for a soft, diffused light oozed through the clouds and turned all things warm and almost summery. But I saw the grounds now in their nakedness because I understood. Hate means strife, and the two together weave the robe that terror wears. Having no so-called religious beliefs myslf, nor belonging to any set of dogmas called a creed, I could stand outside these feelings and observe. Yet they soaked into me sufficiently for me to grasp sympathetically what others, with more cabined souls (I flattered myself), might feel. That picture in the dining-room stalked everywhere, hid behind every tree, peered down upon me from the peaked ugliness of the bourgeois towers, and left the impress of its powerful hand upon every bed of flowers. 'You must not do this, you must not do that,' went past me through the air. 'You must not leave these narrow paths,' said the rigid iron railings of black. 'You shall not walk here,' was written on the lawns. 'Keep to the steps,' 'Don't pick the flowers; make no noise of laughter, singing, dancing,' was placarded all over the rose-garden, and 'Trespassers will be—not prosecuted but—*destroyed*' hung from the crest of monkey-tree and holly. Guarding the ends of each artificial terrace stood gaunt, implacable policemen, warders, gaolers. 'Come with us,' they chanted, 'or be damned eternally.'

I remember feeling quite pleased with myself that I had discovered this obvious explanation of the prison-feeling the place breathed out. That the posthumous influence of heavy old Samuel Franklyn might be an inadequate solution did not occur to me. By 'getting the place straight again,' his widow, of course, meant forgetting the glamour of fear and foreboding his depressing creed had temporarily forced upon her; and Frances, delicately-minded being, did not speak of it because it was the influence of the man her friend had loved. I felt lighter; a load was lifted from me. 'To trace the unfamiliar to the familiar,' came back a sentence I had read somewhere, 'is to understand.' It was a real relief. I could talk with Frances now, even with my hostess, no danger of treading clumsily. For the key was in my hands. I might even help to dissipate the Shadow, 'to get it straight again.' It seemed, perhaps, our long invitation was explained!

I went into the house laughing—at myself a little. 'Perhaps after all the artist's outlook, with no hard and fast dogmas, is as narrow as the others! How small humanity is! And why is there no possible and true combination of *all* outlooks?'

The feeling of 'unsettling' was very strong in me just then, in spite of my big discovery which was to clear everything up. And at the moment I ran into Frances on the stairs, with a portfolio of sketches under her arm.

It came across me then abruptly that, although she had worked a great deal since we came, she had shown me nothing. It struck me suddenly as odd, unnatural. The way she tried to pass me now confirmed my new-born suspicion that—well, that her results were hardly what they ought to be.

'Stand and deliver!' I laughed, stepping in front of her. 'I've seen nothing you've done since you've been here, and as a rule you show me all your things. I believe they are atrocious and degrading!' Then my laughter froze.

She made a sly gesture to slip past me, and I almost decided to let her go, for the expression that flashed across her face shocked me. She looked uncomfortable and ashamed; the colour came and went a moment in he cheeks, making me think of a child detected in some secret naughtiness. It was almost fear.

'It's because they're not finished then?' I said, dropping the tone of banter, 'or because they're too good for me to understand?' For my criticism of painting, she told me, was crude and ignorant sometimes. 'But you'll let me see them later, won't you?'

Frances, however, did not take the way of escape I offered. She changed her mind. She drew the portfolio from beneath her arm instead. 'You can see them if you *really* want to, Bill,' she said quietly, and her tone reminded me of a nurse who says to a boy just grown out of childhood, 'you are old enough now to look upon horror and ugliness—only I don't advise it.'

'I do want to,' I said, and made to go downstairs with her. But, instead, she said in the same low voice as before, 'Come up to my room, we shall be undisturbed there.' So I guessed that she had been on her way to show the paintings to our hostess, but did not care for us all three to see them together.

My mind worked furiously.

'Mabel asked me to do them,' she explained in a tone of submissive horror, once the door was shut, 'in fact, she begged it of me. You know how persistent she is in her quiet way. I—er—had to.'

She flushed and opened the portfolio on the little table by the window, standing behind me as I turned the sketches over—sketches of the grounds and trees and garden. In the first moment of inspection, however, I did not take in clearly why my sister's sense of modesty had been offended. For my attention flashed a second elsewhere. Another bit of the puzzle had dropped into place, defining still further the nature of what I called 'the Shadow'. Mrs. Franklyn, I now remembered, has suggested to me in the library that I might perhaps write something about the place, and I had taken it for one of her banal sentences and paid no further attention. I realised now that it was said in earnest. She wanted our interpretations, as expressed in our respective 'talents', painting and writing. Her invitation *was* explained. She left us to ourselves on purpose.

'I should like to tear them up,' Frances was whispering behind me with a shudder, 'only I promised——' She hesitated a moment.

'Promised not to?' I asked with a queer feeling of distress, my eyes glued to the papers.

'Promised always to show them to her first,' she finished so low I barely caught it.

I have no intuitive, immediate grasp of the value of paintings; results come to me slowly, and though every one believes his own judgment to be good, I dare not claim that mine is worth more than that of any other layman, Frances had too often convicted me of gross ignorance and error. I can only say that I examined these sketches with a feeling of amazement that contained revulsion, if not actually horror and disgust. They were outrageous. I felt hot for my sister, and it was a relief to know she had moved across the room on some pretence or other, and did not examine them with me. Her talent, of course, is mediocre, yet she has her moments of inspiration — moments, that is to say, when a view of Beauty not normally her own flames divinely through her. And these interpretations struck me forcibly as being thus 'inspired'—not her own. They were uncommonly well done; they were also atrocious. The meaning in them, however, was never more than hinted. There the unholy skill and power came in: they suggested so abominably, leaving most to the imagination. To find such significance in a bourgeois villa garden, and to interpret it with such delicate yet legible certainty, was a kind of symbolism that was sinister, even diabolical. The delicacy was her own, but the point of view was another's. And the word that rose in my mind was not the gross description of 'impure', but the more fundamental qualification—'un-pure'.

In silence I turned the sketches over one by one, as a boy hurries through the pages of an evil book lest he be caught.

'What does Mabel do with them?' I asked presently in a low tone, as I neared the end. 'Does she keep them?'

'She makes notes about them in a book and then destroys them,' was the reply from the end of the room. I heard a sigh of relief. 'I'm glad you've seen them, Bill. I wanted you to— but was afraid to show them. You understand?'

'I understand,' was my reply, though it was not a question intended to be answered. All I understood really was that Mabel's mind was as sweet and pure as my sister's, and that she had some good reason for what she did. She destroyed the sketches, but first made notes! It was an interpretation of the place she sought. Brother-like, I felt resentment, though, that Frances should waste her time and talent, when she might be doing work that she could sell. Naturally, I felt other things as well....

'Mabel pays me five guineas for each one,' I heard. 'Absolutely insists.'

I stared at her stupidly a moment, bereft of speech or wit.

'I must either accept, or go away,' she went on calmly, but a little white. 'I've tried everything. There was a scene the third day I was here—when I showed her my first result. I wanted to write to you, but hesitated——'

'It's unintentional, then, on your part—forgive my asking it, Frances, dear?' I blundered, hardly knowing what to think or say. 'Between the lines' of her letter came back to me. 'I mean, you make the sketches in your ordinary way and—the result comes out of itself, so to speak?'

She nodded, throwing her hands out like a Frenchman. 'We needn't keep the money for ourselves, Bill. We can give it away, but—I must either accept or leave,' and she repeated the shrugging gesture. She sat down on the chair facing me, staring helplessly at the carpet.

'You say there was a scene?' I went on presently, 'She insisted?'

'She begged me to continue,' my sister replied very quietly. 'She thinks—that is, she has an idea or theory that there's something about the place—something she can't get at quite.' Frances stammered badly. She knew I did not encourage her wild theories.

'Something she feels—yes,' I helped her, more than curious.

'Oh, you know what I mean, Bill,' she said desperately. 'That the place is saturated with some influence that she is herself too positive or too stupid to interpret. She's trying to make herself negative and receptive, as she calls it, but can't, of course, succeed. Haven't you noticed how dull and impersonal and insipid she seems, as though she had no personality? She thinks impressions will come to her that way. But they don't——'

'Naturally.'

'So she's trying me—us—what she calls the sensitive and impressionable artistic temperament. She says that until she is sure exactly what this influence is, she can't fight it, turn it out, "get the house straight", as she phrases it.'

Remembering my own singular impressions, I felt more lenient than I might otherwise have done. I tried te keep impatience out of my voice.

'And this influence, what—whose is it?'

We used the pronoun that followed in the same breath, for I answered my own question at the same moment as she did:

'*His.*' Our heads nodded involuntarily towards the floor, the dining-room being directly underneath.

And my heart sank, my curiosity died away on the instant; I felt bored. A commonplace haunted house was the last thing in the world to amuse or interest me. The mere thought exasperated, with its suggestions of imagination, overwrought nerves, hysteria, and the rest. Mingled with my other feelings was certainly disappointment. To see a figure or feel a 'presence', and report from day to day strange incidents to each other would be a form of weariness I could never tolerate.

'But really, Frances,' I said firmly, after a moment's pause, 'it's too far-fetched, this explanation. A curse, you know, belongs to the ghost stories of early Victorian days.' And only my positive conviction that there *was* something after all worth discovering, and that it most certainly was *not* this, prevented my suggesting that we terminate our visit forthwith, or as soon as we decently could. 'This is not a haunted house, whatever it is,' I concluded somewhat vehemently, bringing my hand down upon her odious portfolio.

My sister's reply revived my curiosity sharply.

'I was waiting for you to say that. Mabel says exactly the same. *He* is in it—but it's something more than that alone, something far bigger and more complicated.' Her sentence seemed to indicate the sketches, and though I caught the inference I did not take it up, having no desire to discuss them with her just them indeed, if ever.

I merely stared at her and listened. Questions, I felt sure, would be of little use. It was better she should say her thought in her own way.

'He is one influence, the most recent,' she went on slowly, and always very calmly, 'but there are others—deeper layers, as it were—underneath. If his were the only one, something would happen. But nothing ever does happen. The others

111

hinder and prevent—as though each were struggling to pre-dominate.'

I had felt it already myself. The idea was rather horrible. I shivered.

'That's what is so ugly about it—that nothing ever happens,' she said. 'There is this endless anticipation—always on the dry edge of a result that never materialises. It is torture. Mabel is at her wits' end, you see. And when she begged me—what I felt about my sketches—I mean——' She stammered badly as before.

I stopped her. I had judged too hastily. That queer symbolism in her paintings, pagan and yet not innocent, was, I understood, the result of mixture. I did not pretend to understand, but at least I could be patient. I consequently held my peace. We did talk on a little longer, but it was more general talk that avoided successfully our hostess, the paintings, wild theories, and *him*—until at length the emotion Frances had hitherto so successfully kept under burst vehemently forth again. It had hidden between her calm sentences, as it had hidden between the lines of her letter. It swept her now from head to foot, packed tight in the thing she then said.

'Then, Bill, if it is not an ordinary haunted house,' she asked, '*what is it?*'

The words were commonplace enough. The emotion was in the tone of her voice that trembled; in the gesture she made, leaning forward and clasping both hands upon her knees, and in the slight blanching of her cheeks as her brave eyes asked the question and searched my own with anxiety that bordered upon panic. In that moment she put herself under my protection. I winced.

'And why,' she added, lowering her voice to a still and furtive whisper, 'does nothing ever happen? If only,'—this with great emphasis—'something *would* happen—break this awful tension —bring relief. It's the waiting I cannot stand.' And she shivered all over as she said it, a touch of wildness in her eyes.

I would have given much to have made a true and satis-

112

factory answer. My mind searched frantically for a moment, but in vain. There lay no sufficient answer in me. I felt what she felt, though with differences. No conclusive explanation lay within reach. Nothing happened. Eager as I was to shoot the entire business into the rubbish heap where ignorance and superstition discharge their poisonous weeds, I could not honestly accomplish this. To treat Frances as a child, and merely 'explain away' would be to strain her confidence in my protection, so affectionately claimed. It would further be dishonest to myself—weak, besides—to deny that I had also felt the strain and tension even as she did. While my mind continued searching, I returned her stare in silence; and Frances then, with more honesty and insight than my own, gave suddenly the answer herself—an answer whose truth and adequacy, so far as they went, I could not readily gainsay:

'I think, Bill, because it is too big to happen here—to happen anywhere, indeed, all at once—and too awful!'

To have tossed the sentence aside as nonsense, argued it away, proved that it was really meaningless, would have been easy—at any other time or in any other place; and, had the past week brought me none of the vivid impressions it had brought me, this is doubtless what I should have done. My narrowness again was proved. We understand in others only what we have in ourselves. But her explanation, in a measure, I knew was true. It hinted at the strife and struggle that my notion of a Shadow had seemed to cover thinly.

'Perhaps,' I murmured lamely, waiting in vain for her to say more. 'But you said just now that you felt the thing was "in layers", as it were. Do you mean each one—each influence—fighting for the upper hand?'

I used her phraseology to conceal my own poverty. Terminology, after all, was nothing, provided we could reach the idea itself.

Her eyes said yes. She had her clear conception, arrived at independently, as was her way. And, unlike her sex, she kept it clear, unsmothered by too many words.

'One set of influences gets at me, another gets at you. It's according to our temperaments, I think.' She glanced significantly at the vile portfolio. 'Sometimes they are mixed—and therefore false. There has always been in me, more than in you, the pagan thing, perhaps, though never, thank God, like *that*.'

The frank confession of course invited my own, as it was meant to do. Yet it was difficult to find the words.

'What I have felt in this place, Frances, I honestly can hardly tell you, because—er—my impressions have not arranged themselves in any definite form I can describe. The strife, the agony of vainly-sought escape, and the unrest—a sort of prison atmosphere—this I have felt at different times and with varying degrees of strength. But I find, as yet, no final label to attach. I couldn't say pagan, Christian, or anything like that, I mean, as you do. As with the blind and deaf, you may have an intensification of certain senses denied to me, or even another sense altogether in embryo——'

'Perhaps,' she stopped me, anxious to keep to the point, 'you feel it as Mabel does. She feels the whole thing *complete*.'

'That also is possible,' I said very slowly. I was thinking behind my words. Her odd remark that it was 'big and awful' came back upon me as true. A vast sensation of distress and discomfort swept me suddenly. Pity was in it, and a fierce contempt, a savage, bitter anger as well. Fury against some sham authority was part of it.

'Frances,' I said, caught unawares, and dropping all pretence, 'what in the world can it be?' I looked hard at her. For some minutes neither of us spoke.

'Have *you* felt no desire to interpret it?' she asked presently,

'Mabel did suggest my writing something about the house,' was my reply, 'but I've felt nothing imperative. That sort of writing is not my line, you know. My only feeling,' I added, noticing that she waited for more, 'is the impulse to explain, discover, get it out of me somehow, and so get rid of it. Not by writing, though—as yet.' And again I repeated my former question: 'What in the world do you think it is?' My voice had become involuntarily hushed. There was awe in it.

Her answer, given with slow emphasis, brought back all my reserve: the phraseology provoked me rather:—

'Whatever it is, Bill, it is not of God.'

I got up to go downstairs. I believe I shrugged my shoulders. 'Would you like to leave, Frances? Shall we go back to town?' I suggested this at the door, and hearing no immediate reply, I turned back to look. Frances was sitting with her head bowed over and buried in her hands. The attitude horribly suggested tears. No woman, I realised, can keep back the pressure of strong emotion as long as Frances had done, without ending in a fluid collapse. I waited a moment uneasily, longing to comfort, yet afraid to act—and in this way discovered the existence of the appalling emotion in myself, hitherto but half guessed. At all costs a scene must be prevented: it would involve such exaggeration and over-statement. Brutally, such is the weakness of the ordinary man, I turned the handle to go out, but my sister then raised her head. The sunlight caught her face, framed untidily in its auburn hair, and I saw her wonderful expression with a start. Pity, tenderness and sympathy shone in it like a flame. It was undeniable. There shone through all her features the imperishable love and yearning to sacrifice self for others which I have seen in only one type of human being. It was the great mother look.

'We must stay by Mabel and help her get it straight,' she whispered, making the decision for us both.

I murmured agreement. Abashed and half ashamed, I stole softly from the room and went out into the grounds. And the first thing clearly realised when alone was this: that the long scene between us was without definite result. The exchange of confidence was really nothing but hints and vague suggestion. We had decided to stay, but it was a negative decision not to leave rather than a positive action. All our words and questions, our guesses, inferences, explanations, our most subtle allusions and insinuations, even the odious paintings themselves, were without definite result. Nothing had happened.

VI

And instinctively, once alone, I made for the places where she had painted her extraordinary pictures; I tried to see what she had seen. Perhaps, now that she had opened my mind to another view, I should be sensitive to some similar interpretation—and possibly by way of literary expression. If I were to write about the place, I asked myself, how should I treat it? I deliberately invited an interpretation in the way that came easiest to me—writing.

But in this case there came no such revelation. Looking closely at the trees and flowers, the bits of lawn and terrace, the rose-garden and corner of the house where the flaming creeper hung so thickly, I discovered nothing of the odious, unpure thing her colour and grouping had unconsciously revealed. At first, that is, I discovered nothing. The reality stood there, commonplace and ugly, side by side with her distorted version of it that lay in my mind. It seemed incredible. I tried to force it, but in vain. My imagination, ploughed less deeply than hers, or to another pattern, grew different seed. Where I saw the gross soul of an overgrown suburban garden, inspired by the spirit of a vulgar, rich revivalist who loved to preach damnation, she saw this rush of pagan liberty and joy, this strange licence of primitive flesh which, tainted by the other, produced the adulterated, vile result.

Certain things, however, gradually then became apparent, forcing themselves upon me, willy nilly. They came slowly, but overwhelmingly. Not that facts had changed, or natural details altered in the grounds—this was impossible—but that I noticed for the first time various aspects I had not noticed before—trivial enough, yet for me, just then, significant. Some I remembered from previous days; others I saw now as I wandered to and fro, uneasy, uncomfortable,—almost, it seemed, watched by some one who took note of my impressions. The details were so foolish, the total result so formidable. I was half aware that others tried hard to make me see. It was deliberate. My sister's phrase, 'one layer got at me, another gets at you', flashed, undesired, upon me.

For I saw, as with the eyes of a child, what I can only call a goblin garden—house, grounds, trees, and flowers belonged to a goblin world that children enter through the pages of their fairy tales. And what made me first aware of it was the whisper of the wind behind me, so that I turned with a sudden start, feeling that something had moved closer. An old ash tree, ugly and ungainly, had been artificially trained to form an arbour at one end of the terrace that was a tennis lawn, and the leaves of it now went rustling together, swishing as they rose and fell. I looked at the ash tree, and felt as though I had passed that moment between doors into this goblin garden that crouched behind the real one. Below, at a deeper layer perhaps, lay hidden the one my sister had entered.

To deal with my own, however, I call it goblin, because an odd aspect of the quaint in it yet never quite achieved the picturesque. Grotesque, probably, is the truer word, for everywhere I noticed, and for the first time, this slight alteration of the natural due either to the exaggeration of some detail, or to its suppression, generally, I think, to the latter. Life everywhere appeared to me as blocked from the full delivery of its sweet and lovely message. Some counter influence stopped it—suppression; or sent it awry—exaggeration. The house itself, mere expression, of course, of a narrow, limited mind, was sheer ugliness; it required no further explanation. With the grounds and garden, so far as shape and general plan were concerned, this was also true; but that trees and flowers and other natural details should share the same deficiency perplexed my logical soul, and even dismayed it. I stood and stared, then moved about, and stood and stared again. Everywhere was this mockery of a sinister, unfinished aspect. I sought in vain to recover my normal point of view. My mind had found this goblin garden and wandered to and fro in it, unable to escape.

The change was in myself, of course, and so trivial were the details which illustrated it, that they sound absurd, thus mentioned one by one. For me, they proved it, is all I can affirm. The goblin touch lay plainly everywhere: in the forms of the trees, planted at neat intervals along the lawns; in this twisted ash that rustled just behind me; in the shadow of the gloomy wellingtonias, whose sweeping skirts obscured the grass; but especially, I noticed, in the tops and crests of them. For here, the delicate, graceful curves of last year's growth seemed to shrink back into themselves. None of them pointed upwards. Their life had failed and turned aside just when it should have become triumphant. The character of a tree reveals itself chiefly at the extremities, and it was precisely here that they all drooped and achieved this hint of goblin distortion—in the growth, that is, of the last few years. What ought to have been fairy, joyful, natural, was instead uncomely to the verge of the grotesque. Spontaneous expression was arrested. My mind perceived a goblin garden, and was caught in it. The place grimaced at me.

With the flowers it was similar, though far more difficult to detect in detail for description. I saw the smaller vegetable growth as impish, half-malicious. Even the terraces sloped ill, as though their ends had sagged since they had been so lavishly constructed; their varying angles gave a queerly bewildering aspect to their sequence that was unpleasant to the eye. One might wander among their deceptive lengths and get lost—lost among open terraces!—with the house quite close at hand. Unhomely seemed the entire garden, unable to give repose, restlessness in it everywhere, almost strife, and discord certainly.

Moreover, the garden grew into the house, the house into the garden, and in both was this idea of resistance to the natural—the spirit that says No to joy. All over it I was aware of the effort to achieve another end, the struggle to burst forth and escape into free, spontaneous expression that should be happy and natural, yet the effort for ever frustrated by the weight of this dark shadow that rendered it abortive. Life crawled aside into a channel that was a cul-de-sac, then turned horribly upon itself. Instead of blossom and fruit, there were weeds. This approach of life I was conscious of—then dismal

118

failure. There was no fulfilment. Nothing happened.

And so, through this singular mood, I came a little nearer to understand the unpure thing that had stammered out into expression through my sister's talent. For the unpure is merely negative; it has no existence; it is but the cramped expression of what is true, stammering its way brokenly over false boundaries that seek to limit and confine. Great, full expression of anything is pure, whereas here was only the incomplete, unfinished, and therefore ugly. There was a strife and pain and desire to escape. I found myself shrinking from house and grounds as one shrinks from the touch of the mentally arrested, those in whom life has turned awry. There was almost mutilation in it.

Past items, too, now flocked to confirm this feeling that I walked, liberty captured and half-maimed, in a monstrous garden. I remembered days of rain that refreshed the country-side, but left these grounds, cracked with the summer heat, unsatisfied and thirsty; and how the big winds, that cleaned the woods and fields elsewhere, crawled here with difficulty through the dense foliage that protected The Towers from the North and West and East. They were ineffective, sluggish currents. There was no real wind. Nothing happened. I began to realise—far more clearly than in my sister's fanciful explanation about 'layers'—that here were many contrary influences at work, mutually destructive of one another. House and grounds were not haunted merely; they were the arena of past thinking and feeling, perhaps of terrible, impure beliefs, each striving to suppress the others, yet no one of them achieving supremacy because no one of them was strong enough, no one of them was true. Each, moreover, tried to win me over, though only one was able to reach my mind at all. For some obscure reason—possibly because my temperament had a na-tural bias towards the grotesque—it was the goblin layer. With me, it was the line of least resistance....

In my own thoughts this 'goblin garden' revealed, of course, merely my personal interpretation. I felt now objectively what long ago my mind had felt subjectively. My work, essential sign of spontaneous life with me, had stopped dead; production had become impossible. I stood now considerably closer to the cause of this sterility. The Cause, rather, turned bolder, had stepped insolently nearer. Nothing happened anywhere; house, garden, mind alike were barren, abortive, torn by the strife of frustrate impulse, ugly, hateful, sinful. Yet behind it all was still the desire of life—desire to escape—accomplish. Hope—an intolerable hope—I became startlingly aware—crowned torture.

And, realising this, though in some part of me where Reason lost her hold, there rose upon me then another and a darker thing that caught me by the throat and made me shrink with a sense of revulsion that touched actual loathing. I knew instantly whence it came, this wave of abhorrence and disgust, for even while I saw red and felt revolt rise in me, it seemed that I grew partially aware of the layer next below the goblin. I perceived the existence of this deeper stratum. One opened the way for the other, as it were. There were so many, yet all inter-related; to admit one was to clear the way for all. If I lingered I should be caught—horribly. They struggled with such violence for supremacy among themselves, however, that this latest uprising was instantly smothered and crushed back, though not before a glimpse had been revealed to me, and the redness in my thoughts transferred itself to colour my surroundings thickly and appallingly—with blood. This lurid aspect drenched the garden, smeared the terraces, lent to the very soil a tinge as of sacrificial rites, that choked the breath in me, while it seemed to fix me to the earth my feet so longed to leave. It was so revolting that at the same time I felt a dreadful curiosity as of fascination—I wished to stay. Between these contrary impulses I think I actually reeled a moment, transfixed by a fascination of the Awful. Through the lighter goblin veil I felt myself sinking down, down, down into this turgid layer that was so much more violent and so much more ancient. The upper layer, indeed, seemed fairy by comparison with this terror born of the lust for blood, thick with the anguish of human sacrificial victims.

Upper! Then I was already sinking; my feet were caught; I was actually in it! What atavistic strain, hidden deep within me, had been touched into vile response, giving this flash of intuitive comprehension, I cannot say. The coatings laid on by civilisation are probably thin enough in all of us. I made a supreme effort. The sun and wind came back. I could almost swear I opened my eyes. Something very atrocious surged back into the depths, carrying with it a thought of tangled woods, of big stones standing in a circle, motionless, white figures, the one form bound with ropes, and the ghastly gleam of the knife. Like smoke upon a battlefield, it rolled away....

I was standing on the gravel path below the second terrace when the familiar goblin garden danced back again, doubly grotesque now, doubly mocking, yet, by way of contrast, almost welcome. My glimpse into the depths was momentary, it seems, and had passed utterly away. The common world rushed back with a sense of glad relief, yet ominous now for ever, I felt, for the knowledge of what its past had built upon. In street, in theatre, in the festivities of friends, in music-room or playing-field, even indeed in church—how could the memory of what I had seen and felt leave its hideous trace? The very structure of my Thought, it seemed to me, was stained. What has been thought by others can never be obliterated until....

With a start my reverie broke and fled, scattered by a violent sound that I recognised for the first time in my life as wholly desirable. The returning motor meant that my hostess was back. Yet, so urgent had been my temporary obsession, that my first presentation of her was—well, not as I knew her now. Floating along with a face of anguished torture I saw Mabel, a mere effigy captured by others' thinking, pass down into those depths of fire and blood that only just had closed beneath my feet. She dipped away. She vanished, her fading eyes turned to the last towards some saviour who had failed her. And that strange intolerable hope was in her face.

The mystery of the place was pretty thick about me just then. It was the fall of dusk, and the ghost of slanting sunshine was as unreal as though badly painted. The garden stood at attention all about me. I cannot explain it, but I can tell it, I think, exactly as it happened, for it remains vivid in me for ever—that, for the first time, something *almost happened,* myself apparently the combining link through which it pressed towards delivery:

I had already turned towards the house. In my mind were pictures—not actual thoughts—of the motor, tea on the verandah, my sister, Mabel—when there came behind me this tumultuous, awful rush—as I left the garden. The ugliness, the pain, the striving to escape, the whole negative and suppressed agony that *was* the Place, focused that second into a concentrated effort to produce a result. It was a blinding tempest of long-frustrate desire that heaved at me, surging appallingly behind me like an anguished mob. I was in the act of crossing the frontier into my normal self again, when it came, catching fearfully at my skrits. I might use an entire dictionary of descriptive adjectives yet come no nearer to it than this—the conception of a huge assemblage determined to escape with me, or to snatch me back among themselves. My legs trembled for an instant, and I caught my breath—then turned and ran as fast as possible up the ugly terraces.

At the same instant, as though the clanging of an iron gate cut short the unfinished phrase, I *thought* the beginning of an awful thing:

'The Damned...'

Like this it rushed after me from that goblin garden that had sought to keep me:

'The Damned!'

For there was sound in it. I know full well it was subjective, not actually heard at all; yet somehow sound was in it—a great volume, roaring and booming thunderously, far away, and below me. The sentence dipped back into the depths that gave it birth, unfinished. Its completion was prevented. As usual, nothing happened. But it drove behind me like a hurricane as I ran towards the house, and the sound of it I can only liken to those terrible undertones you may hear standing beside Niagara. They lie behind the mere crash of the falling flood, within it somehow, not audible to all—felt rather than definitely heard.

It seemed to echo back from the surface of those sagging terraces as I flew across their sloping ends, for it was somehow underneath them. It was in the rustle of the wind that stirred the skirts of the drooping wellingtonias. The beds of formal flowers passed it on to the creepers, red as blood, that crept over the unsightly building. Into the structure of the vulgar and forbidding house it sank away; The Towers took it home. The uncomely doors and windows seemed almost like mouths that had uttered the words themselves, and on the upper floors at that very moment I saw two maids in the act of closing them again.

And on the verandah, as I arrived breathless, and shaken in my soul, Frances and Mabel, standing by the tea-table, looked up to greet me. In the faces of both were clearly legible the signs of shock. They watched me coming, yet so full of their own distress that they hardly noticed the state in which I came. In the face of my hostess, however, I read another and a bigger thing than in the face of Frances. Mabel *knew*. She had experienced what I had experienced. She had heard that awful sentence I had heard but heard it not for the first time; heard it, moreover, I verily believe, complete and to its dreadful end.

'Bill, did you hear that curious noise just now?' Frances asked it sharply before I could say a word. Her manner was confused; she looked straight at me; and there was a tremor in her voice she could not hide.

'There's wind about,' I said, 'wind in the trees and sweeping round the walls. It's risen rather suddenly.' My voice faltered rather.

'No. It wasn't wind,' she insisted, with a significance meant for me alone, but badly hidden. 'It was more like distant thunder, we thought. How you ran too!' she added. 'What a pace you came across the terraces!'

I knew instantly from the way she said it that they both

had already heard the sound before and were anxious to know if I had heard it, and how. My interpretation was what they sought.

'It was a curiously deep sound, I admit. It may have been big guns at sea,' I suggested, 'forts or cruisers practising. The coast isn't so very far, and with the wind in the right direction——'

The expression on Mabel's face stopped me dead.

'Like huge doors closing,' she said softly in her colourless voice, 'enormous metal doors shutting against a mass of people clamouring to get out.' The gravity, the note of hopelessness in her tones, was shocking.

Frances had gone into the house the instant Mabel began to speak. 'I'm cold,' she had said; 'I think I'll get a shawl.' Mabel and I were alone. I believe it was the first time we had been really alone since I arrived. She looked up from the teacups, fixing her pallid eyes on mine. She had made a question of the sentence.

'You hear it like that?' I asked innocently. I purposely used the present tense.

She changed her stare from one eye to the other; it was absolutely expressionless. My sister's step sounded on the floor of the room behind us.

'If only——' Mabel began, then stopped, and my own feelings leaping out instinctively completed the sentence I felt was in her mind:

'——something would happen.'

She instantly corrected me. I had caught her thought, yet somehow phrased it wrongly.

'We could escape!' She lowered her tone a little, saying it hurriedly. The 'we' amazed and horrified me; but something in her voice and manner struck me utterly dumb. There was ice and teror in it. It was a dying woman speaking— a lost and hopeless soul.

In that atrocious moment I hardly noticed what was said exactly, but I remember that my sister returned with a grey shawl about her shoulders, and that Mabel said, in her ordinary voice again, 'It *is* chilly, yes; let's have tea inside,' and that two maids, one of them the grenadier, speedily carried the loaded trays into the morning-room and put a match to the logs in the great open fireplace. It was, after all, foolish to risk the sharp evening air, for dusk was falling steadily, and even the sunshine of the day just fading could not turn autumn into summer. I was the last to come in. Just as I left the veran-dah a large black bird swooped down in front of me past the pillars; it dropped from overhead, swerved abruptly to one side as it caught sight of me, and flapped heavily towards the shrubberies on the left of the terraces, where it disappeared into the gloom. It flew very low, very close. And it startled me, I think because in some way it seemed like my Shadow materialised—as though the dark horror that was rising every-where from house and garden, then settling back so thickly yet so imperceptibly upon us all, were incarnated in that whirring creature that passed between the daylight and the coming night.

I stood a moment, wondering if it would appear again, before I followed the others indoors, and as I was in the act of closing the windows after me, I caught a glimpse of a figure on the lawn. It was some distance away, on the other side of the shrubberies, in fact where the bird had vanished. But in spite of the twilight that half magnified, half obscured it, the identity was unmistakable. I knew the housekeeper's stiff walk too well to be deceived. 'Mrs. Marsh taking the air,' I said to myself. I felt the necessity of saying it, and I wondered why she was doing so at this particular hour. If I had other thoughts they were so vague, and so quickly and utterly suppres-sed, that I cannot recall them sufficiently to relate them here.

And, once indoors, it was to be expected that there would come explanation, discussion, conversation, at any rate, regar-ding the singular noise and its cause, some uttered evidence of the mood that had been strong enough to drive us all inside. Yet there was none. Each of us purposely, and with various skill, ignored it. We talked little, and when we did it was of anything in the world but that. Personally, I experienced a touch of that same bewilderment which had come over me during my first talk with Frances on the evening of my arrival, for I recall now the acute tension, and the hope, yet dread, that one or other of us must sooner or later introduce the subject. It did not happen, however; no reference was made to it even remotely. It was the presence of Mabel, I felt positive, that prohibited. As soon might we have discussed Death in the bedroom of a dying woman.

The only scrap of conversation I remember, where all was ordinary and commonplace, was when Mabel spoke casually to the grenadier asking why Mrs. Marsh had omitted to do something or other—what it was I forget—and that the maid replied respectfully that 'Mrs. Marsh was very sorry, but her 'and still pained her.' I enquired, though so casually that I scarcely know what prompted the words, whether she had injured herself severely, and the reply, 'She upset a lamp and burnt herself,' was said in a tone that made me feel my curiosity was indiscreet, 'but she always has an excuse for not doing things she ought to do.' The little bit of conversation remained with me, and I remember particularly the quick way Frances interrupted and turned the talk upon the delinquencies of servants in general, telling incidents of her own at our flat with a volubility that perhaps seemed forced, and that certainly did not encourage general talk as it may have been intended to do. We lapsed into silence immediately she finished.

But for all our care and all our calculated silence, each knew that something had, in these last moments, come very close; it had brushed us in passing; it had retired; and I am inclined to think now that the large dark thing I saw, riding the dusk, probably bird of prey, was in some sense a symbol of it in my mind—that actually there had been no bird at all, I mean, but that my mood of apprehension and dismay had formed the vivid picture in my thoughts. It had swept past us, it had retreated, but it was now, at this moment, in hiding very close. And it was watching us.

Perhaps, too, it was mere coincidence that I encountered

Mrs. Marsh, *his* housekeeper, several times that evening in the short interval between tea and dinner, and that on each occasion the sight of this gaunt, half-saturnine woman fed my prejudice against her. Once, on my way to the telephone. I ran into her just where the passage is somewhat jammed by a square table carrying the Chinese gong, a grandfather's clock and a box of croquet mallets. We both gave way, then both advanced, then again gave way—simultaneously. It seemed, impossible to pass. We stepped with decision to the same side, finally colliding in the middle, while saying those futile little things, half apology, half excuse, that are inevitable at such times. In the end she stood upright against the wall for me to pass, taking her place against the very door I wished to open. It was ludicrous.

'Excuse me—I was just going in—to telephone,' I explained. And she sidled off, murmuring apologies, but opening the door for me while she did so. Our hands met a moment on the handle. There was a second's awkwardness—it was too stupid. I remembered her injury, and by way of something to say, I enquired after it. She thanked me; it was entirely healed now, but it might have been much worse; and there was something about the 'mercy of the Lord' that I didn't quite catch. While telephoning, however—a London call, and my attention focused on it—I realised sharply that this was the first time I had spoken with her; also, that I had—touched her.

It happened to be a Sunday, and the lines were clear. I got my connection quickly, and the incident was forgotten while my thoughts went up to London. On my way upstairs, then, the woman came back into my mind, so that I recalled other things about her—how she seemed all over the house, in unlikely places often; how I had caught her sitting in the hall alone that night; how she was for ever coming and going with her lugubrious visage and that untidy hair at the back that had made me laugh three years ago with the idea that it looked singed or burnt; and how the impression on my first arrival at The Towers was that this woman somehow kept alive, though its evidence was outwardly suppressed, the influence of her late employer and of his sombre teachings. Somewhere with her was associated the idea of punishment, vindictiveness, revenge. I remembered again suddenly my odd notion that she sought to keep her present mistress here, a prisoner in this bleak and comfortless house, and that really, in spite of her obsequious silence, she was intensely opposed to the change of thought that had reclaimed Mabel to a happier view of life.

All this in a passing second flashed in review before me, and I discovered, or at any rate reconstructed, the real Mrs. Marsh. She was decidedly in the Shadow. More, she stood in the forefront of it, stealthily leading an assault, as it were, against The Towers and its occupants, as though, consciously or unconsciously, she laboured incessantly to this hateful end.

I can only judge that some state of nervousness in me permitted the series of insignificant thoughts to assume this dramatic shape, and that what had gone before prepared the way and led her up at the head of so formidable a procession. I relate it exactly as it came to me. My nerves were doubtless somewhat on edge by now. Otherwise I should hardly have been a prey to the exaggeration at all. I seemed open to so many strange, impressions.

Nothing else, perhaps, can explain my ridiculous conversation with her, when, for the third time that evening, I came suddenly upon the woman half-way down the stairs, standing by an open window as if in the act of listening. She was dressed in black, a black shawl over her square shoulders and black gloves on her big, broad hands. Two black objects, prayerbooks apparently, she clasped, and on her head she wore a bonnet with shaking beads of jet. At first I did not know her, as I came running down upon her from the landing; it was only when she stood aside to let me pass that I saw her profile against the tapestry and recognised Mrs. Marsh. And to catch her on the front stairs, dressed like this, struck me as incongruous —impertiment. I paused in my dangerous descent. Through the opened window came the sound of bells—church bells—

a sound more depressing to me than superstition, and as nauseating. Though the action was ill-judged, I obeyed the sudden prompting—was it a secret desire to attack, perhaps? —and spoke to her.

'Been to church, I suppose, Mrs. Marsh?' I said. 'Or just going, perhaps?'

Her face, as she looked up a second to reply, was like an iron doll that moved its lips and turned its eyes, but made no other imitation of life at all.

'Some of us still goes, sir,' she said unctuously.

It was respectful enough, yet the implied judgment of the rest of the world made me almost angry. A deferential insolence lay behind the affected meekness.

'For those who believe no doubt it *is* helpful,' I smiled. 'True religion brings peace and happiness, I'm sure—joy, Mrs. Marsh, JOY!' I found keen satisfaction in the emphasis.

She looked at me like a knife. I cannot describe the implacable thing that shone in her fixed, stern eyes, nor the shadow of felt darkness that stole across her face. She glittered. I felt hate in her. I knew—she knew too—who was in the thoughts of us both at that moment.

She replied softly, never forgetting her place for an instant:

'There is joy, sir—in 'eaven—over one sinner that repenteth, and in church there goes up prayer to Gawd for those'oo—well, for the others, sir, 'oo——'

She cut short her sentence thus. The gloom about her as she said it was like the gloom about a hearse, a tomb, a darkness of great hopeless dungeons. My tongue ran on of itself with a kind of bitter satisfaction:

'We must believe there are *no* others, Mrs. Marsh. Salvation, you know, would be such a failure if there were. No merciful, all-foreseeing God could ever have devised such a fearful plan——'

Her voice, interrupting me, seemed to rise out of the bowels of the earth:

'They rejected the salvation when it was offered to them, sir, on earth.'

'But you wouldn't have them tortured for ever because of one mistake in ignorance,' I said, fixing her with my eye. 'Come now, would you, Mrs. Marsh? No God worth worshipping could permit such cruelty. Think a moment what it means.'

She stared at me, a curious expression in her stupid eyes. It seemed to me as though the 'woman' in her revolted, while yet she dared not suffer her grim belief to trip. That is, she would willingly have had it otherwise but for a terror that prevented.

'We may pray for them, sir, and we do—we *may* 'ope'. She dropped her eyes to the carpet.

'Good, good!' I put in cheerfully, sorry now that I had spoken at all. 'That's more hopeful, at any rate isn't it?'

She murmured something about Abraham's bosom, and the 'time of salvation not being for ever,' as I tried to pass her. Then a half gesture that she made stopped me. There was something more she wished to say—to ask. She looked up furtively. In her eyes I saw the 'woman' peering out through fear.

'Per'aps, sir.' she faltered, as though lightning must strike her dead, 'per'aps, would you think, a drop of cold water, given in His name, might moisten——?'

But I stopped her, for the foolish talk had lasted long enough.

'Of course,' I exclaimed, 'of course. For God is love, remember, and love means charity, tolerance, sympathy, and sparing others pain,' and I hurried past her, determined to end the outrageous conversation for which yet I knew myself entirely to blame. Behind me, she stood stock-still for several minutes, half bewildered, half alarmed, as I suspected. I caught the fragment of another sentence, one word of it, rather— 'punishment'—but the rest escaped me. Her arrogance and condescending tolerance exasperated me, while I was at the same time secretly pleased that I might have touched some string of remorse or sympathy in her after all. Her belief was iron; she dared not let it go; yet somewhere underneath there lurked the germ of a wholesome revulsion. She would help 'them'—if she dared. Her question proved it.

Half ashamed of myself, I turned and crossed the hall quickly lest I should be tempted to say more, and in me was a disagreeable sensation as though I had just left the Incurable Ward of some great hospital. A reaction caught me as of nausea. Ugh! I wanted such people cleansed by fire. They seemed to me as centres of contamination whose vicious thoughts flowed out to stain God's glorious world. I saw myself, Frances, Mabel too especially, on the rack, while that odious figure of cruelty and darkness stood over us and ordered the awful handles turned in order that we might be 'saved'—forced, that is, to think and believe exactly as *she* thought and believed.

I found relief for my somewhat childish indignation by letting myself loose upon the organ then. The flood of Bach and Beethoven brought back the sense of proportion. It proved, however, at the same time that there *had* been this growth of distortion in me, and that it had been provided apparently by my closer contact—for the first time—with that funereal personality, the woman who, like her master, believed that all holding views of God that differed from her own, must be damned eternally. It gave me, moreover, some faint clue perhaps, though a clue I was unequal of following up, to the nature of the strife and terror and frustrate influence in the house. That housekeeper had to do with it. She kept it alive. Her thought was like a spell she waved above her mistress's head.

VII

That night I was wakened by a hurried tapping at my door, and before I could answer, Frances stood beside my bed. She had switched on the light as she came in. Her hair fell straggling over her dressing-gown. Her face was deathly pale, its expression so distraught it was almost haggard. The eyes were very wide. She looked almost like another woman.

She was whispering at a great pace: 'Bill, Bill, wake up, quick!'

'I *am* awake. What is it?' I whispered too. I was startled.

131

'Listen!' was all she said. Her eyes stared into vacancy. There was not a sound in the great house. The wind had dropped, and all was still. Only the tapping seemed to continue endlessly in my brain. The clock on the mantelpiece pointed to half-past two.

'I heard nothing, Frances. What is it?' I rubbed my eyes; I had been very deeply asleep.

'Listen!' she repeated very softly, holding up one finger and turning her eyes towards the door she had left ajar. Her usual calmness had deserted her. She was in the grip of some distressing terror.

For a full minute we held our breath and listened. Then her eyes rolled round again and met my own, and her skin went even whiter than before.

'It woke me,' she said beneath her breath, and moving a step nearer to my bed. 'It was the Noise.' Even her whisper trembled.

'The Noise!' The word repeated itself dully of its own accord. I would rather it had been anything in the world but that—earthquake, foreign cannon, collapse of the house above our heads! 'The Noise, Frances! Are you *sure?*' I was playing really for a little time.

'It was like thunder. At first I thought it *was* thunder. But a minute later it came again—from underground. It's appalling.' She muttered the words, her voice not properly under control.

There was a pause of perhaps a minute, and then we both spoke at once. We said foolish, obvious things that neither of us believed in for a second. The roof had fallen in, there were burglars downstairs, the safes had been blown open. It was to comfort each other as children do that we said these things; also it was to gain further time.

'There's some one in the house, of course,' I heard my voice say finally, as I sprang out of bed and hurried into dressing-gown and slippers. 'Don't be alarmed. I'll go down and see,' and from the drawer I took a pistol it was my habit to carry everywhere with me. I loaded it carefully while Frances stood stock-still beside the bed and watched. I moved towards the open door.

'You stay here, Frances,' I whispered, the beating of my heart making the words uneven, 'while I go down and make a search. Lock yourself in, girl. Nothing can happen to you. It was downstairs, you said?'

'Underneath,' she answered faintly, pointing through the floor.

She moved suddenly between me and the door.

'Listen! Hark!' she said, the eyes in her face quite fixed; 'it's coming again,' and she turned her head to catch the slightest sound. I stood there watching her, and while I watched her, shook. But nothing stirred. From the halls below rose only the whirr and quiet ticking of the numerous clocks. The blind by the open window behind us flapped out a little into the room as the draught caught it.

'I'll come with you, Bill—to the next floor,' she broke the silence. 'Then I'll stay with Mabel—till you come up again.' The blind sank down with a long sigh as she said it.

The question jumped to my lips before I could repress it: 'Mabel is awake. She heard it too?'

I hardly know why horror caught me at her answer. All was so vague and terrible as we stood there playing the great game of this sinister house where nothing ever happened.

'We met in the passage. She was on her way to me.'

What shook in me, shook inwardly. Frances, I mean, did not see it. I had the feeling just that the Noise was upon us, that any second it would boom and roar about our ears. But the deep silence held. I only heard my sister's little whisper coming across the room in answer to my question:

'Then what is Mabel doing now?'

And her reply proved that she was yielding at last beneath the dreadful tension, for she spoke at once, unable longer to keep up the pretence. With a kind of relief, as it were, she said it out, looking helplessly at me like a child:

'She is weeping and gna——'

My expression must have stopped her. I believe I clapped both hands upon her mouth, though when I realised things clearly again, I found they were covering my own ears instead. It was a moment of unutterable horror. The revulsion I felt was actually physical. It would have given me pleasure to fire off all the five chambers of my pistol into the air above my head; the sound—a definite, wholesome sound that explained itself—would have been a positive relief. Other feelings, though, were in me too, all over me, rushing to and fro. It was vain to seek their disentanglement; it was impossible. I confess that I experienced, among them, a touch of paralysing fear—though for a moment only; it passèd as sharply as it came, leaving me with a violent flush of blood to the face such as bursts of anger bring, followed abruptly by an icy perspiration over the entire body. Yer I may honestly avow that it was not ordinary personal fear I felt, nor any common dread of physical injury. It was, rather, a vast, impersonal shrinking —a sympathetic shrinking—from the agony and terror that countless others, somewhere, somehow, felt for themselves. The first sensation of a prison overwhelmed me in that instant, of bitter strife and frenzied suffering, and the fiery torture of the yearning to escape that was yet hopelessly uttered.... It was of incredible power. It was real. The vain, intolerable hope swept over me.

I mastered myself, though hardly knowing how, and took my sister's hand. It was as cold as ice, as I led her firmly to the door and out into the passage. Apparently she noticed nothing of my so near collapse, for I caught her whisper as we went. 'You *are* brave, Bill; splendidly brave.'

The upper corridors of the great sleeping house were brightly lit; on her way to me she had turned on every electric switch her hand could reach; and as we passed the final flight of stairs to the floor below, I heard a door shut softly and knew that Mabel had been listening—waiting for us. I led my sister up to it. She knocked, and the door was opened cautiously an inch or so. The room was pitch black. I caught no glimpse of Mabel standing there. Frances turned to me with a hurried whisper, 'Billy, you *will* be careful, won't you?' and went in. I just had time to answer that I would not be long, and Frances

134

to reply, 'You'll find us here——' when the door closed and cut her sentence short before its end.

But it was not alone the closing door that took the final words. Frances—by the way she disappeared I knew it—had made a swift and violent movement into the darkness that was as though she sprang. She leaped upon that other woman who stood back among the shadows, for, simultaneously with the clipping of the sentence, another sound was also stopped— stifled, smothered, choked back lest I should also hear it. Yet not in time. I heard it—a hard and horrible sound that explained both the leap and the abrupt cessation of the whispered words.

I stood irresolute a moment. It was as though all the bones had been withdrawn from my body, so that I must sink and fall. That sound plucked them out, and plucked out my self-possession with them. I am not sure that it was a sound I had ever heard before, though children, I half remembered, made it sometimes in blind rages when they knew not what they did. In a grown-up person certainly I had never known it. I associated it with animals rather—horribly. In the history of the world, no doubt, it has been common enough, alas, but fortunately to-day there can be but few who know it, or would recognise it even when heard. The bones shot back into my body the same instant, but red-hot and burning; the brief instant of irresolution passed; I was torn between the desire to break down the door and enter, and to run—run for my life from a thing I dared not face.

Out of the horrid tumult, then, I adopted neither course. Without reflection, certainly without analysis of what was best to do for my sister, myself or Mabel, I took up my action where it had been interrupted. I turned from the awful door and moved slowly towards the head of the stairs. But that dreadful little sound came with me. I believe my own teeth chattered. It seemed all over the house—in the empty halls that opened into the long passages towards the music-room, and even in the grounds outside the building. From the lawns and barren garden, from the ugly terraces themselves, it rose into the night, and behind it came a curious driving sound, incomplete, unfinished, as of wailing for deliverance, the wailing of desperate souls in anguish, the dull and dry beseeching of hopeless spirits in prison.

That I could have taken the little sound from the bedroom where I actually heard it, and spread it thus over the entire house and grounds, is evidence, perhaps, of the state my nerves were in. The wailing assuredly was in my mind alone. But the longer I hesitated, the more difficult became my task, and, gathering up my dressing-gown, lest I should trip in the darkness, I passed slowly down the staircase into the hall below. I carried neither candle nor matches; every switch in room and corridor was known to me. The covering of darkness was indeed rather comforting than otherwise, for if it prevented seeing, it also prevented being seen. The heavy pistol, knocking against my thigh as I moved, made me feel I was carrying a child's toy, foolishly. I experienced in every nerve that primitive vast dread which is the Thrill of darkness. Merely the child in me was comforted by that pistol.

The night was not entirely black; the iron bars across the glass front door were visible, and, equally, I discerned the big, stiff wooden chairs in the hall, the gaping fireplace, the upright pillars supporting the staircase, the round table in the centre with its books and flower-vases, and the basket that held visitors' cards. There, too, was the stick and umbrella stand and the shelf with railway guides, directory, and telegraph forms. Clocks ticked everywhere with sounds like quiet footfalls. Light fell here and there in patches from the floor above. I stood a moment in the hall, letting my eyes grow more accustomed to the gloom, while deciding on a plan of search. I made out the ivy trailing outside over one of the big windows... and then the tall clock by the front door made a grating noise deep down inside its body—it was the Presentation clock, large and hideous, given by the congregation of his church—and, dreading the booming strike it seemed to threaten, I made a quick decision. If others beside myself were about in the night, the sound of that striking might cover their approach.

So I tiptoed to the right, where the passage led towards the dining-room. In the other direction were the morning- and drawing-rooms, both little used, and various other rooms beyond that had been *his*, generally now kept locked. I thought of my sister, waiting upstairs with that frightened woman for my return. I went quickly, yet stealthily.

And, to my surprise, the door of the dining-room was open. It had been opened. I paused on the threshold, staring about me. I think I fully expected to see a figure blocked in the shadows against the heavy sideboard, or looming on the other side beneath his portrait. But the room was empty; I *felt* it empty. Through the wide bow-windows that gave on to the verandah came an uncertain glimmer that even shone reflected in the polished surface of the dinner-table, and again I per- ceived the stiff outline of chairs, waiting tenantless all round it, two larger ones with high carved backs at either end. The monkey-trees on the upper terrace, too, were visible outside against the sky, and the solemn crests of the wellingtonias on the terraces below. The enormous clock on the mantelpiece ticked very slowly, as though its machinery were running down, and I made out the pale round patch that was its face. Resisting my first inclination to turn the lights up—my hand had gone so far as to finger the friendly knob—I crossed the room so carefully that no single board creaked, nor a single chair, as I rested a hand upon its back, moved on the parquet flooring. I turned neither to the right nor left, nor did I once look back.

I went towards the long corridor filled with priceless *objets d'art,* that led through various antechambers into the spacious music-room, and only at the mouth of this corridor did I next halt a moment in uncertainty. For this long corridor, lit faintly by high windows on the left from the verandah, was very narrow, owing to the mass of shelves and fancy tables it contained. It was not that I feared to knock over precious things as I went, but, that, because of its ungenerous width, there would be no room to pass another person—if I met one. And the certainty had suddenly come upon me that somewhere in this corridor another person at this actual moment stood. Here, somehow, amid all this dead atmosphere of furniture and impersonal emptiness, lay the hint of a living human presence; and with such conviction did it come upon me, that my hand instinctively gripped the pistol in my pocket before I could even think. Either some one had passed along this corridor just before me, or some one lay waiting at its farther end—withdrawn or flattened into one of the little recesses, to let me pass. It was the person who had opened the door. And the blood ran from my heart as I realised it.

It was not courage that sent me on, but rather a strong impulsion from behind that made it impossible to retreat: the feeling that a throng pressed at my back, drawing nearer and nearer; that I was already half surrounded, swept, dragged, coaxed into a vast prison-house where there was wailing and gnashing of teeth, where their worm dieth not and their fire is not quenched. I can neither explain nor justify the storm of irrational emotion that swept me as I stood in that moment, staring down the length of the silent corridor towards the music-room at the far end, I can only repeat that no personal bravery sent me down it, but that the negative emotion of fear was swamped in this vast sea of pity and commiseration for others that surged upon me.

My senses, at least, were no whit confused; if anything, my brain registered impressions with keener accuracy than usual. I noticed, for instance, that the two swinging doors of baize that cut the corridor into definite lengths, making little rooms of the spaces between them, were both wide-open—in the dim light no mean achievement. Also that the fronds of a palm plant, some ten feet in front of me, still stirred gently from the air of some one who had recently gone past them. The long green leaves waved to and fro like hands. Then I went stealthily forward down the narrow space, proud even that I had this command of myself, and so carefully that my feet made no sound upon the Japanese matting on the floor.

It was a journey that seemed timeless. I have no idea how
fast or slow I went, but I remember that I deliberately examined
articles on each side of me, peering with particular closeness
into the recesses of wall and window. I passed the first baize
doors, and the passage beyond them widened out to hold
shelves of books; there were sofas and small reading-tables
against the wall. It narrowed again presently, as I entered the
second stretch. The windows here were higher and smaller,
and marble statuettes of classical subject lined the walls, watching me like figures of the dead. Their white and shining faces
saw me, yet made no sign. I passed next between the second
baize doors. They, too, had been fastened back with hooks
against the wall. Thus all doors were open—had been recently
opened.

And so, at length, I found myself in the final widening of the
corridor which formed an antechamber to the music-room
itself. It had been used formerly to hold the overflow of
meetings. No door separated it from the great hall beyond,
but heavy curtains hung usually to close it off, and these curtains
were invariably drawn. They now stood wide. And here—I
can merely state the impression that came upon me—I knew
myself at last surrounded. The throng that pressed behind
me, also surged in front: facing me in the big room, and waiting
for my entry, stood a multitude; on either side of me, in the
very air above my head, the vast assemblage paused upon my
coming. The pause, however, was momentary, for instantly
the deep. tumultuous movement was resumed that yet was
silent as a cavern underground. I felt the agony that was in it,
the passionate striving, the awful struggle to escape. The
semi-darkness held beseeching faces that fought to press
themselves upon my vision, yearning yet hopeless eyes, lips
scorched and dry, mouths that opened to implore but found
no craved delivery in actual words, and a fury of misery and
hate that made the life in me stop dead, frozen by the horror
of vain pity. That intolerable, vain Hope was everywhere.

And the multitude, it came to me, was not a single multitude, but many; for, as soon as one huge division pressed

too close upon the edge of escape, it was dragged back by another and prevented. The wild host was divided against itself. Here dwelt the Shadow I had 'imagined' weeks ago, and in it struggled armies of lost souls as in the depths of some bottomless pit whence there is no escape. The layers mingled, fighting against themselves in endless torture. It was in this great Shadow I had clairvoyantly seen Mabel, but about its fearful mouth, I now was certain, hovered another figure of darkness, a figure who sought to keep it in existence, since to her thought were due those lampless depths of woe without escape.... Towards me the multitudes now surged.

It was a sound and a movement that brought me back into myself. The great clock at the farther end of the room just then struck the hour of three. That was the sound. And the movement—? I was aware that a figure was passing across the distant centre of the floor. Instantly I dropped back into the arena of my little human terror. My hand again clutched stupidly at the pistol butt. I drew back into the folds of the heavy curtain. And the figure advanced.

I remember every detail. At first it seemed to me enormous—this advancing shadow—far beyond human scale; but as it came nearer, I measured it, though not consciously, by the organ pipes that gleamed in faint colours, just above its gradual soft approach. It passed them, already half-way across the great room. I saw then that its stature was that of ordinary men. The prolonged booming of the clock died away. I heard the footfall, shuffling upon the polished boards. I heard another sound—a voice, low and monotonous, droning as in prayer. The figure was speaking. It was a woman. And she carried in both hands before her a small object that faintly shimmered—a glass of water. And then I recognised her.

There was still an instant's time before she reached me, and I made use of it. I shrank back, flattening myself against the wall. Her voice ceased a moment, as she turned and carefully drew the curtains together behind her, closing them with one hand. Oblivious of my presence, though she actually touched my dressing-gown with the hand that pulled the cords, she resumed her dreadful, solemn march, disappearing at length down the long vista of the corridor like a shadow. But as she passed me, her voice began again, so that I heard each word distinctly as she uttered it, her head aloft, her figure upright, as though she moved at the head of a procession:

'A drop of cold water, given in His name, shall moisten their burning tongues.'

It was repeated monotonously over and over again, droning down into the distance as she went, until at length both voice and figure faded into the shadows at the farther end.

For a time, I have no means of measuring precisely, I stood in that dark corner, pressing my back against the wall, and would have drawn the curtains down to hide me had I dared to stretch an arm out. The dread that presently the woman would return passed gradually away. I realised that the air had emptied, the crowd her presence had stirred into activity had retreated; I was alone in the gloomy under-space of the odious building.... Then I remembered suddenly again the terrified women waiting for me on that upper landing; and realised that my skin was wet and freezing cold after a profuse perspiration. I prepared to retrace my steps. I remember the effort it cost me to leave the support of the wall and covering darkness of my corner, and step out into the grey light of the corridor. At first I sidled, then, finding this mode of walking impossible, turned my face boldly and walked quickly, regardless that my dressing-gown set the precious objects shaking as I passed. A wind that sighed mournfully against the high, small windows seemed to have got inside the corridor as well; it felt so cold; and every moment I dreaded to see the outline of the woman's figure as she waited in recess or angle against the wall for me to pass.

Was there another thing I dreaded even more? I cannot say. I only know that the first baize doors had swung to behind me, and the second ones were close at hand, when the great dim thunder caught me, pouring up with prodigious volume so that it seemed to roll out from another world. It shook the very bowels of the building. I was closer to it than that other time, when it had followed me from the goblin garden. There was strength and hardness in it, as of metal reverberation. Some touch of numbness, almost of paralysis, must surely have been upon me that I felt no actual terror, for I remember even turning and standing still to hear it better. 'That is the Noise,' my thought ran stupidly, and I think I whispered it aloud; '*the Doors are closing.*'

The wind outside against the windows was audible, so it cannot have been really loud, yet to me it was the biggest, deepest sound I have ever heard, but so far away, with such awful remoteness in it, that I had to doubt my own ears at the same time. It seemed underground—the rumbling of earthquake gates that shut remorselessly within the rocky Earth—stupendous ultimate thunder. *They* were shut off from help again. The doors had closed.

I felt a storm of pity, an agony of bitter, futile hate sweep through me. My memory of the figure changed then. The Woman with the glass of cooling water had stepped down from Heaven; but the Man—or was it Men?—who smeared this terrible layer of belief and Thought upon the world!...

I crossed the dining-room—it was fancy, of course, that held my eyes from glancing at the portrait for fear I should see it smiling approval—and so finally reached the hall, where the light from the floor above seemed now quite bright in comparison. All the doors I closed carefully behind me; but first I had to open them. The woman had closed every one. Up the stairs, then, I actually ran, two steps at a time. My sister was standing outside Mabel's door. By her face I knew that she had also heard. There was no need to ask. I quickly made my mind up.

'There's nothing,' I said, and detailed briefly my tour of search. 'All is quiet and undisturbed downstairs.' May God forgive me!

She beckoned to me, closing the door softly behind her. My heart beat violently a moment, then stood still.

'Mabel,' she said aloud.

It was like the sentence of a judge, that one short word.

I tried to push past her and go in, but she stopped me with her arm. She was wholly mistress of herself, I saw.

'Hush!' she said in a lower voice. 'I've got her round again with brandy. She's sleeping quietly now. We won't disturb her.'

She drew me farther out into the landing, and as she did so, the clock in the hall below struck half-past three. I had stood, then, thirty minutes in the corridor below. 'You've been such a long time.' she said simply. 'I feared for you,' and she took my hand in her own that was cold and clammy.

VIII

And then, while that dreadful house stood listening about us in the early hours of this chill morning upon the edge of winter, she told me, with laconic brevity, things about Mabel that I heard as from a distance. There was nothing so unusual or tremendous in the short recital, nothing indeed I might not have already guessed for myself. It was the time and scene, the inference, too, that made it so afflicting: the idea that Mabel believed herself so utterly and hopelessly lost—beyond recovery *damned*.

That she had loved him with so passionate a devotion that she had given her soul into his keeping, this certainly I had not divined—probably because I had never thought about it one way or the other. He had 'converted' her, I knew, but that she had subscribed whole-heartedly to that most cruel and ugly of his dogmas—this was new to me, and came with a certain shock as I heard it. In love, of course, the weaker nature is receptive to all manner of suggestion. This man had 'suggested' his pet brimstone lake so vividly that she had listened and believed. He had frightened her into heaven; and his heaven, a definite locality in the skies, had its foretaste here on earth in miniature—The Towers, house and garden. Into his dolorous scheme of a handful saved and millions damned, his enclosure, as it were, of sheep and goats, he had swept her before she was aware of it. Her mind no longer was her own. And it was Mrs. Marsh who kept the thought-stream open, though tempered, as she deemed, with that touch of craven, superstitious mercy.

But what I found it difficult to understand, and still more difficult to accept, was that, during her year abroad, she had been so haunted with a secret dread of that hideous after-death that she had finally revolted and tried to recover that clearer state of mind she had enjoyed before the religious bully had stunned her—yet had tried in vain. She had returned to The Towers to find her soul again, only to realise that it was lost eternally. The cleaner state of mind lay then beyond recovery. In the reaction that followed the removal of his terrible 'suggestion,' she felt the crumbling of all that he had taught her, but searched in vain for the peace and beauty his teachings had destroyed. Nothing came to replace these. She was empty, desolate, hopeless; craving her former joy and carelessness, she found only hate and diabolical calculation. This man, whom she had loved to the point of losing her soul for him, had bequeathed to her one black and fiery thing—the terror of the damned. His thinking wrapped her in this iron garment that held her fast.

All this Frances told me, far more briefly than I have here repeated it. In her eyes and gestures and laconic sentences lay the conviction of great beating issues and of menacing drama my own description fails to recapture. It was all so incongruous and remote from the world I lived in that more than once a smile, though a smile of pity, fluttered to my lips; but a glimpse of my face in the mirror showed rather the leer of a grimace. There was no real laughter anywhere that night. The entire adventure seemed so incredible, here, in this twentieth century —but yet delusion, that feeble word, did not occur once in the comments my mind suggested though did not utter. I remembered that forbidding Shadow too; my sister's water-colours; the vanished personality of our hostess; the inexplicable, thundering Noise, and the figure of Mrs. Marsh in her midnight ritual that was so childish yet so horrible. I shivered

144

in spite of my own 'emancipated' cast of mind.

'Thete *is* no Mabel,' were the words with which my sister sent another shower of ice down my spine. 'He has killed her in his lake of fire and brimstone.'

I stared at her blankly, as in a nightmare where nothing true or possible ever happened.

'He killed her in his lake of fire and brimstone,' she repeated more faintly.

A desperate effort was in me to say the strong, sensible thing which should destroy the oppressive horror that grew so stiflingly about us both, but again the mirror drew the attempted smile into the merest grin, betraying the distortion that was everywhere in the place.

'You mean,' I stammered beneath my breath, 'that her faith has gone, but that the terror has remained?' I asked it, dully groping. I moved out of the line of the reflection in the glass.

She bowed her head as though beneath a weight; her skin was the pallor of grey ashes.

'You mean,' I said louder, 'that she has lost her—mind?'

'She is terror incarnate,' was the whispered answer. 'Mabel has lost her soul. Her soul is—there!' She pointed horribly below. 'She is seeking it...?'

The word 'soul' stung me into something of my normal self again.

'But her terror, poor thing, is not—cannot be—transferable to *us!*' I exclaimed more vehemently. 'It certainly is not convertible into feelings, sights and—even sounds!'

She interrupted me quickly, almost impatiently, speaking with that conviction by which she conquered me so easily that night.

'It is her terror that revived "the Others." It has brought her into touch with them. They are loose and driving after her. Her efforts at resistance have given them also hope—that escape, after all, *is* possible. Day and night they strive.'

'Escape! Others!' The anger fast rising in me dropped of its own accord at the moment of birth. It shrank into a shuddering beyond my control. In that moment, I think,

I would have believed in the possibility of anything and everything she might tell me. To argue or contradict seemed equally futile.

'His strong belief, as also the beliefs of others who have preceded him,' she replied, so sure of herself that I actually turned to look over my shoulder, 'have left their shadow like a thick deposit over the house and grounds. To them, poor souls imprisoned by thought, it was hopeless as granite walls—until her resistance, her effort to dissipate it—let in light. Now, in their thousands, they are flocking to this little light, seeking escape. Her own escape, don't you see, may release them all!'

It took my breath away. Had his predecessors, former occupants of this house, also preached damnation of all the world but their own exclusive sect? Was this the explanation of her obscure talk of 'layers,' each striving against the other for domination? And if men are spirits, and these spirits survive, could strong Thought thus determine their condition even afterwards?

So many questions flooded into me that I selected no one of them, but stared in uncomfortable silence, bewildered, out of my depth, and acutely, painfully distressed. There was so odd a mixture of possible truth and incredible, unacceptable explanation in it all; so much confirmed, yet so much left darker than before. What she said did, indeed, offer a quasi-interpretation of my own series of abominable sensations—strife, agony, pity, hate, escape—but so far-fetched that only the deep conviction in her voice and attitude made it tolerable for a second even. I found myself in a curious state of mind. I could neither think clearly nor say a word to refute her amazing statements, whispered there beside me in the shivering hours of the early morning with only a wall between ourselves and—Mabel. Close behind her words I remember this singular thing, however—that an atmosphere as of the Inquisition seemed to rise and stir about the room, beating awful wings of black above my head.

Abruptly, then, a moment's common-sense returned to me.

146

I faced her.

'And the Noise?' I said aloud, more firmly, 'the roar of the closing doors? We have *all* heard that! Is that subjective too?'

Frances looked sideways about her in a queer fashion that made my flesh creep again. I spoke brusquely, almost angrily. I repeated the question, and waited with anxiety for her reply.

'What noise?' she asked, with the frank expression of an innocent child. 'What closing doors?'

But her face turned from grey to white, and I saw that drops of perspiration glistened on her forehead. She caught at the back of a chair to steady herself, then glanced about her again with that sidelong look that made my blood run cold. I understood suddenly then. She did not take in what I said. I knew now. She was listening—for something else.

And the discovery revived in me a far stronger emotion than any mere desire for immediate explanation. Not only did I not insist upon an answer, but I was actually terrified lest she *would* answer. More, I felt in me a terror lest I should be moved to describe my own experiences below-stairs, thus increasing their reality and so the reality of all. She might even explain them too!

Still listening intently, she raised her head and looked me in the eyes. Her lips opened to speak. The words came to me from a great distance, it seemed, and her voice had a sound like a stone that drops into a deep well, its fate though hidden, known.

'We are in it with her, too, Bill. We are in it with her. Our interpretations vary—because we are—in parts of it only. Mabel is in it—*all.*'

The desire for violence came over me. If only she would say a definite thing in plain King's English! If only I could find it in me to give utterance to what shouted so loud within me! If only—the same old cry—something would happen! For all this elliptic talk that dazed my mind left obscurity everywhere. Her atrocious meaning, none the less, flashed through me, though vanishing before it wholly divulged itself.

It brought a certain reaction with it. I found my tongue.

Whether I actually believed what I said is more than I can swear to; that it seemed to me wise at the moment is all I remember. My mind was in a state of obscure perception less than that of normal consciousness.

'Yes, Frances, I believe that what you say is the truth, and that we are in it with her'—I meant to say I with loud, hostile emphasis, but instead I whispered it lest she should hear the trembling of my voice—'and for that reason, my dear sister, we leave to-morrow, you and I—to-day, rather, since it is long past midnight—we leave this house of the damned. We go back to London.'

Frances looked up, her face distraught almost beyond recognition. But it was not my words that caused the tumult in her heart. It was a sound—the sound she had been listening for—so faint I barely caught it myself, and had she not pointed I could never have known the direction whence it came. Small and terrible it rose again in the stillness of the night, the sound of gnashing teeth. And behind it came another—the tread of stealthy footsteps. Both were just outside the door.

The room swung round me for a second. My first instinct to prevent my sister going out—she had dashed past me frantically to the door—gave place to another when I saw the expression in her eyes. I followed her lead instead; it was surer than my own. The pistol in my pocket swung uselessly against my thigh. I was flustered beyond belief and ashamed that I was so.

'Keep close to me, Frances,' I said huskily, as the door swung wide and a shaft of light fell upon a figure moving rapidly. Mabel was going down the corridor. Beyond her, in the shadows on the staircase, a second figure stood beckoning, scarcely visible.

'Before they get her! Quick!' was screamed into my ears, and our arms were about her in the same moment. It was a horrible scene. Not that Mabel struggled in the least, but that she collapsed as we caught her and fell with her dead weight, as of a corpse, limp, against us. And her teeth began again. They continued, even beneath the hand that Frances

148

clapped upon her lips....

We carried her back into her own bedroom, where she lay down peacefully enough. It was so soon over.... The rapidity of the whole thing robbed it of reality almost. It had the swiftness of something remembered rather than of something witnessed. She slept again so quickly that it was almost as if we had caught her sleep-walking. I cannot say. I asked no questions at the time; I have asked none since; and my help was needed as little as the protection of my pistol. Frances was strangely competent and collected.... I lingered for some time uselessly by the door, till at length, looking up with a sigh, she made a sign for me to go.

'I shall wait in your room next door,' I whispered, 'till you come.' But, though going out, I waited in the corridor instead, so as to hear the faintest call for help. In that dark corridor upstairs I waited, but not long. It may have been fifteen minutes when Frances reappeared, locking the door softly behind her. Leaning over the banisters, I saw her.

'I'll go in again about six o'clock,' she whispered, 'as soon as it gets light. She is sound asleep now. Please don't wait. If anything happens I'll call—you might leave your door ajar, perhaps.' And she came up, looking like a ghost.

But I saw her first safely into bed, and the rest of the night I spent in an armchair close to my opened door, listening for the slightest sound. Soon after five o'clock I heard Frances fumbling with the key, and, peering over the railing again, I waited till she reappeared and went back into her own room. She closed her door. Evidently she was satisfied that all was well.

Then, and then only, did I go to bed myself, but not to sleep. I could not get the scene out of my mind, especially that odious detail of it which I hoped and believed my sister had not seen— the still, dark figure of the housekeeper waiting on the stairs below—waiting, of course, for Mabel.

IX

It seems I became a mere spectator after that; my sister's lead was so assured for one thing, and, for another, the responsibility of leaving Mabel alone—Frances laid it bodily upon my shoulders—was a little more than I cared about. Moreover, when we all three met later in the day, things went on so exactly as before, so absolutely without friction or distress, that to present a sudden, obvious excuse for cutting our visit short seemed ill-judged. And on the lowest grounds it would have been desertion. At any rate, it was beyond my powers, and Frances was quite firm that *she* must stay. We therefore did stay. Things that happen in the night always seem exaggerated and distorted when the sun shines brightly next morning; no one can reconstruct the terror of a nightmare afterwards, nor comprehend why it seemed so overwhelming at the time.

I slept till ten o'clock, and when I rang for breakfast, a note from my sister lay upon the tray, its message of counsel couched in a calm and comforting strain. Mabel, she assured me, was herself again and remembered nothing of what had happened; there was no need of any violent measures; I was to treat her exactly as if I knew nothing. 'And, if you don't mind, Bill, let us leave the matter unmentioned between ourselves as well. Discussion exaggerates; such things are best not talked about. I'm sorry I disturbed you so unnecessarily; I was stupidly excited. Please forget all the things I said at the moment.' She had written 'nonsense' first instead of 'things', then scratched it out. She wished to convey that hysteria had been abroad in the night, and I readily gulped the explanation down, though it could not satisfy me in the smallest degree.

There was another week of our visit still, and we stayed it out to the end without disaster. My desire to leave at times became that frantic thing, desire to escape; but I controlled it, kept silent, watched and wondered. Nothing happened. As before, and everywhere, there was no sequence of development, no connection between cause and effect; and climax, none whatever. The thing swayed up and down, backwards and forwards like a great loose curtain in the wind, and I could only vaguely surmise what caused the draught or why there was a curtain at all. A novelist might mould the queer material into coherent sequence that would be interesting but could not be true. It remains, therefore, not a story but a history. Nothing happened.

Perhaps my intense dislike of the fall of darkness was due wholly to my stirred imagination, and perhaps my anger when I learned that Frances now occupied a bed in our hostess's room was unreasonable. Nerves were unquestionably on edge. I was for ever on the look-out for some event that should make escape imperative, but yet that never presented itself. I slept lightly, left my door ajar to catch the slightest sound, even made stealthy tours of the house below-stairs while everybody dreamed in their beds. But I discovered nothing; the doors were always locked; I neither saw the housekeeper again in unreasonable times and places, nor heard a footstep in the passages and halls. The Noise was never once repeated. That horrible, ultimate thunder, my intensest dread of all, lay withdrawn into the abyss whence it had twice arisen. And though in my thoughts it was sternly denied existence, the great black reason for the fact afflicted me unbelievably. Since Mabel's fruitless effort to escape, the Doors kept closed remorselessly. She had failed; *they* gave up hope. For this was the explanation that haunted the region of my mind where feelings stir and hint before they clothe themselves in actual language. Only I firmly kept it there; it never knew expression.

But, if my ears were open, my eyes were opened too, and it were idle to pretend that I did not notice a hundred details that were capable of sinister interpretation had I been weak enough to yield. Some protective barrier had fallen into ruins round me, so that Terror stalked behind the general collapse, feeling for me through all the gaping fissures. Much of this, I admit, must have been merely the elaboration of those sensations I had first vaguely felt, before subsequent events and my talks with Frances had dramatised them into living thoughts. I therefore leave them unmentioned in this history, just as my mind left them unmentioned in that interminable final week.

Our life went on precisely as before—Mabel unreal and outwardly so still; Frances, secretive, anxious, tactful to the point of slyness, and keen to save to the point of self-forget-fulness. There were the same stupid meals, the same wearisome long evenings, the stifling ugliness of house and grounds, the Shadow settling in so thickly that it seemed almost a visible, tangible thing. I came to feel the only friendly things in all this hostile, cruel place were the robins that hopped boldly over the monstrous terraces and even up to the windows of the unsightly house itself. The robins alone knew joy; they danced, believing no evil thing was possible in all God's radiant world. They believed in everybody; *their* god's plan of life had no room in it for hell, damnation and lakes of brim-stone. I came to love the little birds. Had Samuel Franklyn known them, he might have preached a different sermon, bequeathing love in place of terror!...

Most of my time I spent writing; but it was a pretence at best, and rather a dangerous one besides. For it stirred the mind to production, with the result that other things came pouring in as well. With reading it was the same. In the end I found an aggressive, deliberate resistance to be the only way of feasible defence. To walk far afield was out of the question, for it meant leaving my sister too long alone, so that my exercise was confined to nearer home. My saunters in the grounds, however, never surprised the goblin garden again. It was close at hand, but I seemed unable to get wholly into it. Too many things assailed my mind for any one to hold exclusive possession, perhaps.

Indeed, all the interpretations, all the 'layers,' to use my sister's phrase, slipped in by turns and lodged there for a time. They came day and night, and though my reason denied them entrance they held their own as by a kind of squatter's right. They stirred moods already in me, that is, and did not introduce entirely new ones; for every mind conceals ancestral deposits that have been cultivated in turn along the whole line of its descent. Any day a chance shower may cause this one or that to blossom. Thus it came to me, at any rate. After darkness the Inquisition paced the empty corridors and set up ghastly apparatus in the dismal halls; and once, in the library, there swept over me that easy and delicious conviction that by confessing my wickedness I could resume it later, since Confession is expression, and expression brings relief and leaves one ready to accumulate again. And in such mood I felt bitter and unforgiving towards all others who thought differently. Another time it was a Pagan thing that assaulted me—so trivial yet oh, so significant at the time—when I dreamed that a herd of centaurs rolled up with a great stamping of hoofs round the house to destroy it, and then woke to hear the horses tramping across the field below the lawns; they neighed ominously and their noisy panting was audible as if it were just outside my windows.

But the tree episode, I think, was the most curious of all—except, perhaps, the incident with the children which I shall mention in a moment—for its closeness to reality was so unforgettable. Outside the east window of my room stood a giant wellingtonia on the lawn, its head rising level with the upper sash. It grew some twenty feet away, planted on the highest terrace, and I often saw it when closing my curtains for the night, noticing how it drew its heavy skirts about it, and how the light from other windows threw glimmering streaks and patches that turned it into the semblance of a towering, solemn image. It stood there then so strikingly, somehow like a great old-world idol, that it claimed attention. Its appearance was curiously formidable. Its branches rustled without visibly moving and it had a certain portentous, forbidding air, so grand and dark and monstrous in the night that I was always glad when my curtains shut it out. Yet, once in bed, I had never thought about it one way or the other, and by day had certainly never sought it out.

One night, then, as I went to bed and closed this window against a cutting easterly wind, I saw—that there were two of these trees. A brother wellingtonia rose mysteriously beside it, equally huge, equally towering, equally monstrous. The menacing pair of them faced me there upon the lawn. But in this new arrival lay a strange suggestion that frightened me before I could argue it away. Exact counterpart of its giant companion, it revealed also that gross, odious quality that all my sister's paintings held. I got the odd impression that the rest of these trees, stretching away dimly in a troop over the farther lawns, were similar, and that, led by this enormous pair, they had all moved boldly closer to my windows. At the same moment a blind was drawn down over an upper room; the second tree disappeared into the surrounding darkness. It was, of course, this chance light that had brought it into the field of vision, but when the black shutter dropped over it, hiding it from view, the manner of its vanishing produced the queer effect that it had slipped into its companion—almost that it had been an emanation of the one I so disliked, and not really a tree at all! In this way the garden turned vehicle for expressing what lay behind it all!...

The behaviour of the doors, the little, ordinary doors, seems scarcely worth mention at all, their queer way of opening and shutting of their own accord; for this was accountable in a hundred natural ways, and to tell the truth, I never caught one in the act of moving. Indeed, only after frequent repetitions did the detail force itself upon me, when, having noticed one, I noticed all. It produced, however, the unpleasant impression of a continual coming and going in the house, as though, screened cleverly and purposely from actual sight, some one in the building held constant invisible intercourse with—others.

Upon detailed descriptions of these uncertain incidents I do not venture, individually so trival, but taken all together so impressive and so insolent. But the episode of the children, mentioned above, was different. And I give it because it showed how vividly the intuitive child-mind received the impression—one impression, at any rate—of what was in the air. It may be told in a very few words. I believe they were the coachman's children, and that the man had been in Mr. Franklyn's service; but of neither point am I quite positive.

I heard screaming in the rose-garden that runs along the stable walls—it was one afternoon not far from the tea-hour—and on hurrying up I found a little girl of nine or ten fastened with ropes to a rustic seat, and two other children—boys, one about twelve and one much younger—gathering sticks beneath the climbing rose-trees. The girl was white and frightened, but the others were laughing and talking among themselves so busily while they picked that they did not notice my abrupt arrival. Some game, I understood, was in progress, but a game that had become too serious for the happiness of the prisoner, for there was a fear in the girl's eyes that was a very genuine fear indeed. I unfastened her at once; the ropes were so loosely and clumsily knotted that they had not hurt her skin; it was not that which made her pale. She collapsed a moment upon the bench, then picked up her tiny skirts and dived away at full speed into the safety of the stable-yard. There was no response to my brief comforting, but she ran as though for her life, and I divined that some horrid boys' cruelty had been afoot. It was probably mere thoughtlessness, as cruelty with children usually is, but something in me decided to discover exactly what it was.

And the boys, not one whit alarmed at my intervention, merely laughed shyly when I explained that their prisoner had escaped, and told me frankly what their 'gime' had been. There was no vestige of shame in them, nor any idea, of course, that they aped a monstrous reality. That it was mere pretence was neither here nor there. To them, though make-believe, it was a make-believe of something that was right and natural and in no sense cruel. Grown-ups did it too. It was necessary for her good.

'We was going to burn her up, sir,' the older one informed me, answering my 'Why?' with the explanation, 'Because she wouldn't believe what we wanted 'er to believe.'

And, game though it was, the feeling of reality about the little episode was so arresting, so terrific in some way, that only with difficulty did I confine my admonitions on this occasion to mere words. The boys slunk off, frightened in their turn, yet not, I felt, convinced that they had erred in principle. It was their inheritance. They had breathed it in with the atmosphere of their bringing-up. They would renew the salutary torture when they could—till she 'believed' as they did.

I went back into the house, afflicted with a passion of mingled pity and distress impossible to describe, yet on my short way across the garden was attacked by other moods in turn, each more real and bitter than its predecessor. I received the whole series, as it were, at once. I felt like a diver rising to the surface through layers of water at different temperatures, though here the natural order was reversed, and the cooler strata were uppermost, the heated ones below. Thus, I was caught by the goblin touch of the willows that fringed the field; by the sensuous curving of the twisted ash that formed a gateway to the little grove of sapling oaks where fauns and satyrs lurked to play in the moonlight before Pagan altars; and by the cloaking darkness, next, of the copse of stunted pines, close gathered each to each, where hooded figures stalked behind an awful cross. The episode with the children seemed to have opened me like a knife. The whole Place rushed at me.

I suspect this synthesis of many moods produced in me that climax of loathing and disgust which made me feel the limit of bearable emotion had been reached, so that I made straight to find Frances in order to convince her that at any rate *I* must leave. For, although this was our last day in the house, and we had arranged to go next day, the dread was in me that she would still find some persuasive reason for staying on. And an unexpected incident then made my dread unnecessary. The front door was open and a cab stood in the drive; a tall, elderly man was gravely talking in the hall with the parlourmaid we called the Grenadier. He held a piece of paper in his hand. 'I have called to see the house,' I heard him say, as I ran up the stairs to Frances, who was peering like an inquisitive child over the banisters....

'Yes,' she told me with a sigh, I know not whether of resignation or relief, 'the house *is* to be let or sold. Mabel has decided. Some Society or other, I believe——'

I was overjoyed: this made our leaving right and possible. 'You never told me, Frances!'

'Mabel only heard of it a few days ago. She told me herself this morning. It is a chance, she says. Alone she cannot get it "straight". '

'Defeat?' I asked, watching her closely.

'She thinks she has found a way out. It's not a family, you see, it's a Society, a sort of Community—they go in for thought——'

'A Community!' I gasped. 'You mean religious?'

She shook her head. 'Not exactly,' she said smiling, 'but some kind of association of men and women who want a head-quarters in the country—a place where they can write and meditate—*think*—mature their plans and all the rest—I don't know exactly what.'

'Utopian dreamers?' I asked, yet feeling an immense relief come over me as I heard. But I asked in ignorance, not cynically. Frances would know. She knew all this kind of thing.

'No, not that exactly,' she smiled. 'Their teachings are grand and simple—old as the world too, really—the basis of every religion before men's minds perverted them with their manu-factured creeds——'

Footsteps on the stairs, and the sound of voices, interrupted our odd impromptu conversation, as the Grenadier came up, followed by the tall, grave gentleman who was being shown over the house. My sister drew me along the corridor towards her room, where she went in and closed the door behind me, yet not before I had stolen a good look at the caller—long enough, at least, for his face and general appearance to have made a definite impression on me. For something strong and peaceful emanated from his presence; he moved with such quiet dignity; the glance of his eyes was so steady and reassuring, that my mind labelled him instantly as a type of man one would turn to in an emergency and not be disappointed. I had seen him but for a passing moment, but I had seen him twice, and the way he walked down the passage, looking competently about him, conveyed the same impression as when I saw him

157

standing at the door—fearless, tolerant, wise. 'A sincere and kindly character,' I judged instantly, 'a man whom some big kind of love has trained in sweetness towards the world; no hate in him anywhere.' A great deal, no doubt, to read in so brief a glance! Yet his voice confirmed my intuition, a deep and very gentle voice, great firmness in it too.

'Have I become suddenly sensitive to people's atmospheres in this extraordinary fashion?' I asked myself, smiling, as I stood in the room and heard the door close behind me. 'Have I developed some clairvoyant faculty here?' At any other time I should have mocked.

And I sat down and faced my sister, feeling strangely comforted and at peace for the first time since I had stepped beneath The Towers' roof a month ago. Frances, I then saw, was smiling a little as she watched me.

'You know him?' I asked.

'You felt it too?' was her question in reply. 'No,' she added, 'I don't know him—beyond the fact that he is a leader in the Movement and has devoted years and money to its objects. Mabel felt the same thing in him that you have felt—and jumped at it.'

'But you've seen him before?' I urged, for the certainty was in me that he was no stranger to her.

She shook her head. 'He called one day early this week, when you were out. Mabel saw him. I believe——' she hesitated a moment, as though expecting me to stop her with my usual impatience of such subjects—'I believe he has explained everything to her—the beliefs he embodies, she declares, are her salvation—might be, rather, if she could adopt them.'

'Conversion again!' For I remembered her riches, and how gladly a Society would gobble them.

'The layers I told you about,' she continued calmly, shrugging her shoulders slightly—'the deposits that are left behind by strong thinking and *real* belief—but especially by ugly, hateful belief, because, you see—unfortunately there's more vital passion in that sort——'

'Frances, I don't understand a bit,' I said out loud, but said it a little humbly, for the impression the man had left was still strong upon me and I was grateful for the steady sense of peace and comfort he had somehow introduced. The horrors had been so dreadful. My nerves, doubtless, were more than a little overstrained. Absurd as it must sound, I classed him in my mind with the robins, the happy, confiding robins who believed in everybody and thought no evil! I laughed a moment at my ridiculous idea, and my sister, encouraged by this sign of patience in me, continued more fluently.

'Of course you don't understand, Bill? Why should you? You've never thought about such things. Needing no creed yourself, you think all creeds are rubbish.'

'I'm open to conviction—I'm tolerant,' I interrupted.

'You're as narrow as Sam Franklyn, and as crammed with prejudice,' she answered, knowing that she had me at her mercy.

'Then, pray, what may be his, or his Society's beliefs?' I asked, feeling no desire to argue, 'and how are they going to prove your Mabel's salvation? Can they bring beauty into all this aggressive hate and ugliness?'

'Certain hope and peace,' she said, 'that peace which is understanding, and that understanding which explains *all* creeds and therefore tolerates them.'

'Toleration! The one word a religous man loathes above all others! His pet word is damnation——'

'Tolerates them,' she repeated patiently, unperturbed by my explosion, 'because it includes them all.'

'Fine, if true' I admitted, 'very fine. But how, pray, does it include them all?'

'Because the key-word, the motto, of their Society is, "There is no religion higher than Truth," and it has no single dogma of any kind. Above all,' she went on, 'because it claims that no individual can be "lost." It teaches universal salvation. To damn outsiders is uncivilised, childish, impure. Some take longer than others—it's according to the way they think and live—but all find peace, through development, in the end. What the creeds call a hopeless soul, it regards as a soul having further to go. There is no damnation——'

'Well, well,' I exclaimed, feeling that she rode her hobby horse too wildly, too roughly over me, 'but what is the bearing of all this upon this dreadful place, and upon Mabel? I'll admit that there is this atmosphere—this—er—inexplicable horror in the house and grounds, and that if not of damnation exactly, it is certainly damnable. I'm not too prejudiced to deny *that,* for I've felt it myself.'

To my relief she was brief. She made her statement, leaving me to take it or reject it as I would.

'The thought and belief its former occupants—have left behind. For there has been coincidence here, a coincidence that must be rare. The site on which this modern house now stands was Roman, before that Early Britain, with burial mounds, before that again, Druid—the Druid stones still lie in that copse below the field, the Tumuli among the ilexes behind the drive. The older building Sam Franklyn altered and practically pulled down was a monastery; he changed the chapel into a meeting hall, which is now the music room; but, before he came here, the house was occupied by Manetti, a violent Catholic without tolerance or vision; and in the interval between these two, Julius Weinbaum had it, Hebrew of most rigid orthodox type imaginable—so they all have left their——'

'Even so,' I repeated, yet interested to hear the rest, 'what of it?'

'Simply this,' said Frances with conviction, 'that each in turn has left his layer of concentrated thinking and belief behind him; because each believed intensely, absolutely, beyond the least weakening of any doubt—the kind of strong belief and thinking that is rare anywhere to-day, the kind that wills, impregnates objects, saturates the atmosphere, haunts, in a word. And each, believing he was utterly and finally right, damned with equally positive conviction the rest of the world. One and all preached that implicitly if not explicitly. It's the root of every creed. Last of the bigoted, grim series came Samuel Franklyn.'

I listened in amazement that increased as she went on.
Up to this point her explanation was so admirable. It was,
indeed, a pretty study in psychology if it were true.

'Then why does nothing ever happen?' I enquired mildly.
'A place so thickly haunted ought to produce a crop of no
ordinary results!'

'There lies the proof,' she went on in a lowered voice, 'the
proof of the horror and the ugly reality. The thought and
belief of each occupant in turn kept all the others under.
They gave no sign of life at the time. But the results of thinking
never die. They crop out again the moment there's an opening.
And, with the return of Mabel in her negative state, believing
nothing positive heself, the place for the first time found itself
free to reproduce its buried stores. Damnation, hell-fire, and
the rest—the most permanent and vital thought of all those
creeds, since it was applied to the majority of the world—broke
loose again, for there was no restraint to hold it back. Each
sought to obtain its former supremacy. None conquered.
There results a pandemonium of hate and fear, of striving to
escape, of agonised, bitter warring to find safety, peace—salvation. The place is saturated by that appalling stream of
thinking—the terror of the damned. It concentrated upon
Mabel, whose negative attitude furnished the channel of deliverance. You and I, according to our sympathy with her,
were similarly involved. Nothing happened, because no one
layer could ever gain the supremacy.'

I was so interested—I dare not say amused—that I stared
in silence while she paused a moment, afraid that she would
draw rein and end the fairy tale too soon.

'The beliefs of this man, of his Society rather, vigorously
thought and therefore vigorously given out here, will put
the whole place straight. It will act as a solvent. These vitriolic
layers actively denied, will fuse and disappear in the stream of
gentle, tolerant sympathy which is love. For each member,
worthy of the name, loves the world, and all creeds go into the
melting-pot; Mabel, too, if she joins them out of real conviction,
will find salvation——'

161

'Thinking, I know, is of the first importance,' I objected, 'but don't you, perhaps, exaggerate the power of feeling and emotion which in religion are *au fond* always hysterical?'

'What *is* the world,' she told me, 'but thinking and feeling? An individual's world is entirely what that individual thinks and believes—interpretation. There is no other. And unless he really thinks and really believes, he has no permanent world at all. I grant that few people think, and still fewer believe, and that most take ready-made suits and make them do. Only the strong make their own things; the lesser fry, Mabel among them, are merely swept up into what has been manufactured for them. They get along somehow. You and I have made for ourselves, Mabel has not. She is a nonentity, and when her belief is taken from her, she goes with it.'

It was not in me just then to criticise the evasion, or pick out the sophistry from the truth. I merely waited for her to continue.

'None of us have Truth, my dear Frances,' I ventured presently, seeing that she kept silent.

'Precisely,' she answered, 'but most of us have beliefs. And what one believes and thinks affects the world at large. Consider the legacy of hatred and cruelty involved in the doctrines men have built into their creeds where the *sine qua non* of salvation is absolute acceptance of one particular set of views or else perishing everlastingly—for only by repudiating history can they disavow it——'

'You're not quite accurate,' I put in. 'Not all the creeds teach damnation, do they? Franklyn did, of course, but the others are a bit modernised now surely?'

'Trying to get out of it,' she admitted, 'perhaps they are, but damnation of unbelievers—of most of the world, that is—is their rather favourite idea if you talk with them.'

'I never have.'

She smiled. 'But I have,' she said significantly, 'so, if you consider what the various occupants of this house have so strongly held and thought and believed, you need not be surprised that the influence they have left behind them should be a dark and dreadful legacy. For thought, you know, does leave——'

The opening of the door, to my great relief, interrupted her, as the Grenadier led in the visitor to see the room. He bowed to both of us with a brief word of apology, looked round him, and withdrew, and with his departure the conversation between us came naturally to an end. I followed him out. Neither of us in any case, I think, cared to argue further.

And, so far as I am aware, the curious history of The Towers ends here too. There was no climax in the story sense. Nothing ever really happened. We left next morning for London. I only know that the Society in question took the house and have since occupied it to their entire satisfaction, and that Mabel, who became a member shortly afterwards, now stays there frequently when in need of repose from the arduous and unselfish labours she took upon herself under its aegis. She dined with us only the other night, here in our tiny Chelsea flat, and a jollier, saner, more interesting and happy guest I could hardly wish for. She was vital—in the best sense; the lay-figure had come to life. I found it difficult to believe she was the same woman whose fearful effigy had floated down those dreary corridors and almost disappeared in the depths of that atrocious Shadow.

What her beliefs were now I was wise enough to leave unquestioned, and Frances, to my great relief, kept the conversation well away from such inappropriate topics. It was clear, however, that the woman had in herself some secret source of joy, that she was now an aggressive, positive force, sure of herself, and apparently afraid of nothing in heaven or hell. She radiated something very like hope and courage about her, and talked as though the world were a glorious place and everybody in it kind and beautiful. Her optimism was certainly infectious.

The Towers were mentioned only in passing. The name of Marsh came up—not *the* Marsh, it so happened, but a name in some book that was being discussed—and I was unable to restrain myself. Curiosity was too strong. I threw out a casual enquiry Mabel could leave unanswered if she wished. But there was no desire to avoid it. Her reply was frank and smiling.

'Would you believe it? She married,' Mabel told me, though obviously surprised that I remembered the housekeeper at all; 'and is happy as the day is long. She's found her right niche in life. A sergeant——'

'The army!' I ejaculated.

'Salvation Army,' she explained merrily.

Frances exchanged a glance with me. I laughed too, for the information took me by surprise. I cannot say why exactly, but I expected at least to hear that the woman had met some dreadful end, not impossibly by burning.

'And The Towers, now called the Rest House,' Mabel chattered on, 'seems to me the most peaceful and delightful spot in England——'

'Really,' I said politely.

'When I lived there in the old days—while you were there, perhaps, though I won't be sure,' Mabel went on, 'the story got abroad that it was haunted. Wasn't it odd? A less likely place for a ghost I've never seen. Why, it had no atmosphere at all.' She said this to Frances, glancing up at me with a smile that apparently had no hidden meaning. 'Did *you* notice anything queer about it when you were there?'

This was plainly addressed to me.

'I found it—er—difficult to settle down to anything,' I said, after an instant's hesitation. 'I couldn't work there——'

'But I thought you wrote that wonderful book on the Deaf and Blind while you stayed with me,' she asked innocently.

I stammered a little. 'Oh no, not then. I only made a few notes—er—at The Towers. My mind, oddly enough, refused to produce at all down there. But—why do you ask? Did anything—was anything *supposed* to happen there?'

She looked searchingly into my eyes a moment before she answered:

'Not that I know of,' she said simply.

WAYFARERS

I missed the train at Evian, and, after infinite trouble, discovered a motor that would take me, ice-axe and all, to Geneva. By hurrying, the connection might be just possible. I telegraphed to Haddon to meet me at the station, and lay back comfortably, dreaming of the precipices of Haute Savoie. We made good time; the roads were excellent, traffic of the slightest, when—crash! There was an instant's excruciating pain, the sun went out like a snuffed candle, and I fell into something as soft as a bed of flowers and as yielding to my weight as warm water....

It was *very* warm. There was a perfume of flowers. My eyes opened, focused vividly upon a detailed picture for a moment, then closed again. There was no context—at least, none that I could recall—for the scene, though familiar as home, brought nothing that I definitely remembered. Broken away from any sequence, unattached to any past, unaware even of my own identity, I simply saw this picture as a camera snaps it off from the world, a scene apart, with meaning only for those who knew the context:

The warm, soft thing I lay in was a bed—big, deep, comfortable; and the perfume came from flowers that stood beside it on a little table. It was in a stately, ancient chamber, with lofty ceiling and immense open fireplace of stone; old-fashioned pictures—familiar portraits and engravings I knew intimately—hung upon the walls; the floor was bare, with dignified, carved furniture of oak and mahogany, huge chairs and massive cupboards. And there were latticed windows set within deep embrasures of grey stone, where clambering roses patterned the sunshine that cast their moving shadows on the polished boards. With the perfume of the flowers there mingled, too, that delicate, elusive odour of age—of wood, of musty tapestries on spacious halls and corridors, and of chambers long unopened to the sun and air.

By the door that stood ajar far away at the end of the room—
very far away it seemed—an old lady, wearing a little cap of
silk embroidery, was whispering to a man of stern, uncompro-
mising figure, who, as he listened, bent down to her with
a grave and even solemn face. A wide stone corridor was
just visible through the crack of the open door behind her.

The picture flashed, and vanished. The numerous details
I took in because they were well known to me already. That
I could not supply the context was merely a trick of the mind,
the kind of trick that dreams play. Darkness swamped vision
again. I sank back into the warm, soft, comfortable bed of
delicious oblivion. There was not the slightest desire to know;
sleep and soft forgetfulness were all I craved.

But a little later—or was it a very great deal later?—when
I opened my eyes again, there was a thin trail of memory.
I remembered my name and age. I remembered vaguely, as
though from some unpleasant dream, that I was on the way to
meet a climbing friend in the Alps of Haute Savoie, and that
there was need to hurry and be very active. Something had
gone wrong, it seemed. There had been a stupid, violent
disaster, pain in it somewhere, an accident. Where were my
belongings? Where, for instance, was my precious ice-axe—tried
old instrument on which my life and safety depended? A rush
of jumbled questions poured across my mind. The effort to
sort them hurt atrociously....

A figure stood beside my bed. It was the same old lady I had
seen a moment ago—or was it a month ago, even last year
perhaps? And this time she was alone. Yet, though familiar
to me as my own right hand, I could not for the life of me
attract her name. Searching for it brought the pain again.
Instead, I asked an easier question; it seemed the most important
somehow, though a feeling of shame came with it, as though
I knew I was talking nonsense:

'My ice-axe—is it safe? It should have stood any ordinary
strain. It's ash....' My voice failed absurdly, caught away
by a whisper half-way down my throat. What *was* I talking
about? There was vile confusion somewhere.

166

She smiled tenderly, sweetly, as she placed her small, cool hand upon my forehead. Her touch calmed me as it always did, and the pain retreated a little.

'All your things are safe,' she answered, in a voice so soft beneath the distant ceiling it was like a bird's note singing in the sky. 'And *you* are also safe. There is no danger now. The bullet has been taken out and all is going well. Only you must be patient, and lie very still, and rest.' And then she added the morsel of delicious comfort she knew quite well I waited for: 'Marion is near you all day long, and most of the night besides. She rarely leaves you. She is in and out all day.'

I stared, thirsting for more. Memory put certain pieces in their place again. I heard them click together as they joined. But they only tried to join. There were several pieces missing They must have been lost in the disaster. The pattern was too ridiculous.

'I ought to tel—telegraph——' I began, seizing at a fragment that poked its end up, then plunged out of sight again before I could read more of it. The pieces fell apart; they would not hold together without these missing fragments. Anger flamed up in me.

'They're badly made,' I said, with a petulance I was secretly ashamed of; 'you have chosen the wrong pieces! I'm not a child—to be treated——' A shock of heat tore through me, led by a point of iron, with blasting pain.

'Sleep, my poor dear Félix, sleep,' she murmured soothingly, while her tiny hand stroked my forehead, just in time to prevent that pointed, hot thing entering my heart. 'Sleep again now, and a little later you shall tell me their names, and I will send on horseback quickly——'

'Telegraph——' I tried to say, but the word went lost before I could pronounce it. It was a nonsense word, caught up from dreams. Thought fluttered and went out.

'I will send,' she whispered, 'in the quickest possible way. You shall explain to Marion. Sleep first a little longer; promise me to lie quite still and sleep. When you wake again, she will come to you at once.'

She sat down gently on the edge of the enormous bed, so that I saw her outline against the window where the roses clambered to come in. She bent me—or was it a rose that bent in the wind across the stone embrasure? I saw her clear blue eyes—or was it two raindrops upon a withered rose-leaf that mirrored the summer sky?

'Thank you,' my voice murmured with intense relief, as everything sank away and the old-world garden seemed to enter by the latticed windows. For there was a power in her way that made obedience sweet, and her little hand, besides, cushioned the attack of that cruel iron so that I hardly felt its entrance. Before the fierce heat could reach me, darkness again put out the world....

Then, after a prodigious interval, my eyes once more opened to the stately, old-world chamber that I knew so well; and this time I found myself alone. In my brain was a stinging, splitting sensation, as though Memory shook her pieces together with angry violence, pieces, moreover, made of clashing metal. A degrading nausea almost vanquished me. Against my feet was a heated metal body, too heavy for me to move, and bandages were tight round my neck and the back of my head. Dimly, it came back to me that hands had been about me hours ago, soft, ministering hands that I loved. Their perfume lingered still. Faces and names fled in swift procession past me, yet without my making any attempt to bid them stay. I asked myself no questions. Effort of any sort was utterly beyond me. I lay and watched and waited, helpless and strangely weak.

One or two things alone were clear. They came, too, without the effort to think them:

There had been a disaster; they had carried me into the nearest house; and—the mountain heights, so keenly longed for, were suddenly denied me. I was being cared for by kind people somewhere far from the world's high routes. They were familiar people, yet for the moment I had lost the name. But it was the bitterness of losing my holiday climbing that chiefly savaged me, so that strong desire returned upon itself unfulfilled. And, knowing the danger of frustrated yearnings, and the curious states of mind they may engender, my tumbling brain registered a decision automatically:

'Keep careful watch upon yourself,' it whispered.

For I saw the peaks that towered above the world, and felt the wind rise from the hidden valleys. The perfume of lonely ridges came to me, and I saw the snow against the blue-black sky. Yet I could not reach them. I lay, instead, broken and useless upon my back, in a soft, deep, comfortable bed. And I loathed the thought. A dull and evil fury rose within me. Where was Haddon? He would get me out of it if any one could. And where was my dear, old trusted ice-axe? Above all, who were these gentle, old-world people who cared for me?... And, with this last thought, came some fairy touch of sweetness so delicious that I was conscious of sudden resignation—more, even of delight and joy.

This joy and anger ran races for possession of my mind, and I knew not which to follow: both seemed real, and both seemed true. The cruel confusion was an added torture. Two sets of places and people seemed to mingle.

'Keep a careful watch upon yourself,' repeated the automatic caution.

Then, with returning, blissful darkness, came another thing —a tiny point of wonder, where light entered in. I thought of a woman.... It was a vehement, commanding thought; and though at first it was very close and real—as much of To-day as Haddon and my precious ice-axe—the next second it was leagues away in another world somewhere. Yet, before the confusion twisted it all askew, I knew her; I remembered clearly even where she lived; that I knew her husband, too—had stayed with them in—in Scotland—yes, in Scotland. Yet no word in this life had ever crossed my lips, for she was not free to come. Neither of us, with eyes or lips or gesture, had ever betrayed a hint to the other of our deeply hidden secret. And although for me she was *the* woman, my great yearning—long, long ago it was, in early youth—had been sternly put aside and buried with all the vigour nature gave me. Her husband was my friend as well.

Only, now, the shock had somehow strained the prison bars, and the yearning escaped for a moment full-fledged, and vehement with passion long denied. The inhibition was destroyed. The knowledge swept deliciously upon me that we had the right to be together, because we always *were* together. I had the right to ask for her.

My mind was certainly a mere field of confused, ungoverned images. No thinking was possible, for it hurt too vilely. But this one memory stood out with violence. I distinctly remember that I called to her to come, and that she had the right to come because my need was so peremptory. To the one most loved of all this life had brought me, yet to whom I had never spoken because she was in another's keeping, I called for help, and called, I verily believe, aloud:

'Please come!' Then, close upon its heels, the automatic warning again: 'Keep close watch upon yourself....!'

It was as though one great yearning had loosed the other that was even greater, and had set it free.

Disappearing consciousness then followed the cry for an incalculable distance. Down into subterraneans within myself that were positively frightening it plunged away. But the cry was real; the yearning appeal held authority in it as of command. Love gave the right, supplied the power as well. For it seemed to me a tiny answer came, but from so far away that it was scarcely audible. And names were nowhere in it, either in answer or appeal.

'I am always here. I have never, never left you!'

The unconsciousness that followed was not complete, apparently. There was a memory of effort in it, of struggle, and, as it were, of searching. Some one was trying to get at me. I tossed in a troubled sea upon a piece of wreckage that another swimmer also fought to reach. Huge waves of transparent green now brought this figure nearer, now concealed it, but it came steadily on, holding out a rope. My exhaustion was too great for me to respond, yet this swimmer swept up nearer, brought by enormous rollers that threatened to engulf us both. The rope was for my safety, too. I saw hands outstretched. In the deep water I saw the outline of the body, and once I even saw the face. But for a second, merely. The wave that bore it crashed with a horrible roar that smothered us both and swept me from my piece of wreckage. In the violent flood of water the rope whipped against my feeble hands. I grasped it. A sense of divine security at once came over me —an intolerable sweetness of utter bliss and comfort, then blackness and suffocation as of the grave. The white-hot point of iron struck me. It beat audibly against my heart. I heard the knocking. The pain brought me up to the surface, and the knocking of my dreams was in reality a knocking on the door. Some one was gently tapping.

Such was the confusion of images in my painracked mind, that I expected to see the old lady enter, bringing ropes and ice-axes, and followed by Haddon, my mountaineering friend; for I thought that I had fallen down a deep crevasse and had waited hours for help in the cold, blue darkness of the ice. I was too weak to answer, and the knocking for that matter was not repeated. I did not even hear the opening of the door, so softly did she move into the room. I only knew that before I actually saw her, this wave of intolerable sweetness drenched me once again with bliss and peace and comfort, my pain retreated, and I closed my eyes, knowing I should feel that cool and soothing hand upon my forehead.

The same minute I did feel it. There was a perfume of old gardens in the air. I opened my eyes to look the gratitude I could not utter, and saw, close against me—not the old lady, but the young and lovely face my worship had long made familiar. With lips that smiled their yearning and eyes of brown that held tears of sympathy, she sat down beside me on the bed. The warmth and fragrance of her atmosphere enveloped me. I sank away into a garden where spring melts magically into summer. Her arms were round my neck. Her face dropped down, so that I felt her hair upon my cheek and eyes. And then, whispering my name twice over, she kissed me on the lips.

'Marion,' I murmured.

'Hush! Mother sends you this,' she answered softly. 'You are to take it all; she made it with her own hands. But *I* bring it to you. You must be quite obedient, please.'

She tried to rise, but I held her against my breast.

'Kiss me again and I'll promise obedience always,' I strove to say. But my voice refused so long a sentence, and anyhow her lips were on my own before I could have finished it. Slowly, very carefully, she disentangled herself, and my arms sank back upon the coverlet. I sighed in happiness. A moment longer she stood beside my bed, gazing down with love and deep anxiety into my face.

'And when all is eaten, all, mind, *all*,' she smiled, 'you are to sleep until the doctor comes this afternoon. You are much better. Soon you shall get up. Only, remember,' shaking her finger with a sweet pretence of looking stern, 'I shall exact complete obedience. You must yield your will utterly to mine. You are in my heart, and my heart must be kept very warm and happy.'

Her eyes were tender as her mother's and I loved the authority and strength that were so real in her. I remembered how it was this strength that had sealed the contract her beauty first drew up for me to sign. She bent down once more to arrange my pillows.

'What happened to—to the motor?' I asked hesitatingly, for my thoughts *would* not regulate themselves. The mind presented such incongruous fragments.

'The—what?' she asked, evidently puzzled. The word seemed strange to her. 'What is that?' she repeated, anxiety in her eyes.

I made an effort to tell her, but I could not. Explanation was suddenly impossible. The whole idea dived away out of sight. It utterly evaded me. I had again invented a word that was without meaning. I was talking nonsense. In its place my dream came up. I tried to tell her how I had dreamed of climbing dangerous heights with a stranger, and had spoken another

172

language with him than my own—English, was it?—at any
rate, not my native French.

'Darling,' she whispered close into my ear, 'the bad dreams
will not come back. You are safe here, quite safe.' She put
her little hand like a flower on my forehead and drew it softly
down the cheek. 'Your wound is already healing. They took
the bullet out four days ago. I have got it,' she added with
a touch of shy embarrassment, and kissed me tenderly upon
my eyes.

'How long have you been away from me?' I asked, feeling
exhaustion coming back.

'Never once for more than ten minutes,' was the reply.
'I watched with you all night. Only this morning, while mother
took my place, I slept a little. But, hush!' she said, with dear
authority again; 'you are not to talk so much. You must eat
what I have brought, then sleep again. You must rest and
sleep. Good-bye, good-bye, my love. I shall come back in
an hour, and I shall always be within reach of your dear voice.'

Her tall, slim figure, dressed in the grey I loved, crossed
silently to the door. She gave me one more look—there was
all the tenderness of passionate love in it—and then was gone.

I followed instructions meekly, and when a delicious sleep
stole over me soon afterwards, I had forgotten utterly the ugly
dream that I was climbing dangerous heights with another man,
forgotten as well everything else, except that it seemed so many
days since my love had come to me, and that my bullet wound
would after all be healed in time for our wedding on the day
so long, so eagerly waited for.

And when, several hours later, her mother came in with
the doctor—his face less grave and solemn this time—the
news that I might get up next day and lie a little in the garden,
did more to heal me than a thousand bandages or twice that
quantity of medical instructions.

I watched them as they stood a moment by the open door.
They went out very slowly together, speaking in whispers.
But the only thing I caught was the mother's voice, talking
brokenly of the great wars. Napoleon, the doctor was saying

173

in a low, hushed tone, was in full retreat from Moscow, though the news had only just come through. They passed into the corridor then, and there was a sound of weeping as the old lady murmured something about her son and the cruelty of Heaven. 'Both will be taken from me,' she was sobbing softly, while he stooped to comfort her; 'one in marriage, and the other in death.' They closed the door then, and I heard no more.

I

Convalescence seemed to follow very quickly then, for I was utterly obedient as I had promised, and never spoke of what could excite me to my own detriment—the wars and my own unfortunate part in them. We talked instead of our love, our already too-long engagement, and of the sweet dream of happines that life held waiting for us in the future. And, indeed, I was sufficiently weary of the world to prefer repose to much activity, for my body was almost incessantly in pain, and this old garden where we lay between high walls of stone, aloof from the busy world and very peaceful, was far more to my taste just then than wars and fighting.

The orchards were in blossom, and the winds of spring showered their rain of petals upon the long, new grass. We lay, half in sunshine, half in shade, beneath the poplars that lined the avenue towards the lake, and behind us rose the ancient grey stone towers where the jackdaws nested in the ivy and the pigeons cooed and fluttered from the woods beyond.

There was loveliness everywhere, but there was sadness too, for though we both knew that the wars had taken her brother whence there is no return, and that only her aged, failing mother's life stood between ourselves and the stately property, there hid a sadness yet deeper than either of these thoughts in both our hearts. And it was, I think, the sadness that comes with spring. For spring, with her lavish, short-lived promises of eternal beauty, is ever a symbol of passing human happiness, incomplete and always unfulfilled. Promises made on earth are playthings, after all, for children. Even while we make them so solemnly, we seem to know they are not meant to hold. They are made, as spring is made, with a glory of soft, radiant blossoms that pass away before there is time to realise them. And yet they come again with the return of spring, as unashamed and glorious as if Time had utterly forgotten.

And this sadness was in her too. I mean it was part of her and she was part of it. Not that our love could change to pass or die, but that its sweet, so-long-desired accomplishment must hold away, and, like the spring, must melt and vanish before it had been fully known. I did not speak of it. I well understood that the depression of a broken body can influence the spirit with its poisonous melancholy, but it must have betrayed itself in my words and gestures, even in my manner too. At any rate, she was aware of it. I think, if truth be told, she felt it too. It seemed so painfully inevitable.

My recovery, meanwhile, was rapid, and from spending an hour or two in the garden, I soon came to spend the entire day. For the spring came on with a rush, and the warmth increased deliciously. While the cuckoos called to one another in the great beech-woods behind the chateau, we sat and talked and sometimes had our simple meals or coffee there together, and I particularly recall the occasion when solid food was first permitted me and she gave me a delicate young *bondelle,* fresh caught that very morning in the lake. There were leaves of sweet, crisp lettuce with it, and she picked the bones out for me with her own white hands.

The day was radiant, with a sky of cloudless blue, soft airs stirred the poplar crests; the little waves fell on the pebbly beach not fifty metres away, and the orchard floor was carpeted with flowers that seemed to have caught from heaven's stars the patterns of their yellow blossoms. The bees droned peacefully among the fruit trees; the air was full of musical deep hummings. My former vigour stirred delightfully in blood, and I knew no pain, beyond occasional dull twinges in the head that came with a rush of temporary darkness over my mind. The scar was healed, however, and the hair had grown

175

over it again. This temporary darkness alarmed her more than it alarmed me. There were grave complications, apparently, that I did not know of.

But the deep-lying sadness in me seemed independent of the glorious weather, due to causes so intangible, so far off that I never could dispel them by arguing them away. For I could not discover what they actually were. There was a vague, distressing sense of restlessness that I ought to have been elsewhere and otherwise, that we were together for a few days only, and that these few days I had snatched unlawfully from stern, imperative duties. These duties were immediate, but neglected. In a sense I had no right to this springtide of bliss her presence brought me. I was playing truant somehow, somewhere. It was *not* my absence from the regiment; that I know. It was infinitely deeper, set to some enormous scale that vaguely frightened me, while it deepened the sweetness of the stolen joy.

Like a child, I sought to pin the sunny hours against the sky and make them stay. They passed with such a mocking swiftness, snatched momentarily from some big oblivion. The twilights swallowed our days together before they had been properly tasted, and on looking back, each afternoon of happiness seemed to have been a mere moment in a flying dream. And I must have somehow betrayed the aching mood, for Marion turned of a sudden and gazed into my face with yearning and anxiety in the sweet brown eyes.

'What is it, dearest?' I asked, 'and why do your eyes bring questions?'

'You sighed,' she answered, smiling a little sadly; 'and sighed so deeply. You are in pain again. The darkness, perhaps, is over you?' And her hand stole out to meet my own. 'You are in pain?'

'Not physical pain,' I said, 'and not *the* darkness either. I see *you* clearly,' and would have told her more, as I carried her soft fingers to my lips, had I not divined from the expression in her eyes that she read my heart and knew all my strange, mysterious forebodings in herself.

'I know,' she whispered before I could find speech, 'for I feel it too. It is the shadow of separation that oppresses you— yet of no common, measurable separation you can understand. Is it not that?'

Leaning over then, I took her close into my arms, since words in that moment were mere foolishness. I held her so that she could not get away; but even while I did so it was like trying to hold the spring, or fasten the flying hour with a fierce desire. All slipped from me, and my arms caught at the sunshine and the wind.

'We have both felt it all these weeks,' she said bravely, as soon as I had released her, 'and we both have struggled to conceal it. But now——' she hesitated for a second, and with so exquisite a tenderness that I would have caught her to me again but for my anxiety to hear her further words—'now that you are well, we may speak plainly to each other, and so lessen our pain by sharing it.' And then she added, still more softly: 'You feel there is "something" that shall take you from me—yet what it is you cannot discover nor divine. Tell me, Félix—all your thought, that I in turn may tell you mine.'

Her voice floated about me in the sunny air. I stared at her, striving to focus the dear face more clearly for my sight. A shower of apple blossoms fell about us, and her words seemed floating past me like those passing petals of white. They drifted away. I followed them with difficulty and confusion. With the wind, I fancied, a veil of indefinable change slipped across her face and eyes.

'Yet nothing that could alter feeling,' I answered; for she had expressed my own thought completely. 'Nor anything that either of us can control. Only—perhaps, that everything must fade and pass away, just as this glory of the spring must fade and pass away——'

'Yet leaving its sweetness in us,' she caught me up passionately, 'and to come again, my beloved, to come again in every subsequent life, each time with an added sweetness in it too!' Her little face showed suddenly the courage of a lion in its eyes. Her heart was ever braver than my own, a vigorous, fighting soul. She spoke of lives, I prattled of days and hours merely.

A touch of shame stole over me. But that delicate, swift change in her spread too. With a thrill of ominous warning I noticed how it rose and grew about her. From within, outwards, it seemed to pass—like a shadow of great blue distance. Shadow was somewhere in it, so that she dimmed a little before my very eyes. The dreadful yearning searched and shook me, for I could not understand it, try as I would. She seemed going from me—drifting like her words and like the apple blossoms.

'But when we shall no longer be here to know it,' I made answer quickly, yet as calmly as I could, 'and when we shall have passed to some other place—to other conditions—where we shall not recognise the joy and wonder. When barriers of mist shall have rolled between us—our love and passion so made-over that we shall not know each other'—the words rushed out feverishly, half beyond control— 'and perhaps shall not even dare to speak to each other of our deep desire——'

I broke off abruptly, conscious that I was speaking out of some unfamiliar place where I floundered, helpless among strange conditions. I was saying things I hardly understood myself. Her bigger, deeper mood spoke through me, perhaps.

Her darling face came back again; she moved close within reach once more.

'Hush, hush!' she whispered, terror and love both battling in her eyes. 'It is the truth, perhaps, but you must not say such things. To speak them brings them closer. A chain is about our hearts, a chain of fashioning lives without number, but do not seek to draw upon it with anxiety or fear. To do so can only cause the pain of wrong entanglement, and interrupt the natural running of the iron links.' And she placed her hand swiftly upon my mouth, as though divining that the bleak attack of anguish was again upon me with its throbbing rush of darkness.

But for once I was disobedient and resisted. The physical pain, I realised vividly, was linked closely with this spiritual torture. One caused the other somehow. The disordered brain

178

received, though brokenly, some hints of darker and unusual knowledge. It had stammered forth in me, but through her it flowed easily and clear. I saw the change move more swiftly then across her face. Some ancient look passed into both her eyes.

And it was inevitable; I must speak out, regardless of mere bodily well-being.

'We shall have to face them some day,' I cried, although the effort hurt abominably, 'then why not now?' And I drew her hand down and kissed it passionately over and over again. 'We are not children, to hide our faces among shadows and pretend we are invisible. At least we have the Present—the Moment that is here and now. We stand side by side in the heart of this deep spring day. This sunshine and these flowers, this wind across the lake, this sky of blue and this singing of the birds—all, all are ours *now*. Let us use the moment that Time gives, and so strengthen the chain you speak of that shall bring us again together times without number. We shall then, perhaps, remember. Oh, my heart, think what that would mean—to remember!'

Exhaustion caught me, and I sank back among my cushions. But Marion rose up suddenly and stood beside me. And as she did so, another Sky dropped softly down upon us both, and I smelt again the incense of old, old gardens that brought long-forgotten perfumes, incredibly sweet, but with it an ache of far-off, passionate remembrance that was pain. This great ache of distance swept over me like a wave.

I know not what grand change then was wrought upon her beauty, so that I saw her defiant and erect, commanding Fate because she understood it. She towered over me, but it was her soul that towered. The rush of internal darkness in me blotted out all else. The familiar, present sky grew dim, the sunshine faded, the lake and flowers and poplars dipped away. Conditions a thousand times more vivid took their place. She stood out, clear and shining in the glory of an undressed soul, brave and confident with an eternal love that separation strengthened but could never, never change. The deep sadness

179

I abruptly realised, was very little removed from joy—because, somehow, it was the condition of joy. I could not explain it more than that.

And her voice, when she spoke, was firm with a note of steel in it; intense, yet devoid of the wasting anger that passion brings. She was determined beyond Death itself, upon a foundation sure and lasting as the stars. The heart in her was calm, because she *knew*. She was magnificent.

'We are together—always,' she said, her voice rich with the knowledge of some unfathomable experience, 'for separation is temporary merely, forging new links in the ancient chain of lives that binds our hearts eternally together.' She looked like one who has conquered the adversity Time brings, by accepting it. 'You speak of the Present as though our souls were already fitted now to bid it stay, needing no further fashioning. Looking only to the Future, you forget our ample Past that has made us what we are. Yet our Past is here and now, beside us at this very moment. Into the hollow cups of weeks and months, of years and centuries, Time pours its flood beneath our eyes. Time is our schoolroom.... Are you so soon afraid? Does not separation achieve that which companionship never could accomplish? And how shall we dare eternity together of we cannot be strong in separation first?'

I listened while a flood of memories broke up through film upon film and layer upon layer that had long covered them.

'This Present that we seem to hold between our hands,' she went on in that earnest, distant voice, '*is* our moment of sweet remembrance that you speak of, of renewal, perhaps, too, of reconciliation—a fleeting instant when we may kiss again and say good-bye, but with strengthened hope and courage revived. But we may not stay together finally—we *cannot*—until long discipline and pain shall have perfected sympathy and schooled our love by searching, difficult tests, that it may last for ever.'

I stretched my arms out dumbly to take her in. Her face shone down upon me, bathed in an older, fiercer sunlight. The change in her seemed in an instant then complete. Some

180

big, soft wind blew both of us ten thousand miles away. The centuries gathered us back together.

'Look, rather, to the Past,' she whispered grandly, 'where first we knew the sweet opening of our love. Remember, if you can, how the pain and separation have made it so worth while to continue. And be braver thence.'

She turned her eyes more fully upon my own, so that their light persuaded me utterly away with her. An immense new happiness broke over me. I listened, and with the stirrings of an ampler courage. It seemed I followed her down an interminable vista of remembrance till I was happy with her among the flowers and fields of our earliest pre-existence.

Her voice came to me with the singing of birds and the hum of summer insects.

'Have you so soon forgotten,' she sighed, 'when we knew together the perfume of the hanging Babylonian Gardens, or when the Hesperides were so soft, to us in the dawn of the world? And do you not remember,' with a little rise of passion in her voice, 'the sweet plantations of Chaldea, and how we tasted the odour of many a drooping flower in the gardens of Alcinous and Adonis, when the bees of olden time picked out the honey for our eating? It is the fragrance of those first hours we knew together that still lies in our hearts to-day, sweetening our love to this apparent suddenness. Hence comes the full, deep happiness we gather so easily To-day.... The breast of every ancient forest is torn with storms and lightning... that's why it is so soft and full of little gardens. You have forgotten too easily the glades of Lebanon, where we whispered our earliest secrets while the big winds drove their chariots down those earlier skies...'

There rose an indescribable tempest of remembrance in my heart as I strove to bring the pictures into focus; but words failed me, and the hand I eagerly stretched out to touch her own, met only sunshine and the rain of apple blossoms.

'The myrrh and frankincense,' she continued in a sighing voice that seemed to come with the wind from invisible caverns in the sky, 'the grapes and pomegranates—have they all passed from you, with the train of apes and peacocks, the tigers and the ibis, and the hordes of dark-faced slaves? And this little sun that plays so lightly here upon our woods of beech and pine—does it bring back nothing of the old-time scorching when the olive slopes, the figs and ripening cornfields heard our vows and watched our love mature?... Our spread encampment in the Desert—do not these sands upon our little beach revive its lonely majesty for you, and have you forgotten the gleaming towers of Semiramis ... or, in Sardis, those strange lilies that first tempted our souls to their divine disclosure...?'

Conscious of a violent struggle between pain and joy, both too deep for me to understand, I rose to seize her in my arms. But the effort dimmed the flying pictures. The wind that bore her voice down the stupendous vista fled back into the caverns whence it came. And the pain caught me in a vice of agony so searching that I could not move a muscle. My tongue lay dry against my lips. I could not frame a word of any sentence....

Her voice presently came back to me, but fainter, like a whisper from the stars. The light dimmed everywhere; I saw no more the vivid, shining scenery she had summoned. A mournful dusk instead crept down upon the world she had momentarily revived.

'... we may not stay together,' I heard her little whisper, 'until long discipline shall have perfected sympathy, and schooled our love to last. For this love of ours *is* for ever, and the pain that tries it is the furnace that fashions precious stones....'

Again I stretched my arms out. Her face shone a moment longer in that forgotten fiercer sunlight, then faded very swiftly. The change, like a veil, passed over it. From the place of prodigious distance where she had been, she swept down towards me with such dizzy speed. As she was To-day I saw her again, more and more.

'Pain and separation, then, are welcome,' I tried to stammer, 'and we will desire them'—but my thought got no further into expression than the first two words. Aching blotted out coherent utterance.

She bent down very close against my face. Her fragrance was about my lips. But her voice ran off like a faint thrill of music, far, far away. I caught the final words, dying away as wind dies in high branches of a wood. And they reached me this time through the droning of bees and of waves that murmured close at hand upon the shore.

'... for our love is of the soul and our souls are moulded in Eternity. It is not yet, it is not now, our perfect consummation. Nor shall our next time of meeting know it. We shall not even speak.... For I shall not be free....' was what I heard. She paused.

'You mean we shall not know each other?' I cried, in an anguish of spirit that mastered the lesser physical pain.

I barely caught her answer:

'My discipline then will be in another's keeping—yet only that I may come back to you ... more perfect ... in the end....'

The bees and waves then cushioned her whisper with their humming. The trail of a deeper silence led them far away. The rush of temporary darkness passed and lifted. I opened my eyes. My love sat close beside me in the shadow of the poplars. One hand held both my own, while with the other she arranged my pillows and stroked my aching head. The world dropped back into a tiny scale once more.

'You have had the pain again,' Marion murmured anxiously, 'but it is better now. It is passing.' She kissed my cheek. 'You must come in....'

But I would not let her go. I held her to me with all the strength that was in me. 'I had it, but it's gone again. An awful darkness came with it,' I whispered in the little ear that was so close against my mouth. 'I've been dreaming,' I told her, as memory dipped away, 'dreaming of you and me— together somewhere—in old gardens, or forests—where the sun was——'

But she would not let me finish. I think, in any case, I could not have said more, for thought evaded me, and any language of coherent description was in the same instant beyond my power. Exhaustion came upon me, that vile, compelling nausea with it.

'The sun here is too strong for you, dear love,' I heard her saying, 'and you must rest more. We have been doing too much these last few days. You must have more repose.' She rose to help me move indoors.

'I have been unconscious then?' I asked, in the feeble whisper that was all I could manage.

'For a little while. You slept, while I watched over you.'

'But I was away from you! Oh, how could you let me sleep, when our time together is so short?'

She soothed me instantly in the way she knew we both loved so. I clung to her until she released herself again.

'Not away from me,' she smiled, 'for I was with you in your dreaming.'

'Of course, of course you were'; but already I knew not exactly why I said it, nor caught the deep meaning that struggled up into my words from such unfathomable distance.

'Come,' she added, with her sweet authority again, 'we must go in now. Give me your arm, and I will send out for the cushions. Lean on me. I am going to put you back to bed.'

'But I shall sleep again,' I said petulantly, 'and we shall be separated.'

'We shall dream together,' she replied, as she helped me slowly and painfully towards the old grey walls of the château.

II

Half an hour later I slept deeply, peacefully, upon my bed in the big stately chamber where the roses watched beside the latticed windows.

And to say I dreamed again is not correct, for it can only be expressed by saying that I saw and knew. The figures round the bed were actual, and in life. Nothing could be more real than the whisper of the doctor's voice—that solemn, grave-faced man who was so tall—as he said, sternly yet brokenly, to some one: 'You must say good-bye; and you had better say it *now*.' Nor could anything be more definite and sure, more charged with the actuality of living, than the figure of Marion, as she stooped over me to obey the terrible command. For I saw her face float down towards me like a star, and a shower of pale spring blossoms rained upon me with her hair. The perfume of old, old gardens rose about me as she slipped to her knees beside the bed and kissed my lips—so softly it was like the breath of wind from lake and orchard, and so lingeringly it was as though the blossoms lay upon my mouth and grew into flowers that she planted there.

'Good-bye, my love; be brave. It is only separation.'

'It is death,' I tried to say, but could only feebly stir my lips against her own.

I drew her breath of flowers into my mouth ... and there came then the darkness which is final.

The voices grew louder. I heard a man stuggling with an unfamiliar language. Turning restlessly, I opened my eyes— upon a little, stuffy room, with white walls whereon no pictures hung. It was very hot. A woman was standing beside the bed, and the bed was very short. I stretched, and my feet kicked against the boarding at the end.

'Yes, he *is* awake,' the woman said in French. 'Will you come in? The doctor said you might see him when he woke. I think he'll know you.' She spoke in French. I just knew enough to understand.

And of course I knew him. It was Haddon. I heard him thanking her for all her kindness, as he blundered in. His French, if anything, was worse than my own. I felt inclined to laugh. I did laugh.

'By Jove! old man, this is bad luck, isn't it? You've had a narrow shave. This good lady telegraphed——'

'Have you got my ice-axe? Is it all right?' I asked. I re-membered clearly the motor accident—everything.

'The ice-axe is right enough,' he laughed, looking cheerfully at the woman, 'but what about yourself? Feel bad still? Any

185

pain, I mean?'

'Oh, I feel all right,' I answered, searching for the pain of broken bones, but finding none. 'What happened? I was stunned, I suppose?'

'Bit stunned, yes,' said Haddon. 'You got a nasty knock on the head, it seems. The point of the axe ran into you, or something.'

'Was that all?'

He nodded. 'But I'm afraid it's knocked our climbing on the head. Shocking bad luck, isn't it?'

'I telegraphed last night,' the kind woman was explaining.

'But I couldn't get there till this morning,' Haddon said. 'The telegram didn't find me till midnight, you see.' And he turned to thank the woman in his voluble, dreadful French. She kept a little pension on the shores of the lake. It was the nearest house, and they had carried me in there and got the doctor to me all within the hour. It proved slight enough, apart from the shock. It was not even concussion. I had merely been stunned. Sleep had cured me, as it seemed.

'Jolly little place,' said Haddon, as he moved me that afternoon to Geneva, whence, after a few days' rest, we went on into the Alps of Haute Savoie, 'and lucky the old body was so kind and quick. Odd, wasn't it?' He glanced at me.

Something in his voice betrayed he hid another thought. I saw nothing 'odd' in it at all, only very tiresome.

'What's its name?' I asked, taking a shot at a venture.

He hesitated a second. Haddon, the climber, was not skilled in the delicacies of tact.

'Don't know its present name,' he answered, looking away from me across the lake, 'but it stands on the site of an old château—destroyed a hundred years ago—the Château de Bellerive.'

And then I understood my old friend's absurd confusion. For Bellerive chanced also to be the name of a married woman I knew in Scotland—at least, it was her maiden name, and she was of French extraction.

THE SEA FIT

THE sea that night sang rather than chanted; all along the far-running shore a rising tide dropped thick foam, and the waves, white-crested, came steadily in with the swing of a deliberate purpose. Overhead, in a cloudless sky, that ancient Enchantress, the full moon, watched their dance across the sheeted sands, guiding them carefully while she drew them up. For through that moonlight, through that roar of surf, there penetrated a singular note of earnestness and meaning—almost as though these common processes of Nature were instinct with the flush of an unusual activity that sought audaciously to cross the borderland into some subtle degree of conscious life. A gauze of light vapour clung upon the surface of the sea, far out—a transparent carpet through which the rollers drove shorewards in a moving pattern.

In the low-roofed bungalow among the sand-dunes the three men sat. Foregathered for Easter, they spent the day fishing and sailing, and at night told yarns of the days when life was younger. It was fortunate that there were three—and later four—because in the mouths of several witnesses an extraordinary thing shall be established—when they agree. And although whisky stood upon the rough table made of planks nailed to barrels, it is childish to pretend that a few drinks invalidate evidence, for alcohol, up to a certain point, intensifies the consciousness, focuses the intellectual powers, sharpens observation; and two healthy men, certainly three, must have imbibed an absurd amount before they all see, or omit to see, the same things.

The other bungalows still awaited their summer occupants. Only the lonely tufted sand-dunes watched the sea, shaking their hair of coarse white grass to the winds. The men had the whole spit to themselves—with the wind, the spray, the flying gusts of sand, and that great Easter full moon. There was Major Reese of the Gunners and his half-brother, Dr. Malcolm

Reese, and Captain Erricson, their host, all men whom the
kaleidoscope of life had jostled together a decade ago in many
adventures, then flung for years apart about the globe. There
was also Erricson's body-servant, 'Sinbad,' sailor of big seas,
and a man who had shared on many a ship all the lust of strange
adventure that distinguished his great blonde-haired owner—an
ideal servant and dog-faithful, divining his master's moods
almost before they were born. On the present occasion, besides
crew of the fishing-smack, he was cook, valet, and steward
of the bungalow smoking-room as well.

'Big Erricson', Norwegian by extraction, student by adop-
tion, wanderer by blood, a Viking reincarnated if ever there
was one, belonged to that type of primitive man in whom burns
an inborn love and passion for the sea that amounts to positive
worship—devouring tide, a lust and fever in the soul. 'All
genuine votaries of the old sea-gods have it,' he used to say,
by way of explaining his carelessness of worldly ambitions.
'We're never at our best away from salt water—never quite
right. I've got it bang in the heart myself. I'd do a bit before
the mast sooner than make a million on shore. Simply can't
help it, you see, and never could! It's our gods calling us to
worship.' And he had never tried to 'help it', which explains
why he owned nothing in the world on land except this tumble-
down, one-storey bungalow—more like a ship's cabin than
anything else, to which he sometimes asked his bravest and
most faithful friends—and a store of curious reading gathered
in long, becalmed days at the ends of the world. Heart and
mind, that is, carried a queer cargo. 'I'm sorry if you poor
devils are uncomfortable in her. You must ask Sinbad for
anything you want and don't see, remember.' As though Sinbad
could have supplied comforts that were miles away, or converted
a draughty wreck into a snug, taut, brand-new vessel.

Neither of the Reeses had cause for grumbling on the score
of comfort, however, for they knew the keen joys of roughing
it, and both weather and sport besides had been glorious.
It was on another score this particular evening that they found
cause for uneasiness, if not for actual grumbling. Erricson had

one of his queer sea fits on—the Doctor was responsible for the term—and was in the thick of it, plunging like a straining boat at anchor, talking in a way that made them both feel vaguely uncomfortable and distressed. Neither of them knew exactly perhaps why he should have felt this growing *malaise*, and each was secretly vexed with the other for confirming his own unholy instinct that something uncommon was astir. The loneliness of the sandspit and that melancholy singing of the sea before their very door may have had something to do with it, seeing that both were landsmen; for Imagination is ever Lord of the Lonely Places, and adventurous men remain children to the last. But, whatever it was that affected both men in different fashion, Malcolm Reese, the doctor, had not thought it necessary to mention to his brother that Sinbad had tugged his sleeve on entering and whispered in his ear significantly: 'Full moon, sir, please, and he's better without too much! These high spring tides get him all caught off his feet sometimes—clean sea-crazy'; and the man had contrived to let the doctor see the hilt of a small pistol he carried in his hip-pocket.

For Erricson had got upon his old subject: that the gods were not dead, but merely withdrawn, and that even a single true worshipper was enough to draw them down again into touch with the world, into the sphere of humanity, even into active and visible manifestation. He spoke of queer things he had seen in queerer places. He was serious, vehement, voluble; and the others had let it pour out unchecked, hoping thereby for its speedier exhaustion. They puffed their pipes in comparative silence, nodding from time to time, shrugging their shoulders, the soldier mystified and bewildered, the doctor alert and keenly watchful.

'And I like the old idea,' he had been saying, speaking of these departed pagan deities, 'that sacrifice and ritual feed their great beings, and that death is only the final sacrifice by which the worshipper becomes absorbed into them. The devout worshipper'—and there was a singular drive and power behind the words—'should go to his death singing, as to a wedding—

189

the wedding of his soul with the particular deity he has loved
and served all his life.' He swept his tow-coloured beard with
one hand, turning his shaggy head towards the window, where
the moonlight lay upon the procession of shaking waves.
'It's playing the whole game, I always think, man-fashion....
I remember once, some years ago, down there off the coast
by Yucatan——'

And then, before they could interfere, he told an extraordinary
tale of something he had seen years ago, but told it with such
a horrid earnestness of conviction—for it was dreadful, though
fine, this adventure—that his listeners shifted in their wicker
chairs, struck matches, unnecessarily, pulled at their long
glasses, and exchanged glances that attempted a smile yet did
not quite achieve it. For the tale had to do with sacrifice of
human life and a rather haunting pagan ceremonial of the sea,
and at its close the room had changed in some indefinable
manner—was not exactly as it had been before perhaps—as
though the savage earnestness of the language had introduced
some new element that made it less cosy, less cheerful, even
less warm. A secret lust in the man's heart, born of the sea,
and of his intense admiration of the pagan gods called a light
into his eye not altogether pleasant.

'They were great Powers, at any rate, those ancient fellows,'
Erricson went on, refilling his huge pipe bowl; 'too great to
disappear altogether, though to-day they may walk the earth
in another manner. I swear they're still going it—especially
the——' (he hesitated for a mere second) 'the old water Powers—the Sea Gods. Terrific beggars, every one of 'em.'

'Still move the tides and raise the winds, eh?' from the
Doctor.

Erricson spoke again after a moment's silence, with impressive
dignity. 'And I like, too, the way they manage to keep their
names before us,' he went on, with a curious eagerness that
did not escape the Doctor's observation, while it clearly
puzzled the soldier. 'There's old Hu, the Druid god of justice,
still alive in "Hue and Cry"; there's Typhon hammering his
way against us in the typhoon; there's the mighty Hurakar,

serpent god of the winds, you know, shouting to us in hurricane and *ouragan*; and there's——'

'Venus still at it as hard as ever,' interrupted the Major, facetiously, though his brother did not laugh because of their host's almost sacred earnestness of manner and uncanny grimness of face. Exactly how he managed to introduce that element of gravity—of conviction—into such talk neither of his listeners quite understood, for in discussing the affair later they were unable to pitch upon any definite detail that betrayed it. Yet there it was, alive and haunting, even distressingly so. All day he had been silent and morose, but since dusk, with the turn of the tide, in fact, these queer sentences, half mystical, half unintelligible, had begun to pour from him, till now that cabin-like room among the sand-dunes fairly vibrated with the man's emotion. And at last Major Reese, with blundering good intention, tried to shift the key from this portentous subject of sacrifice to something that might eventually lead towards comedy and laughter, and so relieve this growing pressure of melancholy and incredible things. The Viking fellow had just spoken of the possibility of the old gods manifesting themselves visibly, audibly, physically, and so the Major caught him up and made light mention of spiritualism and the so-called 'materialisation séances,' where physical bodies were alleged to be built up out of the emanations of the medium and the sitters. This crude aspect of the Supernatural was the only possible link the soldier's mind could manage. He caught his brother's eye too late, it seems, for Malcolm Reese realised by this time that something untoward was afoot, and no longer needed the memory of Sinbad's warning to keep him sharply on the look-out. It was not the first time he had seen Erricson 'caught' by the sea; but he had never known him quite so bad, nor seen his face so flushed and white alternately, nor his eyes so oddly shining. So that Major Reese's well-intentioned allusion only brought wind to fire.

The man of the sea, once Viking, roared with a rush of boisterous laughter at the comic suggestion, then dropped his voice to a sudden hard whisper, awfully earnest, awfully intense. Any one must have started at the abrupt change and the life-and-death manner of the big man. His listeners undeniably both did.

'Bunkum!' he shouted, 'bunkum, and be damned to it all! There's only one real materialisation of these immense Outer Beings possible, and that's when the great embodied emotions, which are their sphere of action'—his words became wildly incoherent, painfully struggling to get out—'derived, you see, from their honest worshippers the world over—constituting their Bodies, in fact—come down into matter and get condensed, crystallised into form—to claim that final sacrifice I spoke about just now, and to which any man might feel himself proud and honoured to be summoned.... No dying in bed or fading out from old age, but to plunge full-blooded and alive into the great Body of the god who has deigned to descend and fetch you——'

The actual speech may have been even more rambling and incoherent than that. It came out in a torrent at white heat. Dr. Reese kicked his brother beneath the table, just in time. The soldier looked thoroughly uncomfortable and amazed, utterly at a loss to know how he had produced the storm. It rather frightened him.

'I know it because I've seen it,' went on the sea man, his mind and speech slightly more under control. 'Seen the ceremonies that brought these whopping old Nature gods down into form—seen 'em carry off a worshipper into themselves—seen that worshipper, too, go off singing and happy to his death, proud and honoured to be chosen.'

'Have you really—by George!' the Major exclaimed. 'You tell us a queer thing, Erricson'; and it was then for the fifth time that Sinbad cautiously opened the door, peeped in and silently withdrew after giving a swiftly comprehensive glance round the room.

The night outside was windless and serene, only the growing thunder of the tide near the full woke muffled echoes among the sand-dunes.

'Rites and ceremonies,' continued the other, his voice booming with a singular enthusiasm, but ignoring the interruption, 'are simply means of losing one's self by temporary ecstasy in the God of one's choice—the God one has worshipped all one's life—of being partially absorbed into his being. And sacrifice completes the process——'

'At death, you said?' asked Malcolm Reese, watching him keenly.

'Or voluntary,' was the reply that came flash-like. 'The devotee becomes wedded to his Deity—goes bang into him, you see, by fire or water or air—as by a drop from a height—according to the nature of the particular God; at-one-ment, of course. A man's death that! Fine, you know!'

The man's inner soul was on fire now. He was talking at a fearful pace, his eyes alight, his voice turned somehow into a kind of sing-song that chimed well, singularly well, with the booming of waves outside, and from time to time he turned to the window to stare at the sea and the moon-blanched sands. And then a look of triumph would come into his face—that giant face framed by slow-moving wreaths of pipe smoke.

Sinbad entered for the sixth time without any obvious purpose, busied himself unnecessarily with the glasses and went out again, lingeringly. In the room he kept his eye hard upon his master. This time he contrived to push a chair and a heap of netting between him and the window. No one but Dr. Reese observed the manoeuvre. And he took the hint.

'The port-holes fit badly, Erricson,' he laughed, but with a touch of authority. 'There's a five-knot breeze coming through the cracks worse than an old wreck!' And he moved up to secure the fastening better.

'The room *is* confoundedly cold,' Major Reese put in; 'has been for the last half-hour, too.' The soldier looked what he felt—cold—distressed—creepy. 'But there's no wind really, you know,' he added.

Captain Erricson turned his great bearded visage from one to the other before he answered; there was a gleam of sudden suspicion in his blue eyes. 'The beggar's got that back door open again. If he's sent for any one, as he did once before, I swear I'll drown him in fresh water for his impudence—or perhaps—can it be already that he expects——?' He left the sentence incomplete and rang the bell, laughing with a boisterousness that was clearly feigned. 'Sinbad, what's this cold in the place? You've got the back door open. Not expecting any one, are you——?'

'Everything's shut tight, Captain. There's a bit of a breeze coming up from the east. And the tide's drawing in at a raging pace——'

'We can all hear *that*. But are you expecting any one? I asked,' repeated his master, suspiciously, yet still laughing. One might have said he was trying to give the idea that the man had some land flirtation on hand. They looked one another square in the eye for a moment, these two. It was the straight stare of equals who understood each other well.

'Some one—might be—on the way, as it were, Captain. Couldn't say for certain.'

The voice almost trembled. By a sharp twist of the eye, Sinbad managed to shoot a lightning and significant look at the Doctor.

'But this cold—this freezing, damp cold in the place? Are you sure no one's come—by the back ways?'insisted the master. He whispered it. 'Across the dunes, for instance?' His voice conveyed awe and delight, both kept hard under.

'It's all over the house, Captain, already,' replied the man, and moved across to put more sea-logs on the blazing fire. Even the soldier noticed then that their language was tight with allusion of another kind. To relieve the growing tension and uneasiness in his own mind he took up the word 'house' and made fun of it.

'As though it were a mansion,' he observed, with a forced chuckle, 'instead of a mere sea-shell!' Then, looking about him, he added: 'But, all the same, you know, there *is* a kind of fog getting into the room—from the sea, I suppose; coming up with the tide, or something, eh?' The air had certainly in the last twenty minutes turned thickish; it was not all tobacco smoke, and there was a moisture that began to precipitate on the objects in tiny, fine globules. The cold, too, fairly bit.

'I'll take a look round,' said Sinbad, significantly, and went out. Only the Doctor perhaps noticed that the man shook, and was white down to the gills. He said nothing, but moved his chair nearer to the window and to his host. It was really a little bit beyond comprehension how the wild words of this old sea-dog in the full sway of his 'sea fit' had altered the very air of the room as well as the personal equations of its occupants, for an extraordinary atmosphere of enthusiasm that was almost splendour pulsed about him, yet vilely close to something that suggested terror! Through the armour of every-day common sense that normally clothed the minds of these other two, had crept the faint wedges of a mood that made them vaguely wonder whether the incredible could perhaps sometimes—by way of bewildering exceptions— actually come to pass. The moods of their deepest life, that is to say, were already affected. An inner, and thoroughly unwelcome, change was in progress. And such psychic disturbances once started are hard to arrest. In this case it was well on the way before either the Army or Medicine had been willing to recognise the fact. There was something coming— coming from the sand-dunes or the sea. And it was invited, welcomed at any rate, by Erricson. His deep, volcanic enthusiasm and belief provided the channel. In lesser degree they, too, were caught in it. Moreover, it was terrific, irresistible.

And it was at this point—as the comparing of notes aferwards established—that Father Norden came in, Norden, the big man's nephew, having bicycled over from some point beyond Corfe Castle and raced along the hard Studland sand in the moonlight, and then hullood till a boat had ferried him across the narrow channel of Poole Harbour. Sinbad simply brought him in without any preliminary question or announcement. He could not resist the splendid night and the spring air, explained Norden. He felt sure his uncle could 'find a hammock' for him somewhere aft, as he put it. He did not add that Sinbad had telegraphed for him just before sundown from the coast-guard hut. Dr. Reese already knew him, but he was introduced to the Major. Norden was a member of the Society of Jesus, an ardent, not clever, and unselfish soul.

Erricson greeted him with obviously mixed feelings, and with an extraordinary sentence: 'It doesn't really matter,' he exclaimed, after a few commonplaces of talk, 'for all religions are the same if you go deep enough. All teach sacrifice, and, without exception, all seek final union by absorption into their Deity.' And then, under his breath, turning sideways to peer out of the window, he added a swift rush of half-smothered words that only Dr. Reese caught: 'The Army, the Church, the Medical Profession, and Labour—if they would only all come! What a fine result, what a grand offering! Alone—I seem so unworthy—insignificant...!'

But meanwhile young Norden was speaking before any one could stop him, although the Major did make one or two blundering attempts. For once the Jesuit's tact was at fault. He evidently hoped to introduce a new mood — to shift the current already established by the single force of his own personality. And he was not quite man enough to carry it off.

It was an error of judgment on his part. For the forces he found established in the room were too heavy to lift and alter, their impetus being already acquired. He did his best, anyhow. He began moving with the current—it was not the first sea fit he had combated in this extraordinary personality—then found, too late, that he was carried along with it himself like the rest of them.

'Odd—but couldn't find the bungalow at first,' he laughed, somewhat hardly. 'It's got a bit of seafog all to itself that hides it. I thought perhaps my pagan uncle——'

The Doctor interrupted him hastily, with great energy. 'The fog *does* lie caught in these sand hollows—like steam in a cup, you know,' he put in. But the other, intent on his own procedure, missed the cue.

196

'——thought it was smoke at first, and that you were up to some heathen ceremony or other,' laughing in Erricson's face; 'sacrificing to the full moon or the sea, or the spirits of the desolate places that haunt sand-dunes, eh?'

No one spoke for a second, but Erricson's face turned quite radiant.

'My uncle's such a pagan, you know,' continued the priest, 'that as I flew along those deserted sands from Studland I almost expected to hear old Triton blow his wreathed horn... or see fair Thetis's tinsel-slippered feet....'

Erricson, suppressing violent gestures, highly excited, face happy as a boy's, was combing his great yellow beard with both hands, and the other two men had begun to speak at once, intent on stopping the flow of unwise allusion. Norden, swallowing a mouthful of cold soda-water, had put the glass down, spluttering over its bubbles, when the sound was first heard at the window. And in the back room the manservant ran, calling something aloud that sounded like 'It's coming, God save us, it's coming in...!' Though the Major swears some name was mentioned that he afterwards forgot—Glaucus —Proteus—Pontus—or some such word. The sound itself, however, was plain enough—a kind of imperious tappling on the window-panes as of a multitude of objects. Blown sand it might have been or heavy spray or, as Norden suggested later, a great water-soaked branch of giant seaweed. Every one started up, but Erricson was first upon his feet, and had the window wide open in a twinkling. His voice roared forth over those moonlit sand-dunes and out towards the line of heavy surf ten yards below.

'All along the shore of the Aegean,' he bellowed, with a kind of hoarse triumph that shook the heart, 'that ancient cry once rang. But it was a lie, a thumping and audacious lie. And He is not the only one. Another still lives—and, by Poseidon, He comes! He knows His own and His own know Him— and His own shall go to meet Him...!'

That reference to the Aegean 'cry'! It was so wonderful. Every one, of course, except the soldier, seized the allusion.

It was a comprehensive, yet subtle, way of suggesting the idea. And meanwhile all spoke at once, shouted rather, for the Invasion was somehow—monstrous.

'Damn it—that's a bit too much. Something's caught my throat!' The Major, like a man drowning, fought with the furniture in his amazement and dismay. Fighting was his first instinct, of course. 'Hurts so infernally—takes the breath,' he cried, by way of explaining the extraordinarily violent impetus that moved him, yet half ashamed of himself for seeing nothing he could strike. But Malcolm Reese struggled to get between his host and the open window, saying in tense voice something like 'Don't let him get out! Don't let him get out!' While the shouts of warning from Sinbad in the little cramped back offices added to the general confusion. Only Father Norden stood quiet—watching with a kind of admiring wonder the expression of magnificence that had flamed into the visage of Erricson.

'Hark, you fools! Hark!' boomed the Viking figure, standing erect and splendid.

And through that open window, along the far-drawn line of shore from Canford Cliffs to the chalk bluffs of Studland Bay, there certainly ran a sound that was no common roar of surf. It was articulate— message from the sea—an announcement—a thunderous warning of approach. No mere surf breaking on sand could have compassed so deep and multitudinous a voice of dreadful roaring—far out over the entering tide, yet at the same time close in along the entire sweep of shore, shaking all the ocean, both depth and surface, with its deep vibrations. Into the bungalow chamber came—the SEA!

Out of the night, from the moonlit spaces where it had been steadily accumulating, into that little cabined room so full of humanity and tobacco smoke, came invisibly—the Power of the Sea. Invisible, yes, but mighty, pressed forward by the huge draw of the moon, soft-coated with brine and moisture —the great Sea. And with it, into the minds of those three other men, leaped instantaneously, not to be denied, overwhelming suggestions of water-power, the tear and strain of thousand-mile currents, the irresistible pull and rush of tides, the suction of giant whirlpools—more, the massed and awful impetus of whole driven oceans. The air turned salt and briny, and a welter of seaweed clamped t. eir very skins.

'Glaucus! I come to Thee, great God of the deep Waterways.... Father and Master!' Erricson cried aloud in a voice that most marvellously conveyed supreme joy.

The little bungalow trembled as from a blow at the foundations, and the same second the big man was through the window and running down the moonlit sands towards the foam.

'God in Heaven! Did you all see *that*?' shouted Major Reese, for the manner in which the great body slipped through the tiny window-frame was incredible. And then, first tottering with a sudden weakness, he recovered himself and rushed round by the door, followed by his brother. Sinbad, invisible, but not inaudible, was calling aloud from the passage at the back. Father Norden, slimmer than the others—well controlled, too—was through the little window before either of them reached the fringe of beach beyond the sand-dunes. They joined forces halfway down to the water's edge. The figure of Erricson, towering in the moonlight, flew before them, coasting rapidly along the wave-line.

No one of them said a word; they tore along side by side, Norden a trifle in advance. In front of them, head turned seawards, bounded Erricson in great flying leaps, singing as he ran, impossible to overtake.

Then, what they witnessed, all three witnessed; the weird grandeur of it in the moonshine was too splendid to allow the smaller emotions of personal alarm, it seems. At any rate, the divergence of opinion afterwards was unaccountably insignificant. For, on a sudden, that heavy roaring sound far out at sea came close in with a swift plunge of speed, followed simultaneously—accompanied, rather—by a dark line that was no mere wave moving: enormously, up and across, between the sea and sky it swept close in to shore. The moonlight caught it for a second as it passed, in a cliff of her bright silver.

And Erricson slowed down, bowed his great head and shoulders, spread his arms out and...

And what? For no one of those amazed witnesses could swear exactly what then came to pass. Upon this impossibility of telling it in language they all three agreed. Only those eyeless dunes of sand that watched, only the white and silent moon overhead, only that long, curved beach of empty and deserted shore retain the complete record, to be revealed some day perhaps when a later Science shall have learned to develop the photographs that Nature takes incessantly upon her secret plates. For Erricson's rough suit of tweed went out in ribbons across the air; his figure somehow turned dark like strips of tide-sucked seaweed; something enveloped and overcame him, half shrouding him from view. He stood for one instant upright, his hair wild in the moonshine, towering, with arms again outstretched; then bent forward, turned, drew out most curiously sideways, uttering the singing sound of tumbling waters. The next instant, curving over like a falling wave, he swept along the glistening surface of the sands—and was gone. In fluid form, wave-like, his being slipped away into the Being of the Sea. A violent tumult convulsed the surface of the tide near in, but at once, and with amazing speed, passed careering away into the deeper water—far out. To his singular death, as to a wedding, Erricson had gone, singing, and well content.

'May God, who holds the sea and all its powers in the hollow of His mighty hand, take them *both* into Himself!' Norden was on his knees, praying fervently.

The body was never recovered ... and the most curious thing of all was that the interior of the cabin, where they found Sinbad shaking with terror when they at length returned, was splashed and sprayed, almost soaked, with salt water. Up into the bigger dunes beside the bungalow, and far beyond the reach of normal tides, lay, too, a great streak and furrow as of a large invading wave, caking the dry sand. A hundred tufts of the coarse grass tussocks had been torn away.

The high tide that night, drawn by the Easter full moon, of course, was known to have been exceptional, for it fairly flooded Poole Harbour, flushing all the coves and bays towards the mouth of the Frome. And the natives up at Arne Bay and Wych always declare that the noise of the sea was heard far inland even up to the nine Barrows of the Purbeck Hills—triumphantly singing.

THE ATTIC

THE forest-girdled village upon the Jura slopes slept soundly, although it was not yet many minutes after ten o'clock. The clang of the *couvre-feu* had indeed just ceased, its notes swept far into the woods by a wind that shook the mountains. This wind now rushed down the deserted street. It howled about the old rambling building called La Citadelle, whose roof towered gaunt and humped above the smaller houses—Château left unfinished long ago by Lord Wemyss, the exiled Jacobite. The families who occupied the various apartments listened to the storm and felt the building tremble. 'It's the mountain wind. It will bring the snow,' the mother said, without looking up from her knitting. 'And how sad it sounds.'

But it was not the wind that brought sadness as we sat round the open fire of peat. It was the wind of memories. The lamplight slanted along the narrow room towards the table where breakfast things lay ready for the morning. The double windows were fastened. At the far end stood a door ajar, and on the other side of it the two elder children lay asleep in the big bed. But beside the window was a smaller unused bed, that had been empty now a year. And to-night was the anniversary....

And so the wind brought sadness and long thoughts. The little chap that used to lie there was already twelve months gone, far, far beyond the Hole where the Winds came from, as he called it; yet it seemed only yesterday that I went to tell him a tuck-up story, to stroke Riquette, the old motherly cat that cuddled against his back and laid a paw beside his pillow like a human being, and to hear his funny little earnest whisper say, 'Oncle, tu sais, j'ai prié pour Petavel.' For La Citadelle had its unhappy ghost—of Petavel, the usurer, who had hanged himself in the attic a century gone by, and was known to walk its dreary corridors in search of peace—and this wise Irish mother, calming the boys' fears with wisdom, had told him,

'If you pray for Petavel, you'll save his soul and make him happy, and he'll only love you.' And, thereafter, this little imaginative boy had done so every night. With a passionate seriousness he did it. He had wonderful, delicate ways like that. In all our hearts he made his fairy nests of wonder. In my own, I know, he lay closer than any joy imaginable, with his big blue eyes, his queer soft questionings, and his splendid child's unselfishness—a sun-kissed flower of innocence that, had he lived, might have sweetened half a world.

'Let's put more peat on,' the mother said, as a handful of rain like stones came flinging against the windows; 'that must be hail.' And she went on tiptoe to the inner room. 'They're sleeping like two puddings,' she whispered, coming presently back. But it struck me she had taken longer than to notice merely that; and her face wore an odd expression that made me uncomfortable. I thought she was somehow just about to laugh or cry. By the table a second she hesitated. I caught the flash of indecision as it passed. 'Pan,' she said suddenly—it was a nickname, stolen from my tuck-up stories, *he* had given me—'I wonder how Riquette got in.' She looked hard at me. 'It wasn't you, was it?' For we never let her come at night since he had gone. It was too poignant. The beastie always went cuddling and nestling into that empty bed. But this time it was not my doing, and I offered plausible explanations. 'But—she's on the bed. Pan, *would* you be so kind——' She left the sentence unfinished, but I easily understood, for a lump had somehow risen in my own throat too, and I remembered now that she had come out from the inner room so quickly—with a kind of hurried rush almost. I put 'mère Riquette' out into the corridor. A lamp stood on the chair outside the door of another occupant further down, and I urged her gently towards it. She turned and looked at me—straight up into my face; but, instead of going down as I suggested, she went slowly in the opposite direction. She stepped softly towards a door in the wall that led up broken stairs into the attics. There she sat down and waited. And so I left her, and came back hastily to the peat fire and companionship. The wind rushed in behind me and slammed the door.

And we talked then somewhat busily of cheerful things; of the children's future, the excellence of the cheap Swiss schools, of Christmas presents, ski-ing, snow, tobogganing. I led the talk away from mournfulness; and when these subjects were exhausted I told stories of my own adventures in distant parts of the world. But 'mother' listened the whole time—not to me. Her thoughts were all elsewhere. And her air of intently, secretly listening, bordered, I felt, upon the uncanny. For she often stopped her knitting and sat with her eyes fixed upon the air before her; she stared blankly at the wall, her head slightly on one side, her figure tense, attention strained—elsewhere. Or, when my talk positively demanded it, her nod was oddly mechanical and her eyes looked through and past me. The wind continued very loud and roaring; but the fire glowed, the room was warm and cosy. Yet she shivered, and when I drew attention to it, her reply, 'I do feel cold, but I didn't know I shivered,' was given as though she spoke across the air to some one else. But what impressed me even more uncomfortably were her repeated questions about Riquette. When a pause in my tales permitted, she would look up with 'I wonder where Riquette went?' or, thinking of the inclement night, 'I hope mère Riquette's not out of doors. Perhaps Madame Favre has taken her in?' I offered to go and see. Indeed I was already half-way across the room when there came the heavy bang at the door that rooted me to the ground where I stood. It was not wind. It was something alive that made it rattle. There was a second blow. A thud on the corridor boards followed, and then a high, odd voice that at first was as human as the cry of a child.

It is undeniable that we both started, and for myself I can answer truthfully that a chill ran down my spine; but what frightened me more than the sudden noise and the eerie cry was the way 'mother' supplied the immediate explanation. For behind the words 'It's only Riquette; she sometimes springs at the door like that; perhaps we'd better let her in,'

was a certain touch of uncanny quiet that made me feel she
had known the cat would come, and knew also *why* she came.
One cannot explain such impressions further. They leave
their vital touch, then go their way. Into the little room,
however, in that moment there came between us this uncomfortable sense that the night held other purposes than our
own—and that my companion was aware of them. There
was something going on far, far removed from the routine
of life as we were accustomed to it. Moreover, our usual
routine was the eddy, while this was the main stream. It felt
big, I mean.

And so it was that the entrance of the familiar, friendly
creature brought this thing both itself and 'mother' *knew*,
but whereof I as yet was ignorant. I held the door wide. The
draught rushed through behind her, and sent a shower of
sparks about the fireplace. The lamp flickered and gave a little
gulp. And Riquette marched slowly past, with all the impressive
dignity of her kind, towards the other door that stood ajar.
Turning the corner like a shadow, she disappeared into the
room where the two children slept. We heard the soft thud
with which she leaped upon the bed. Then, in a lull of the
wind, she came back again and sat on the oilcloth, staring
into 'mother's' face. She mewed and put a paw out, drawing
the black dress softly with half-opened claws. And it was all
so horribly suggestive and pathetic, it revived such poignant
memories, that I got up impulsively—I think I had actually
said the words, 'We'd better put her out, mother, after all'—
when my companion rose to her feet and forestalled me.
She said another thing instead. It took my breath away to
hear it. 'She wants us to go with her. Pan, will you come too?'
The surprise on my face must have asked the question, for
I do not remember saying anything. 'To the attic,' she said
quietly.

She stood there by the table, a tall, grave figure dressed
in black, and her face above the lamp-shade caught the full
glare of light. Its expression positively stiffened me. She
seemed so secure in her singular purpose. And her familiar

appearance had so oddly given place to something wholly strange to me. She looked like another person—almost with the unwelcome transformation of the sleep-walker about her. Cold came over me as I watched her, for I remembered suddenly her Irish second-sight, her story years ago of meeting a figure on the attic stairs, the figure of Petavel. And the idea of this motherly, sedate, and wholesome woman, absorbed day and night in prosaic domestic duties, and yet 'seeing' things, touched the incongruous almost to the point of alarm. It was so distressingly convincing.

Yet she knew quite well that I would come. Indeed, following the excited animal, she was already by the door, and a moment later, still without answering or protesting, I was with them in the draughty corridor. There was something inevitable in her manner that made it impossible to refuse. She took the lamp from its nail on the wall, and following our four-footed guide, who ran with obvious pleasure just in front, she opened the door into the courtyard. The wind nearly put the lamp out, but a minute later we were safe inside the passage that led up flights of creaky wooden stairs towards the world of tenantless attics overhead.

And I shall never forget the way the excited Riquette first stood up and put her paws upon the various doors, trotted ahead, turned back to watch us coming, and then finally sat down and waited on the threshold of the empty, raftered space that occupied the entire length of the building underneath the roof. For her manner was more that of an intelligent dog than of a cat, and sometimes more like that of a human mind than either.

We had come up without a single word. The howling of the wind as we rose higher was like the roar of artillery. There were many broken stairs, and the narrow way was full of twists and turnings. It was a dreadful journey. I felt eyes watching us from all the yawning spaces of the darkness, and the noise of the storm smothered footsteps everywhere. Troops of shadows kept us company. But it was on the threshold of this big, chief attic, when 'mother' stopped abruptly to put down the lamp, that real feat took hold of me. For Riquette marched steadily forward into the middle of the dusty flooring, picking her way among the fallen tiles and mortar, as though she went towards—some one. She purred loudly and uttered little cries of excited pleasure. Her tail went up into the air, and she lowered her head with the unmistakable intention of being stroked. Her lips opened and shut. Her green eyes smiled. She *was* being stroked.

It was an unforgettable performance. I would rather have witnessed an execution or a murder than watch that mysterious creature twist and turn about in the way she did. Her magnified shadow was as large as a pony on the floor and rafters. I wanted to hide the whole thing by extinguishing the lamp. For, even before the mysterious action began, I experienced the sudden rush of conviction that others besides ourselves were in this attic—and standing very close to us indeed. And, although there was ice in my blood, there was also a strange swelling of the heart that only love and tenderness could bring.

But, whatever it was, my human companion, still silent, knew and understood. She *saw*. And her soft whisper that ran with the wind among the rafters, 'Il a prié pour Petavel et le bon Dieu l'a entendu,' did not amaze me one quarter as much as the expression I then caught upon her radiant face. Tears ran down the cheeks, but they were tears of happiness. Her whole figure seemed lit up. She opened her arms— picture of great Motherhood, proud, blessed, and tender beyond words. I thought she was going to fall, for she took quick steps forward; but when I moved to catch her, she drew me aside instead with a sudden gesture that brought fear back in the place of wonder.

'Let them pass,' she whispered grandly. 'Pan, don't you see.... He's leading him into peace and safety ... by the hand!' And her joy seemed to kill the shadows and fill the entire attic with white light. Then, almost simultaneously with her words, she swayed. I was in time to catch her, but as I did so, across the very spot where we had just been standing—two figures, I swear, went past us like a flood of light.

There was a moment next of such confusion that I did not see what happened to Riquette, for the sight of my companion kneeling on the dusty boards and praying with a curious sort of passionate happiness, while tears pressed between her covering fingers—the strange wonder of this made me utterly oblivious to minor details....

We were sitting round the peat fire again, and 'mother' was saying to me in the gentlest, tenderest whisper I ever heard from human lips—'Pan, I think perhaps that's why God took him....'

And when a little later we went in to make Riquette cosy in the empty bed, ever since kept sacred to her use, the mournfulness had lifted; and in the place of resignation was proud peace and joy that knew no longer sad or selfish questionings.

THE HEATH FIRE

The men at luncheon in Rennie's Surrey cottage that September day were discussing, of course, the heat. All agreed it had been exceptional. But nothing unusual was said until O'Hara spoke of the heath fires. They had been rather terrific, several in a single day, devouring trees and bushes, endangering human life, and spreading with remarkable rapidity. The flames, too, had been extraordinarily high and vehement for heath fires. And O'Hara's tone had introduced into the commonplace talk something new—the element of mystery; it was nothing definite he said, but manner, eyes, hushed voice and the rest conveyed it. And it was genuine. What he *felt* reached the others rather than what he said. The atmosphere in the little room, with the honeysuckle trailing sweetly across the open windows, changed; the talk became of a sudden less casual, frank, familiar; and the men glanced at one another across the table, laughing still, yet with an odd touch of constraint marking little awkward, unfilled pauses. Being a group of normal Englishmen, they disliked mystery; it made them feel uncomfortable; for the things O'Hara hinted at had touched that kind of elemental terror that lurks secretly in all human beings. Guarded by 'culture', but never wholly concealed, the unwelcome thing made its presence known—the hint of primitive dread that, for instance, great thunder-storms, tidal waves, or violent conflagrations rouse.

And instinctively they fell at once to discussing the obvious causes of the fires. The stockbroker, scenting imagination, edged mentally away, sniffing. But the journalist was full of brisk information, 'simply given'.

'The sun starts them in Canada, using a dewdrop as a lens,' he said, 'and an engine's spark, remember, carries an immense distance without losing its heat.'

'But hardly miles,' said another, who had not been really listening.

'It's my belief,' put in the critic keenly, 'that a lot were done on purpose. Bits of live coal wrapped in cloth were found, you know.' He was a little, weasel-faced iconoclast, dropping the acid of doubt and disbelief wherever he went, but offering nothing in the place of what he destroyed. His head was turret-shaped, lips tight and thin, nose and chin running to points like gimlets, with which he bored into the unremunerative clays of life.

'The general unrest, yes,' the journalist supported him, and tried to draw the conversation on to labour questions. But their host preferred the fire talk. 'I must say,' he put in gravely, 'that some of the blazes hereabouts were uncommonly —er—queer. They started, I mean, so oddly. You remember, O'Hara, only last week that suspicious one over Kettlebury way——?'

It seemed he wished to draw the artist out, and that the artist, feeling the general opposition, declined.

'Why seek an unusual explanation at all?' the critic said at length, impatiently. 'It's all natural enough, if you ask me.'

'Natural! Oh yes!' broke in O'Hara, with a sudden vehemence that betrayed feeling none had as yet suspected; 'provided you don't limit the word to mean only what we understand. There's nothing anywhere—unnatural.'

A laugh cut short the threatened tirade, and the journalist expressed the general feeling with 'Oh *you*, Jim! You'd see a devil in a dust-storm, or a fairy in the tea-leaves of your cup!'

'And why not, pray? Devils and fairies are every bit as true as formulae.'

Some one tactfully guided them away from a profitless discussion, and they talked glibly of the damage done, the hideousness of the destroyed moors, the gaunt, black, ugly slopes, fifty-foot flames, roaring noises, and the splendour of the enormous smoke-clouds that had filled the skies. And Rennie, still hoping to coax O'Hara, repeated tales the beaters had brought in that crying, as though living things were caught, had been heard in places, and that some had seen tall shapes of fire passing headlong through the choking smoke. For the note O'Hara had struck refused to be ignored. It went on sounding underneath the commonest remark; and the atmosphere to the end retained that curious tinge that he had given to it—of the strange, the ominous, the mysterious and unexplained. Until, at last, the artist, having added nothing further to the talk, got up with some abruptness and left the room. He complained briefly that the fever he had suffered from still bothered him and he would go and lie down a bit. The heat, he said, oppressed him.

A silence followed his departure. The broker drew a sigh as though the market had gone up. But Rennie, old, comprehending friend, looked anxious. 'Excitement,' he said, 'not oppression, is the word he meant. He's always a bit strung up when that Black Sea fever gets him. He brought it with him from Batoum.' And another brief silence followed.

'Been with you most of the summer, hasn't he?' enquired the journalist, on the trail of a 'par', 'painting those wild things of his that no one understands.' And their host, weighing a moment how much he might in fairness tell, replied—among friends it was—'Yes; and this summer they have been more—er—wild and wonderful than usual—an extraordinary rush of colour——splendid schemes, "conceptions", I believe you critics call 'em, of fire, as though, in a way, the unusual heat had possessed him for interpretation.'

The group expressed its desultory interest by uninspired interjections.

'That was what he meant just now when he said the fires had been mysterious, required explanation, or something—the way they started, rather,' concluded Rennie.

Then he hesitated. He laughed a moment, and it was an uneasy, apologetic little laugh. How to continue he hardly knew. Also, he wished to protect his friend from the cheap jeering of miscomprehension. 'He is very imaginative, you know,' he went on, quietly, as no one spoke. 'You remember that glorious mad thing he did of the Fallen Lucifer—driving a star across the heavens till the heat of the descent set a light to half the planets, scorched the old moon to the white cinder that she now is, and passed close enough to earth to send our oceans up in a single jet of steam? Well, this time—he's been at something every bit as wild, only truer—finer. And what is it? Briefly, then, he's got the idea, it seems, that the unusual heat from the sun this year has penetrated deep enough—in places—especially on these unprotected heaths that retain their heat so cleverly—to reach another kindred expression—to waken a response—in sympathy, you see—from the central fires of the earth.'

He paused again a moment awkwardly, conscious how clumsily he expressed it. 'The parent getting into touch again with its lost child, eh? See the idea? Return of the Fire Prodigal, as it were?'

His listeners stared in silence, the broker looking his obvious relief that O'Hara was not on 'Change, the critic's eyes glancing sharply down that pointed, boring nose of his.

'And the central fires have felt it and risen in response,' continued Rennie in a lower voice. 'You see the idea? It's big, to say the least. The volcanoes have answered too—there's old Etna, the giant of 'em all, breaking out in fifty new mouths of flame. Heat is latent in everything, only waiting to be called out. That match you're striking, this coffee-pot, the warmth in our bodies, and so on—their heat comes first from the sun, and is therefore an actual part of the sun, the origin of all heat and life. And so O'Hara, you know, who sees the universe as a single homogeneous *One* and—and—well, I give it up. Can't explain it, you see. You must get him to do that. But somehow this year—cloudless—the protecting armour of water all gone too—the sun's rays managed to sink in and reach their kind buried deep below. Perhaps, later, we may get him to show us the studies that he's made—whew!—the most—er—amazing things you ever saw!'

The 'superiority' of unimaginative minds was inevitable, making Rennie regret that he had told so much. It was almost as if he had been untrue to his friend. But at length the group broke up for the afternoon. They left messages for O'Hara. Two motored, and the journalist took the train. The critic followed his sharp nose to London, where he might ferret out the failures that his mind delighted in. And when they were gone the host slipped quickly upstairs to find his friend. The heat was unbearable to suffocation, the little bedroom like an oven. But Jim O'Hara was not in it.

For, instead of lying down as he had said, a fierce revolt, stirred by the talk of those unvisioned minds below, had wakened, and the deep, sensitive, poet's soul in him had leaped suddenly to the acceptance of an impossible thing. He had escaped, driven forth by the secret call of wonder. He made full speed for the destroyed moors. Fever or no fever, he must see for himself. Did no one understand? Was he the only one?... Walking quickly, he passed the Frensham Ponds, came through that spot of loneliness and beauty, the Lion's Mouth, noting that even there the pool of water had dried up and the rushes waved in the hot air over a bed of hard, caked mud, and so reached within the hour the wide expanse of Thursley Common. On every side the world stretched dark and burnt, a cemetery of cinders. Great thrills rushed through his heart; and with the power of a tide that yet came at flashing speed the truth rose up in him... Half running now, he plunged forward another mile or two, and found himself, the only living thing, amid the great waste of heatherland. The blazing sunlight drenched it. It lay, a sheet of weird dark beauty, spreading like a black, enormous garden as far as the eye could reach.

Then, breathless, he paused and looked about him. Within his heart something, long smouldering, ran into sudden flame. Light blazed upon his inner world. For as the scorch of vehement passion may quicken tracts of human consciousness that lie ordinarily inert and unproductive, so here the surface of the earth had turned alive. He knew; he saw; he understood.

Here, in these open sun-traps that gathered and retained the

213

heat, the fire of the Universe had dropped and lain, increasing week by week. These parched, dry months, the soil, free from rejecting and protective moisture, had let it all accumulate till at length it had sunk downwards, inwards, and the sister fires below, responding to the touch of their ancient parent source, too long unfelt, had answered with a swift uprising roar. They had come up with answering joy, and here and there had actually reached the surface, and had leaped out with dancing cry, wild to escape from an age-long prison back to their huge, eternal origin.

This sunshine, ah! what was it? These farthing dips of heat men complained about in their tiny, cage-like houses! It scorched the grass and fields, yes; but the surface never held it long enough to let it sink to union with its kindred of the darker fires beneath! These cried for it, but union was ever denied and stifled by the weight of cooled and cooling rock. And the ages of separation had almost cooled remembrance too—fire—the kiss and strength of fire—the flaming embrace and burning lips of the father sun himself.... He could have cried with the fierce delight of it all, and the picture he would paint rose there before him, burnt gloriously into the canvas of the entire heavens. Was not his own heat and life also from the sun?...

He stared about him in the deep silence of the afternoon. The world was still. It basked in the windless heat. No living thing stirred, for the common forms of life had fled away. Earth waited. He, too, waited. And then some touch of intuition, blown to white heat, supplied the link the pedestrian intellect missed, and he knew that what he waited for was on the way. For he would *see*. The message he should paint would come before his outer eye as well, though not, as he had first stupidly expected, on some grand, enormous scale. Rather would it be the equivalent of that still, small voice that once had inspired an entire nation....

The wind passed very softly across the unburnt patch of heather where he lay; he heard it rustling in the skeletons of scorched birch trees, and in the gorse and furze bushes that the flame had left so ghostly pale. Farther off it sang in the isolated pines, dying away like surf upon some far-off reef. He smelt the bitter perfume of burnt soil, the pungent, acrid odour of beaten ashes. The purple-black of the moors yawned like openings in the side of the earth. In all directions for miles stretched the deep emptiness of the heather-lands, an immense, dark, magic garden, still black with the feet of wonder that had flown across it and left it so beautifully scarred. The shadow of the terrible embrace still trailed and lingered as through Midnight had screened a time of passion with this curtain of her softest plumes.

And *they* had called it ugly, had spoken of its marred beauty, its hideousness! He laughed exultantly as he drank it in, for the weird and savage splendour everywhere broke loose and spread, passing from the earth into the receptive substance of his own mind. Even the roots of gorse and heather, like petrified, shadow-eating snakes, charged with the mystery of that eternal underworld whence they had risen, lay waiting for the return of the night of sleep whence Fire had wakened them. Lost ghosts of a salamander army that the flame had swept above the ground, they lay anguished and frightened in the glare of the unaccustomed sun....

And waiting, he stared about him in the deep silence of the afternoon. Hazy with distance he saw the peak of Crooksbury, dim in its sheet of pines, waving a blue-plumed crest into the sky for signal; and close about him rose the more sombre glory of the lesser knolls and boulders, still cloaked in the swarthy magic of the smoke. Amid pools of ashes in the nearer hollows he saw the blue beauty of the fire-weed that rushes instantly into life behind all conflagrations. It was ulowing softly in the wind. And here and there, set like emeralds bpon some dusky bosom, lay the brilliant spires of young bracken that rose to clap a thousand tiny hands in the heart of exquisite desolation. In a cloud of green they rustled in the wind above the sea of black.... And so within himself O'Hara realised the huge excitement of the flame this fragment of the earth had felt. For Fire, mysterious symbol of universal

215

life, spirit that prodigally gives itself without itself diminishing, had passed in power across this ancient heather-land, leaving the soul of it all naked and unashamed. The sun had loved it. The fires below had risen up and answered. They had known that union with their source which some call death....

And the fires were rising still. The poet's heart in him became suddenly and awfully aware. Ye stars of fire! This patch of unburnt heather where he lay had been untouched as yet, but now the flame in his soul had brought the little needed link and he would *see*. The thing of wonder that the Universe should teach him how to paint was already on the way. Called by the sun, tremendous, splendid parent, the central fires were still rising.

And he turned, weakness and exultation racing for possession of him. The wind passed softly over his face, and with it came a faint, dry sound. It was distant and yet close beside him. At the stir of it there rose also in himself a strange vast thing that was bigger than the bulk of the moon and wide as the extension of swept forests, yet small and gentle as a blade of grass that pricks the lawn in spring. And he realised then that 'within' and 'without' had turned one, and that over the entire moorland arrived this thing that was happening too in a whitehot point of his own heart. He was linked with the sun and the farthest star, and in his little finger glowed the heat and fire of the universe itself. In sympathy *his own fires were rising too*.

The sound was born—a faint, light noise of crackling in the heather at his feet. He bent his head and searched, and among the obscure and tiny underways of the roots he saw a tip of curling smoke rise slowly upwards. It moved in a thin, blue spiral past his face. Then terror took him that was like a terror of the mountains, yet with it at the same time a realisation of beauty that made the heart leap within him into dazzling radiance. For the incense of this fairy column of thin smoke drew his soul with it—upwards towards its source. He rose to his feet, trembling....

He watched the line rise slowly to the sky and vanish into

blue. The whole expanse of blackened heather-land watched too. Wind sank away; the sunshine dropped to meet it. A sense of deep expectancy, profound and reverent, lay over all that sun-baked moor; and the entire sweep of burnt world about him knew with joy that what was taking place in that wee, isolated patch of Surrey heather was the thing the Hebrew mystic knew when the Soul of the Universe became manifest in the bush that burned, yet never was consumed. In that faint sound of crackling, as he stood aside to listen and to watch, O'Hara knew a form of the eternal Voice of Ages. There was no flame, but it seemed to him that all his inner being passed in fiery heat outwards towards its source.... He saw the little patch of dried-up heather sink to the level of the black surface all about it—a sifted pile of delicate, pale-blue ashes. The tiny spiral vanished; he watched it disappear, winding upwards out of sight in a little ghostly trail of beauty. So small and soft and simple was this wonder of the world. It was gone. And something in himself had broken, dropped in ashes, and passed also outwards like a tiny mounting flame.

But the picture O'Hara had thought himself designed to paint was never done. It was not even begun. The great canvas of 'The Fire Worshipper' stood empty on the easel, for the artist had not strength to lift a brush. Within two days the final breath passed slowly from his lips. The strange fever that so perplexed the doctor by its rapid development and its fury took him so easily. His temperature was extra-ordinary. The heat, as of an internal fire, fairly devoured him, and the smile upon his face at the last—so Rennie declared—was the most perplexingly wonderful thing he had ever seen. 'It was like a great, white flame,' he said.

THE RETURN

It was curious—that sense of dull uneasiness that came over him so suddenly, so stealthily at first he scarcely noticed it, but with such marked increase after a time that he presently got up and left the theatre. His seat was on the gangway of the dress circle, and he slipped out awkwardly in the middle of what seemed to be the best and jolliest song of the piece. The full house was shaking with laughter; so infectious was the gaiety that even strangers turned to one another as much as to say: 'Now, isn't *that* funny——?'

It was curious, too, the way the feeling first got into him at all, here in the full swing of laughter, music, light-heartedness, for it came as a vague suggestion: 'I've forgotten something—something I meant to do—something of importance. What in the world was it, now?' And he thought hard, searching vainly through his mind; then dismissed it as the dancing caught his attention. It came back a little later again, during a passage of long-winded talk that bored him and set his attention free once more, but came more strongly this time, insisting on an answer. What could it have been that he had overlooked, left undone, omitted to see to? It went on nibbling at the sub-conscious part of him. Several times this happened, this dismissal and return, till at last the thing declared itself more plainly—and he felt bothered, troubled, distinctly uneasy.

He was wanted somewhere. There was somewhere else he ought to be. That describes it best, perhaps. Some engage-ment of moment had entirely slipped his memory—an engage-ment that involved another person, too. But where, what, with whom? And at length, this vague uneasiness amounted to positive discomfort, so that he felt unable to enjoy the piece—and left abruptly. Like a man to whom comes suddenly the horrible idea that the match he lit his cigarette with and flung into the waste-paper basket on leaving was not really out—a sort of panic distress—he jumped into a taxi-cab and hurried to his flat: to find everything in order, of course; no smoke, no fire, no smell of burning.

But his evening was spoilt. He sat smoking in his armchair at home—this business man of forty, practical in mind, of character some called stolid—cursing himself for an imaginative fool. It was now too late to go back to the theatre; the club bored him; he spent an hour with the evening papers, dipping into books, sipping a long cool drink; doing odds and ends about the flat; 'I'll go to bed early for a change,' he laughed, but really all the time fighting—yes, deliberately fighting—this strange attack of uneasiness that so insidiously grew upwards, outwards from the buried depths of him that sought so strenuously to deny it. It never occurred to him that he was ill. He was *not* ill. His health was thunderingly good. He was robust as a coal-heaver.

The flat was roomy, high up on the top floor, yet in a busy part of town, so that the roar of traffic mounted round it like a sea. Through the open windows came the fresh night air of June. He had never noticed before how sweet the London night air could be, and that not all the smoke and dust could smother a certain touch of wild fragrance that tinctured it with perfume—yes, almost perfume—as of the country. He swallowed a draught of it as he stood there, staring out across the tangled world of roofs and chimney-pots. He saw the procession of the clouds; he saw the stars; he saw the moonlight falling in a shower of silver spears upon the slates and wires and steeples. And something in him quickened—something that had never stirred before.

He turned with a horrid start, for the uneasiness had of a sudden leaped within him like an animal. There was some one in the flat.

Instantly, with action, even this slight action, the fancy vanished; but, all the same, he switched on the electric lights and made a search. For it seemed to him that some one had crept up close behind him while he stood there watching the Night—some one, moreover, whose silent presence fingered with unerring touch both this new thing that had quickened

219

in his hear *and* that sense of original deep uneasiness. He was amazed at himself, angry; indignant that he could be thus foolishly upset over nothing, yet at the same time profoundly distressed at this vehement growth of a new thing in his well-ordered personality. Growth? He dismissed the word the moment it occurred to him. But it had occurred to him. It stayed. While he searched the empty flat, the long passages, the gloomy bedroom at the end, the little hall where he kept his overcoats and golf sticks—it stayed. Growth! It was oddly disquieting. Growth, to him, involved—though he neither acknowledged nor recognised the truth perhaps—some kind of undesirable changeableness, instability, unbalance.

Yet, singular as it all was, he realised that the uneasiness and the sudden appreciation of Beauty that was so new to him had both entered by the same door into his being. When he came back to the front room he noticed that he was perspiring. There were little drops of moisture on his forehead. And down his spine ran positively chills—little, faint quivers of cold. He was shivering.

He lit his big meerschaum pipe, and left the lights all burning. The feeling that there was something he had overlooked, forgotten, left undone, had vanished. Whatever the original cause of this absurd uneasiness might be—he called it absurd on purpose, because he now realised in the depths of him that it was really more vital then he cared about—it was much nearer to discovery than before. It dodged about just below the threshold of discovery. It was as close as that. Any moment he would know what it was: he would remember. Yes, he would *remember*. Meanwhile, he was in the right place. No desire to go elsewhere afflicted him, as in the theatre. Here was the place, here in the flat.

And then it was, with a kind of sudden burst and rush—it seemed to him the only way to phrase it—memory gave up her dead.

At first he only caught her peeping round the corner at him, drawing aside a corner of an enormous curtain, as it were; striving for more complete entrance as though the mass

220

of it were difficult to move. But he understood; he knew; he recognised. It was enough for that. An entrance into his being—heart, mind, soul—was being attempted, and the entrance, because of his stolid temperament, was difficult of accomplishment. There was effort, strain. Something in him had first to be opened up, widened, made soft and ready as by an operation, before full entrance could be effected. This much he grasped, though for the life of him he could not have put it into words. Also, he knew *who* it was that sought an entrance. Deliberately from himself he withheld the name. But he knew, as surely as though Straughan stood in the room and faced him with a knife, saying, 'Let me in, let me in. I wish you to know I'm here. I'm clearing a way...! You recall our promise...?'

He rose from his chair and went to the open window again, the strange fear slowly passing. The cool air fanned his cheeks. Beauty, till now, had scarcely ever brushed the surface of his soul. He had never troubled his head about it. It passed him by, indifferent; and he had ever loathed the mouthy prating of it on others' lips. He was practical; beauty was for dreamers, for women, for men who had means and leisure. He had not exactly scorned it; rather it had never touched his life, to sweeten, cheer, uplift. Artists for him were like monks—another sex almost, useless beings who never helped the world go round. He was for action always, work, activity, achievement—as he saw them. He remembered Straughan vaguely—Straughan, the ever impecunious, friend of his youth, always talking of colour, sound—mysterious, ineffective things. He even forgot what they had quarrelled about, if they *had* quarrelled at all even; or why they had gone apart all these years ago. And, certainly, he had forgotten any promise. Memory, as yet, only peeped round the corner of that huge curtain at him, tentatively, suggestively yet—he was obliged to admit it—somewhat winningly. He was conscious of this gentle, sweet seductiveness that now replaced his fear.

And, as he stood now at the open window, peering over huge London, Beauty came close and smote him between the eyes. She came blindingly, with her train of stars and clouds and perfumes. Night, mysterious, myriad-eyed, and flaming across her sea of haunted shadows, invaded his heart and shook him with her immemorial wonder and delight. He found no words, of course, to clothe the new, unwonted sensations. He only knew that all his former dread, uneasiness, distress, and with them this idea of 'growth' that had seemed so repugnant to him, were merged, swept up, and gathered magnificently home into a wave of Beauty that enveloped him. 'See it ... and understand,' ran a secret inner whisper across his mind. He saw. He understood....

He went back and turned the lights out. Then he took his place again at that open window, drinking in the night. He saw a new world; a species of intoxication held him. He sighed ... as his thoughts blundered for expression among words and sentences that knew him not. But the delight was there, the wonder, the mystery. He watched, with heart alternately tightening and expanding, the transfiguring play of moon and shadow over the sea of buildings. He saw the dance of the hurrying clouds, the open patches into outer space, the veiling and unveiling of that ancient silvery face; and he caught strange whispers of the hierophantic, sacerdotal Power that had echoed down the world since Time began and dropped strange magic phrases into every poet's heart since first 'God dawned on Chaos'—the Beauty of the Night....

A long time passed—it may have been one hour, it may have been three—when at length he turned away and went slowly to his bedroom. A deep peace lay over him. Something quite new and blessed had crept into his life and thought. He could not quite understand it all. He only knew that it uplifted. There was no longer the least sign of affliction or distress. Even the inevitable reaction that, of course, set in could not destroy that.

And then, as he lay in bed, nearing the borderland of sleep, suddenly and without any obvious suggestion to bring it, he remembered another thing. He remembered the promise. Memory got past the big curtain for an instant, and showed her face. She looked into his eyes. It must have been a dozen years ago when Straughan and he had made that foolish, solemn promise that whoever died first should show himself, if possible, to the other.

He had utterly forgotten it—till now. But Straughan had not forgotten it. The letter came three weeks later, from India. That very evening Straughan had died—at nine o'clock. And he had come back—in the Beauty that he loved.

THE TRANSFER

THE child first began to cry in the early afternoon—about three o'clock, to be exact. I remember the hour, because I had been listening with secret relief to the sound of the departing carriage. Those wheels fading into distance down the gravel drive with Mrs. Frene, and her daughter Gladys to whom I was governess, meant for me some hours' welcome rest, and the June day was oppressively hot. Moreover, there was this excitement in the little country household that had told upon us all, but especially upon myself. This excitement, running delicately behind all the events of the morning, was due to some mystery, and the mystery was of course kept concealed from the governess. I had exhausted myself with guessing and keeping on the watch. For some deep and unexplained anxiety possessed me, so that I kept thinking of my sister's dictum that I was really much too sensitive to make a good governess, and that I should have done far better as a professional clairvoyante.

Mr. Frene, senior, 'Uncle Frank', was expected for an unusual visit from town about tea-time. That I knew. I also knew that his visit was concerned somehow with the future welfare of little Jamie, Gladys' seven-year-old brother. More than this, indeed, I never knew, and this missing link makes my story in a fashion incoherent—an important bit of the strange puzzle left out. I only gathered that the visit of Uncle Frank was of a condescending nature, that Jamie was told he must be upon his very best behaviour to make a good impression, and that Jamie, who had never seen his uncle, dreaded him horribly already in advance. Then, trailing thinly through the dying crunch of the carriage wheels this sultry afternoon, I heard the curious little wail of the child's crying, with the effect, wholly unaccountable, that every nerve in my body shot its bolt electrically, bringing me to my feet with a tingling of unequivocal alarm. Positively, the water ran into my eyes.

I recalled his white distress that morning when told that Uncle Frank was motoring down for tea and that he was to be 'very nice indeed' to him. It had gone into me like a knife. All through the day, indeed, had run this nightmare quality of terror and vision.

'The man with the 'normous face?' he had asked in a little voice of awe, and then gone speechless from the room in tears that no amount of soothing management could calm. That was all I saw; and what he meant by 'the 'normous face' gave me only a sense of vague presentiment. But it came as anti-climax somehow—a sudden revelation of the mystery and excitement that pulsed beneath the quiet of the stifling summer day. I feared for him. For of all that commonplace household I loved Jamie best, though professionally I had nothing to do with him. He was a high-strung, ultra-sensitive child, and it seemed to me that no one understood him, least of all his honest, tender-hearted parents; so that his little wailing voice brought me from my bed to the window in a moment like a call for help.

The haze of June lay over that big garden like a blanket; the wonderful flowers, which were Mr. Frene's delight, hung motionless; the lawns, so soft and thick, cushioned all other sounds; only the limes and huge clumps of guelder roses hummed with bees. Through this muted atmosphere of heat and haze the sound of the child's crying floated faintly to my ears—from a distance. Indeed, I wonder now that I heard it at all, for the next moment I saw him down beyond the garden, standing in his white sailor suit alone, two hundred yards away. He was down by the ugly patch where nothing grew—the Forbidden Corner. A faintness then came over me at once, a faintness as of death, when I saw him *there* of all places—where he never was allowed to go, and where, more-over, he was usually too terrified to go. To see him standing solitary in that singular spot, above all to hear him crying there, bereft me momentarily of the power to act. Then, before I could recover my composure sufficiently to call him in, Mr. Frene came round the corner from the Lower Farm with the dogs, and, seeing his son, performed that office for me. In his loud, goodnatured, hearty voice he called him, and Jamie turned and ran as though some spell had broken just in time— ran into the open arms of his fond but uncomprehending father, who carried him indoors on his shoulder, while asking 'what all this hubbub was about?' And, at their heels, the tail- less sheep-dogs followed, barking loudly, and performing what Jamie called their 'Gravel Dance', because they ploughed up the moist, rolled gravel with their feet.

I stepped back swiftly from the window lest I should be seen. Had I witnessed the saving of the child from fire or drowning the relief could hardly have been greater. Only Mr. Frene, I felt sure, would not say and do the right thing quite. He would protect the boy from his own vain imagin- ings, yet not with the explanation that could really heal. They disappeared behind the rose trees, making for the house. I saw no more till later, when Mr. Frene, senior, arrived.

To describe the ugly patch as 'singular' is hard to justify, perhaps, yet some such word is what the entire family sought, though never—oh, never!—used. To Jamie and myself, though equally we never mentioned it, that treeless, flowerless spot was more than singular. It stood at the far end of the magnificent rose garden, a bald, sore place, where the black earth showed uglily in winter, almost like a piece of dangerous bog, and in summer baked and cracked with fissures where green lizards shot their fire in passing. In contrast to the rich luxuriance of the whole amazing garden it was like a glimpse of death amid life, a centre of disease that cried for healing lest it spread. But it never did spread. Behind it stood the thick wood of silver birches and, glimmering beyond, the orchard meadow, where the lambs played.

The gardeners had a very simple explanation of its barren- ness—that the water all drained off it owing to the lie of the slope immediately about it, holding no remnant to keep the soil alive. I cannot say. It was Jamie—Jamie who felt its spell and haunted it, who spent whole hours there, even while afraid, and for whom it was finally labelled 'strictly out of bounds' because it stimulated his already big imagination, not wisely but too darkly—it was Jamie who buried ogres there and heard it crying in an earthy voice, swore that it shook its surface sometimes while he watched it, and secretly gave it food in the form of birds or mice of rabbits he found dead upon his wanderings. And it was Jamie who put so extraordinarily into words the *feeling* that the horrid spot had given me from the moment I first saw it.

'It's bad, Miss Gould,' he told me.

'But Jamie, nothing in Nature is bad—exactly; only different from the rest sometimes.'

'Miss Gould, if you please, then it's empty. It's not fed. It's dying because it can't get the food it wants.'

And when I stared into the little pale face where the eyes shone so dark and wonderful, seeking within myself for the right thing to say to him, he added, with an emphasis and conviction that made me suddenly turn cold: 'Miss Gould'—he always used my name like this in all his sentences—'it's hungry, don't you see? But *I* know what would make it feel all right.'

Only the conviction of an earnest child, perhaps, could have made so outrageous a suggestion worth listening to for an instant; but for me, who felt that things an imaginative child believed were important, it came with a vast disquieting shock of reality. Jamie, in this exaggerated way, had caught at the edge of a shocking fact—a hint of dark, undiscovered truth had leaped into that sensitive imagination. Why there lay horror in the words I cannot say, but I think some power of darkness trooped across the suggestion of that sentence at the end, 'I know what would make it feel all right.' I remember that I shrank from asking explanation. Small groups of other words, veiled forunately by his silence, gave life to an unspeakable possibility that hitherto had lain at the back of my own consciousness. The way it sprang to life proves, I think, that my mind already contained it. The blood rushed from my heart as I listened. I remember that my knees shook. Jamie's idea was—had been all along—my own as well.

And now, as I lay down on my bed and thought about it all, I understood why the coming of his uncle involved somehow an experience that wrapped terror at its heart. With a sense of nightmare certainty that left me too weak to resist the preposterous idea, too shocked, indeed, to argue or reason it away, this certainty came with its full, black blast of conviction; and the only way I can put it into words, since nightmare horror really is not properly tellable at all, seems this: that there *was* something missing in that dying patch of garden; something lacking that it ever searched for; something, once found and taken, that would turn it rich and living as the rest; more—that there *was* some living person who could do this for it. Mr. Frene, senior, in a word, 'Uncle Frank,' was this person who out of his abundant life could supply the lack—unwittingly.

For this connection between the dying, empty patch and the person of this vigorous, wealthy, and successful man had already lodged itself in my subconsciousness before I was aware of it. Clearly it must have lain there all along, though hidden. Jamie's words, his sudden pallor, his vibrating emotion of fearful anticipation had developed the plate, but it was his weeping alone there in the Forbidden Corner that had printed it. The photograph shone framed before me in the air. I hid my eyes. But for the redness—the charm of my face goes to pieces unless my eyes are clear—I could have cried. Jamie's words that morning about the ''normous face' came back upon me like a battering-ram.

Mr. Frene, senior, had been so frequently the subject of conversation in the family since I came, I had so often heard him discussed, and had then read so much about him in the papers—his energy, his philanthropy, his success with everything he laid his hand to—that a picture of the man had grown complete within me. I knew him as he was—within; or, as my sister would have said—clairvoyantly. And the only time I saw him (when I took Gladys to a meeting where he was chairman, and later *felt* his atmosphere and presence while for a moment he patronisingly spoke with her) had justified the portrait I had drawn. The rest, you may say, was a woman's wild imagining; but I think rather it was that kind of divining intuition which women share with children. If souls could be made visible, I would stake my life upon the truth and accuracy of my portrait.

For this Mr. Frene was a man who drooped alone, but grew vital in a crowd—because he used their vitality. He was a supreme, unconscious artist in the science of taking the fruits of others' work and living—for his own advantage. He vampired, unknowingly no doubt, every one with whom he came in contact; left them exhausted, tired, listless. Others fed him, so that while in a full room he shone, alone by himself and with no life to draw upon he languished and declined. In the man's immediate neighbourhood you felt his presence draining you; he took your ideas, your strength, your very words, and later used them for his own benefit and aggrandisement. Not evilly, of course; the man was good enough; but you felt that he was dangerous owing to the facile way he absorbed into himself all loose vitality that was to be had. His eyes and voice and presence devitalised you. Life, it seemed, not highly organised enough to resist, must shrink from his too near approach and hide away for fear of being appropriated, for fear, that is, of—death.

Jamie, unknowingly, put in the finishing touch to my unconscious portrait. The man carried about with him some silent, compelling trick of drawing out all your reserves— then swiftly pocketing them. At first you would be conscious of taut resistance; this would slowly shade off into weariness; the will would become flaccid; then you either moved away or yielded—agreed to all he said with a sense of weakness pressing ever closer upon the edges to collapse. With a male antagonist it might be different, but even then the effort of resistance would generate force that *he* absorbed and not the other. He never gave out. Some instinct taught him how to protect himself from that. To human beings, I mean, he never gave out. This time it was a very different matter. He had no more chance than a fly before the wheels of a huge—what

Jamie used to call—'attraction' engine.

So this was how I saw him—a great human sponge, crammed and soaked with the life, or proceeds of life, absorbed from others—stolen. My idea of a human vampire was satisfied. He went about carrying these accumulations of the life of others. In this sense his 'life' was not really his own. For the same reason, I think, it was not so fully under his control as he imagined.

And in another hour this man would be here. I went to the window. My eye wandered to the empty patch, dull black there amid the rich luxuriance of the garden flowers. It struck me as a hideous bit of emptiness yawning to be filled and nourished. The idea of Jamie playing round its bare edge was loathsome. I watched the big summer clouds above, the stillness of the afternoon, the haze. The silence of the overheated garden was oppressive. I had never felt a day so stifling, motionless. It lay there waiting. The household, too, was waiting—waiting for the coming of Mr. Frene from London in his big motor-car.

And I shall never forget the sensation of icy shrinking and distress with which I heard the rumble of the car. He had arrived. Tea was all ready on the lawn beneath the lime trees, and Mrs. Frene and Gladys, back from their drive, were sitting in wicker chairs. Mr. Frene, junior, was in the hall to meet his brother, but Jamie, as I learned afterwards, had shown such hysterical alarm, offered such bold resistance, that it had been deemed wiser to keep him in his room. Perhaps, after all, his presence might not be necessary. The visit clearly had to do with something on the uglier side of life—money, settlements, or what not; I never knew exactly; only that his parents were anxious, and that Uncle Frank had to be propitiated. It does not matter. That has nothing to do with the affair. What has to do with it—or I should not be telling the story—is that Mrs. Frene sent for me to come down 'in my nice white dress, if I didn't mind,' and that I was terrified, yet pleased, because it meant that a pretty face would be considered a welcome addition to the visitor's landscape. Also, most odd it was, I felt my presence was somehow inevitable, that in some way it was intended that I should witness what I did witness. And the instant I came upon the lawn—I hesitate to set it down, it sounds so foolish, disconnected—I could have sworn, as my eyes met his, that a kind of sudden darkness came, taking the summer brilliance out of everything, and that it was caused by troops of small black horses that raced about us from his person—to attack.

After a first momentary approving glance he took no further notice of me. The tea and talk went smoothly; I helped to pass the plates and cups, filling in pauses with little under-talk to Gladys. Jamie was never mentioned. Outwardly all seemed well, bur inwardly everything was awful—skirting the edge of things unspeakable, and so charged with danger that I could not keep my voice from trembling when I spoke.

I watched his hard, bleak face; I noticed how thin he was, and the curious, oily brightness of his steady eyes. They did not glitter, but they drew you with a sort of soft, creamy shine like Eastern eyes. And everything he said or did announced what I may dare to call the *suction* of his presence. His nature achieved this result automatically. He dominated us all, yet so gently that until it was accomplished no one noticed it.

Before five minutes had passed, however, I was aware of one thing only. My mind focused exclusively upon it, and so vividly that I marvelled the others did not scream, or run, or do something violent to prevent it. And it was this: that, separated merely by some dozen yards of so, this man, vibrating with the acquired vitality of others, stood within easy reach of that spot of yawning emptiness, waiting and eager to be filled. Earth scented her prey.

These two active 'centres' were within fighting distance; he so thin, so hard, so keen, yet really spreading large with the loose 'surround' of others' life he had appropriated, so practised and triumphant; that other so patient, deep, with so mighty a draw of the whole earth behind it, and—ugh!—so obviously aware that its opportunity at last had come.

231

I saw it all as plainly as though I watched two great animals prepare for battle, both unconsciously; yet in some inexplicable way I saw it, of course, within me, and not externally. The conflict would be hideously unequal. Each side had already sent out emissaries, how long before I could not tell, for the first evidence *he* gave that something was going wrong with him was when his voice grew suddenly confused, he missed his words, and his lips trembled a moment and turned flabby. The next second his face betrayed that singular and horrid change, growing somehow loose about the bones of the cheek, and larger, so that I remembered Jamie's miserable phrase. The emissaries of the two kingdoms, the human and the vegetable, had met, I make it out, in that very second. For the first time in his long career of battening on others, Mr. Frene found himself pitted against a vaster kingdom than he knew and, so finding, shook inwardly in that little part that was his definite actual self. He felt the huge disaster coming.

'Yes, John,' he was saying, in his drawling, self-congratulating voice, 'Sir George gave me that car—gave it to me as a present. Wasn't it char——?' and then broke off abruptly, stammered, drew breath, stood up, and looked uneasily about him. For a second there was a gaping pause. It was like the click which starts some huge machinery moving—that instant's pause before it actually starts. The whole thing, indeed, then went with the rapidity of machinery running down and beyond control. I thought of a giant dynamo working silently and invisible.

'What's that?' he cried, in a soft voice charged with alarm. 'What's that horrid place? And some one's crying there—who is it?'

He pointed to the empty patch. Then, before any one could answer, he started across the lawn towards it, going every minute faster. Before any one could move he stood upon the edge. He leaned over—peering down into it.

It seemed a few hours passed, but really they were seconds, for time is measured by the quality and not the quantity of sensations it contains. I saw it all with merciless, photographic detail, sharply etched amid the general confusion. Each side was intensely active, but only one side, the human, exerted *all* its force—in resistance. The other merely stretched out a feeler, as it were, from its vast, potential strength; no more was necessary. It was such a soft and easy victory. Oh, it was rather pitiful! There was no bluster of great effort, on one side at least. Close by his side I witnessed it, for I, it seemed, alone had moved and followed him. No one else stirred, though Mrs. Frene clattered noisily with the cups, making some sudden impulsive gesture with her hands, and Gladys, I remember, gave a cry—it was like a litle scream—'Oh, mother, it's the heat, isn't it?' Mr. Frene, her father, was speechless, pale as ashes.

But the instant I reached his side, it became clear what had drawn me there thus instinctively. Upon the other side, among the silver birches, stood little Jamie. He was watching. I experienced—for him—one of those moments that shake the heart; a liquid fear ran all over me, the more effective because unintelligible really. Yet I felt that if I could know all, what lay actually behind, my fear would be more than justified; that the thing *was* awful, full of awe.

And then it happened—a truly wicked sight—like watching a universe in action, yet all contained within a small square foot of space. I think he understood vaguely that if some one could only take his place he might be saved, and that was why, discerning instinctively the easiest substitute within reach, he saw the child and called aloud to him across the empty patch, 'James, my boy, come here!'

His voice was like a thin report, but somehow flat and lifeless, as when a rifle misses fire, sharp, yet weak; it had no 'crack' in it. It was really supplication. And, with amazement, I heard my own ring out imperious and strong, though I was not conscious of saying it, 'Jamie, don't move. Stay where you are!' But Jamie, the little child, obeyed neither of us. Moving up nearer to the edge, he stood there—laughing! I heard that laughter, but could have sworn it did not come from him. The empty, yawning patch gave out that sound.

Mr. Frene turned sideways, throwing up his arms. I saw

his hard, bleak face grow somehow wider, spread through the air, and downwards. A similar thing, I saw, was happening at the same time to his entire person, for it drew out into the atmosphere in a stream of movement. The face for a second made me think of those toys of green indiarubber that children pull. It grew enormous. But this was an external impression only. What actually happened, I clearly understood, was that all this vitality and life he had transferred from others to himself for years was now in turn being taken from him and transferred—elsewhere.

One moment on the edge he wobbled horribly, then with that queer sideways motion, rapid yet ungainly, he stepped forward into the middle of the patch and fell heavily upon his face. His eyes, as he dropped, faded shockingly, and across the countenance was written plainly what I can only call an expression of destruction. He looked utterly destroyed. I caught a sound—from Jamie?—but this time not of laughter. It was like a gulp; it was deep and muffled and it dipped away into the earth. Again I thought of a troop of small black horses galloping away down a subterranean passage beneath my feet—plunging into the depths—their tramping growing fainter and fainter into buried distance. In my nostrils was a pungent smell of earth.

And then—all passed. I came back into myself. Mr. Frene, junior, was lifting his brother's head from the lawn where he had fallen from the heat, close beside the tea-table. He had never really moved from there. And Jamie, I learned afterwards, had been the whole time asleep upon his bed upstairs, worn out with his crying and unreasoning alarm. Gladys came running out with cold water, sponge and towel, brandy too—all kinds of things. 'Mother, it *was* the heat, wasn't it?' I heard her whisper, but I did not catch Mrs. Frene's reply. From her face it struck me that she was bordering on collapse herself. Then the butler followed, and they just picked him up and carried him into the house. He recovered even before the doctor came.

But the queer thing to me is that I was convinced the others all had seen what I saw, only that no one said a word about it; and to this day no one *has* said a word. And that was, perhaps, the most horrid part of all.

From that day to this I have scarcely heard a mention of Mr. Frene, senior. It seemed as if he dropped suddenly out of life. The papers never mentioned him. His activities ceased, as it were. His after-life, at any rate, became singularly ineffective. Certainly he achieved nothing worth public mention. But it may be only that, having left the employ of Mrs. Frene, there was no particular occasion for me to hear anything.

The after-life of that empty patch of garden, however, was quite otherwise. Nothing, so far as I know, was done to it by gardeners, or in the way of draining it or bringing in new earth, but even before I left in the following summer it had changed. It lay untouched, full of great, luscious, driving weeds and creepers, very strong, full-fed, and bursting thick with life.

CLAIRVOYANCE

In the darkest corner, where the firelight could not reach him, he sat listening to the stories. His young hostess occupied the corner on the other side; she was also screened by shadows; and between them stretched the horse-shoe of eager, frightened faces that seemed all eyes. Behind yawned the blackness of the big room, running as it were without a break into the night.

Some one crossed on tiptoe and drew a blind up with a rattle, and at the sound all started: through the window, opened at the top, came a rustle of the poplar leaves that stirred like footsteps in the wind. 'There's a strange man walking past the shrubberies,' whispered a nervous girl; 'I saw him crouch and hide. I saw his eyes!' 'Nonsense!' came sharply from a male member of the group; 'it's far too dark to see. You heard the wind.' For mist had risen from the river just below the lawn, pressing close against the windows of the old house like a soft grey hand, and through it the stir of leaves was faintly audible.... Then, while several called for lights, others remembered that hop-pickers were still about in the lanes, and the tramps this autumn overbold and insolent. All, perhaps, wished secretly for the sun. Only the elderly man in the corner sat quiet and unmoved, contributing nothing. He had told no fearsome story. He had evaded, indeed, many openings expressly made for him, though fully aware that to his well-known interest in psychical things was partly due his presence in the week-end party. 'I never have experiences— that way,' he said shortly when some one asked him point blank for a tale; 'I have no unusual powers.' There was per- haps the merest hint of contempt in his tone, but the hostess from her darkened corner quickly and tactfully covered his retreat. And he wondered. For he knew why she invited him. The haunted room, he was well aware, had been specially allotted to him.

And then, most opportunely, the door opened noisily and the host came in. He sniffed at the dakrness, rang at once for lamps, puffed at his big curved pipe, and generally, by his mere presence, made the group feel rather foolish. Light streamed past him from the corridor. His white hair shone like silver. And with him came the atmosphere of common sense, of shooting, agriculture, motors, and the rest. Age entered at that door. And his young wife sprang up instantly to greet him, as though his disapproval of this kind of entertainment might need humouring.

It may have been the light—that witchery of half-lights from the fire and the corridor, or it may have been the abrupt entrance of the Practical upon the soft Imaginative that traced the outline with such pitiless, sharp conviction. At any rate, the contrast—for those who had this inner clairvoyant sight all had been prating of so glibly!—was unmistakably revealed. It was poignantly dramatic, pain somewhere in it—naked pain. For, as she paused a moment there beside him in the light, this childless wife of three years' standing, picture of youth and beauty, there stood upon the threshold of that room the presence of a true ghost story.

And most marevellously she changed—her lineaments, her very figure, her whole presentment. Etched against the gloom, the delicate, unmarked face shone suddenly keen and anguished, and a rich maturity, deeper than any mere age, flushed all her little person with its secret grandeur. Lines started into being upon the pale skin of the girlish face, lines of pleading, pity, and love the daylight did not show, and with them an air of magic tenderness that betrayed, though for a second only, the full soft glory of a motherhood denied, yet somehow mysteriously enjoyed. About her slenderness rose all the deep-bosomed sweetness of maternity, a potential mother of the world, and a mother, though she might know no dear fulfilment, who yet yearned to sweep into her immense embrace all the little helpless things that ever lived.

Light, like emotion, can play strangest tricks. The change pressed almost upon the edge of revelation.... Yet, when a moment later lamps were brought, it is doubtful if any but the silent guest who had told no marvellous tale, knew no psychical experience, and disclaimed the smallest clairvoyant faculty, had received and registered the vivid, poignant picture. For an instant it had flashed there, mercilessly clear for all to see who were not blind to subtle spiritual wonder thick with pain. And it was not so much mere picture of youth and age ill-matched, as of youth that yearned with the oldest craving in the world, and of age that had slipped beyond the power of sympathetically divining it.... It passed, and all was as before.

The husband laughed with genial good-nature, not one whit annoyed. 'They've been frightening you with stories, child,' he said in his jolly way, and put a protective arm about her. 'Haven't they now? Tell me the truth. Much better,' he added, 'have joined me instead at billiards, or for a game of Patience, eh?' She looked up shyly into his face, and he kissed her on the forehead. 'Perhaps they have—a little, dear,' she said, 'but now that you've come, I feel all right again.' 'Another night of this,' he added in a graver tone, 'and you'd be at your old trick of putting guests to sleep in the haunted room. I was right after all, you see, to make it out of bounds.' He glanced fondly, paternally down upon her. Then he went over and poked the fire into a blaze. Some one struck up a waltz on the piano, and couples danced. All trace of nervousness vanished, and the butler presently brought in the tray with drinks and biscuits. And slowly the group dispersed. Candles were lit. They passed down the passage into the big hall, talking in lowered voices of to-morrow's plans. The laughter died away as they went up the stairs to bed, the silent guest and the young wife lingering a moment over the embers.

'You have not, after all then, put me in your haunted room?' he asked quietly. 'You mentioned, you remember, in your letter——'

'I admit,' she replied at once, her manner gracious beyond her years, her voice quite different, 'that I wanted you to sleep there—some one, I mean, who really knows, and is not merely curious. But—forgive my saying so—when I *saw* you'—she laughed very slowly—'and when you told no marvellous story like the others, I somehow felt——'

'But I never *see* anything——' he put in hurriedly.

'You *feel*, though,' she interrupted swiftly, the passionate tenderness in her voice but half suppressed. 'I can tell it from your——'

'Others, then,' he interrupted abruptly, almost bluntly, 'have slept there—sat up, rather?'

'Not recently. My husband stopped it.' She paused a second, then added, 'I had that room — for a year—when first we married.'

The other's anguished look flew back upon her little face like a shadow and was gone, while at the sight of it there rose in himself a sudden deep rush of wonderful amazement beckoning almost towards worship. He did not speak, for his voice would tremble.

'I had to give it up,' she finished, very low.

'Was it so terrible?' after a pause he ventured.

She bowed her head. 'I had to change,' she repeated softly.

'And since then—*now*—you see nothing?' he asked.

Her reply was singular. 'Because I will not, not because it's gone.' ... He followed her in silence to the door, and as they passed along the passage, again that curious great pain of emptiness, of loneliness, of yearning rose upon him, as of a sea that never, never can swim beyond the shore to reach the flowers that it loves ...

'Hurry up, child, or a ghost will catch you,' cried her husband, leaning over the banisters, as the pair moved slowly up the stairs towards him. There was a moment's silence when they met. The guest took his lighted candle and went down the corridor. Good-nights were said again. They moved away, she to her loneliness, he to his unhaunted room. And at his door he turned. At the far end of the passage, silhouetted against the candle-light, he watched them—the fine old man with his silvered hair and heavy shoulders, and the slim young wife with that amazing air as of some great bountiful mother of the world for whom the years yet passed hungry and unharvested. They turned the corner, and he went in and closed his door.

Sleep took him very quickly, and while the mist rose up and veiled the countryside, something else, veiled equally for all other sleepers in that house but two, drew on towards its climax.... Some hours later he awoke; the world was still, and it seemed the whole house listened; for with that clear vision which some bring out of sleep, he remembered that there had been no direct denial, and of a sudden realised that this big, gaunt chamber where he lay was after all the haunted room. For him, however, the entire world, not merely separate rooms in it, was ever haunted; and he knew no terror to find the space about him charged with thronging life quite other than his own.... He rose and lit the candle, crossed over to the window where the mist shone grey, knowing that no barriers of walls or door or ceiling could keep out this host of Presences that poured so thickly everywhere about him. It was like a wall of being, with peering eyes, small hands stretched out, a thousand pattering wee feet, and tiny voices crying in a chorus very faintly and beseeching.... The haunted room! Was it not, rather, a temple vestibule, prepared and sanctified by yearning rites few men might ever guess, for all the childless women of the world? How could she know that *he* would understand—this woman he had seen but twice in all his life? And how entrust to him so great a mystery that was her secret? Had she so easily divined in him a similar yearning to which, long years ago, death had denied fulfilment? Was she clairvoyant in the true sense, and did all faces bear on them so legibly this great map that sorrow traced?...

And then, with awful suddenness, mere feelings dipped away, and something concrete happened. The handle of the door had faintly rattled. He turned. The round brass knob was slowly moving. And first, at the sight, something of common fear did grip him, as though his heart had missed a beat, but on the instant he heard the voice of his own mother, now long beyond the stars, calling to him to go softly yet with speed. He watched a moment the feeble efforts to undo the door, yet never afterwards could swear that he saw actual movement, for something in him, tragic as blindness, rose through a mist of tears and darkened vision utterly....

He went towards the door. He took the handle very gently, and very softly then he opened it. Beyond was darkness. He saw the empty passage, the edge of the banisters where the great hall yawned below, and, dimly, the outline of the Alpine photograph and the stuffed deer's head upon the wall. And then he dropped upon his knees and opened wide his arms to something that came in upon uncertain, viewless feet. All the young winds and flowers and dews of dawn passed with it ... filling him to the brim ... covering closely his breast and eyes and lips. There clung to him all the small beginnings of life that cannot stand alone ... the little helpless hands and arms that have no confidence ... and when the wealth of tears and love that flooded his heart seemed to break upon the frontiers of some mysterious yet impossible fulfilment, he rose and went with curious small steps towards the window to taste the cooling, misty air of that other dark Emptiness that waited so patiently there above the entire world. He drew the sash up. The air felt soft and tender as though there were somewhere children in it too—children of stars and flowers, of mists and wings and music, all that the Universe contains unborn and tiny.... And when at length he turned again the door was closed. The room was empty of any life but that which lay so wonderfully blessed within himself. And this, he felt, had marvellously increased and multiplied....

Sleep then came back to him, and in the morning he left the house before the others were astir, pleading some overlooked engagement. For he had seen Ghosts indeed, but yet no ghost that he could talk about with others round an open fire.

THE GOLDEN FLY

I⊤ fell upon him out of a clear sky just when existence seemed on its very best behaviour, and he savagely resented the undeserved affliction of it. Involving him in an atrocious scandal that reflected directly upon his honour, it destroyed in a moment the erection his entire life had so laboriously built up—his reputation. In the eyes of the world he was a broken, discredited man, at the very moment, moreover, when his most cherished ambitions touched fulfilment. And the cruelty of it appalled his sense of justice, for it was impossible to vindicate himself without inculpating others who were dearer to him than life. It seemed more than he could bear; and the grim course he contemplated—decision itself as yet hung darkly waiting in the background—appeared the only way of escape that offered.

He had discussed the matter with friends until his brain whirled. Their sympathy maddened him, with hints of *qui s'excuse s'accuse*, and he turned at last in desperation to something that could not answer back. For the first time in his life he turned to Nature—to that dead, inanimate Nature he had left to poets and rhapsodising women: 'I must face it alone,' he put it. For the Finger of God was a phrase without meaning to him, and his entire being contained no trace of the religious instinct. He was a business man, honest, selfish, and ambitious; and the collapse of his worldly position was paramount to the collapse of the universe itself—his universe, at any rate. This 'crumbling of the universe' was the thought he took out with him. He left the house by the path that led into solitude, and reached the heathery expanse that formed one of the breathing-places of the New Forest. There he flung himself down wearily in the shadow of a little pine-copse. And his crumbled universe lay down with him, for he could not escape it.

Taking the pistol from the hip-pocket where it hurt him, he lay upon his back and watched the clouds. Half stunned, half dazed, he stared into the sky. The perfumed wind played

242

softly on his eyes; he smelt the heather-honey; golden flies hung motionless in the air, like coloured pins fastening the sunshine against the blue curtain of the summer, while dragon-flies, like darting shuttles, wove across its pattern their threads of gleaming bronze. He heard the petulant crying of the peewits, and watched their tumbling flight. Below him tinkled a rivulet, its brown water rippling between banks of peaty earth. Everywhere was singing, peace, and careless unconcern.

And this lordly indifference of Nature calmed and soothed him. Neither human pain nor the injustice of man could shift the key of the water, alter the peewits' cry a single tone, nor influence one fraction of an inch those cloudy frigates of vapour that sailed the sky. The earth bulged sunwards as she had bulged for centuries. The power of her steady gait, superbly calm, breathed everywhere with grandeur—undismayed, unhasting, and supremely confident.... And, like the flash of those golden flies, there leaped suddenly upon him this vivid thought: that his world of agony lay neatly buttoned up within the tiny space of his own brain. Outside himself it had no existence at all. His mind contained it—the minute interior he called his heart. From this vaster world about him it lay utterly apart, like deeds in the black boxes of japanned tin he kept at the office, shut off from the universe, huddled in an overcrowded space within his skull.

How this commonplace thought reached him, garbed in such startling novelty, was odd enough; for it seemed as though the fierceness of his pain had burned away something. His thoughts it merely enflamed; but this other thing it consumed. Something that had obscured clear vision shrivelled before it as a piece of paper, eaten up by fire, dwindles down into a thimbleful of unimportant ashes. The thicket of his mind grew half transparent. At the farther end he saw, for the first time—light. The perspective of his inner life, hitherto so enormous, telescoped into the proportions of a miniature. Just as momentous and significant as before, it was somehow abruptly different—seen from another point of view. The suffering had burned up rubbish he himself had piled over the head of a little Fact. Like a point of metal that glows yet will not burn, he discerned in the depths of him the essential shining fact that not all this ruinous conflagration could destroy. And this brilliant, indestructible kernel was—his Innocence. The rest was self-reared rubbish: opinion of the world. He had magnified an atom into a universe....

Pain, as it seemed, had cleared a way for the sublimity of Nature to approach him. The calm old Universe rolled past. The deep, majestic Day gave him a push, as though the shoulder of some star had brushed his own. He had thought his feelings were the world: instead, they were merely his way of looking at it. The actual 'world' was some glorious, unchanging thing he never saw direct. His attitude of mind was but a peephole into it. The choice of his particular peephole, moreover, lay surely within the power of his individual will. The anguish, centred upon so small a point, had seemed to affect the entire spread universe around him, whereas in reality it affected nothing but his attitude of mind towards it. The truism struck him like a blow between the eyes, that a man is what he thinks or feels himself to be. It leaped the barrier between words and meaning. The intellectual concept became a hard-edged fact, because he realised it—for the first time in his very circumscribed life. And this dreadful pain that had made even suicide seem desirable was entirely a fabrication of his own mind. The universe about him rolled on just the same in the majesty of its eternal purpose. His tiny inner world was clouded, but the glory of this stupendous world about him was undimmed, untroubled, unaffected. Even death itself....

With a swift smash of the hand he crushed the golden fly that settled on his knee. The murder was done impulsively, utterly without intention. He watched the little point of gold quiver for a moment among the hairs of the rough tweed; then lie still for ever ... but the scent of heather-honey filled the air as before; the wind passed sighing through the pines; the clouds still sailed their uncharted sea of blue. There lay the whole spread surface of the Forest in the sun. Only the attitude of the golden fly towards it all was gone. A single, tiny point of view had disappeared. Nature passed on calmly and unhasting; she took no note.

Then, with a rush of awe, another thought flashed through him: Nature *had* taken note. There was a difference everywhere. Not a sparrow falleth, he remembered, without God knowing. God was certainly in Nature somewhere. His clumsy senses could not register this difference, yet it was there. His own small world, fed by these senses, was after all the merest little corner of Existence. To the whole of Existence, that included himself, the golden fly, the sun, and all the stars, he must somehow answer for his crime. It was a wanton interference with a sublime and sovereign Purpose that he now divined for the first time. He looked at the wee point of gold lying still and silent in the forest of hairs. He realised the enormity of his act. It could not have been graver had he put out the sun, or the little, insignificant flame of his own existence. He had done a criminal, evil thing, for he had put an end to a certain point of view; had wiped it out; made it impossible. Had the fly been quicker, less easily overwhelmed, or more tenacious of the scrap of universal life it used, Nature would at this instant be richer for its little contribution to the whole of things—to which he himself also belonged. And wherein, he asked himself, did he differ from that fly in the importance, the significance of his contribution to the universe? The soul ...? He had never given the question a single thought; but if the scrap of life he owned was called a soul, why should that point of golden glory not comprise one too? Its minute size, its trivial purpose, its few hours of apparently futile existence ... these formed no true criterion ...!

Similarly, the thought rushed over him, a Hand was being stretched out to crush himself. His pain was the shadow of its approach; anger in his heart, the warning. Unless he were quick enough, adroit and skilled enough, he also would be wiped out, while Nature continued her slow, unhasting way without him. His attitude towards the personal pain was really the test of his ability, of his merit—of his right to survive. Pain teaches, pain develops, pain brings growth: he had heard it since his copybook days. But now he realised it, as again thought leaped the barrier between familiar words and meaning. In his attitude of mind to his catastrophe lay his salvation or his ... death.

In some such confused and blundering fashion, because along unaccustomed channels, the truth charged into him to overwhelm, yet bringing with it an unwonted sense of joy that seemed to break a crust which long had held back—life. Thus tapped, these sources gushed forth and bubbled over, spread about his being, flooded him with hope and courage, above all with—calmness. Nature held forces just as real and living as human sympathy, and equally able to modify the soul. And Nature was always accessible. A sense of huge companionship, denied him by the littleness of his fellow-men, stole sweetly over him It was amazingly uplifting, yet fear came close behind it, as he realised the presumption of his former attitude of cynical indifference. These Powers were aware of his petty insolence, yet had not crushed him.... It was, of course, the awakening of the religious instinct in a man who hitherto had worshipped merely a rather low-grade form of intellect.

And, while the enormous confusion of it shook him, this sense of incommunicable sweetness remained. Bright haunting eyes, with love in them, gazed at him from the blue; and this thing that came so close, stood also far away upon the line of the horizon. It was everywhere. It filled the hollows, but towered over him as well towards the pinnaces of cloud. It was in the sharpness of the peewits' cry, and in the water's murmur. It whispered in the pine-boughs, and blazed in every patch of sunlight. And it was glory, pure and simple. It filled him with a sense of strength for which he could find but one description—Triumph.

And so, first, the anger faded from his mind and crept away. Resentment then slunk after it. Revolt and disappointment also melted, and bitterness gave place to the most marvellous peace the man had ever known. Then came resignation to fill the empty places. Pain, as a means and not an end, had cleared the way, though the accomplishment was like a miracle. But Conversion *is* a miracle. No ordinary pain can bring it. This anguish he understood now in a new relation to life—as something to be taken willingly into himself and dealt with, all regardless of public opinion. What people said and thought was in their world, not in his. It was less than nothing. The pain cultivated dormant tracts. The terror also purged. It disclosed....

He watched the wind, and even the wind brought revelation; for without obstacles in its path it would be silent. He watched the sunshine, and the sunshine taught him too; for without obstacles to fling it back against his eye, he could never see it. He would neither hear the tinkling water nor feel the summer heat unless both one and other overcame some reluctant medium in their pathways. And, similarly with his moral being—his pain resulted from the friction of his personal ambitions against the stress of some noble Power that sought to lift him higher. That Power he could not know direct, but he recognised its strain against him by the resistance it generated in the inertia of his selfishness. His attitude of mind had switched completely round. It was what the preachers termed development through suffering.

Moreover, he had acquired this energy of resistance somehow from the wind and sun and the beauty of a common summer's day. Their peace and strength had passed into himself. Unconsciously on his way home he drew upon it steadily. He tossed the pistol into a pool of water. Nature had healed him; and Nature, should he turn weak again, was always there. It was very wonderful. He wanted to sing....

SPECIAL DELIVERY

MEIKLEJOHN the curate, was walking through the Jura when this thing happened to him. There is only his word to vouch for it, for the inn and its proprietor are now both of the past, and the local record of the occurrence has long since assumed the proportions of a picturesque but inaccurate legend. As a true story, however, it stands out from those of its kidney by the fact that there seems to have been a deliberate intention in it. It saved a life—a life the world had need of. And this singular rescue of a man of value to the best order of things makes one feel that there was some sense, even logic, in the affair.

Moreover, Meiklejohn asserts that it was the only psychic experience he ever knew. Things of the sort were not a 'habit' with him. His rescue, thus was not one of those meaningless interventions that puzzle the man in the street while they exhilarate the psychologist. It was a deliberate and very determined affair.

Meiklejohn found himself that hot August night in one of the valleys that slip like blue shadows hidden among pinewoods between the Swiss frontier and France. He had passed Ste. Croix earlier in the day; Les Rasses had been left behind about four o'clock; Buttes, and the Val de Travers, where the cement of many a London street comes from, was his goal. But the light failed long before he reached it, and he stopped at an inn that appeared unexpectedly round a corner of the dusty road, built literally against the great cliffs that formed one wall of the valley. He was so footsore, and his knapsack so heavy, that he turned in without more ado.

Le Guillaume Tell was the name of the inn—dirty white walls, with thin, almost mangy vines scrambling over the door, and the stream brawling beneath shuttered windows with green and white stripes all patched by sun and rain. His room was sevenpence, his dinner of soup, omelette, fruit, cheese, and coffee, a franc. The prices suited his pocket and

248

made him feel comfortable and at home. Immediately behind the hotel—the only house visible, except the sawmill across the road, rose the ever-crumbling ridges and precipices that formed the flanks of Chasseront and ran on past La Sagne towards the grey Aiguilles de Baulmes. He was in the Jura fastnesses where tourists rarely penetrate.

Through the low doorway of the inn he carried with him the strong atmosphere of thoughts that had accompanied him all day—dreams of how he intended to spend his life, plans of sacrifice and effort. For his hopes of great achievement, even then at twenty-five, were a veritable passion in him, and his desire to spend himself for humanity a devouring flame. So occupied, indeed, was his mind with the emotions belonging to this line of thinking, that he hardly noticed the singular, though exceedingly faint, sense of alarm that stirred somewhere in the depths of his being as he passed within that doorway where the dropping vine-leaves clutched at his hat. He remembered it a little later. The sense of danger had been touched in him. He felt at the moment only a hint of discomfort, too vague to claim definite recognition. Yet it was there—the instant he stepped within the threshold—and afterwards he distinctly recalled its sudden and unaccountable advent.

His bedroom, though stuffy, as from windows long unopened, was clean; carpetless, of course, and primitive, with white pine floor and walls, and the short bed, smothered under its duvet, very creaky. And very short! For Meiklejohn was well over six feet.

'I shall have to curl up, as usual, in a knot,' was his reflection as he measured the bed with his eye; 'though to-night I think— after my twenty miles in this air——'

The thought refused to complete itself. He was going to add that he was tired enough to have slept on a stone floor, but for some undefined reason the same sense of alarm that had tapped him on the shoulder as he entered the inn returned now when he contemplated the bed. A sharp repugnance for that bed, as sudden and unaccountable as it was curious, swept into him—and was gone again before he had time to seize it wholly. It was in reality so slight that he dismissed it immediately as the merest fancy; yet, at the same time, he was aware that he would rather have slept on another bed, had there been one in the room—and then the queer feeling that, after all, perhaps, he would *not* sleep there in the end at all. How this idea came to him he never knew. He records it, however, as part of the occurrence.

After eight o'clock a few peasants, and workmen from the sawmill, came in to drink their *demi-litre* of red wine in the common room downstairs, to stare at the unexpected guest, and to smoke their vile tobacco. They were neither picturesque nor amusing—simply dirty and slightly malodorous. At nine o'clock Meiklejohn knocked the ashes from his briar pipe upon the limestone window-ledge, and went upstairs, overpowered with sleep. The sense of alarm had utterly disappeared; his mind was busy once more with his great dreams of the future—dreams that materialised themselves, as all the world knows, in the famous Meiklejohn Institutes....

Berthoud, the proprietor, short and sturdy, with his faded brown coat and no collar, slightly confused with red wine and a 'tourist' guest, showed him the way up. For, of course, there was no *femme de chambre*.

'You have the corridor all to yourself,' the man said; showed him the best corner of the landing to shout from in case he wanted anything—there being no bell—eyed his boots, knapsack, and flask with considerable curiosity, wished him goodnight, and was gone. He went downstairs with a noise like a horse, thought the curate, as he locked the door after him.

The windows had been open now for a couple of hours, and the room smelt sweet with the odours of sawn wood and shavings, the resinous perfume of the surrounding hosts of pines, and the sharp, delicate touch of a lonely mountain valley where civilisation has not yet tainted the air. Whiffs of coarse tobacco, pungent without being offensive, came invisibly through the cracks of the floor. Primitive and simple it all was—a—sort of vigorous 'backwoods' atmosphere. Yet, once again, as he turned to examine the room after Berthoud's steps had blundered down below into the passage, something rose faintly within him to set his nerves mysteriously a-quiver.

Out of these perfectly simple conditions, without the least apparent cause, the odd feeling again came over him that he was—in danger.

The curate was not much given to analysis. He was a man of action pure and simple, as a rule. But to-night, in spite of himself, his thoughts went plunging, searching, asking. For this singular message of dread that emanated as it were from the room, or from some article of furniture in the room perhaps—that bed still touched his mind with a peculiar repugnance—demanded somewhat insistently for an explanation. And the only explanation that suggested itself to his unimaginative mind was that the forces of nature hereabouts were—overpowering; that, after the slum streets and factory chimneys of the last twelve months, these towering cliffs and smothering pine-forests communicated to his soul a word of grandeur that amounted to awe. Inadequate and far-fetched as the explanation seems, it was the only one that occurred to him; and its value in this remarkable adventure lies in the fact that he connected his sense of danger partly with the bed and partly with the mountains.

'I felt once or twice,' he said afterwards, 'as though some powerful agency of a spiritual kind were all the time trying to beat into my stupid brain a message of warning.' And this way of expressing it is more true and graphic than many paragraphs of attempted analysis.

Meiklejohn hung his clothes by the open window to air, washed, read his Bible, looked several times over his shoulder without apparent cause, and then knelt down to pray. He was a simple and devout soul; his Self lost in the yearning, young but sincere, to live for humanity. He prayed, as usual, with intense earnestness that his life might be preserved for use in the world, when in the middle of his prayer—there came a knocking at the door.

Hastily rising from his knees, he opened. The sound of rushing water filled the corridor. He heard the voices of the workmen below in the drinking-room. But only darkness stood in the passages, filling the house to the very brim. No one was there. He returned to his interrupted devotions.

'I imagined it,' he said to himself. He continued his prayers, however, longer than usual. At the back of his thoughts, dim, vague, half-defined only, lay this lurking sense of uneasiness—that he was in danger. He prayed earnestly and simply, as a child might pray, for the preservation of his life....

Again, just as he prepared to get into bed, struggling to make the heaped-up duvet spread all over, came that knocking at the bedroom door. It was soft, wonderfully soft, and something within him thrilled curiously in response. He crossed the floor to open—then hesitated. Suddenly he understood that that knocking at the door was connected with the sense of danger in his heart. In the region of subtle intuitions the two were linked. With this realisation there came over him, he declares, a singular mood in which, as in a revelation, he knew that Nature held forces that might somehow communicate directly and positively with—human beings. This thought rushed upon him out of the night, as it were. It arrested his movements. He stood there upon the bare pine boards, hesitating to open the door.

The delay thus described lasted actually only a few seconds, but in those few seconds these thoughts tore rapidly and like fire through his mind. The beauty of this lost and mysterious valley was certainly in his veins. He felt the strange presence of the encircling forests, soft and splendid, their million branches sighing in the night airs. The crying of the falling water touched him. He longed to transfer their peace and power to the hearts of suffering thousands of men and women and children. The towering precipices that literally dropped their pale walls over the roof of the inn lifted his thoughts to their own wind-swept heights; he longed to convey their message of inflexible strength to the weak-kneed folk in the slums where he worked. He was peculiarly conscious of the presence of these forces of Nature—the irresistible powers that regenerate as easily as they destroy.

All this, and far more, swept his soul like a huge wind as he stood there, waiting to open the door in answer to that mysterious soft knocking.

And there, when at length he opened, stood the figure of a man—staring at him and smiling.

Disappointment seized him instantly. He had expected, almost believed, that he would see something un-ordinary; and instead, there stood a man who had merely mistaken the door of his room, and was now bowing his apology for the interruption. Then, to his amazement, he saw that the man beckoned: the figure was some one who sought to draw him out.

'Come with me,' it seemed to say.

But Meiklejohn only realised this afterwards, he says, when it was too late and he had already shut the door in the stranger's face. For the man had withdrawn into the darkness a little, and the curate had taken the movement for a mere acknowledgment of his mistake instead of—as he afterwards felt—a sign that he should follow.

'And the moment the door was shut,' he says, 'I felt that it would have been better for me to have gone out into the passage to see what he wanted. It came over me that the man had something important to say to me. I had missed it.'

For some seconds, it seemed, he resisted the inclination to go after him. He argued with himself; then turned to his bed, pulled back the sheets and heavy duvet, and was met sharply again with the sense of repugnance, almost of fear, as before. It leaped out upon him—as though the drawing back of the blankets had set free some cold blast of wind that struck him across the face and made him shiver.

At the same moment a shadow fell from behind his shoulder and dropped across the pillow and upper half of the bed. It may, of course, have been the magnified shadow of the moth that buzzed about the pale-yellow electric light in the ceiling. He does not pretend to know. It passed swiftly, however, and was gone; and Meiklejohn, feeling less sure of himself than ever before in his life, crossed the floor quickly, almost running, and opened the door to go after the man who had knocked—twice. For in reality less than half a minute had passed since the shutting of the door and its reopening.

But the corridor was empty. He marched down the pine-board floor for some considerable distance. Below he saw the glimmer of the hall, and heard the voices of the peasants and workmen from the sawmill as they still talked and drank their red wine in the public room. That sound of falling water, as before, filled the air. Darkness reigned. But the person—the *messenger*—who had twice knocked at his door was gone utterly.... Presently a door opened downstairs, and the peasants clattered out noisily. He turned and went back to bed. The electric light was switched off below. Silence fell. Conquering his strange repugnance, Meiklejohn, with a prayer on his lips, got into bed, and in less than ten minutes was sound asleep.

'I admit,' he says, in telling the story, 'that what happened afterwards came so swiftly and so confusingly, yet with such a storm of overwhelming conviction of its reality, that its sequence may be somewhat blurred in my memory, while, at the same time, I see it after all these years as though it was a thing of yesterday. But in my sleep, first of all, I again heard that soft, mysterious tapping—not in the course of a dream of any sort, but sudden and alone out of the dark blank of forgetfulness. I tried to wake. At first, however, the bonds of unconsciousness held me tight. I had to struggle in order to return to the waking world. There was a distinct effort before I opened my eyes; and in that slight interval I became aware that the person who had knocked at the door had mean-while opened it and passed into the room. I had left the lock unturned. The person was close beside me in the darkness—not in utter darkness, however, for a rising three-quarter moon shed its faint silver upon the floor in patches, and as I sprang swiftly from the bed, I noticed something alive moving towards me across the carpetless boards. Upon the edges of a patch of moonlight, where the fringe of silver and shadow mingled, it stopped. Three feet away from it I, too, stopped, shaking in every muscle. It lay there crouching at my very feet, staring up at me. But was it man or was it animal? For at first I took it certainly for a human being on all fours; but the next moment, with a spasm of genuine terror that half stopped my breath, it was borne in upon me that the creature was—nothing human. Only in this way can I describe it. It was identical with the human figure who had knocked before and beckoned to me to follow, but it was another presentation of that figure.

'And it held (or brought, if you will) some tremendous message for me—some message of tremendous importance, I mean. The first time I had argued, resisted, refused to listen. Now it had returned in a form that ensured obedience. Some quite terrific power emanated from it—a power that I understood instinctively belonged to the mountains and the forests and the untamed elemental forces of Nature. Amazing as it may sound in cold blood, I can only say that I felt as though the towering precipices outside had sent me a direct warning—that my life was in immediate danger.

'For a space that seemed minutes, but was probably less than a few seconds, I stood there trembling on the bare boards, my eyes riveted upon the dark, uncouth shape that covered all the floor beyond. I saw no limbs or features, no suggestion of outline that I could connect with any living form I know, animate or inanimate. Yet it moved and stirred all the time— *whirled within itself*, describes it best; and into my mind sprang a picture of an immense dark wheel, turning, spinning, whizzing so rapidly that it appears motionless, and uttering that low and ominous thunder that fills a great machinery-room of a factory. Then I thought of Ezekiel's vision of the Living Wheels....

'And it must have been at this instant, I think, that the muttering and deep note that issued from it formed itself into words within me. At any rate, I heard a voice that spoke with unmistakable intelligence:

' "Come!" it said. "Come out—at once!" And the sense of power that accompanied the Voice was so splendid that my fear vanished and I obeyed instantly without thinking more. I followed; it led. It altered in shape. The door *was* open. It ran silently in a form that was more like a stream of deep black water than anything else I can think of—out of the room, down the stairs, across the hall, and up to the deep shadows that lay against the door leading into the road. There I lost sight of it.'

Meiklejohn's only desire, he says, then was to rush after it—to escape. This he did. He understood that somehow it had passed through the door into the open air. Ten seconds later, perhaps even less, he, too, was in the open air. He acted almost automatically; reason, reflection, logic all swept away. Nowhere, however, in the soft moonlight about him was any sign of the extraordinary apparition that had succeeded in drawing him out of the inn, out of his bedroom, out of his—bed. He stared in a dazed way at everything—just beginning to get control of his faculties a bit—wondering what in the world it all meant. That huge spinning form, he felt convinced, lay hidden somewhere close beside him, waiting for the end. The danger it had enabled him to avoid was close at hand.... He *knew* that, he says....

There lay the meadows, touched here and there with wisps of floating mist; the stream roared and tumbled down its rocky bed to his left; across the road the sawmill lifted its skeleton-like outline, moonlight shining on the dew-covered shingles of the roof, its lower part hidden in shadow. The cold air of the valley was exquisitely scented.

To the right, where his eye next wandered, he saw the thick black woods rising round the base of the precipices that soared into the sky, sheeted with silvery moonlight. His gaze ran up them to the far ridges that seemed to push the very stars farther into the heavens. Then, as he saw those stars crowding the night, he staggered suddenly backwards, seizing the wall of the road for support, and catching his breath. For the top of the cliff, he fancied, moved. A group of stars was for a fraction of a second—hidden. The earth—the scenery of the valley, at least—turned about him. Something prodigious was happening to the solid structure of the world. The precipices seemed to bend over upon the valley. The far, uppermost ridge of those beetling cliffs shifted downwards. Meiklejohn declares that the way its movement hid momentarily a group of stars was the most startling—for some reason horrible—thing he had ever witnessed.

Then came the roar and crash and thunder as the mass toppled, slid, and finally—took the frightful plunge. How long the forces of rain and frost had been chiselling out the slow detachment of the giant slabs that fell, or whence came the particular extra little push that drove the entire mass out from the parent rock, no one can know. Only one thing is certain: that it was due to no chance, but to the nicely and exactly calculated results of balanced cause and effect. From the beginning of time it had been known—it might have been accurately calculated, rather—that this particular thousand tons of rock would break away from the crumbling tops of the precipices and crash downwards with the roar of many tempests into the lost and mysterious mountain valley where Meiklejohn the curate spent such and such a night of such and such a holiday. It was just as sure as the return of Halley's comet.

'I watched it,' he says, 'because I couldn't do anything else. I would far rather have run—I was so frightfully close to it all—but I couldn't move a muscle. And in a few seconds it was over. A terrific wind knocked me backwards against the stone wall; there was a vast clattering of smaller stones, set rolling down the neighbouring couloirs; a steady roll of echoes ran thundering up and down the valley; and then all was still again exactly as it had been before. And the curious thing was—ascertained a little later, as you may imagine, and not at once—that the inn, being so closely built up against the cliffs, had almost entirely escaped. The great mass of rock and trees had taken a leap farther out, and filled the meadows, blocked the road, crushed the sawmill like a matchbox, and dammed up the stream; but the inn itself was almost untouched.

'*Almost*—for a single block of limestone, about the size

of a grand piano, had dropped straight upon one corner of the roof and smashed its way through my bedroom, carrying everything it contained down to the level of the cellar, so terrific was the momentum of its crushing journey. Not a stick of the furniture was afterwards discoverable—as such. The bed seems to have been caught by the very middle of the fallen mass.'

The confusion in Meiklejohn's mind may be imagined— the rush of feeling and emotion that swept over him. Berthoud and the peasants mustered in less than a dozen minutes, talking, crying, praying. Then the stream, dammed up by the accumulation of rock, carried off the debris of the broken roof and walls in less than half an hour. The rock, however, that swept the room and the *empty* bed of Meiklejohn the curate into dust, still lies in the valley where it fell.

'The only other thing that I remember,' he says, in telling the story, 'is that, as I stood there, shaking with excitement and the painful terror of it all, before Berthoud and the peasants had come to count over their number and learn that no one was missing—while I stood there, leaning against the wall of the road, something rose out of the white dust at my feet, and, with a noise like the whirring of some immense projectile, passed swiftly and invisibly away up into space—so far as I could judge, towards the distant ridges that reared their motionless outline in moonlight beneath the stars.'

THE DESTRUCTION
OF SMITH

Ten years ago, in the western States of America, I once met Smith. But he was no ordinary member of the clan: he was Ezekiel B. Smith of Smithville. He *was* Smithville, for he founded it and made it live.

It was in the oil region, where towns spring up on the map in a few days like mushrooms, and may be destroyed again in a single night by fire and earthquake. On a hunting expedition Smith stumbled upon a natural oil well, and instantly staked his claim; a few months later he was rich, grown into affluence as rapidly as that patch of wilderness grew into streets and houses where you could buy anything from an evening's gambling to a tin of Boston baked pork-and-beans. Smith was really a tremendous fellow, a sort of human dynamo of energy and pluck, with rare judgment in his great square head—the kind of judgment that in higher walks of life makes statesmen. His personality cut through the difficulties of life with the clean easy force of putting his whole life into anything he touched. 'God's own luck,' his comrades called it; but really it was sheer ability and character and personality. The man had power.

From the moment of that 'oil find' his rise was very rapid, but while his brains went into a dozen other big enterprises, his heart remained in little Smithville, the flimsy mushroom town he had created. His own life was in it. It was his baby. He spoke tenderly of its hideousness. Smithville was an intimate expression of his very self.

Ezekiel B. Smith I saw once only, for a few minutes; but I have never forgotten him. It was the moment of his death. And we came across him on a shooting trip where the forests melt away towards the vast plains of the Arizona desert. The personality of the man was singularly impressive. I caught myself thinking of a mountain, or of some elemental force of Nature so sure of itself that hurry is never necessary. And his gentleness was like the gentleness of women. Great strength often—the greatest always—has tenderness in it, a depth of tenderness unknown to pettier life.

Our meeting was coincidence, for we were hunting in a region where distances are measured by hours and the chance of running across white men very rare. For many days our nightly camps were pitched in spots of beauty where the loneliness is akin to the loneliness of the Egyptian Desert. On one side the mountain slopes were smothered with dense forest, hiding wee meadows of sweet grass like English lawns; and on the other side, stretching for more miles than a man can count, ran the desolate alkali plains of Arizona where tufts of sage-brush are the only vegetation till you reach the lips of the Colorado Canyons. Our horses were tethered for the night beneath the stars. Two backwoodsmen were cooking dinner. The smell of bacon over a wood fire mingled with the keen and fragrant air—when, suddenly, the horses neighed, signalling the approach of one of their own kind. Indians, white men—probably another hunting party—were within scenting distance, though it was long before my city ears caught any sound, and still longer before the cause itself entered the circle of our firelight.

I saw a square-faced man, tanned like a redskin, in a hunting shirt and a big sombrero, climb down slowly from his horse and move towards us keenly searching with his eyes; and at the same moment Hank, looking up from the frying-pan where the bacon and venison spluttered in a pool of pork-fat, exclaimed, 'Why, it's Ezekiel B.!' The next words, addressed to Jake, who held the kettle, were below his breath: 'And if he ain't all broke up! Jest look at the eyes on him!' I saw what he meant—the face of a human being distraught by some extraordinary emotion, a soul in violent distress, yet betrayal well kept under. Once, as a newspaper man, I had seen a murderer walk to the electric chair. The expression was similar. Death was *behind* the eyes, not in them. Smith brought in with him—terror.

In a dozen words we learned he had been hunting for some

weeks, but was now heading for Tranter, a 'stop-off' station where you could flag the daily train 140 miles south-west. He was making for Smithville, the little town that was the apple of his eye. Something 'was wrong' with Smithville. No one asked him what—it is the custom to wait till information is volunteered. But Hank, helping him presently to venison (which he hardly touched), said casually, 'Good hunting, Boss, your way?'; and the brief reply told much, and proved how eager he was to relieve his mind by speech. 'I'm glad to locate your camp, boys,' he said. 'That's luck. There's something going wrong'—and a catch came into his voice— 'with Smithville.' Behind the laconic statement emerged somehow the terror the man experienced. For Smith to confess cowardice and in the same breath admit mere 'luck', was equivalent to the hysteria that makes city people laugh or cry. It was genuinely dramatic. I have seen nothing more impressive by way of human tragedy—though hard to explain why—than this square-jawed, dauntless man, sitting there with the firelight on his rugged features, and saying this simple thing. For how in the world could he know it——?

In the pause that followed, his Indians came gliding in, tethered the horses, and sat down without a word to eat what Hank distributed. But nothing was to be read on their impassive faces. Redskins, whatever they may feel, show little. Then Smith gave us another pregnant sentence. '*They* heard it too,' he said, in a lower voice, indicating his three men; 'they saw it jest as I did.' He looked up into the starry sky a second. 'It's hard upon our trail right now,' he added, as though he expected something to drop upon us from the heavens. And from that moment I swear we all felt creepy. The darkness round our lonely camp hid terror in its folds; the wind that whispered through the dry sage-brush brought whispers and the shuffle of watching figures; and when the Indians went softly out to pitch the tents and get more wood for the fire, I remember feeling glad the duty was not mine. Yet this feeling of uneasiness is something one rarely experiences in the open. It belongs to houses, overwrought imaginations, and the presence of evil men. Nature gives peace and security. That we all felt it proves how real it was. And Smith, who felt it most, of course, had brought it.

'There's something gone wrong with Smithville' was an ominous statement of disaster. He said it just as a man in civilised lands might say, 'My wife is dying; a telegram's just come. I must take the train.' But how he felt so sure of it, a thousand miles away in this uninhabited corner of the wilderness, made us feel curiously uneasy. For it was an incredible thing—yet true. We all felt *that*. Smith did not imagine things. A sense of gloomy apprehension settled over our lonely camp, as though things were about to happen. Already they stalked across the great black night, watching us with many eyes. The wind had risen, and there were sounds among the trees. I, for one, felt no desire to go to bed. The way Smith sat there, watching the sky and peering into the sheet of darkness that veiled the Desert, set my nerves all jangling. He expected something—but what? It was following him. Across this tractless wilderness, apparently above him against the brilliant stars, Something was 'hard upon his trail.'

Then, in the middle of painful silences, Smith suddenly turned loquacious—further sign with him of deep mental disturbance. He asked questions like a schoolboy—asked them of me too, as being 'an edicated man.' But there were such queer things to talk about round an Arizona camp-fire that Hank clearly wondered for his sanity. He knew about the 'wilderness madness' that attacks some folks. He let his green cigar go out and flashed me signals to be cautious. He listened intently, with the eyes of a puzzled child, half cynical, half touched with superstitious dread. For, briefly, Smith asked me what I knew about stories of dying men appearing at a distance to those who loved them much. He had read such tales, 'heard tell of 'em,' but 'are they dead true, or are they jest little feery tales?' I satisfied him as best I could with one or two authentic stories. Whether he believed or not I cannot say; but his swift mind jumped in a flash to the point. 'Then, if that kind o' stuff is true,' he asked, simply, 'it looks as though a feller had a dooplicate of himself—sperrit maybe—that gits loose and active at the time of death, and heads straight for the party it loves best. Ain't that so, Boss?' I admitted the theory was correct. And then he startled us with a final question that made Hank drop an oath below his breath—sure evidence of uneasy excitement in the old backwoodsman. Smith whispered it, looking over his shoulder into the night: 'Ain't it jest possible then,' he asked, 'seeing that men an' Nature is all made of a piece like, that places too have this dooplicate appearance of theirselves that gits loose when they go under?'

It was difficult, under the circumstances, to explain that such a theory *had* been held to account for visions of scenery people sometimes have, and that a city may have a definite personality made up of all its inhabitants—moods, thoughts, feelings, and passions of the multitude who go to compose its life and atmosphere, and that hence is due the odd changes in man's individuality when he goes from one city to another. Nor was there any time to do so, for hardly had he asked his singular question when the horses whinnied, the Indians leaped to their feet as if ready for an attack, and Smith himself turned the colour of the ashes theat lay in a circle of whitish-grey about the burning wood. There was an expression in his face of death, or, as the Irish peasants say, 'destroyed.'

'That's Smithville,' he cried, springing to his feet, then tottering so that I thought he must fall into the flame; 'that's my baby town—got loose and huntin' for me, who made it, and love it better'n anything on Gawd's green earth!' And then he added with a kind of gulp in his throat as of a man who wanted to cry but couldn't: 'And it's going to bits—it's dying—and I'm not thar to save it——!'

He staggered and I caught his arm. The sound of his frightened, anguished voice, and the shuffling of our many feet among the stones, died away into the night. We all stood, staring. The darkness came up closer. The horses ceased their whinnying. For a moment nothing happened. Then Smith turned slowly round and raised his head towards the stars as though he saw something. 'Hear that?' he whispered. 'It's coming up close. That's what I've bin hearing now, on and off, two days and nights. Listen!' His whispering voice broke horribly; the man was suffering atrociously. For a moment he became vastly, horribly animated—then stood still as death.

But in the hollow silence, broken only by the sighing of the wind among the spruces, we at first heard nothing. Then most curiously, something like rapid driven mist came trooping down the sky, and veiled a group of stars. With it, as from an enormous distance, but growing swiftly nearer, came noises that were beyond all question the noises of a city rushing through the heavens. From all sides they came; and with them there shot a reddish, streaked appearance across the misty veil that swung so rapidly and softly between the stars and our eyes. Lurid it was, and in some way terrible. A sense of helpless bewilderment came over me, scattering my faculties as in scenes of fire, when the mind struggles violently to possess itself and act for the best. Hank, holding his rifle ready to shoot, moved stupidly round the group, equally at a loss, and swearing incessantly below his breath. For this overwhelming certainty that Something living had come upon us from the sky possessed us all, and I, personally, felt as if a gigantic Being swept against me through the night, destructive and enveloping, and yet that it was not one, but many. Power of action left me. I could not even observe with accuracy what was going on. I stared, dizzy and bewildered, in all directions; but my power of movement was gone, and my feet refused to stir. Only I remember that the Redskins stood like figures of stone, unmoved.

And the sounds about us grew into a roar. The distant murmur came past us like a sea. There was a babel of shouting. Here, in the deep old wilderness that knew no living human beings for hundreds of leagues, there was a tempest of voices calling, crying, shrieking; men's hoarse clamouring, and the high screaming of women and children. Behind it ran a booming sound like thunder. Yet all of it, while apparently so close above our heads, seemed in some inexplicable way far off in the distance—muted, faint, thinning out among the quiet stars. More like a *memory* of turmoil and tumult it seemed than the actual uproar heard at first hand. And through it ran the crash of big things tumbling, breaking, falling in destruction with an awful detonating thunder of collapse. I thought the hills were toppling down upon us. A shrieking city, it seemed, fled past us through the sky.

How long it lasted it is impossible to say, for my power of measuring time had utterly vanished. A dreadful wild anguish summed up all the feelings I can remember. It seemed I watched, or read, or dreamed some desolating scene of disaster in which human life went overboard wholesale, as though one threw a hatful of insects into a blazing fire. This idea of burning, of thick suffocating smoke and savage flame, coloured the entire experience. And the next thing I knew was that it had passed away as completely as though it had never been at all; the stars shone down from an air of limpid clearness, and—there was a smell of burning leather in my nostrils. I just stepped back in time to save my feet. I had moved in my excitement against the circle of hot ashes. Hank pushed me back roughly with the barrel of his rifle.

But, strangest of all, I understood, as by some flash of divine intuition, the reason of this abrupt cessation of the horrible tumult. The Personality of the town, set free and loosened in the moment of death, had returned to him who gave it birth, who loved it, and of whose life it was actually an expression. The Being of Smithville was literally a projection, an emanation of the dynamic, vital personality of its puissant creator. And, in death, it had returned on him with the shock of an accumulated power impossible for a human being to resist. For years he had provided it with life—but *gradually*. It now rushed back to its source, thus concentrated, in a single terrific moment.

'That's him,' I heard a voice saying from a great distance as it seemed. 'He's fired his last shot—!' and saw Hank turning the body over with his riflebutt. And, though the face itself was calm beneath the stars, there was an attitude of limbs and body that suggested the bursting of an enormous shell that had twisted every fibre by its awful force yet somehow left the body as a whole intact.

We carried 'it' to Tranter, and at the first real station along the line we got the news by telegraph: 'Smithville wiped out by fire. Burned two days and nights. Loss of life, 3000.' And all the way in my dreams I seemed still to hear that curious, dreadful cry of Smithville, the shrieking city rushing headlong through the sky.

THE TRYST

As he got out of the train at the little wayside station he remembered the conversation as if it had been yesterday, instead of fifteen years ago—and his heart went thumping against his ribs so violently that he almost heard it. The original thrill came over him again with all its infinite yearning. He felt it as he had felt it *then*—not with that tragic lessening the interval had brought to each repetition of its memory. Here, in the familiar scenery of its birth, he realised with mingled pain and wonder that the subsequent years had not destroyed, but only dimmed it. The forgotten rapture flamed back with all the fierce beauty of its genesis, desire at white heat. And the shock of the abrupt discovery shattered time. Fifteen years became a negligible moment; the crowded experiences that had intervened seemed but a dream. The farewell scene, the conversation on the steamer's deck, were clear as of the day before. He saw the hand holding her big hat that fluttered in the wind, saw the flowers on the dress where the long coat was blown open a moment, recalled the face of a hurrying steward who had jostled them; he even heard the voices—his own and hers:

'Yes,' she said simply; 'I promise you. You have my word. I'll wait——'

'Till I come back,' he interrupted.

Steadfastly she repeated his actual words, then added: 'Here; at home—that is.'

'I'll come to the garden gate as usual,' he told her, trying to smile. 'I'll knock. You'll open the gate—as usual—and come out to me.'

These words, too, she attempted to repeat, but her voice failed, her eyes filled suddenly with tears; she looked into his face and smiled. It was just then that her little hand went up to hold the hat on—he saw the very gesture still. He remembered that he was vehemently tempted to tear his ticket

267

up there and then, to go ashore with her, to stay in England, to brave all opposition—when the siren roared its third horrible warning ... and the ship put out to sea.

Fifteen years, thick with various incident, had passed between them since that moment. His life had risen, fallen, crashed, then risen again. He had come back at last, fortune won by a lucky coup—at thirty-five; had come back to find her, come back, above all, to keep his word. Once every three months they had exchanged the brief letter agreed upon: 'I am well; I am waiting; I am happy; I am unmarried. Yours——.' For his youthful wisdom had insisted that no 'man' had the right to keep 'any woman' too long waiting; and she, thinking that letter brave and splendid, had insisted likewise that he was free—if freedom called him. They had laughed over this last phrase in their agreement. They put five years as the possible limit of separation. By then he would have won success, and obstinate parents would have nothing more to say.

But when five years ended he was 'on his uppers' in a western mining town, and with the end of ten in sight those uppers, though changed, were little better, apparently, than patched and mended. It was just then, too, that the change which had been stealing over him first betrayed itself. He realised it abruptly, a sense of shame and horror in him. The discovery was made unconsciously: it disclosed itself. He was reading her letter as a labourer on a Californian fruit farm: 'Funny she doesn't marry—someone else!' he heard himself say. The words were out before he knew it, and certainly before he could suppress them. They just slipped out, startling him into the truth; and he knew instantly that the thought was fathered in him by a hidden wish.... He was older. He had lived. It was a memory he loved.

Despising himself in a contradictory fashion—both vaguely and fiercely—he yet held true to his boyhood's promise. He did not write and offer to release her as he knew they did in stories; he persuaded himself that he meant to keep his word. There was this fine, stupid, selfish obstinacy in his character. In any case, she would misunderstand and think he wanted to set free—himself. 'Besides—I'm still—awfully fond of her,' he asserted. And it was true; only the love, it seemed, had gone its way. Not that another woman took it; he kept himself clean, held firm as steel. The love, apparently, just faded of its own accord; her image dimmed, her letters had ceased to thrill, then ceased to interest him.

Subsequent reflection made him realise other details about himself. In the interval he had suffered hardships, had learned the uncertainty of life that depends for its continuance on a little food, but that food often hard to come by, and had seen so many others go under that he held it more cheaply than of old. The wandering instinct, too, had caught him, slowly killing the domestic impulse; he lost his desire for a settled place of abode, the desire for children of his own, lost the desire to marry at all. Also—he reminded himself with a smile—he had lost other things: the expression of youth *she* was accustomed to and held always in her thoughts of him, two fingers of one hand, his hair! He wore glasses, too. The gentlemen-adventurers of life get scarred in those wild places where he lived. He saw himself a rather battered specimen well on the way to middle age.

There was confusion in his mind, however, *and* in his heart: a struggling complex of emotions that made it difficult to know exactly what he did feel. The dominant clue concealed itself. Feelings shifted. A single, clear determinant did not offer. He was an honest fellow. 'I can't quite make it out,' he said. 'What is it I really feel? And why?' His motive seemed obscured. To keep the flame alight for the long buffeting years was no small achievement; better men had succumbed in half the time. Yet something in him still held fast to the girl as with a band of steel that *would* not let her go entirely. Occasionally there came strong reversions, when he ached with longing, yearning, hope; when he loved her again; re-membered passionately each detail of the far-off courtship days in the forbidden rectory garden beyond the small, white garden gate. Or was it merely the image and the memory he loved 'again'? He hardly knew himself. He could not tell.

That 'again' puzzled him. It was the wrong word surely....
He still wrote the promised letter, however; it was so easy;
those short sentences could not betray the dead or dying fires.
One day, besides, he would return and claim her. He meant
to keep his word.

And he had kept it. Here he was, this calm September
afternoon, within three miles of the village where he first
had kissed her, where the marvel of first love had come to
both; three short miles between him and the little white garden
gate of which at this very moment she was intently thinking,
and behind which some fifty minutes later she would be standing, waiting for him....

He had purposely left the train at an earlier station; he would
walk the three miles in the dusk, climb the familiar steps,
knock at the white gate in the wall as of old, utter the promised
words, 'I have come back to find you,' enter, and—keep his
word. He had written from Mexico a week before he sailed;
he had made careful, even accurate calculations: 'In the dusk,
on the sixteenth of September, I shall come and knock,' he
added to the usual sentences. The knowledge of his coming,
therefore, had been in her possession seven days. Just before
sailing, moreover, he had heard from her—though not in
answer, naturally. She was well; she was happy; she was
unmarried; she was waiting.

And now, as by some magical process of restoration—possible
to deep hearts only, perhaps, though even to them quite
inexplicable—the state of first love had blazed up again in
him. In all its radiant beauty it lit his heart, burned unextinguish-
ed in his soul, set body and mind on fire. The years had merely
veiled it. It burst upon him, captured, overwhelmed him
with the suddenness of a dream. He stepped from the
train. He met it in the face. It took him prisoner. The familiar
trees and hedges, the unchanged countryside, the 'fields-smells
known in infancy,' all these, with something subtly added
to them, rolled back the passion of his youth upon him in
a flood. No longer was he bound upon what he deemed,
perhaps, an act of honourable duty; it was love that drove

him, as it drove him fifteen years before. And it drove him with the accumulated passion of desire long forcibly repressed; almost as if, out of some fancied notion of fairness to the girl, he had deliberately, yet still unconsciously, said 'No' to it; that *she* had not faded, but that he had decided, '*I* must forget her.' That sentence: 'Why dosen't she marry—someone else?' had not betrayed change in himself. It surprised another motive: 'It's not fair to—her!'

His mind worked with a curious rapidity, but worked within one circle only. The stress of sudden emotion was extraordinary. He remembered a thousand things; yet, chief among them, those occasional reversions when he had felt he 'loved her again.' Had he not, after all, deceived himself? Had she ever really 'faded' at all? Had he not felt he ought to let her fade—release her that way? And the change in himself?—that sentence on the Californian fruit-farm—what did they mean? Which had been true, the fading or the love?

The confusion in his mind was hopeless, but, as a matter of fact, he did not think at all: he only felt. The momentum, besides, was irresistible, and before the shattering onset of the sweet revival he did not stop to analyse the strange result. He knew certain things, and cared to know no others: that his heart was leaping, his blood running with the heat of twenty, that joy recaptured him, that he must see, hear, touch her, hold her in his arms—and marry her. For the fifteen years had crumbled to a little thing, and at thirty-five he felt himself but twenty, rapturously, deliciously in love.

He went quickly, eagerly, down the little street to the inn, still feeling only, not thinking anything. The vehement uprush of the old emotion made reflection of any kind impossible. He gave no further thought to those long years 'out there,' when her name, her letters, the very image of her in his mind had found him, if not cold, at least without keen response. All that was forgotten as though it had not been. The steadfast thing in him, this strong holding to a promise which had never wilted, ousted the recollection of fading and decay that, whatever caused them, certainly had existed. And this steadfast thing now took command. This enduring quality in his character led him. It was only towards the end of the hurried tea he first received the singular impression—vague, indeed, but undeniably persistent—that he was *being* led.

Yet, though aware of this, he did not pause to argue or reflect. The emotional displacement in him, of course, had been more than considerable: there had been upheaval, a change whose abruptness was even dislocating, fundamental in a sense he could not estimate—shock. Yet he took no count of anything but the one mastering desire to get to her as soon as possible, knock at the small, white garden gate, hear her answering voice, see the low wooden door swing open—take her. There was joy and glory in his heart, and a yearning sweet delight. At this very moment she was expecting him. And he—had come.

Behind these positive emotions, however, there lay concealed all the time others that were of a negative character. Consciously, he was not aware of them, but they were there; they revealed their presence in various little ways that puzzled him. He recognised them absent-mindedly, as it were; did not analyse or investigate them. For, through the confusion upon his faculties, rose also a certain hint of insecurity that betrayed itself by a slight hesitancy or miscalculation in one or two unimportant actions. There was a touch of melancholy, too, a sense of something lost. It lay, perhaps, in that tinge of sadness which accompanies the twilight of an autumn day, when a gentler, mournful beauty veils a greater beauty that is past. Some trick of memory connected it with a scene of early boyhood, when, meaning to see the sunrise, he overslept, and, by a brief half-hour, was just—too late. He noted it merely, then passed on; he did not understand it; he hurried all the more, this hurry the only sign that it *was* noted. 'I must be quick,' flashed up across his strongly positive emotions.

And, due to this hurry, possibly, were the slight miscalculations that he made. They were very trivial. He rang for sugar, though the bowl stood just before his eyes, yet when the girl

came in he forgot completely what he rang for—and inquired
instead about the late trains back to London. And, when the
time-table was laid before him, he examined it without intelligence, then looked up suddenly into the maid's face with
a question about flowers. Were there flowers to be had in
the village anywhere? What kind of flowers? 'Oh, a bouquet
or a'—he hesitated, searching for a word that tried to present
itself, yet was not the word *he* wanted to make use of—'or
a wreath—of some sort?' he finished. He took the very word
he did not want to take. In several things he did and said,
this hesitancy and miscalculation betrayed themselves—such
trivial things, yet significant in and elusive way that he disliked.
There was sadness, insecurity somewhere in them. And he
resented them, though aware of their existence only because
they qualified his joy. There was a whispered 'No' floating
somewhere in the dusk. Almost—he felt disquiet. He hurried, more and more eager to be off upon his journey—the final
part of it.

Moreover, there were other signs of an odd miscalculation—
dislocation, perhaps, properly speaking—in him. Though
the inn was familiar from his boyhood days, kept by the same
old couple, too, he volunteered no information about himself,
nor asked a single question about the village he was bound
for. He did not even inquire if the rector—her father—still
were living. And when he left he entirely neglected the gilt-
framed mirror above the mantelpiece of plush, dusty pampas-
grass in waterless vases on either side. It did not matter,
apparently, whether he looked well or ill, tidy or untidy.
He forgot that when his cap was off the absence of thick,
accustomed hair must alter him considerably, forgot also
that two fingers were missing from one hand, the right hand,
the hand that she would presently clasp. Nor did it occur
to him that he wore glasses, which must change his expression
and add to the appearance of the years he bore. None of these
obvious and natural things seemed to come into his thoughts
at all. He was in a hurry to be off. He did not think. But
though his mind may not have noted these slight betrayals

with actual sentences, his attitude, nevertheless, expressed them. This was, it seemed, the feeling in him: 'What could such details matter to her *now*? Why, indeed, should he give to them a single thought? It was himself she loved and waited for, not separate items of his external, physical image.' As well think of the fact that she, too, must have altered—outwardly. It never once occurred to him. Such details were of To-day.... He was only impatient to come to her quickly, very quickly, instantly, if possible. He hurried.

There was a flood of boyhood's joy in him. He paid for his tea, giving a tip that was twice the price of the meal, and set out gaily and impetuously along the winding lane. Charged to the brim with a sweet picture of a small, white garden gate, the loved face close behind it, he went forward at a headlong pace, singing 'Nancy Lee' as he used to sing it fifteen years before.

With action, then, the negative sensations hid themselves, obliterated by the positive ones that took command. The former, however, merely lay concealed; they waited. Thus, perhaps, does vital emotion, overlong restrained, denied, indeed, of its blossoming altogether, take revenge. Repressed element in his psychic life asserted themselves, selecting, as though naturally a dramatic form.

The dusk fell rapidly, mist rose in floating strips along the meadows by the stream; the old, familiar details beckoned him forwards, then drove him from behind as he went swiftly past them. He recognised others rising through the thickening air beyond; they nodded, peered, and whispered, sometimes they almost sang. And each added to his inner happiness; each brought its sweet and precious contribution, and built it into the reconstructed picture of the earlier, long-forgotten rapture. It was an enticing and enchanted journy that he made, something impossibly blissful in it, something, too, that seemed curiously irresistible.

For the scenery had not altered all these years, the details of the country were unchanged, everything he saw was rich with dear and precious association, increasing the momentum of the tide that carried him along. Yonder was the stile over whose broken step he had helped her yesterday, and there the slippery plank across the stream where she looked above her shoulder to ask for his support; he saw the very bramble bushes where she scratched her hand, a-blackberrying, the day before ... and, finally, the weather-stained signpost, 'To the Rectory.' It pointed to the path through the dangerous field where Farmer Sparrow's bull provided such a sweet excuse for holding, leading—protecting her. From the entire landscape rose a stream of recent memory, each incident alive, each little detail brimmed with its cargo of fond association.

He read the rough black lettering on the crooked arm—it was rather faded, but he knew it too well to miss a single letter —and hurried forward along the muddy track; he looked about him for a sign of Farmer Sparrow's bull; he even felt in the misty air for the little hand, that he might take and lead her into safety. The thought of her drew him on with such irresistible anticipation that it seemed as if the cumulative drive of vanished and unsated years evoked the tangible phantom almost. He actually felt it, soft and warm and clinging in his own, that was no longer incomplete and mutilated.

Yet it was not he who led and guided now, but, more and more, he who was being led. The hint had first betrayed its presence at the inn; it now openly declared itself. It had crossed the frontier into a positive sensation. Its growth, swiftly increasing all this time, had accomplished itself; he had ignored, somehow, both its genesis and quick development; the result he plainly recognised. She was expecting him, indeed, but it was more than expectation; there was calling in it—she summoned him. Her thought and longing reached him along that old, invisible track love builds so easily between true, faithful hearts. All the forces of her being, her very voice, came towards him through the deepening autumn twilight. He had not noticed the curious physical restoration in his hand, but he was vividly aware of this more magical alteration—that *she* led and guided him, drawing him ever more swiftly towards the little, white garden gate where

275

she stood at this very moment, waiting. Her sweet strength compelled him; there was this new touch of something irresistible about the familiar journey, where formerly had been delicious yielding only, shy, tentative advance.

His footsteps hurried, faster and ever faster; so deep was the allurement in his blood, he almost ran. He reached the narrow, winding lane, and raced along it. He knew each bend, each angle of the holly hedge, each separate incident of ditch and stone. He could have plunged blindfold down it at top speed. The familiar perfumes rushed at him—dead leaves and mossy earth and ferns and dock leaves, bringing the bewildering currents of strong emotion in him all together as in a rising wave. He saw, then, the crumbling wall, the cedars topping it with spreading branches, the chimneys of the rectory. On his right bulked the outline of the old, grey church; the twisted, ancient yews, the company of gravestones, upright and leaning, dotting the ground like listening figures. But he looked at none of these. For, a little beyond, he already saw the five rough steps of stone that led from the lane towards a small, white garden gate. That gate at last shone before him, rising through the misty air. He reached it.

He stopped dead a moment. His heart, it seemed, stopped too, then took to violent hammering in his brain. There was a roaring in his mind, and yet a marvellous silence—just behind it. Then the roar of emotion died away. There was utter stillness. This stillness, silence, was all about him. The world seemed preternaturally quiet.

But the pause was too brief to measure. For the tide of emotion had receded only to come on again with redoubled power. He turned, leaped forward, clambered impetuously up the rough stone steps, and flung himself, breathless and exhausted, against the trivial barrier that stood between his eyes and—hers. In his wild, half violent impatience, however, he stumbled. That roaring, too, confused him. He fell forward, it seemed, for twilight had merged in darkenss, and he misjudged the steps, the distances he yet knew so well. For a moment, certainly, he lay at full length upon the uneven

276

ground against the wall; the steps had tripped him. And then he raised himself and knocked. His right hand struck upon the small, white garden gate. Upon the two lost fingers he felt the impact. 'I am here,' he cried, with a deep sound in his throat as though utterance was choked and difficult. 'I have come back.'

For a fraction of a second he waited, while the world stood still and waited with him. But there was no delay. Her answer came at once: 'I am well.... I am happy.... I am waiting.'

And the voice was dear and marvellous as of old. Though the words were strange, reminding him of something dreamed, forgotten, lost, it seemed, he did not take special note of them. He only wondered that she did not open instantly that he might see her. Speech could follow, but sight came surely first! There was this lightning-flash of disappointment in him. Ah, she was lengthening out the marvellous moment, as often and often she had done before. It was to tease him that she made him wait. He knocked again; he pushed against the unyielding surface. For he noticed that it was unyielding; and there was a depth in the tender voice that he could not understand.

'Open!' he cried again, but louder than before. 'I have come back!' And, as he said it, the mist struck cold against his face.

But her answer froze his blood.

'I cannot open.'

And a sudden anguish of despair rose over him; the sound of her voice was strange; in it was faintness, distance as well as depth. It seemed to echo. Something frantic seized him then—the panic sense.

'Open, open! Come out to me!' he tried to shout. His voice failed oddly; there was no power in it. Something appalling struck him between the eyes. 'For God's sake, open. I'm waiting here! Open, and come out to me!'

The reply was muffled by distance that already seemed increasing; he was conscious of freezing cold about him—in his heart:

'I cannot. You must come in to me.'

He knew not exactly then what happened, for the cold grew dreadful and the icy mist was in his throat. No words would come. He rose to his knees, and from his knees to his feet. He stooped. With all his force he knocked again; in a blind frenzy of despair he hammered and beat against the unyielding barrier of the small, white garden gate. He battered it till the skin of his knuckles was torn and bleeding—the first two fingers of a hand already mutilated. He remembered the torn and broken skin, for he noticed in the gloom that stains upon the gate bore witness to his violence; it was not till afterwards that he remembered the other fact—that the hand had already suffered mutilation, long, long years ago. The power of sound was feebly in him; he called aloud; there was no answer. He tried to scream, but the scream was muffled in his throat before it issued properly; it was a nightmare scream. As a last resort he flung himself bodily upon the unyielding gate, with such precipitate violence, moreover, that his face struck against its surface.

From the friction, then, along the whole length of his cheek he knew that the surface was not smooth. Cold and rough that surface was; but also—it was not of wood. Moreover, there was writing on it he had not seen before. How he deciphered it in the gloom, he never knew. The lettering was deeply cut. Perhaps he traced it with his fingers; his right hand certainly lay stretched upon it. He made out a name, a date, a broken verse from the Bible, and strange words: *'Je suis la première au rendez-vous. Je vous attends.'* The lettering way sharply cut with edges that were new. For the date was of a week ago; the broken verse ran, 'When the shadows flee away ...' and the small, white garden gate was unyielding because it was of—stone.

At the inn he found himself staring at a table from which the tea things had not been cleared away. There was a railway time-table in his hands, and his head was bent forwards over it, trying to decipher the lettering in the growing twilight.

Beside him, still fingering a florin, stood the serving-girl; her other hand held a brown tray with a running dog painted upon its dented surface. It swung to and fro a little as she spoke, evidently continuing a conversation her customer had begun. For she was giving information—in the colourless, disinterested voice such persons use:

'We all went to the funeral, sir, all the country people went. The grave was her father's—the family grave....' Then, seeing that her customer was too absorbed in the time-table to listen further, she said no more but began to pile the tea things on to the tray with noisy clatter.

Ten minutes later, in the road, he stood hesitating. The signal at the station just opposite was already down. The autumn mist was rising. He looked along the winding road that melted away into the distance, then slowly turned and reached the platform just as the London train came in. He felt very old—too old to walk three miles....

THE WINGS OF HORUS

BINOVITCH had the bird in him somewhere: in his features, certainly, with his piercing eye and hawk-like nose; in his movements, with his quick way of flitting, hopping, darting; in the way he perched on the edge of a chair; in the manner he pecked at his food; in his twittering, high-pitched voice as well; and, above all, in his airy, flashing mind. He skimmed all subjects and picked their heart out neatly, as a bird skims lawn or air to snatch its prey. He had the bird's-eye view of everything. He loved birds and understood them instinctively; could imitate their whistling notes with astonishing accuracy. Their one quality he had not was poise and balance. He was a nervous little man; he was neurasthenic. And he was in Egypt by doctor's orders.

Such imaginative, unnecessary ideas he had! Such uncommon beliefs!

'The old Egyptians,' he said laughingly yet with a touch of solemn conviction in his manner, 'were a great people. Their consciousness was different from ours. The bird idea, for instance, conveyed a sense of deity to them—of bird deity, that is: they had sacred birds—hawks, ibis, and so forth—and worshipped them.' And he put his tongue out as though to saywith challenge, 'Ha, ha!'

'They also worshipped cats and crocodiles and cows,' grinned Palazov. Binovitch seemed to dart across the table at his adversary. His eyes flashed; his nose pecked the air. Almost one could imagine the beating of his angry wings.

'Because everything alive,' he half screamed, 'was a symbol of some spiritual power to them. Your mind is as literal as a dictionary and as incoherent. Pages of ink without connected meaning! Verb always in the infinitive! If you were an old Egyptian, you—you'—he flashed and spluttered, his tongue shot out again, his keen eyes blazed—'you would take all those words and spin them into a great interpretation of life,

280

a cosmic romance, as they did. Instead, you get the bitter, dead taste of ink in your mouth, and spit it over us—like that'—he made a quick movement of his whole body as a bird that shakes itself—'in empty phrases.'

Khilkoff ordered another bottle of champagne, while Vera, his sister, said half nervously, 'Let's go for a drive: it's moonlight.' There was enthusiasm at once. Another of the party called the head waiter and told him to pack food and drink in baskets. It was only eleven o'clock. They would drive out into the desert, have a meal at two in the morning, tell stories, sing, and see the dawn.

It was in one of those cosmopolitan hotels in Egypt which attract the ordinary tourists as well as those who are doing a 'cure,' and all these Russians were ill with one thing or another. All were ordered out for their health, and all were the despair of their doctors. They were as unmanageable as a bazaar and as incoherent. Excess and bed were their routine. They lived, but none of them got better. Equally, none of them got angry. They talked in this strange personal way without a shred of malice or offence. The English, French, and Germans in the hotel watched them with remote amazement, referring to them as 'that Russian lot'. Their energy was elemental. They never stopped. They merely disappeared when the pace became too fast, then reappeared after a day or two, and resumed their 'living' as before. Binovitch, despite his neurasthenia, was the life of the party. He was also a special patient of Dr. Plitzinger, the famous psychiatrist, who took a peculiar interest in his case. It was not surprising. Binovitch was a man of unusual ability and of genuine, deep culture. But there was something more about him that stimulated curiosity. There was this striking originality. He said and did surprising things.

'I could fly if I wanted to,' he said once when the airmen came to astonish the natives with their biplanes over the desert, 'but without all that machinery and noise. It's only a question of believing and understanding——'

'Show us!' they cried. 'Let's see you fly!'

'He's got it! He's off again! One of his impossible, delightful moments!'

These occasions when Binovitch let himself go always proved wildly entertaining. He said monstrously incredible things as though he really believed them. They loved his madness, for it gave them new sensations.

'It's only levitation, after all, this flying,' he exclaimed, shooting out his tongue between the words, as his habit was when excited; 'and what is levitation but a power of the air? None of you can hang an orange in space for a second, with all your scientific knowledge; but the moon is always levitated perfectly. And the stars. D'you think they swing on wires? What raised the enormous stones of ancient Egypt? D'you really believe it was heaped-up sand and ropes and clumsy leverage and all our weary and laborious mechanical contrivances? Bah! It was levitation. It was the powers of the air. Believe in those powers, and gravity becomes a mere nursery trick—true where it is, but true nowhere else. To know the fourth dimension is to step out of a locked room and appear instantly on the roof or in another country altogether. To know the powers of the air, similarly, is to annihilate what you call weight—and fly.'

'Show us, show us!' thy cried, roaring with delighted laughter.

'It's a question of belief,' he repeated, his tongue appearing and disappearing like a pointed shadow. 'It's in the heart; the power of the air gets into your whole being. Why should I show you? Why should I ask my deity to persuade your scoffing little minds by any miracle? For it is deity, I tell you, and nothing else. I know it. Follow *one* idea like that, as I follow my bird-idea—follow it with the impetus and undeviating concentration of a projectile—and you arrive at power. You know deity—the bird-idea of deity, that is. *They* knew that. The old Egyptians knew it.'

'Oh show us, show us!' they shouted impatiently, wearied of his nonsense-talk. 'Get up and fly! Levitate yourself, as they did! Become a star!'

282

Binovitch turned suddenly very pale, and an odd light shone in his keen brown eyes. He rose slowly from the edge of the chair where he was perched. Something about him changed. There was silence instantly.

'I *will* show you,' he said calmly, to their intense amazement; 'not to convince your disbelief, but to prove it to myself. For the powers of the air are with me here. I believe. And Horus, great falcon-headed symbol, is my patron god.'

The suppressed energy in his voice and manner was indescribable. There was a sense of lifting, upheaving power about him. He raised his arms; his face turned upward; he inflated his lungs with a deep, long breath, and his voice broke into a kind of singing cry, half prayer, half chant:

'O Horus,
Bright-eyed deity of wind,
[1]Feather my soul
Through earth's thick air,
To know thy awful swiftness—'

He broke off suddenly. He climbed lightly and swiftly upon the nearest table—it was in a deserted card-room, after a game in which he had lost more pounds than there are days in the year—and leaped into the air. He hovered a second, spread his arms and legs in space, appeared to float a moment —then buckled, rushed down and forward, and dropped in a heap upon the floor, while everyone roared with laughter.

But the laughter died out quickly, for there was something in his wild performance that was peculiar and unusual. It was uncanny, not quite natural. His body had seemed, as with Mordkin and Nijinski, literally to hang upon the air a moment. For a second he gave the distressing impression of overcoming gravity. There was a touch in it of that faint horror which appals by its very vagueness. He picked himself up unhurt, and his face was as grave as a portrait in the Academy, but with a new expression in it that everybody noticed with this strange, half-shocked amazement. And it was this

[1]The original is untraslatable. The phrase means, 'Give my life wings.'

expression that extinguished the claps of laughter as wind takes away the sound of bells. Like many ugly men, he was an inimitable actor, and his facial repertory was endless and incredible. But this was neither acting nor clever manipulation of expressive features. There was something in his curious Russian physiognomy that made the heart beat slower. And that was why the laughter died away so suddenly.

'You ought to have flown farther,' cried someone. It expressed what all had felt.

'Icarus didn't drink champagne,' another replied, with a laugh; but nobody laughed with him.

'You went too near to Vera,' said Palazov, 'and passion melted the wax.' But his face twitched oddly as he said it. There was something he did not understand, and so heartily disliked.

The strange expression on the features deepened. It was arresting in a disagreeable, almost in a horrible way. The talk stopped dead; all stared; there was a feeling of dismay in everybody's heart, yet unexplained. Some lowered their eyes, or else looked stupidly elsewhere; but the women of the party felt a kind of fascination. Vera, in particular, could not move her sight away. The joking reference to his passionate admiration for her passed unnoticed. There was a general and individual sense of shock. And a chorus of whispers rose instantly:

'Look at Binovitch! What's happened to his face?'

'He's changed—he's changing!'

'God! Why he looks like a—bird!'

But no one laughed. Instead, they chose the names of birds —hawk, eagle, even owl. The figure of a man leaning against the edge of the door, watching them closely, they did not notice. He had been passing down the corridor, had looked in unobserved, and then had paused. He had seen the whole performance. He watched Binovitch narrowly now with calm, discerning eyes. It was Dr. Plitzinger, the great psychiatrist.

For Binovitch had picked himself up from the floor in a way that was oddly self-possessed, and precluded the least possibility of the ludicrous. He looked neither foolish nor abashed. He looked surprised, but also he looked half angry and half frightened. As someone had said, he 'ought to have flown farther.' That was the incredible impression his acrobatics had produced—incredible, yet somehow actual. This uncanny idea prevailed, as at a séance where nothing genuine is expected to happen, and something genuine, after all, does happen. There was no pretence in this: Binovitch had flown.

And now he stood there, white in the face—with terror and with anger white. He looked extraordinary, this little, neurasthenic Russian, but he looked at the same time half terrific. Another thing, not commonly experienced by men, was in him, breaking out of him, affecting *directly* the minds of his companions. His mouth opened; blood and fury shone in his blazing eyes; his tongue shot out like an ant-eater's, though even in this the comic had no place. His arms were spread like flapping wings, and his voice rose poignantly:

'He failed me, he failed me!' he tried to shout. 'Horus, my falcon-headed deity, my power of the air, deserted me! Hell take him! Hell burn his wings and blast his piercing sight! Hell scorch him into dust for his false prophecies! I curse him —I curse Horus!'

The voice that should have roared across the silent room emitted, instead, this high-pitched, bird-like scream. The added touch of sound, the reality it lent, was ghastly. Yet it was marvellously done and acted. The entire thing was a bit of instantaneous inspiration—his voice, his words, his gestures, his whole wild appearance. Only—here was the reality that caused the sense of shock—the expression on his altered features was genuine. *That* was not assumed. There was something new and alien in him, something cold and difficult to human life, something alert and swift and cruel, of another element than earth. A strange, rapacious grandeur had leaped upon the struggling features. The face looked hawk-like.

And he came forward suddenly and sharply toward Vera, whose fixed, staring eyes had never once ceased to watch him with a kind of anxious yet eager fascination. She was both drawn and beaten back. Binovitch advanced on tiptoe. No doubt he still was acting, still pretending this mad nonsense that he worshipped Horus, the falcon-headed deity of forgotten days, and that Horus had failed him in his hour of need; but somehow there was just a hint of too much reality in the way he moved and looked. The girl, a little creature, with fluffy golden hair, opened her lips; her cigarette fell to the floor; she shrank back; she looked for a moment like some smaller, coloured bird trying to escape from a great pursuing hawk; she screamed. Binovitch, his arms wide, his bird-like face thrust forward, had swooped upon her. He leaped. Almost he caught her.

No one could say exactly what happened. Play, become suddenly and unexpectedly too real, confuses the emotions. The change of key was swift. From fun to terror is a dislocating jolt upon the mind. Someone—it was Khilkoff, the brother—upset a chair; everybody spoke at once; everybody stood up. An unaccountable feeling of disaster was in the air, as with those drinkers' quarrels that blaze out from nothing, and end in a pistol-shot and death, no one able to explain clearly how it came about. It was the silent, watching figure in the doorway who saved the situation. Before anyone had noticed his approach, there he was among the group, laughing, talking, applauding—between Binovitch and Vera. He was vigorously patting his patient on the back, and his voice rose easily above the general clamour. He was a strong, quiet personality; even in his laughter there was authority. And his laughter now was the only sound in the room, as though by his mere presence peace and harmony were restored. Confidence came with him. The noise subsided; Vera was in her chair again. Khilkoff poured out a glass of wine for the great man.

'The Czar!' said Plitzinger, sipping his champagne, while all stood up, delighted with his compliment and tact. 'And to your opening night with the Russian ballet,' he added quickly a second toast, 'or to your first performance at the Moscow Théâtre des Arts!' Smiling significantly, he glanced at Binovitch; he clinked glasses with him. Their arms were already

286

linked, but it was Palazov who noticed that the doctor's fingers
seemed rather tight upon the creased black coat. All drank,
looking with laughter, yet with a touch of respect, toward
Binovitch, who stood there dwarfed beside the stalwart
Austrian, and suddenly as meek and subdued as any mole.
Apparently the abrupt change of key had taken his mind
successfully off something else.

'Of course—"The Fire-Bird." ' exclaimed the little man,
mentioning the famous Russian ballet. 'The very thing!' he
exclaimed. 'For *us*,' he added, looking with devouring eyes
at Vera. He was greatly pleased. He began talking vociferously
about dancing and the rationale of dancing. They told him he
was an undiscovered master. He was delighted. He winked
at Vera and touched her glass again with his. 'We'll make our
début together,' he cried. 'We'll begin at Covent Garden,
in London. I'll design the dresses and the posters 'The Hawk
and the Dove!' *Magnifique!* I in dark grey, and you in blue
and gold! Ah, dancing, you know, is sacred. The little self
is lost, absorbed. It is ecstasy, it is divine. And dancing in air—
the passion of the birds and stars—ah! they are the movements
of the gods. You know deity that way—by living it.'

He went on and on. His entire being had shifted with a leap
upon this new subject. The idea of realising divinity by dancing
it absorbed him. The party discussed it with him as though
nothing else existed in the world, all sitting now and talking
eagerly together. Vera took the cigarette he offered her, lighting
it from his own; their fingers touched; he was as harmless
and normal as a retired diplomat in a drawing room. But it
was Plitzinger whose subtle manoeuvring had accomplished
the change so cleverly, and it was Plitzinger who presently
suggested a game of billiards, and led him off, full now of
a fresh enthusiasm for cannons, balls, and pockets, into another
room. They departed arm in arm, laughing and talking together.

Their departure, it seemed, made no great difference at first.
Vera's eyes watched him out of sight, then turned to listen to
Baron Minski, who was describing with gusto how he caught
wolves alive for coursing purposes. The speed and power of

the wolf, he said, was impossible to realise; the force of their awful leap, the strength of their teeth, which could bite through metal stirrup-fastenings. He showed a scar on his arm and another on his lip. He was telling truth, and everybody listened with deep interest. The narrative lasted perhaps the minutes or more, when Minski abruptly stopped. He had come to an end; he looked about him; he saw his glass, and emptied it. There was a general pause. Another subject did not at once present itself. Sighs were heard; several fidgeted; fresh cigarettes were lighted. But there was no sign of boredom, for where one or two Russians are gathered together there is always life. They produce gaiety and enthusiasm as wind produces waves. Like great children, they plunge wholeheartedly into whatever interest presents itself at the moment. There is a kind of uncouth gambolling in their way of taking life. It seems as if they are always fighting that deep, underlying, national sadness which creeps into their very blood.

'Midnight!' then exclaimed Palazov, abruptly, looking at his watch; and the others fell instantly to talking about that watch, admiring it and asking questions. For the moment that very ordinary timepiece became the centre of observation. Palazov mentioned the price. 'It never stops,' he said proudly, 'not even under water'. He looked up at everybody, challenging admiration. And he told how, at a country house, he made a bet that he would swim to a certain island in the lake, and won the bet. He and a girl were the winners, but as it was a horse they had bet, he got nothing out of it for himself, giving the horse to her. It was a genuine grievance in him. One felt he could have cried as he spoke of it. 'But the watch went all the time,' he said delightedly, holding the gunmetal object in his hand to show, 'and I was twelve minutes in the water with my clothes on.'

Yet this fragmentary talk was nothing but pretence. The sound of clicking billiard-balls was audible from the room at the end of the corridor. There was another pause. The pause, however, was intentional. It was not vacuity of mind or absence of ideas that caused it. There was another subject,

an unfinished subject, that each member of the group was still
considering. Only no one cared to begin about it, till at last,
unable to resist the strain any longer, Palazov turned to Khilkoff,
who was saying he would take a 'whisky-soda,' as the champagne was too sweet, and whispered something beneath his
breath; whereupon Khilkoff, forgetting his drink, glanced
at his sister, shrugged his shoulders, and made a curious
grimace. 'He's all right now'—his reply was just audible—'he's
with Plitzinger.' He cocked his head sidewise to indicate that
the clicking of the billiard-balls still was going on.

The subject was out: all turned their heads; voices hummed
and buzzed; questions were asked and answered or half answered; eyebrows were raised, shoulders shrugged, hands spread
out expressively. There came into the atmosphere a feeling
of presentiment, of mystery, of things half understood; primitive, buried instinct stirred a little, the kind of racial dread
of vague emotions that might gain the upper had if encouraged.
They shrank from looking something in the face, while yet
this unwelcome influence drew closer round them all. They
discussed Binovitch and his astonishing performance. Pretty
little Vera listened with large and troubled eyes, though saying
nothing. The Arab waiter had put out the lights in the corridor,
and only a solitary cluster burned now above their heads,
leaving their faces in shadow. In the distance the clicking of
the billiard-balls still continued.

'It was not play; it was real,' exclaimed Minski vehemently.
'I can catch wolves,' he blurted; 'but birds—ugh!—and human
birds!' He was half inarticulate. He had witnessed something
he could not understand, and it had touched instinctive terror
in him. 'It was the way he leaped that put the wolf first into
my mind, only it was not a wolf at all.' The others agreed and
disagreed. 'It was play at first, but it was reality at the end,'
another whispered; 'and it was no animal he mimicked, but
a bird, and a bird of prey at that!'

Vera thrilled. In the Russian woman hides that touch of
savagery which loves to be caught, mastered, swept helplessly
away, captured utterly and deliciously by the one strong enough

to do it thoroughly. She left her chair and sat down beside an older woman in the party, who took her arm quietly at once. Her little face wore a perplexed expression, mournful, yet somehow wild. It was clear that Binovitch was not indifferent to her.

'It's become an *idée fixe* with him,' this older woman said. 'The bird-idea lives in his mind. He lives it in his imagination. Ever since that time at Edfu, when he pretended to worship the great stone flacons ouside the temple—the Horus figures— he's been full of it.' She stopped. The way Binovitch had behaved at Edfu was better lefet unmentioned at the moment, perhaps. A slight shiver ran round the listening group, each one waiting for someone else to focus their emotion, and so explain it by saying the convincing thing. Only no one ventured. Then Vera abruptly gave a little jump.

'Hark!' she exclaimed, in a staccato whisper, speaking for the first time. She sat bolt upright. She was listening. 'Hark!' she repeated. 'There it is again, but nearer than before. It's coming closer. I hear it.' She trembled. Her voice, her manner, above all her great staring eyes, startled everybody. No one spoke for several seconds; all listened. The halls and corridors lay in darkness, and gloom was over the big hotel. Everybody was in bed. But the clicking of the billiard-balls had ceased.

'Hear what?' asked the older woman soothingly, yet with a perceptible quaver in her voice, too. She was aware that the girl's hand tightened upon her arm.

'Do you not hear it, too?' the girl whispered.

All listened without speaking. All watched her paling face. Something wonderful, yet half incomprehensible, seemed in the air about them. There was a dull murmur, audible, faint, remote, its direction hard to tell. It had come suddenly from nowhere. They shivered. That strange racial thrill again passed into the group, unwelcome, unexplained. It was aboriginal; it belonged to the unconscious primitive mind, half childish, half terrifying.

'*What* do you hear?' her brother asked angrily—the irritable anger of nervous fear.

'When he came at me,' she answered very low, 'I heard it first. I hear it now again. Listen! He's coming.'

And at that minute, out of the dark mouth of the corridor, emerged two human figures, Plitzinger and Binovitch. Their game was over; they were going up to bed. They passed the open door of the card-room. But Binovitch was being half dragged, half restrained, for he was apparently attempting to run down the passage with flying, dancing leaps. He bounded. It was like a huge bird trying to rise for flight, while his companion kept him down by force upon the earth. As they entered the strip of light, Plitzinger changed his own position, placing himself swiftly between his companion and the group in the dark corner of the room. He hurried Binovitch along as though he sheltered him from view. They passed into the shadows down the passage. They disappeared. And everyone looked significantly, questioningly at his neighbour, though at first saying no word. It seemed that a curious disturbance of the air had followed them audibly.

Vera was the first to open her lips. 'You heard it *then*,' she said breathlessly, her face whiter than the ceiling.

'Damn!' exclaimed her brother furiously. 'It was wind against the outside walls—wind in the desert. The sand is driving.'

Vera looked at him. She shrank closer against the side of the older woman, whose arm was tight about her.

'It was *not* wind,' she whispered simply.

She paused. All waited uneasily for the completion of her sentence. They stared into her face like peasants who expected a miracle.

'Wings,' she whispered. 'It was the sound of wings.'

And at four o'clock in the morning, when they all returned exhausted from their excursion into the desert, little Binovitch was sleeping soundly and peacefully in his bed. They passed his door on tiptoe. But he did not hear them. He was dreaming. His spirit was at Edfu, experiencing with that ancient diety who was master of all flying life those strange enjoyments upon

291

which his own troubled human heart was passionately set. Safe with that mighty falcon whose powers his lips had scorned a few hours before, his soul, released in vivid dream, went sweetly flying. It was amazing, it was gorgeous. He shimmed the Nile at lightning speed. Dashing down headlong from the height of the great Pyramid, he chased with faultless accuracy a little dove that sought vainly to hide from his terrific pursuit beneath the palm trees. For what he loved must worship where he worshipped, and the majesty of those tremendous effigies had fired his imagination to the creative point where expression was imperative.

Then suddenly, at the very moment of delicious capture, the dream turned horrible, becoming awful with the nightmare touch. The sky lost all its blue and sunshine. Far, far below him the little dove enticed him into nameless depths, so that he flew faster and faster, yet never fast enough to overtake it. Behind him came a great thing down the air, black, hovering, with gigantic wings outstretched. It had terrific eyes, and the beating of its feathers stole his wind away. It followed him, crowding space. He was aware of a colossal beak, curved like a scimitar and pointed wickedly like a troth of steel. He dropped. He faltered. He tried to scream.

Through empty space he fell, caught by the neck. The huge spectral falcon was upon him. The talons were in his heart. And in sleep he remembered then that he had cursed. He recalled his reckless language. The curse of the ignorant is meaningless; that of the worshipper is real. This attack was on his soul. He had invoked it. He realised next, with a shock of ghastly horror, that the dove he chased was, after all, the bait that had lured him purposely to destruction ... and awoke with a suffocating terror upon him, and his entire body bathed in icy perspiration. Outside the open window he heard a sound of wings retreating with powerful strokes into the surrounding darkness of the sky.

The nightmare made its impression upon Binovitch's impressionable and dramatic temperament. It aggravated his tendencies. He related it next day to Mme. de Drühn, the friend of Vera, telling it with that somewhat boisterous laughter some minds use to disguise less kind emotions. But he received no encouragement. The mood of the previous night was not recoverable; it was already ancient hitory. Russians never make the banal mistake of repeating a sensation till it is exhausted; they hurry on to novelties. Life flashes and rushes with them, never standing still for exposure before the cameras of their minds. Mme. de Drühn, however, took the trouble to mention the matter to Plitzinger, for Plitzinger, like Freud of Vienna, held that dreams revealed subconscious tendencies which sooner or later must betray themselves in action.

'Thank you for telling me,' he smiled politely; 'but I have already heard it from him.' He watched her eyes a moment, really examining her soul. 'Binovitch, you see,' he continued, apparently satisfied with what he saw, 'I regard as that rare phenomenon—a genius without an outlet. His spirit, intensely creative, finds no adequate expression. His power of production is enormous and prolific; yet he accomplishes nothing.' He paused an instant. 'Binovitch, therefore, is in danger of poisoning—himself.' He looked steadily into her face, as a man who weighs how much he may confide. 'Now,' he continued, '*if* we can find an outlet for him, a field wherein his bursting imaginative genius can produce results—above all, *visible* results'—he shrugged his shoulders—'the man is saved. Otherwise'—he looked extraordinarily impressive—'there is bound to be sooner or later——'

'Madness?' she asked very quietly.

'An explosion, let us say,' he replied gravely. 'For instance, take this Horus obsession of his, quite wrong archaeologically though it is. *Au fond* it is megalomania of a most unusual kind. His passionate interet, his love, his worship of birds, wholesome enough in themselves, find no satisfying outlet. A man who really loves birds neither keeps them in cages, nor shoots, nor stuffs them. What, then can, he do? The commonplace bird-lover observes them through glasses, studies their habits, then writes a book about them. But a man like Binovitch, overflowing with this intense creative power of mind and imagination, is not content with that. He wants to know them from within. He wants to feel what they feel, to live their life. He wants to *become* them.... You follow me? Not quite. Well, he seeks to be identified with the object of his sacred, passionate adoration. All genius seeks to know the thing-itself from its own point of view. It desires union. That tendency, unrecognised by himself, perhaps, and therefore subconscious, hides in his very soul.' He paused a moment. 'And the sudden sight of those majestic figures at Edfu—that crystallisation of his *idée fixe* in granite—took hold of this excess in him, so to speak—and is now focusing it toward some definite act. Binovitch sometimes—feels himself a bird! You noticed what occurred last night?'

She nodded; a slight shiver passed over her.

'A most curious performance,' she murmured; 'an exhibition I never want to see again.'

'The most curious part,' replied the doctor coolly, 'was its truth.'

'Its truth!' she exclaimed beneath her breath. She was frightened by something in his voice and by the uncommon gravity in his eyes. It seemed to arrest her intelligence. She felt upon the edge of things beyond her. 'You mean that Binovitch did for a moment—hang—in the air?' The other verb, the right one, she could not bring herself to use.

The great man's face was enigmatical. He talked to her sympathy, perhaps, rather than to her mind.

'Real genius,' he said smilingly, 'is as rare as talent, even great talent, is common. It means that the personality, if only for one second, becomes everything; becomes the universe; becomes the soul of the world. It gets the flash. It is identified with the universal life. Being everything and everywhere, all is possible to it—in that second of vivid realisation. It can brood with the crystal, grow with the plant, leap with the animal and fly with the bird: genius unifies all three. That is the meaning of 'creative.' It is faith. Knowing it, you can pass through fire and not be burned, walk on water and not sink, move a mountain, fly. Because you *are* fire, water, earth, air. Genius, you see, is madness in the magnificent sense of being superhuman. Binovitch has it.'

He broke off abruptly, seeing he was not understood. Some great enthusiasm in him he deliberately suppressed.

'The point is,' he resumed, speaking more carefully, 'that we must try to lead this passionately constructive genius of the man into some human channel that will absorb it, and therefore render it harmless.'

'He loves Vera,' the woman said, bewildered, yet seizing this point correctly.

'But would he marry her?' asked Plitzinger at once.

'He is already married.'

The doctor looked steadily at her a moment, hesitating whether he should utter all his thought.

'In that case,' he said slowly after a pause, 'it is better he or she should leave.'

His tone and manner were exceedingly impressive.

'You mean there's danger?' she asked.

'I mean, rather,' he replied earnestly, 'that this great creative flood in him, so curiously focused now upon his Horus falcon-bird idea, may result in some act of violence——'

'Which would be madness,' she said, looking hard at him. 'Which would be disastrous,' he corrected her. And then he added slowly: 'Because in the mental moment of creation he might overlook material laws.'

The costume ball two nights later was a great success. Palazov was a Bedouin, and Khilkoff an Apache; Mme. de Drühn wore a national headdress; Minski looked almost natural as Don Quixote; and the entire Russian 'set' was cleverly, if somewhat extravagantly, dressed. But Binovitch and Vera were the most successful of all the two hundred dancers who took part. Another figure, a big man dressed as a Pierrot, also claimed exceptional attention, for though the costume was commonplace enough, there was something of dignity in his appearance that drew the eyes of all upon him. But he wore a mask, and his identity was not discoverable.

It was Binovitch and Vera, however, who must have won the prize, if prize there had been, for they not only looked their parts, but acted them as well. The former in his dark grey feather tunic, and his falcon mask, complete even to the brown hooked beak and tufted talons, looked fierce and splendid. The disguise was so admirable, yet so entirely natural, that it was uncommonly seductive. Vera, in blue and gold, a charming head-dress of a dove upon her loosened hair, and a pair of little dove-pale wings fluttering from her shoulders, her tiny twinkling feet and slender ankles well visible, too, was equally successful and admired. Her large and timid eyes, her flitting movements, her light and dainty way of dancing—all added touches that made the picture perfect.

How Binovitch contrived his dress remained a mystery, for the layers of wings upon his back were real; the large black kites that haunt the Nile, soaring in their hundreds over Cairo and the bleak Mokattam Hills, had furnished them. He had procured them none knew how. They measured five feet across from tip to tip; they swished and rustled as he swept along; they were true falcons' wings. He danced with nautch girls and Egyptian princesses and Rumanian gipsies; he danced well, with beauty, grace, and lightness. But with Vera he did not dance at all; with her he simply flew. A kind of passionate abandon was in him as he skimmed the floor with her in a way that made everybody turn to watch them. They seemed to leave the ground together. It was delightful, an amazing sight; but it was peculiar. The strangeness of it was on many lips. Somehow its queer extravagance communicated itself to the entire ball-room. They became the centre of observation. There were whispers.

'There's that extraordinary bird-man! Look! He goes by like a hawk. And he's always after that dove-girl. How marvellously he does it! It's rather awful. Who is he? I don't envy *her*.'

People stood aside when he rushed past. They got out of his way. He seemed for ever pursuing Vera, even when dancing with another partner. Word passed from mouth to mouth.

A kind of telepathic interest was established everywhere. It was a shade too real sometimes, something unduly earnest in the chasing wildness, something unpleasant. There was even alarm.

'It's rowdy; I'd rather not see it; it's quite disgraceful,' was heard. '*I* think it's horrible; you can see she's terrified.'

And once there was a little scene, trivial enough, yet betraying this reality that many noticed and disliked. Binovitch came up to claim a dance, programme clutched in his great tufted claws, and at the same moment the big Pierrot appeared abruptly round the corner with a similar claim. Those who saw it assert he had been waiting, and came on purpose, and that there was something protective and authoritative in his bearing. The misunderstanding was ordinary enough—both men had written her name against the dance but 'No. 13, Tango' also included the supper interval, and neither Hawk nor Pierrot would give way. They were very obstinate. Both men wanted her. It was awkward.

'The Dove shall decide between us,' smiled the Hawk politely, yet his taloned fingers working nervously. Pierrot, however, more experienced in the ways of dealing with women, or more bold, said suavely:

'I am ready to abide by her decision'—his voice poorly cloaked this aggravating authority, as though he had the right to her—'only I engaged this dance before Mis Majesty Horus appeared upon the scene at all, and therefore it is clear that Pierrot has the right of way.'

At once, with a masterful air, he took her off. There was no withstanding him. He meant to have her and he got her. Both yielding and resisting, she was swept away. They vanished among the maze of coloured dancers, leaving the Hawk, disconsolate and vanquished, amid the titters of the onlookers His swiftness, as against this steady power, was of no avail.

It was then that the singular phenomenon was witnessed first. Those who saw it affirm that he changed absolutely into the part he played. It was dreadful; it was not possible. A frightened whisper ran about the rooms and corridors:

'An extraordinary thing is in the air!'

Some shrank away, while others flocked to see. There were those who swore that a curious, rushing sound was audible, the atmosphere visibly disturbed and shaken; that a shadow fell upon the spot the couple had vacated; that a cry was heard, a high, wild, searching cry: 'Horus! bright deity of wind,' it began, then died away. One man was positive that the windows had been opened and that something had flown in. It was the obvious explanation. The thing spread rapidly. As in a fire panic, there was consternation and excitement. Confusion caught the feet of all the dancers. The music fumbled and lost time. The leading pair of tango dancers halted and looked round. It seemed that everybody pressed back, hiding, shuffling, eager to see, yet more eager not to be seen, as though something unusual, dangerous, terrible, had broken loose. In rows against the wall they stood. For a great space had made itself in the middle of the ball-room, and into this empty space reappeared suddenly the Pierrot and the Dove.

It was like a challenge. A sound of applause, half voices, half clapping of gloved hands, was heard. The couple danced exquisitely into the arena. All stared. There was an impression that a set piece had been prepared, and that this was its beginning. The music again took heart. Pierrot was strong and dignified, no whit nonplussed by this abrupt publicity. The Dove, though faltering, seemed deliciously obedient. They danced together like a single outline. She was captured utterly. And to the man who needed her the sight was naturally agonising—the protective way the Pierrot held her, the right and strength of it, the mastery the complete possession.

'He's still got her!' someone breathed too loud, uttering the thought of all. 'Good thing it's not the Hawk!'

And, to the absolute amazement of the throng, this sight was then apparent. A figure dropped through space. That high, shrill cry again was heard:

'Feather my soul ... to know thy awful swiftness!'

Its singing loveliness touched the heart, its appealing, passionate sweetness was marvellous, as from an upper gallery this figure of a man, dressed as a strong, dark bird, shot down with splendid grace and ease. The feathers swept; the wings spread out as sails that take the wind. Like a hawk that darts with unerring power and aim upon its prey, this thing of mighty wings rushed down into the empty space where the couple danced. Observed by all, he entered, swooping beautifully, stretching his wings like any eagle. He dropped. He fixed his point of landing with consummate skill close beside the astonished dancers. He landed.

It happened with such swiftness that it brought the dazzle and blindness as when lighting strikes. People in different parts of the room saw different details; a few saw nothing at all after the first startling shock, closing their eyes, or holding their arms before their faces as in self-protection. The touch of panic fear caught the entire room. The nameless thing that all the evening had been vaguely felt was come. It had suddenly materialised.

For this incredible thing occurred in the full blaze of light upon the open floor. Binovitch, grown in some sense formidable, opened his dark, big wings about the girl. He drew her to him. The long grey feathers moved, causing powerful draughts of wind that made a rushing sound. An aspect of the terrible was about him, like an emanation. The great beaked head was poised to strike, the tufted claws were raised like fingers that shut and opened, and the whole presentiment of his amazing figure focused in an attitude of attack that was magnificent and terrible. No one who saw it doubted. Yet there were those who swore that it was not Binovitch at all, but that another outline monstrous and shadowy, towered above him, draping his lesser proportions with two colossal wings of darkness. That some touch of strange divinity lay in it may be claimed, however confused the wild descriptions afterward. For many lowered their heads and bowed their shoulders. There was terror. There was also awe. The onlookers swayed as though some power passed over them across the air.

A sound of wings was certainly in the room.

Then someone screamed; a shriek broke high and clear; and emotion, ordinary, human emotion, unaccustomed to terrific things, swept loose. The Hawk and Vera flew—the girl with willing happiness, the man with power. Beaten back against the wall as by a stroke of whirlwind, the Pierrot staggered. He watched them go. Out of the lighted room they flew, out of the crowded human atmosphere, out of the heat and artificial light, the walled-in, airless halls that were a cage. All this they left behind. They seemed things of wind and air, made free happily of another element. Earth held them not. Toward the open night they raced with this extraordinary lightness as of birds, down the long corridor and on to the southern terrace, where great coloured curtains were hung suspended from the columns. A moment they were visible. Then the fringe of one huge curtain, lifted by the wind, showed their dark outline for a second against the starry sky. There was a cry, a leap. The curtain flapped again and closed. They vanished. And into the ball-room swept the cold draught of night air from the desert.

But three figures instantly were close upon their heels. The throng of half dazed, half stupefied onlookers, it seemed, projected them as though by some explosive force. The general mass held back, but, like projectiles, these three flung themselves after the fugitives down the corridor at high speed—the Apache, Don Quixote, and, last of them, the Pierrot. For Khilkoff, the brother, and Baron Minski, the man who caught wolves alive, had been for some time keenly on the watch, while Dr. Plitzinger, reading the symptoms clearly, never far away, had been faithfully observant of every movement. His mask tossed aside, the great psychiatrist was now recognised by all. They reached the parapet just as the curtain flapped back heavily into place; the next second all three were out of sight behind it. Khilkoff was first, however, urged forward at frantic speed by the warning words the doctor had whispered as they ran. Some thirty yards beyond the terrace was the brink of the crumbling cliff on which the great hotel was built, and there was a drop of sixty feet to the desert floor below. Only a low stone wall marked the edge.

Accounts varied. Khilkoff, it seems, arrived in time—in the nick of time—to seize his sister, virtually hovering on the brink. He heard the loose stones strike the sand below. There was a moment's violent struggle. She resisted the interference passionately and with all her strength at first. In a sence she was beside—outside—herself. And he did a characteristic thing; he not only brought her back into the ball-room, but he *danced* her back. It was admirable. Nothing could have calmed the general excitement better. The pair of them danced in together as though nothing was amiss. Accustomed to the strenuous practice of his Cossack regiment, this young cavalry officer's muscles were equal to the semi-dead weight in his arms. At most the onlookers thought her tired, perhaps. Confidence was restored—such is the psychology of a crowd—and in the middle of a thrilling Viennese waltz he easily smuggled her out of the room, administered brandy, and got her up to bed.... The absence of the Hawk, meanwhile, was hardly noticed; comments were made and then forgotten; it was Vera in whom the strange, anxious sympathy had centred. And, with her obvious safety, the moment of primitive, childish panic passed away. Don Quixote, too, was presently seen dancing gaily as though nothing untoward had happened; supper intervened; the incident was over; it had melted into the general wildness of the evening's irresponsibility. The fact that Pierrot did not appear again was noticed by no single person.

But Dr. Plitzinger was otherwise engaged, his heart and mind and soul all deeply exercised. A death-certificate is not always made out quite so simply as the public thinks. That Binovitch had died of suffocation in his swift descent through merely sixty feet of air was not conceivable; yet that his body lay so neatly placed upon the desert after such a fall was stranger still. It was not crumpled, it was not torn; no single bone was broken, no muscle wrenched; there was no bruise. There was no indenture in the sand. The figure lay sidewise as though in sleep, no sign of violence visible anywhere, the dark wings folded as a great bird folds them when it creeps away to die in loneliness. Beneath the Horus mask the face was smiling. It seemed he had floated into death upon the element he loved. And only Vera had seen the enormous wings that, hovering invitingly above the dark abyss, bore him so softly into another world. Plitzinger, that is, saw them, too, but he said firmly that they belonged to the big black falcons that haunt the Mokattam Hills and roost upon these ridges, close beside the hotel, at night. Both he and Vera, however, agreed on one thing: the high, sharp cry in the air above them, wild and plaintive, was certainly the black kite's cry—the note of the falcon that passionately seeks its mate. It was the pause of a second, when she stood to listen, that made her rescue possible. A moment later and she, too, would have flown to death with Binovitch.

INITIATION

A FEW years ago, on a Black Sea steamer heading for the Caucasus, I fell into conversation with an American. He mentioned that he was on his way to the Baku oil-fields, and I replied that I was going up into the mountains. He looked at me questioningly a moment. 'Your first trip?' he asked with interest. I said it was. A conversation followed; it was continued the next day, and renewed the following day, until we parted company at Batoum. I don't know why he talked so freely to me in particular. Normally, he was a taciturn, silent man. We had been fellow travellers from Marseilles, but after Constantinople we had the boat pretty much to ourselves. What struck me about him was his vehement, almost passionate, love of natural beauty—in seas and woods and sky, but above all in mountains. It was like a religion in him. His taciturn manner hid deep poetic feeling.

And he told me it had not always been so with him. A kind of friendship sprang up between us. He was a New York business man—buying and selling exchange between banks—but was English born. He had gone out forty years before, and become naturalised. His talk was exceedingly 'American', slangy, and almost Western. He said he had roughed it in the West for several years first. But what he chiefly talked about was mountains. He said it was in the mountains an unusual experience had come to him that had opened his eyes to many things, but principally to the beauty that was now everything to him, and to the—insignificance of death.

He knew the Caucasus well where I was going. I think that was why he was interested in me and my journey. 'Up there,' he said, 'you'll feel things—and maybe find out things you never knew before.'

'What kind of things?' I asked.

'Why, for one,' he replied with emotion and enthusiasm in his voice, 'that living and dying ain't either of them of much account. That if you know Beauty, I mean, and Beauty is in your life, you live on in it and with it for others—even when you're dead.'

The conversation that followed is too long to give here, but it led to his telling me the experience in his own life that had opened his eyes to the truth of what he said. 'Beauty is imperishable,' he declared, 'and if you live with it, why, you're imperishable too!'

The story, as he told it verbally in his curious language, remains vividly in my memory. But he had written it down, too, he said. And he gave me the written account, with the remark that I was free to hand it on to others if I 'felt that way'. He called it 'Initiation'. It runs as follows:

1

In my own family this happened, for Arthur was my nephew. And a remote Alpine valley was the place. It didn't seem to me in the least suitable for such occurrences, except that it was Catholic, and the 'Church', I understand—at least, scholars who ought to know have told me so—has subtle Pagana origins incorporated unwittingly in its observations of certain Saints' Days, as well as in certain ceremonials. All this kind of thing is Dutch to me, a form of poetry or superstition, for I am interested chiefly in the buying and selling of exchange, with an office in New Yok City, just off Wall Street, and only come to Europe now occasionally for a holiday. I like to see the dear old musty cities, and go to the Opera, and take a motor run through Shakespeare's country or round the Lakes, get in touch again with London and Paris at the Ritz Hotels—and then back again to the greatest city on earth, where for years now I've been making a good thing out of it. Repton and Cambridge, long since forgotten, had their uses. They were all right enough at the time. But I'm now 'on the make,' with a good fat partnership, and have left all that truck behind me.

My half-brother, however—he was my senior and got the

cream of the family wholesale chemical works—has stuck to the trade in the Old Country, and is making probably as much as I am. He approved my taking the chance that offered, and is only sore now because his son, Arthur, is on the stupid side. He agreed that finance suited my temperament far better than drugs and chemicals, though he warned me that all American finance was speculative and therefore dangerous. 'Arthur is getting on,' he said in his last letter, 'and will some day take the director's place you would be in now had you cared to stay. But he's a plodder, rather.' That meant, I knew, that Arthur was a fool. Business, at any rate, was not suited to his temperament. Some years ago, when I came home with a month's holiday to be used in working up connections in English banking circles, I saw the boy. He was fifteen years of age at the time, a delicate youth, with an artist's dreams in his big blue eyes, if my memory goes for anything, but with a tangle of yellow hair and features of classical beauty that would have made half the young girls of my New York set in love with him, and a choice of heiresses at his disposal when he wanted them.

I have a clear recollection of my nephew then. He struck me as having grit and character, but as being wrongly placed. He had his grandfather's tastes. He ought to have been, like him, a great scholar, a poet, and editor of marvellous old writings in new editions. I couldn't get much out of the boy, except that he 'liked the chemical business fairly', and meant to please his father by 'knowing it thoroughly' so as to qualify later for his directorship. But I have never forgotten the evening when I caught him in the hall, staring up at his grandfather's picture, with a kind of light about his face, and the big blue eyes all rapt and tender (moist, too, as if from tears), and replying, when I asked him what was up: '*That* was worth living for. He brought Beauty back into the world!'

'Yes,' I said, 'I guess that's right enough. He did. But there was no money in it to speak of.'

The boy looked at me and smiled. He twigged somehow or other that deep down in me, somewhere below the money-making instinct, a poet, but a dumb poet, lay in hiding. 'You know what I mean,' he said. 'It's in you too.'

The picture was a copy—my father had it made—of the presentation portrait given to Balliol, and 'the grandfather' was celebrated in his day for the translations he made of Anacreon and Sappho, of Homer, too, if I remember rightly, as well as for a number of classical studies and essays that he wrote. A lot of stuff like that he did, and made a name at it too. His 'Lives of the Gods' went into six editions. They said—the big critics of his day—that he was 'a poet who wrote no poetry, yet lived it passionately in the spirit of old-world, classical Beauty', and I know he was a wonderful felllow in his way and made the dons and schoolmasters all sit up. We're proud of him all right. After thirty years of successful 'exchange' in New York City, I confess I am unable to appreciate all that, feeling more in touch with the commercial and financial spirit of the age, progress, development and the rest. But, still, I'm not ashamed of the classical old boy, who seems to have been a good deal of a Pagan, judging by the records we have kept. However, Arthur peering up at that picture in the dusk, his eyes half moist with emotion, and his voice gone positively shaky, is a thing I never have forgotten. He stimulated my curiosity uncommonly. It stirred something deep down in me that I hardly cared to acknowledge on Wall Street—something burning.

And the next time I saw him was in the summer of 1910, when I came to Europe for a two months' look around—my wife at Newport with the children—and hearing that he was in Switzerland, learning a bit of French to help him in the business, I made a point of dropping in upon him just to see how he was shaping generally and what new kinks his mind had taken on. There was something in Arthur I never could quite forget. Whenever his face came into my mind I began to think. A kind of longing came over me — a desire for Beauty, I guess, it was. It made me dream.

I found him at an English tutor's—a lively old dog, with a fondness for the cheap native wines and a financial interest in the tourist development of the village. The boys learnt French in the mornings, possibly, but for the rest of the day were free to amuse themselves exactly as they pleased and without a trace of supervision—provided the parents footed the bills without demur.

This suited everybody all round; and as long as the boys came home with an accent and a vocabulary, all was well. For myself, having learned in New York to attend strictly to my own business—exchange between different countries with a profit—I did not deem it necessary to exchange letters and opinions with my brother—with no chance of profit anywhere. But I got to know Arthur, and had a queer experience of my own into the bargain. Oh, there was profit in it for me. I'm drawing big dividends to this day on the investment.

I put up at the best hotel in the village, a one-horse show, differing from the other inns only in the prices charged for a lot of cheap decoration in the dining-room, and went up to surprise my nephew with a call the first thing after dinner. The tutor's house stood some way back from the narrow street, among fields where there were more flowers than grass, and backed by a forest of fine old timber that stretched up several thousand feet to the snow. The snow at least was visible, peeping out far overhead just where the dark line of forest stopped; but in reality, I suppose, that was an effect of foreshortening, and big slopes and pastures intervened between the trees and the snow-fields. The sunset, long since out of the valley, still shone on those white ridges, where the peaks stuck up like the teeth of a gigantic saw. I guess it meant five or six hours' good climbing to get up to them—and nothing to do when you got there. Switzerland, anyway, seemed a poor country, with its little bit of watch-making, sour wines, and every square yard hanging upstairs at an angle of 60 degrees used for hay. Picture post cards, chocolate and cheap tourists kept it going apparently, but I dare say it was all right enough to learn French in—and cheap as Hoboken to live in.

Arthur was out; I just left a card and wrote on it that I would be very pleased if he cared to step down to take luncheon with me at my hotel next day. Having nothing better to do, I strolled homewards by way of the forest.

Now what came over me in that bit of dark pine forest is more than I can quite explain, but I think it must have been due to the height—the village was 4,000 feet above sea-level—and the effect of the rarefied air upon my circulation. The nearest thing to it in my experience is rye whisky, the queer touch of wildness, of self-confidence, a kind of whooping rapture and the reckless sensation of being a tin god of sorts that comes from a lot of alcohol—a memory, please understand, of years before, when I thought it a grand thing to own the earth and paint the old town red. I seemed to walk on air, and there was a smell about those trees that made me suddenly—well, that took my mind clean out of its accustomed rut. It was just too lovely and wonderful for me to describe it. I had got well into the forest and lost my way a bit. The smell of an old-world garden wasn't in it. It smelt to me as if someone had just that minute turned out the earth all fresh and new. There was moss and tannin, a hint of burning, something between smoke and incense, say, and a fine clean odour or pitch-pine bark when the sun gets on it after rain—and a flavour of the sea thrown in for luck. That was the first I noticed, for I had never smelt anything half so good since my camping days on the coast of Maine. And I stood still to enjoy it. I threw away my cigar for fear of mixing things and spoiling it. 'If that could be bottled,' I said to myself, 'it'd sell for two dollars a pint in every city in the Union!'

And it was just then, while standing and breathing it in, that I got the queer feeling of someone watching me. I kept quite still. Someone was moving near me. The sweat went trickling down my back. A kind of childhood thrill got hold of me.

It was very dark. I was not afraid exactly, but I was a stranger in these parts and knew nothing about the habits of the mountain peasants. There might be tough customers lurking around after dark on the chance of striking some guy of a tourist with money in his pockets. Yet, somehow, that wasn't the kind of feeling that came to me at all, for, though I had a pocket Browning at my hip, the notion of getting at it did not even occur to me. The sensation was new—a kind of lifting, exciting sensation that made my heart swell out with exhilaration. There was happiness in it. A cloud that *weighed* seemed to roll off my mind, same as that light-hearted mood when the office door is locked and I'm off on a two months' holiday—with gaiety and irresponsibility at the back of it. It was invigorating. I felt youth sweep over me.

I stood there, wondering what on earth was coming on me, and half expecting that any moment someone would come out of the darkness and show himself; and as I held my breath and made no movement at all the queer sensation grew stronger. I believe I even resisted a temptation to kick up my heels and dance, to let out a flying shout as a man with liquor in him does. Instead of this, however, I just kept dead still. The wood was black as ink all round me, too black to see the tree-trunks separately, except far below where the village lights came up twinkling between them, and the only way I kept the path was by the soft feel of the pine-needles that were thicker than a Brussels carpet. But nothing happened, and no one stirred. The idea that I was being watched remained, only there was no sound anywhere except the roar of falling water that filled the entire valley. Yet someone was very close to me in the darkness.

I can't say how long I might have stood there, but I guess it was the best part of ten minutes, and I remember it struck me that I had run up against a pocket of extra-rarefied air that had a lot of oxygen in it—oxygen or something similar—and that was the cause of my elation. The idea was nonsense, I have no doubt; but for the moment it half explained the thing to me. I realised it was all *natural* enough, at any rate—and so moved on. It took a longish time to reach the edge of the wood, and a footpath led me—oh, it was quite a walk, I tell you—into the village street again. I was both glad and sorry to get there. I kept myself busy thinking the whole thing over again. What

309

caught me all of a heap was that million-dollar sense of beauty, youth, and happiness. Never in my born days had I felt anything to touch it. And it hadn't cost a cent!

Well, I was sitting there enjoying my smoke and trying to puzzle it all out, and the hall was pretty full of people smoking and talking and reading papers, and so forth, when all of a sudden I looked up and caught my breath with such a jerk that I actually bit my tongue. There was grandfather in front of my chair! I looked into his eyes. I saw him as clear and solid as the porter standing behind his desk across the lounge, and it gave me a touch of cold all down the back that I needn't forget unless I want to. He was looking into my face, and he had a cap in his hand, and he was speaking to me. It was my grandfather's picture come to life, only much thinner and younger and a kind of light in his eyes like fire.

'I beg your pardon, but you *are*—Uncle Jim, aren't you?'

And then, with another jump of my nerves, I understood.

'You, Arthur! Well, I'm jiggered. So it is. Take a chair, boy. I'm right glad you found me. Shake! Sit down.' And I took his hand and pushed a chair up for him. I was never so surprised in my life. The last time I set eyes on him he was a boy. Now he was a young man, and the very image of his ancestor.

He sat down, fingering his cap. He wouldn't have a drink and he wouldn't smoke. 'All right,' I said, 'let's talk then. I've lots to tell you and I've lots to hear. How are you, boy?'

He didn't answer at first. He eyed me up and down. He hesitated. He was as handsome as a young Greek god.

'I say, Uncle Jim,' he began presently, 'it *was* you—just now—in the wood—wasn't it?' It made me start, that question put so quietly.

'I *have* just come through that wood up there,' I answered, pointing in the direction as well as I could remember, 'if that's what you mean. But why? *You* weren't there, were you?' It gave me a queer sort of feeling to hear him say it. What in the name of heaven did he mean?

He sat back in his chair with a sigh of relief.

310

'Oh, that's all right then,' he said, 'if it *was* you. Did you see,' he asked suddenly, 'did you see—anything?'

'Not a thing,' I told him honestly. 'It was far too dark.' I laughed. I fancied I twigged his meaning. But I was not the sort of uncle to come prying on him. Life must be dull enough, I remembered, in this mountain village.

But he didn't understand my laugh. He didn't mean what I meant.

And there came a pause between us. I discovered that we were talking different lingoes. I leaned over towards him.

'Look here, Arthur,' I said in a lower voice, 'what is it, and what do you mean? I'm all right, you know, and you needn't be afraid of telling me. What d'you mean by—did I see anything?'

We looked at each other squarely in the eye. He saw he could trust me, and I saw—well, a whole lot of things, perhaps, but I felt chiefly that he liked me and would tell me things later, all in his own good time. I liked him all the better for that too.

'I only meant' he answered slowly, 'whether you really *saw*—anything?'

'No,' I said straight, 'I didn't see a thing, but, by the gods, I *felt* something.'

He started. I started too. An astonishing big look came swimming over his fair, handsome face. His eyes seemed all lit up. He looked as if he'd just made a cool million in wheat or cotton.

'I knew—you were that sort,' he whispered. 'Though I hardly remembered what you looked like.'

'Then what on earth was it?' I asked.

His reply staggered me a bit. 'It was just that,' he said—'the Earth!'

And then, just when things were getting interesting and promising a dividend, he shut up like a clam. He wouldn't say another word. He asked after my family and business, my health, what kind of crossing I'd had, and all the rest of the common stock. It fairly bowled me over. And I couldn't change him either.

311

I suppose in America we get pretty free and easy, and don't quite understand reserve. But this young man of half my age kept me in my place as easily as I might have kept a nervous customer quiet in my own office. He just refused to take me on. He was polite and cool and distant as you please, and when I got pressing sometimes he simply pretended he didn't understand. I could no more get him back again to the subject of the wood than a customer could have gotten me to tell him about the prospects of exchange being cheap or dear—when I didn't know myself but wouldn't let him see I didn't know. He was charming, he was delightful, enthusiastic and even affectionate; downright glad to see me, too, and to chin with me—but I couldn't draw him worth a cent. And in the end I gave up trying.

And the moment I gave up trying he let down a little—but only a very little.

'You'll stay here some time, Uncle Jim, won't you?'

'That's my idea,' I said, 'if I can see you, and you can show me round some.'

He laughed with pleasure. 'Oh, rather. I've got lots of time. After three in the afternoon I'm free till—any time you like. There's a lot to see,' he added.

'Come along to-morrow then,' I said. 'If you can't take lunch, perhaps you can come just afterwards. You'll find me waiting for you—right here.'

'I'll come at three,' he replied, and we said good night.

2

He turned up sharp on time, and I liked his punctuality. I saw him come swinging down the dusty road; tall, deep-chested, his broad shoulders a trifle high, and his head set proudly. He looked like a young chap in training, a thoroughbred, every inch of him. At the same time there was a touch of something a little too refined and delicate for a man, I thought. That was the poetic, scholarly vein in him, I guess—grandfather cropping out. This time he wore no cap. His thick light hair, not brushed back like the London shop-boys, but parted on the side, yet untidy for all that, suited him exactly and gave him a touch of wildness.

'Well,' he asked, 'what would you like to do, Uncle Jim? I'm at your service, and I've got the whole afternoon till supper at seven-thirty.' I told him I'd like to go through that wood. 'All right,' he said, 'come along. I'll show you.' He gave me one quick glance, but said no more. 'I'd like to see if I feel anything this time,' I explained. 'We'll locate the very spot, maybe.' He nodded. 'You know where I mean, don't you?' I asked, 'because you saw me there?' He just said yes, and then we started.

It was hot, and air was scarce. I remember that we went uphill, and that I realised there was considerable difference in our ages. We crossed some fields first—smothered in flowers so thick that I wondered how much grass the cows got out of it!—and then came to a sprinkling of fine young larches that looked as soft as velvet. There was no path, just a wild mountain side. I had very little breath on the steep zigzags, but Arthur talked easily—and talked mighty well, too: the light and shade, the colouring, and the effect of all this wilderness of lonely beauty on the mind. He kept all this suppressed at home in business. It was safety valves. I twigged *that*. It was the artist in him talking. He seemed to think there was nothing in the world but Beauty—with a big B all the time. And the odd thing was he took for granted that I felt the same. It was cute of him to flatter me that way. 'Daulis and the lone Cephissian vale,' I heard; and a few moments later—with a sort of reverence in his voice like worship—he called out a great singing name: '*Astarte!*'

> 'Day is her face, and midnight is her hair,
> And morning hours are but the golden stair
> By which she climbs to Night.'

'Steady on, boy! I've forgotten all my classics ages ago,' I cried.

He turned and gazed down on me, his big eyes glowing,

and not a sign of perspiration on his skin.

'That's nothing,' he exclaimed in his musical, deep voice. 'You know it, or you'd never have felt things in this wood last night; and you wouldn't have wanted to come out with me now!'

'How?' I gasped. 'How's that?'

'You've come,' he continued quietly, 'to the only valley in this artificial country that has atmosphere. This valley is *alive*—especially this end of it. There's superstition here, thank God! Even the peasants know things.'

It was here first that a queer change began to grow upon me too.

I stared at him. 'See here, Arthur,' I objected. 'I'm not a Cath. And I don't know a thing—at least it's all dead in me and forgotten—about poetry or classics or your gods and pan—pantheism—in spite of grandfather——'

His face turned like a dream face.

'Hush!' he said quickly. 'Don't mention *him*. There's a bit of him in you as well as in me, and it was here, you know, he wrote——'

I didn't hear the rest of what he said. A creep came over me. I remembered that this ancestor of ours lived for years in the isolation of some mountain forest where he claimed—he used that setting for his writing—to have found the exiled gods, their ghosts, their beauty, their eternal essence—or something astonishing of that sort. I had clean forgotten it till this moment. It all rushed back upon me, a memory of my boyhood.

And, as I say, a creep came over me—something as near to awe as ever could be. The sunshine on the field of yellow daisies and blue forget-me-nots turned paler. The warm valley wind had a touch of snow in it. And, ashamed and frightened of my baby mood, I looked at Arthur, meaning to choke him off with all this rubbish—and then saw something in his eyes that fairly scared me stiff.

I admit it. What's the use? There was an expression on his face that made my blood go curdled. I got cold feet right there. It mastered me. In him, behind him, near him—blest if I know which, *through* him probably—came an ernormous thing that turned me insignificant. It downed me utterly.

It was over in a second, the flash of a wing. I recovered instantly. No mere boy should come these muzzy tricks on me, scholar or no scholar. For the change in me was on the increase, and I shrank.

'See here, Arthur,' I said plainly once again, 'I don't know what your game is, but—there's something queer up here I don't quite get at. I'm only a business man, with classics and poetry all gone dry in me twenty years ago and more——'

He looked at me so strangely that I stopped, confused.

'But, Uncle Jim,' he said as quietly as though we talked tobacco brands, 'you needn't be alarmed. It's natural you should feel the place. You and I belong to it. We've both got *him* in us. You're just as proud of him as I am, only in a different way.' And then he added, with a touch of disappointment: 'I thought you'd like it. You weren't afraid last night. You felt the beauty *then*.'

Flattery is a darned subtle thing at any time. To see him standing over me in that superior way and talking down at my poor business mind—well, it just came over me that I was laying my cards on the table a bit too early. After so many years of city life——!

Anyway, I pulled myself together. 'I was only kidding you, boy,' I laughed. 'I feel this beauty just as much as you do. Only, I guess, you're more accustomed to it than I am. Come on now,' I added with energy, getting upon my feet, 'let's push on and see the wood. I want to find that place again.'

He pulled me with a hand of iron, laughing as he did so. Gee! I wished I had his teeth, as well as the muscles in his arm. Yet I, too, felt younger, somehow—youth flowed more and more into my veins. I had forgotten how sweet the winds and woods and flowers could be. Something melted in me. For it was Spring, and the whole world was singing like a dream. Beauty was creeping over me. I don't know. I began to feel all big and tender and open to a thousand wonderful sensations.

The thought of streets and houses seemed like death....

We went on again, not talking much; my breath got shorter and shorter, and he kept looking about him as though he expected something. But we passed no living soul, not even a peasant; there were no chalets, no cattle, no cattle-shelters even. And then I realised that the valley lay at our feet in haze and that we had been climbing at least a couple of hours. 'Why, last night I got home in twenty minutes at the outside,' I said. He shook his head, smiling. 'It seemed like that,' he replied, 'but you really took much longer. It was long after ten when I found you in the hall.' I reflected a moment. 'Now I come to think of it, you're right, Arthur. Seems curious, though, somehow.' He looked closely at me. 'I followed you all the way,' he said.

'You followed me!'

'And you went at a good pace too. It was your feelings that made it seem so short—you were singing to yourself and happy as a dancing faun. We kept close behind you for a long way.'

I think it was 'we' he said, but for some reason or other I didn't care to ask.

'Maybe,' I answered shortly, trying uncomfortably to recall what particular capers I had cut. 'I guess that's right.' And then I added something about the loneliness, and how deserted all this slope of mountain was. And he explained that the peasants were afraid of it and called it No Man's Land. From one year's end to another no human foot went up or down it; the hay was never cut; no cattle grazed along the splendid pastures; no chalet had even been built within a mile of the wood we slowly made for. 'They're superstitious,' he told me. 'It was just the same a hundred years ago when *he* discovered it—there was a little natural cave on the edge of the forest where he used to sleep sometimes—I'll show it to you presently —but for generations this entire mountain-side has been undisturbed. You'll never meet a living soul in any part of it.' He stopped and pointed above us to where the pine wood hung in mid-air, like a dim blue carpet. 'It's just the place for

316

Them, you see.'

And a thrill of power went smashing through me. I can't describe it. It drenched me like a waterfall. I thought of Greece—Mount Ida and a thousand songs! Something in me—it was like the click of a shutter—announced that the 'change' was suddenly complete. I was another man; or rather a deeper part of me had come on top. My very language showed it.

The calm of halcyon weather lay over all. Overhead the peaks rose clear as crystal; below us the village lay in a bluish smudge of smoke and haze, as though a great finger had rubbed them softly into the earth. Absolute loneliness fell upon me like a clap. From the world of human beings we seemed quite shut off. And there began to steal over me again the strange elation of the night before.... We found ourselves almost at once against the edge of the wood.

It rose in front of us, a big wall of splendid trees, motionless as if cut out of dark green metal, the branches hanging stiff, and the crowd of trunks lost in the blue dimness underneath. I shaded my eyes with one hand, trying to peer into the solemn gloom. The contrast between the brilliant sunshine on the pastures and this region of heavy shadows blurred my sight.

'It's like the entrance to another world,' I whispered.

'It is,' said Arthur, watching me. 'We will go in. You shall pluck asphodel....'

And, before I knew it, he had me by the hand. We were advancing. We left the light behind us. The cool air dropped upon me like a sheet. There was a temple silence. The sun ran down behind the sky, leaving a marvellous blue radiance everywhere. Nothing stirred. But through the stillness there rose power, power that has no name, power that hides at the foundations somewhere—foundations that are changeless, invisible, everlasting. What do I mean? My mind grew to the dimensions of a planet. We were among the roots of life—whence issues that *one thing* in infinite guise that seeks so many temporary names from the protean minds of men.

'You shall pluck asphodel in the meadows this side of Erebus,'

Arthur was chanting. 'Hermes himself, the Psychopomp, shall lead, and Malahide shall welcome us.'

Malahide...!

To hear him use that name, the name of our scholar-ancestor, now dead and buried close upon a century—the way he half chanted it—gave me the goose-flesh. I stopped against a tree-stem, thinking of escape. No words came to me at the moment, for I didn't know what to say; but, on turning to find the bright green slopes just left behind, I saw only a crowd of trees and shadows hanging thick as a curtain—as though we had walked a mile. And it was a shock. The way out was lost. The trees closed up behind us like a tide.

'It's all right,' said Arthur; 'just keep an open mind and a heart alive with love. It has a shattering effect at first, but that will pass.' He saw I was afraid, for I shrank visibly enough. He stood beside me in his grey flannel suit, with his brilliant eyes and his great shock of hair, looking more like a column of light than a human being. 'It's all quite right and natural,' he repeated; 'we have passed the gateway, and Hecate, who presides over gateways, will let us out again. Do not make discord by feeling fear. This is a pine wood, and pines are the oldest, simplest trees; they are true primitives. They are an open channel; and in a pine wood where no human life has ever been you shall often find gateways where Hecate is kind to such as us.'

He took my hand—he must have felt mine trembling, but his own was cool and strong and felt like silver—and led me forward into the depths of a wood that seemed to me quite endless. It felt endless, that is to say. I don't know what came over me. Fear slipped away, and elation took its place.... As we advanced over ground that seemed level, or slightly undulating, I saw bright pools of sunshine here and there upon the forest floor. Great shafts of light dropped in slantingly between the trunks. There was movement everywhere, though I never could see what moved. A delicious, scented air stirred through the lower branches. Running water sang not very far away. Figures I did not actually see; yet there were limbs and flowing draperies and flying hair from time to time, ever just beyond the pools of sunlight. Surprise went from me too. I was on air. The atmosphere of dream came round me, but a dream of something just hovering outside the world I knew—a dream wrought in gold and silver, with shining eyes, with graceful beckoning hands, and with voices that rang like bells of music ... And the pools of light grew larger, merging one into another, until a delicate soft light shone equably throughout the entire forest. Into this zone of light we passed together. Then something fell abruptly at our feet, as though thrown down... two marvellous, shining sprays of blossom such as I had never seen in all my days before!

'Asphodel!' cried my companion, stooping to pick them up and handing one to me. I took it from him with a delight I could not understand. 'Keep it,' he murmured; 'it is the sign that we are welcome. For Malahide has dropped these on our path.'

And at the use of that ancestral name it seemed that a spirit passed before my face and the hair of my head stood up. There was a sense of violent, unhappy contrast. A composite picture presented itself, then rushed away. What was it? My youth in England, music and poetry at Cambridge and my passionate love of Greek that lasted two terms at most, when Malahide's great books formed part of the curriculum. Over against this, then, the drag and smother of solid worldly business, the sordid weight of modern ugliness, the bitterness of an ambitious, over-striving life. And abruptly—beyond both pictures—a shining, marvellous Beauty that scattered stars beneath my feet and scarved the universe with gold.

All this flashed before me with the utterance of that old family name. An alternative sprang up. There seemed some radical, elemental choice presented to me—to what I used to call my soul. My soul could take it or leave it as it pleased....

I looked at Arthur moving beside me like a shaft of light. What had come over me? How had our walk and talk and mood, our quite recent everyday and ordinary view, our normal relationship with the things of the world—how had it all slipped into this? So insensibly, so easily, so naturally!

'Was it worth while?'

The question—*I* didn't ask it—jumped up in me of its own accord. Was 'what' worth while? Why, my present life of commonplace and grubbing toil, of course; my city existence, with its meagre, unremunerative ambitions. Ah, it was this new Beauty calling me, this shining dream that lay beyond the two pictures I have mentioned.... I did not argue it, even to myself. But I understood. There was a radical change in me. The buried poet, too long hidden, rushed into the air like some great singing bird.

I glanced again at Arthur moving along lightly by my side, half dancing almost in his brimming happiness. 'Wait till you see Them,' I heard him singing. 'Wait till you hear the call of Artemis and the footsteps of her flying nymphs. Wait till Orion thunders overhead and Selene, crowned with the crescent moon, drives up the zenith in her white-horsed chariot. The choice will be beyond all question then...!'

A great silent bird, with soft brown plumage, whirred across our path, pausing an instant as though to peep, then disappearing with a muted sound into an eddy of the wind it made. The big trees hid it. It was an owl. The same moment I heard a rush of liquid song come pouring through the forest with a gush of almost human notes, and another pair of glossy wings flashed past us, swerving upwards to find the open sky—blue-black, pointed wings.

'His favourites!' exclaimed my companion with clear joy in his voice. 'They all are here! Athene's bird, Procne and Philomela too! The owl—the swallow—and the nightingale! Tereus and Itys are not far away.' And the entire forest, as he said it, stirred with movement, as though that great bird's quiet wings had waked the sea of ancient shadows. There were voices too—ringing, laughing voices, as though his words woke echoes that had been listening for it. For I heard sweet singing in the distance. The names he had used perplexed me. Yet even I, stranger as I was to such refined delights, could not mistake the passion of the nightingale and the dart of the eager swallow. That wild burst of music, that curve of swift escape, were unmistakable.

And I struck a stalwart tree-stem with my open hand, feeling the need of hearing, touching, sensing it. My link with known, remembered things was breaking. I craved the satisfaction of the commonplace. I got that satisfaction; but I got something more as well. For the trunk was round and smooth and comely. It was no dead thing I struck. Somehow it brushed me into intercourse with inanimate Nature. And next the desire came to hear my voice—my own familiar, high-pitched voice with the twang and accent the New World climate brings, so-called American:

'Exchange Place, Noo York City. I'm in that business, buying and selling of exchange between the banks of two civilised countries, one of them stoopid and old-fashioned, the other leading all creation...!'

It was an effort, but I made it firmly. Only it sounded odd, remote, unreal.

'Sunlit woods and a wind among the branches,' followed close and sweet upon my words. But who, in the name of Wall Street, said it?

'England's buying gold,' I tried again. 'We've had a private wire. Cut in quick. First National is selling!'

Great-faced Hephaestus, how ridiculous! It was like saying, 'I'll take your scalp unless you give me meat.' It was barbaric, savage, centuries ago. Again there came another voice that caught up my own and turned it into common syntax. Some heady beauty of the Earth rose about me like a cloud.

'Hark! Night comes, with the dusk upon her eyelids. She brings those dreams that every dew-drop holds at dawn. Daughter of Thanatos and Hypnos...!'

But again—who said the words? It surely was not Arthur, my nephew Arthur, of To-day, learning French in a Swiss mountain village! I felt—well, what did I feel? In the name of the Stock Exchange and Wall Street, what was the cash surrender of my amazing feelings?

3

AND, turning to look at him, I made a discovery. I don't know how to tell it quite; such shadowy marvels have never been my line of goods. He looked several things at once—taller, slighter, sweeter, but chiefly—it sounds so crazy when I write it down—grander is the word, I think. And radiating with some power that flowed like Spring when it pours upon a landscape. Eternally young and glorious—young, I mean, in the sense that a field of flowers in the Spring looks young; and glorious in the sense the sky looks glorious at dawn or sunset. Something big shone through him like a storm, something that would go on for ever just as the Earth goes on, always renewing itself; something of gigantic life that in the human sense could never age at all—something the old gods had. But the figure, so far as there was any figure at all, was that old family picture come to life. Our great ancestor and Arthur were one being, and that one being was vaster than a million people. Yet it was Malahide I saw....

'They laid me in the earth I loved,' he said in a low, penetrating voice like running wind and water, 'and I found eternal life. I live now for ever in Their divine existence. I share the life that changes yet can never pass away.'

I felt myself rising like a cloud as he said it. A rising beauty captured me completely. If I could tell it in honest newspaper language—the common language used in flats and offices—why, I guess I could patent a new meaning in ordinary words, a new power of expression, the thing that all the churches and poets and thinkers have been trying to say since the world began. I caught on to a fact so fine and simple that it knocked me silly to think I'd never realised it before. I had read about it, yes; but now I *knew* it. The Earth, the whole bustling universe, was nothing after all but a visible production of eternal, living Powers—spiritual powers, mind you—that just happened to include the particular little type of strutting creature we called mankind. And these Powers, as seen in Nature, were the gods. It was our refusal of their grand appeal, so wild and sweet and beautiful, that caused 'evil'. It was this barrier between ourselves and the rest of....

My thoughts and feelings swept away upon the rising flood as the 'figure' came upon me like a shaft of moonlight, melting the last remnant of opposition that was in me. I took my brain, my reason, chucking them aside for the futile little mechanism I suddenly saw them to be. In place of them came—oh, God, I hate to say it, for only nursery talk can get within a mile of it, and yet what I need is something simpler even than the words that children use. Under one arm I carried a whole forest breathing in the wind, and beneath the other a hundred meadows full of singing streams with golden marigolds and blue forget--me-nots along their banks. Upon my back and shoulders lay the clouded hills with dew and moonlight in their brimmed, capacious hollows. Thick in my hair hung the unaging powers that are stars and sunlight; though the sun was far away, it sweetened the currents of my blood with liquid gold. Breast and throat and face, as I advanced, met all the rivers of the world and all the winds of heaven, their strength and swiftness melting into me as light melts into everything it touches. And into my eyes passed all the radiant colours that weave the cloth of Nature as she takes the sun. I mean that the beauty of the world which never dies was one with the beauty in my soul—imperishable.

And this 'figure', pouring upon me like a burst of moonlight, spoke:

'They all are in you—air, and fire, and water....'

'And I—my feet stand—on the *Earth*,' my own voice interrupted, power lifting through the sound of it.

'The Earth! He laughed gigantically. He spread. He seemed everywhere about me. He seemed a race of men. My life swam forth in waves of some immense sensation that issued from the mountain and the forest, then returned to them again. I reeled. I became afraid. I clutched at something in me that was slipping beyond control, slipping down a bank towards a deep, dark river flowing at my feet. A shadowy boat appeared, a still more shadowy outline at the helm. I was in the act of stepping into it. For the tree I caught at to save myself was only air. I couldn't stop. I tried to scream.

'You have plucked asphodel,' sang the voice beside me, 'and you shall pluck more....'

I slipped and slipped, the speed increasing horribly. Then something caught, as though a cog held fast and stopped me—I remembered my business in New York City.

'Arthur!' I yelled. 'Arthur!' I shouted again as hard as I could shout. There was frantic terror in me. I felt as though I should never get back to myself again. Death!

The answer came in his normal voice: 'Keep close to me. I know the way....'

The scenery dwindled suddenly; the trees came back. I was walking in the forest beside my nephew, and the moonlight lay in patches and little shafts of silver. The crests of the pines just murmured in a wind that scarcely stirred, and through an opening on our right I saw the deep valley clasped about the twinkling village lights. Towering in splendour the spectral snowfields hung upon the sky, huge summits guarding them. And Arthur took my arm—oh, solidly enough this time. Thank heaven, he asked no questions of me.

'There's a smell of myrrh,' he whispered, 'and we are very near the undying, ancient things.'

I said something about the resin from the trees, but he took no notice.

'It enclosed its body in an egg of myrrh,' he went on, smiling down at me; 'then, setting it on fire, rose from the ashes with its life renewed. Once every five hundred years, you see——'

'What did?' I cried, feeling that loss of self stealing over me again. And his answer came like a blow between the eyes:

'The Phœnix. They called it a bird, though, of course, the true...'

'But my life's insured in that,' I cried, for he had named the company that took large yearly premiums from me; 'and I pay...'

'Your life's insured in *this*,' he said quietly, waving his arms to indicate the Earth. 'Your love of Nature and your sympathy with it make you safe.' He gazed at me. There was a marvellous expression in his eyes. I understood why poets talked of stars and flowers in a human face. But behind the face crept back another look as well. There grew about his figure an indeterminate extension. The outline of Malahide again stirred through his own. A pale, delicate hand reached out to take my own. And something broke in me.

I was conscious of two things—a burst of joy that meant losing myself entirely, and a rush of terror that meant staying as I was, a small, painful, struggling item of individual life. Another spray of that awful asphodel fell fluttering through the air in front of my face. It rested on the earth against my feet. And Arthur—this weirdly changing Arthur—stooped to pick it up for me. I kicked it with my foot beyond his reach... then turned and ran as though the Furies of that ancient world were after me. I ran for what I called my 'very life'. How I escaped from that thick wood without banging my body to bits against the trees I can't explain. I ran from something I desired yet feared. I leaped along in a succession of flying bounds. Each tree I passed turned of its own accord and flung after me until the entire forest followed. But I got out. I reached the open. Upon the sloping field in the full, clear light of the moon I collapsed in a panting heap. The Earth drew back with a great shuddering sigh behind me. There was this strange, tumultuous sound upon the night. I lay beneath the open heavens that were full of moonlight. I was myself—but there were tears in me. Beauty too high for understanding had slipped between my fingers. I had lost Malahide. I had lost the gods of Earth.... Yet I had seen... and felt. I had not lost all. Something remained that I could never lose again....

I don't know how it happened exactly, but presently I heard Arthur saying: 'You'll catch your death of cold if you lie on that soaking grass,' and felt his hand seize mine to pull me to my feet.

'I feel safer on earth,' I believed I answered. And then he said: 'Yes, but it's such a stupid way to die—a chill!'

4

I GOT up then, and we went downhill together towards the village lights. I danced—oh, I admit it—I sang as well. There was a flood of joy and power about me that beat anything I'd ever felt before. I didn't think or hesitate, there was no self-consciousness; I just let it rip for all there was, and if there had been ten thousand people there in front of me, I could have made them feel it too. That was the kind of feeling—power and confidence and a sort of raging happiness. I think I know what it was too. I say this soberly, with reverence... all wool and no fading. There was a bit of God in me, God's power that drives the Earth and pours through Nature—the imperishable Beauty expressed in those old-world nature-deities!

And the fear I'd felt was nothing but the little tickling pain of losing my ordinary two-cent self, the dread of letting go, the shrinking before the plunge—what a fellow feels when he's falling in love, and hesitates, and tries to think it out and hold back, and is afraid to let the enormous tide flow in and drown him.

Oh, yes, I began to think it over a bit as we raced down the mountain-side that glorious night. I've read some in my day; my brain's all right; I've heard of dual personality and subliminal uprush and conversion—no new line of goods, all that. But somehow these stunts of the psychologists and philosophers didn't cut any ice with me just then, because I'd *experienced* what they merely *explained*. And explanation was just a bargain sale. The best things can't be explained at all. There's no real value in a bargain sale.

Arthur had trouble to keep up with me. We were running due east, and the Earth was turning, therefore, with us. We all three ran together at her own pace—terrific! The moonlight danced along the summits, and the snowfields flew like spreading robes, and the forests everywhere, far and near, hung watching us and booming like a thousand organs. There were uncaged winds about; you could hear them whistling among the precipices. But the one great thing I knew was—Beauty, a beauty of the common old familiar Earth, and a beauty that's stayed with me ever since, and given me joy and strength and a source of power and delight I'd never guessed existed before.

As we dropped lower into the thicker air of the valley I sobered down. Gradually the ecstasy passed from me. We slowed up a bit. The lights and the houses and the sight of the hotel where people were dancing in a stuffy ballroom, all this put blotting-paper on something that had been flowing.

Now you'll think this an odd thing too—but when we reached the village street, I just took Arthur's hand and shook it and said good-night and went up to bed and slept like a two-year-old till morning. And from that day to this I've never set eyes on the boy again.

Perhaps it's difficult to explain, and perhaps it isn't. I can explain it to myself in two lines—I was afraid to see him. I was afraid he might explain. I was afraid he might explain away. I just left a note—he never replied to it—and went off by a morning train. Can you understand that? Because if you can't you haven't understood this account I've tried to give of the experience Arthur gave me. Well—anyway—I'll just let it go at that.

Arthur's a director now in his father's wholesale chemical business, and I—well, I'm doing better than ever in the buying and selling of exchange between banks in New York City as before.

But when I said I was still drawing dividends on my Swiss investment, I meant it. And it's not 'scenery.' Everybody gets a thrill from 'scenery.' It's a darned sight more than that. It's those little wayward patches of blue on a cloudy day; those blue pools in the sky just above Trinity Church steeple when I pass out of Wall Street into Lower Broadway; it's the rustle of the sea-wind among the Battery trees; the wash of the waves when the Ferry's starting for Staten Island, and the glint of the sun far down the Bay, or dropping a bit of pearl into the old East River. And sometimes it's the strip of cloud in the west above the Jersey shore of the Hudson, the first star, the sickle of the new moon behind the masts and shipping. But usually it's something nearer, bigger, simpler than all or any of these. It's just the certainty that, when I hurry along the hard stone pavements from bank to bank, I'm walking on the —Earth. It's just that—*the Earth!*

A DESERT EPISODE

1

'BETTER put wraps on now. The sun's getting low,' a girl said.

It was the end of a day's expedition in the Arabian Desert, and they were having tea. A few yards away the donkeys munched their *barsim*; beside them in the sand the boys lay finishing bread and jam. Immense, with gliding tread, the sun's rays slid from crest to crest of the limestone ridges that broke the huge expanse towards the Red Sea. By the time the tea-things were packed the sun hovered, a giant ball of red, above the Pyramids. It stood in the western sky a moment, looking out of its majestic hood across the sand. With a movement almost visible it leaped, paused, then leaped again. It seemed to bound towards the horizon; then, suddenly, was gone.

'It *is* cold, yes,' said the painter, Rivers. And all who heard looked up at him because of the way he said it. A hurried movement ran through the merry party, and the girls were on their donkeys quickly, not wishing to be left to bring up the rear. They clattered off. The boys cried; the thud of sticks was heard; hoofs shuffled through the sand and stones. In single file the picnickers headed for Helouan, some five miles distant. And the desert closed up behind them ast they went, following in a shadowy wave that never broke, noiseless, foamless, unstreaked, driven by no wind, and of a volume undiscoverable. Against the orange sunset the Pyramids turned deep purple. The strip of silvery Nile among its palm trees looked like rising mist. In the incredible Egyptian after-glow the enormous horizons burned a little longer, then went out. The ball of the earth—a huge round globe that bulged—curved visibly as at sea. It was no longer a flat espanse; it turned. Its splendid curves were realised.

'Better put wraps on; it's cold and the sun is low'—and

329

then the curious hurry to get back among the houses and the haunts of men. No more was said, perhaps, than this, yet, the time and place being what they were, the mind became suddenly aware of that quality which ever brings a certain shrinking with it—vastness; and more than vastness: that which is endless because it is also beginningless—eternity. A colossal splendour stole upon the heart; and the senses, unaccustomed to the unusual stretch, reeled a little, as though the wonder was more than could be faced with comfort. Not all, doubtless, realised it, though to two, at least, it came with a staggering impact there was no withstanding. For, while the luminous greys and purples crept round them from the sand wastes, the hearts of these two became aware of certain common things whose simple majesty is usually dulled by mere familiarity. Neither the man nor the girl knew for certain that the other felt it, as they brought up the rear together; yet the fact that each *did* feel it set them side by side in the same strange circle—and made them silent. They realised the immensity of a moment: the dizzy stretch of time that led up to the casual pinning of a veil, to the tightening of a stirrup strap, to the little speech with a companion, to the roar of the vanished centuries that have ground mountains into sand and spread them over the floor of Africa; above all, to the little truth that they themselves existed amid the whirl of stupendous systems all delicately balanced as a spider's web—that they were *alive*.

For a moment this vast scale of reality revealed itself, then hid swiftly again behind the debris of the obvious. The universe, containing their two tiny yet important selves, stood still for an instant before their eyes. They looked at it—realised that they belonged to it. Everything moved and had its being, *lived*—here in this silent, empty desert even more actively than in a city of crowded houses. The quiet Nile, sighing with age, passed down towards the sea; there loomed the menacing Pyramids across the twilight; beneath them, in monstrous dignity, crouched that Shadow from whose eyes of battered stone proceeds the nameless thing that contracts the heart, then opens it again to terror; and everywhere, from towering monoliths as from secret tombs, rose that strange, long whisper which, defying time and distance, laughs at death. The spell of Egypt, which is the spell of immortality, touched their hearts.

Already, as the group of picnickers rode homewards now, the first stars twinkled overhead, and the peerless Egyptian night was on the way. There was hurry in the passing of the dusk. And the cold sensibly increased.

'So you did no painting after all,' said Rivers to the girl who rode a little in front of him, 'for I never saw you touch your sketch-book once.'

They were some distance now behind the others; the line straggled; and when no answer came he quickened his pace, drew up alongside and saw that her eyes, in the reflection of the sunset, shone with moisture. But she turned her head a little, smiling into his face, so that the human and the non-human beauty came over him with an onset that was almost shock. Neither one nor other, he knew, were long for him, and the realisation fell upon him with a pant of actual physical pain. The acuteness, the hopelessness of the realisation, for a moment, were more than he could bear, stern of temper though he was, and he tried to pass in front of her, urging his donkey with resounding strokes. Her own animal, however, following the lead, at once came up with him.

'You felt it, perhaps, as I did,' he said some moments later, his voice quite steady again. 'The stupendous, everlasting thing—the—*life* behind it all.' He hesitated a little in his speech, unable to find the substantive that could compass even a fragment of his thought. She paused, too, similarly inarticulate before the surge of incomprehensible feelings.

'It's—awful,' she said, half laughing, yet the tone hushed and a little quaver in it somewhere. And her voice to him was like the first sound he had ever heard in the world, for the first sound a full-grown man heard in the world would be beyond all telling—magical. 'I shall not try again,' she continued, leaving out the laughter this time; 'my sketch-book is a farce. For, to tell the truth'—and the next three words she

331

said below her breath—'I dare not.'

He turned and looked at her for a second. It seemed to him that the following wave had caught them up, and was about to break above her too. But the big-brimmed hat and the streaming veil shrouded her features. He saw, instead, the Universe. He felt as though he and she had always, always been together, and always, always would be. Separation was inconceivable.

'It came so close,' she whispered. 'It—shook me!'

They were cut off from their companions, whose voices sounded far ahead. Her words might have been spoken by the darkness, or by someone who peered at them from within that following wave. Yet the fanciful phrase was better than any he could find. From the immeasurable space of time and distance men's hearts vainly seek to plumb, it drew into closer perspective a certain meaning that words may hardly compass, a formidable truth that belongs to that deep place where hope and doubt fight their incessant battle. The awe she spoke of was the awe of immortality, of belonging to something that is endless and beginningless.

And he understood that the tears and laughter were one— caused by that spell which takes a little human life and shakes it, as an animal shakes its prey that later shall feed its blood and increase its power of growth. His other thoughts—really but a single thought—he had not the right to utter. Pain this time easily routed hope as the wave came nearer. For it was the wave of death that would shortly break, he knew, over him, but not over her. Him it would sweep with its huge withdrawal into the desert whence it came: her it would leave high upon the shores of life—alone. And yet the separation would somehow not be real. They were together in eternity even now. They were endless as this desert, beginningless as this sky ... immortal. The realisation overwhelmed....

The lights of Helouan seemed to come no nearer as they rode on in silence for the rest of the way. Against the dark background of the Mokattam Hills these fairy lights twinkled brightly, hanging in mid-air, but after an hour they were no closer than before. It was like riding towards the stars. It would take centuries to reach them. There were centuries in which to do so. Hurry has no place in the desert; it is born in streets. The desert stands still; to go fast in it is to go backwards.

Now, in particular, its enormous, uncanny leisure was everywhere—in keeping with that mighty scale the sunset had made visible. His thoughts, like the steps of the weary animal that bore him, had no progress in them. The serpent of eternity, holding its tail in its own mouth, rose from the sand, enclosing himself, the stars—and her. Behind him, in the hollows of that shadowy wave, the procession of dynasties and conquests, the great series of gorgeous civilisations the mind calls Past, stood still, crowded with shining eyes and beckoning faces, still waiting to arrive. There is no death in Egypt. His own death stood so close that he could touch it by stretching out his hand, yet it seemed as much behind him as in front. What man called a beginning was a trick. There was no such thing. He was with this girl—*now*, when Death waited so close for him—yet he had never really begun. Their lives ran always parallel. The hand he stretched to clasp approaching death caught instead in this girl's shadowy hair, drawing her in with him to the centre where he breathed the eternity of the desert. Yet expression of any sort was as futile as it was unnecessary. To paint, to speak, to sing, even the slightest gesture of the soul, became a crude and foolish thing. Silence was here the truth. And they rode in silence towards the fairy lights.

Then suddenly the rocky ground rose up close before them; boulders stood out vividly with black shadows and shining heads; a flatroofed house slid by; three palm trees rattled in the evening wind; beyond, a mosque and minaret sailed upwards, like the spars and rigging of some phantom craft; and the colonnades of the great modern hotel, standing upon its dome of limestone ridge, loomed over them. Helouan was about them before they knew it. The desert lay behind with its huge, arrested billow. Slowly, owing to its prodigious volume, yet with a speed that merged it instantly with the far horizon behind the night, this wave now withdrew a little. There was no hurry. It came, for the moment, no farther. Rivers knew. For he was in it to the throat. Only his head was above the surface. He still could breathe—and speak—and see. Deepening with every hour into an incalculable splendour, it waited.

2

In the street the foremost riders drew rein, and, two and two abreast, the long line clattered past the shops and cafés, the railway station and hotels, stared at by the natives from the busy pavements. The donkeys stumbled, blinded by the electric light. Girls in white dresses flitted here and there, arabîyehs rattled past with people hurrying home to dress for dinner, and the evening train, just in from Cairo, disgorged its stream of passengers. There were dances in several of the hotels that night. Voices rose on all sides. Questions and answers, engagements and appointments were made, little plans and plots and intrigues for seizing happiness on the wing—before the wave rolled in and caught the lot. They chattered gaily:

'You *are* going, aren't you? You promised——'

'Of course I am.'

'Then I'll drive you over. May I call for you?'

'All right. Come at ten.'

'We shan't have finished our bridge by then. Say ten-thirty.'

And eyes exchanged their meaning signals. The group dismounted and dispersed. Arabs standing under the lebbekh trees, or squatting on the pavements before their dim-lit booths, watched them with faces of gleaming bronze. Rivers gave his bridle to a donkey-boy, and moved across stiffly after the long ride to help the girl dismount. 'You feel tired?' he asked gently. 'It's been a long day.' For her face was white as chalk, though the eyes shone brilliantly.

'Tired, perhaps,' she answered, 'but exhilarated too. I

should like to be there now. I should like to go back this minute—if someone would take me.' And, though she said it lightly, there was a meaning in her voice he apparently chose to disregard. It was as if she knew his secret. 'Will you take me—some day soon?'

The direct question, spoken by those determined little lips, was impossible to ignore. He looked close into her face as he helped her from the saddle with a spring that brought her a moment half into his arms. 'Some day—soon,' I will, he said with emphasis; 'when you are—ready.' The pallor in her face, and a certain expression in it he had not known before, startled him. 'I think you have been overdoing it, he added, with a tone in which authority and love were oddly mingled, neither of them disguised.

'Like yourself,' she smiled, shaking her skirts out and looking down at her dusty shoes. 'I've only a few days more—before I sail. We're both in such a hurry, but you are the worse of the two.'

'Because my time is even shorter,' ran his horrified thought—for he said no word.

She raised her eyes suddenly to his, with an expression that for an instant almost convinced him she had guessed—and the soul in him stood rigidly at attention, urging back the rising fires. The hair dropped loosely round the sun-burned neck. Her face was level with his shoulder. Even the glare of the street lights could not make her undesirable. But behind the gaze of the deep brown eyes another thing looked forth imperatively into his own. And he recognised it with a rush of terror, yet of singular exultation.

'It followed us all the way,' she whispered. 'It came after us from the desert—where it *lives*.'

'At the houses,' he said equally low, 'it stopped,'. He gladly adopted her syncopated speech, for it helped him in his struggle to subdue those rising fires.

For a second she hesitated. 'You mean, if we had not left so soon—when it turned cold. If we had not hurried—if we had remained a little longer——'

335

He caught at her hand, unable to control himself, but dropped it again the same second, while she made as though she had not noticed, forgiving him with her eyes. 'Or a great deal longer,' she added slowly—'for ever?'

And then he was certain that she *had* guessed—not that he loved her above all else in the world, for that was so obvious that a child might know it, but that his silence was due to his other, lesser secret: that the great Executioner stood waiting to drop the hood about his eyes. He was already pinioned. Something in her gaze and in her manner persuaded him suddenly that she understood.

His exhilaration increased extraordinarily. 'I mean,' he said very quietly, 'that the spell weakens here among the houses and among the—so-called living.' There was masterfulness, triumph, in his voice. Very wonderfully he saw her smile change; she drew slightly closer to his side, as though unable to resist. 'Mingled with lesser things we should not under-stand completely,' he added softly.

'And that might be a mistake, you mean?' she asked quickly, her face grave again.

It was his turn to hesitate a moment. The breeze stirred the hair about her neck, bringing its faint perfume—perfume of young life—to his nostrils. He drew his breath in deeply, smothering back the torrent of rising words he knew were unpermissible. 'Misunderstanding,' he said briefly. 'If the eye be single——' He broke off, shaken by a paroxysm of coughing. 'You know my meaning,' he continued, as soon as the attack had passed; 'you feel the difference *here*,' pointing round him to the hotels, the shops, the busy stream of people; 'the hurry, the excitement, the feverish, blinding child's play which pretends to be alive, but does not know it——' And again the coughing stopped him. This time she took his hand in her own, pressed it very slightly, then released it. He felt it as the touch of that desert wave upon his soul. 'The reception must be in complete and utter resignation. Tainted by lesser things, the disharmony might be——' he began stammeringly.

Again there came interruption, as the rest of the party called impatiently to know if they were coming up to the hotel. He had not time to find the completing adjective. Perhaps he could not find it ever. Perhaps it does not exist in any modern language. Eternity is not realised to-day; men have no time to know they are alive for ever; they are too busy....

They all moved in a chattering, merry group towards the big hotel. Rivers and the girl were separated.

3

THERE was a dance that evening, but neither of these took part in it. In the great dining-room their tables were far apart. He could not even see her across the sea of intervening heads and shoulders. The long meal over, he went to his room, feeling it imperative to be alone. He did not read, he did not write; but, leaving the light unlit, he wrapped himself up and leaned out upon the broad window-sill into the great Egyptian night. His deep-sunken thoughts, like to the crowding stars, stood still, yet for ever took new shapes. He tried to see behind them, as, when a boy, he had tried so see behind the constellations—out into space—where there is nothing.

Below him the lights of Helouan twinkled like the Pleiades reflected in a pool of water; a hum of queer soft noises rose to his ears; but just beyond the houses the desert stood at attention, the vastest thing he had ever known, very stern, yet very comforting, with its peace beyond all comprehension, its delicate, wild terror, and its awful message of immortality. And the attitude of his mind, though he did not know it, was one of prayer.... From time to time he went to lie on the bed with paroxysms of coughing. He had overtaxed his strength —his swiftly fading strength. The wave had risen to his lips.

Nearer forty than thirty-five, Paul Rivers had come out to Egypt, plainly understanding that with the greatest care he might last a few weeks longer than if he stayed in England. A few more times to see the sunset and the sunrise, to watch the stars, feel the soft airs of earth upon his cheeks; a few more days of intercourse wtih his kind, asking and answering questions, wearing the old, familiar clothes he loved, reading his favourite pages, and then—out into the big spaces—where there is nothing.

Yet no one, from his stalwart, energetic figure, would have guessed—no one but the expert mind, not to be deceived, to whom in the first attack of overwhelming despair and desolation he went for final advice. He left that house, as many had left it before, knowing that soon he would need no earthly protection of roof and walls, and that his soul, if it existed, would be shelterless in the space behind all manifested life. He had looked forward to fame and position in this world; had, indeed, already achieved the first step towards his end; and now, with the vanity of all earthly aims so mercilessly clear before him, he had turned, in somewhat of a nervous, concentrated hurry, to make terms with the Infinite while still the brain was there. And had, of course, found nothing. For it takes a lifetime crowded with experiment and effort to learn even the alphabet of genuine faith; and what could come of a few weeks' wild questioning but confusion and bewilderment of mind? It was inevitable. He came out to Egypt wondering, thinking, questioning, but chiefly wondering. He had grown, that is, more childlike, abandoning the futile tool of Reason, which hitherto had seemed to him the perfect instrument. Its foolishness stood naked before him in the pitiless light of the specialist's decision; for 'Who can by searching find out God?'

To be exceedingly careful of over-exertion was the final warning he brought with him, and within a few hours of his arrival, three weeks ago, he had met this girl and utterly disregarded it. He took it somewhat thus: 'Instead of lingering I'll enjoy myself and go out—a little sooner. I'll *live*. The time is very short.' His was not a nature, anyhow, that could heed a warning. He could not kneel. Upright and unflinching, he went to meet things as they came, reckless, unwise, but certainly not afraid. And this characteristic operated now. He ran to meet Death full tilt in the uncharted spaces that lay behind the stars. With love for a companion, he raced, his speed increasing from day to day, she, as he thought, knowing merely that he sought her, but had not guessed his darker secret that was now his *lesser* secret.

And in the desert, this afternoon of the picnic, the great thing he sped to meet had shown itself with its familiar touch of appalling cold and shadow: familiar, because all minds know of and accept it; appalling, because, until realised close and with the mental power at the full, it remains but a name the heart refuses to believe in. And he had discovered that its name was—Life.

Rivers had seen the wave that sweeps incessant, tireless, but as a rule invisible, round the great curve of the bulging earth, brushing the nations into the deeps behind. It had followed him home to the streets and houses of Helouan. He saw it now, as he leaned from his window, dim and immense, too huge to break. Its beauty was nameless, undecipherable. His coughing echoed back from the wall of its great sides.... And the music floated up at the same time from the ball-room in the opposite wing. The two sounds mingled. Life, which is love, and Death, which is their unchanging partner, held hands beneath the stars.

He leaned out farther to drink in the cool, sweet air. Soon, on this air, his body would be dust, driven, perhaps, against her very cheek, trodden on possibly by her little foot—until, in turn, she joined him too, blown by the same wind loose about the desert. True. Yet at the same time they would always be together, always somewhere side by side, continuing in the vast universe, alive. This new, absolute conviction was in him now. He remembered the curious, sweet perfume in the desert, as of flowers, where yet no flowers are. It was the perfume of life. But in the desert there is no life. Living things that grow and move and utter, are but a protest against death. In the desert they are unnecessary, because death there *is* not. Its overwhelming vitality needs no insolent, visible proof, no protest, no challenge, no little signs of life. The message of the desert is immortality....

He went finally to bed, just before midnight. Hovering magnificently just outside his window, Death watched him while he slept. The wave crept to the level of his eyes. He called her name....

And downstairs, meanwhile, the girl, knowing nothing, wondered where he was, wondered unhappily and restlessly; more—though this she did not understand—wondered mother-ingly. Until to-day, on the ride home, and from their singular conversation together, she had guessed nothing of his reason for being at Helouan, where so many come in order to find life. She only knew her own. And she was but twenty-five....

Then, in the desert, when that touch of unearthly chill had stolen out of the sand towards sunset, she had realised clearly, astonished she had not seen it long ago, that this man loved her, yet that something prevented his obeying the great impulse. In the life of Paul Rivers, whose presence had profoundly stirred her heart the first time she saw him, there was some obstacle that held him back, a barrier his honour must respect. He could never tell her of his love. It could lead to nothing. Knowing that he was not married, her intuition failed her utterly at first. Then, in their silence on the homeward ride, the truth had somehow pressed up and touched her with its hand of ice. In that disjointed conversation at the end, which reads as it sounded, as though no coherent meaning lay behind the words, and as though both sought to conceal by speech what yet both burned to utter, she had divined his darker secret, and knew that it was the same as her own. She under-stood then it was Death that had tracked them from the desert, following with its gigantic shadow from the sandy wastes. The cold, the darkness, the silence which cannot answer, the stupendous mystery which is the spell of its inscrutable Pre-sence, had risen about them in the dusk, and kept them com-pany at a little distance, until the lights of Helouan had bade it halt. Life which may not, cannot end, had frightened her.

His time, perhaps, was even shorter than her own. None knew his secret, since he was alone in Egypt and was caring for himself. Similarly, since she bravely kept her terror to herself her companions had no inkling of her own, aware merely that the disease was in her system and that her orders were to be extremely cautious. This couple, therefore, shared secretly together the two clearest glimpses of eternity life has to offer to the soul. Side by side they looked into the splenid eyes of Love and Death. Life, moreover, with its instinct for simple and terrific drama, had produced this majestic climax, breaking with pathos, at the very moment when it could not be developed—this side of the stars. They stood together upon the stage, a stage emptied of other human players; the audience had gone home and the lights were being lowered; no music sounded; the critics were a-bed. In this great game of Consequences it was known where he met her, what he said and what she answered, possibly what they did and even what the world thought. But 'what the consequence was' would remain unknown, untold. That would happen in the big spaces of which the desert in its silence, its motionless serenity, its shelterless, intolerable vastness, is the perfect symbol. And the desert gives no answer. It sounds no challenge, for it is complete. Life in the desert makes no sign. It *is*.

4

In the hotel that night there arrived by chance a famous International dancer, whise dahabíyeh lay anchored at San Giovanni, in the Nile below Heoľuan; and this woman, with her party, had come to dine and take part in the festivities. The news spread. After twelve the lights were lowered, and while the moonlight flooded the terraces, streaming past pillar and colonnade, she rendered in the shadowed halls the music of the Masters, interpreting with an instinctive genius messages which ternal and divine.

Among the crowd of enthralled and delighted guests, the girl sat on the steps and watched her. The rhythmical interpretation held a power that seemed, in a sense, inspired; there lay in it a certain unconscious something that was pure, unearthly; something that the stars, wheeling in stately movements over the sea and desert, know; something the great

341

winds bring to mountains where they play together; something the forests capture and fix magically into their gathering of big and little branches. It was both passionate and spiritual, wild and tender, intensely human and seductively non-human. For it was original, taught of Nature, a revelation of naked, unhampered life. It comforted, as the desert comforts. It brought the desert awe into the stuffy corridors of the hotel, with the moonlight and the whispering of stars, yet behind it ever the silence of those grey, mysterious, interminable spaces which utter to themselves the wordless song of life. For it was the same dim thing, she felt, that had followed her from the desert several hours before, halting just outside the streets and houses as though blocked from further advance; the thing that had stopped her foolish painting, skilled thought she was, because it hides behind colour and not in it; the thing that veiled the meaning in the cryptic sentences she and he had stammered out together; the thing, in a word, as near as she could approach it by any means of interior expression, that the realisation of death for the first time makes comprehensible—Immortality. It was unutterable, but it *was*. He and she were indissolubly together. Death was no separation. There was no death... It was terrible. It was—she had already used the word—awful, full of awe.

'In the desert,' thought whispered, as she watched spellbound, 'it is impossible even to conceive of death. The idea is meaningless. It simply is not.'

The music and the movement filled the air with life which, being there, must continue always, and continuing always can have never had a beginning. Death, therefore, was the great revealer of life. Without it none could realise that they are alive. Others had discovered this before her, but she did not know it. In the desert no one can realise death: it is hope and life that are the only certainty. The entire conception of the Egyptian system was based on this—the conviction, sure and glorious, of life's endless continuation. Their tombs and temples, their pyramids and sphinxes surviving after thousands of years, defy the passage of time and laugh at death; the very

bodies of their priests and kings, of their animals even, their
fish, their insects, stand to-day as symbols of their stalwart
knowledge.

And this girl, as she listened to the music and watched the
inspired dancing, remembered it. The message poured into
her from many sides, though the desert brought it clearest.
With death peering into her face a few short weeks ahead, she
thought instead of—life. The desert, as it were, became for
her a little fragment of eternity, focused into an intelligible
point for her mind to rest upon with comfort and comprehension. Her steady, thoughtful nature stirred towards an
objective far beyond the small enclosure of one narrow lifetime.
The scale of the desert stretched her to the grandeur of its
own imperial meaning, its divine repose, its unassailable and
everlasting majesty. She looked beyond the wall.

Eternity! That which is endless; without pause, without
beginning, without divisions or boundaries. The fluttering
of her brave yet frightened spirit ceased, aware with awe of its
own everlastingness. The swiftest motion produces the effect
of immobility; excessive light is darkness; size, run loose into
enormity, is the same as the minutely tiny. Similarly, in the
desert, life, too overwhelming and terrific to know limit or
confinement, lies undetailed and stupendous, still as deity,
a revelation of nothingness because it is all. Turned golden
beneath its spell that the music and the rhythm made even more
comprehensible, the soul in her, already lying beneath the
shadow of the great wave, sank into rest and peace, too certain
of itself to fear. And panic fled away. 'I am immortal...
because I *am*. And what I love is not apart from me. It is
myself. We are together endlessly because we *are*.'

Yet in reality, though the big desert brought this, it was
Love, which, being of similar parentage, interpreted its vast
meaning to her little heart—that sudden love which, without
a word of preface or explanation, had come to her a short three
weeks before.... She went up to her room soon after midnight, abruptly, unexpectedly stricken. Someone, it seemed,
had called her name. She passed his door.

The lights had been turned up. The clamour of praise was loud round the figure of the weary dancer as she left in a carriage for her dahabîyeh on the Nile. A low wind whistled round the walls of the great hotel, blowing chill and bitter between the pillars of the colonnades. The girl heard the voices float up to her through the night, and once more, behind the confused sound of the many, she heard her own name called, but more faintly than before, and from very far away. It came through the spaces beyond her open window; it died away again; then—but for the sighing of that bitter wind—silence, the deep silence of the desert.

And these two, Paul Rivers and the girl, between them merely a floor of that stone that built the Pyramids, lay a few moments before the Wave of Sleep engulfed them. And, while they slept, two shadowy forms hovered above the roof of the quiet hotel, melting presently into one, as dreams stole down from the desert and the stars. Immortality whispered to them. On either side rose Life and Death, towering in splendour. Love, joining their spreading wings, fused the gigantic outlines into one. The figures grew smaller, comprehensible. They entered the little windows. Above the beds they paused a moment, watching, waiting, and then, like a wave that is just about to break, they stooped....

And in the brilliant Egyptian sunlight of the morning, as she went downstairs, she passed his door again. She had awakened, but he slept on. He had preceded her. It was next day she learned his room was vacant.... Within the month she joined him, and within the year the cool north wind that sweetens Lower Egypt from the sea blew the dust across the desert as before. It is the dust of kings, of queens, of priests, princesses, lovers. It is the dust no earthly power can annihilate. It, too, lasts for ever. There was a little more of it... the desert's message slightly added to: Immortality.

TRANSITION

JOHN MUDBURY was on his way home from the shops, his arms full of Christmas Presents. It was after six o'clock and the streets were very crowded. He was an ordinary man, lived in an ordinary suburban flat, with an ordinary wife and ordinary children. *He* did not think them ordinary, but everybody else did. He had ordinary presents for each one, a cheap blotter for his wife, a cheap air-gun for the boy, and so forth. He was over fifty, bald, in an office, decent in mind and habits, of uncertain opinions, uncertain politics, and uncertain religion. Yet he considered himself a decided, positive gentleman, quite unaware that the morning newspaper determined his opinions for the day. He just lived—from day to day. Physically, he was fit enough, except for a weak heart (which never troubled him); and his summer holiday was bad golf, while the children bathed and his wife read Garvice on the sands. Like the majority of men, he dreamed idly of the past, muddled away the present, and guessed vaguely—after imaginative reading on occasions—at the future.

'I'd like to survive all right,' he said, 'provided it's better than this,' surveying his wife and children, and thinking of his daily toil. 'Otherwise——!' and he shrugged his shoulders as a brave man should.

He went to church regularly. But nothing in church convinced him that he did survive, just as nothing in church enticed him into hoping that he would. On the other hand, nothing in life persuaded him that he didn't, wouldn't, couldn't. 'I'm an Evolutionist,' he loved to say to thoughtful cronies (over a glass), having never heard that Darwinism had been questioned.

And so he came home gaily, happily, with his bunch of Christmas Presents 'for the wife and little ones,' stroking himself upon their keen enjoyment and excitement. The night before he had taken 'the wife' to see *Magic* at a select

345

London theatre where the Intellectuals went—and had been extraordinarily stirred. He had gone questioningly, yet expecting something out of the common. 'It's *not* musical,' he warned her, 'nor farce, nor comedy, so to speak'; and in answer to her question as to what the critics had said, he had wriggled, sighed, and put his gaudy neck-tie straight four times in quick succession. For no Man in the Street, with any claim to self-respect, could be expected to understand what the critics had said, even if he understood the Play. And John had answered truthfully: 'Oh, they just said things. But the theatre's always full—and that's the only test.'

And just now, as he crossed the crowded Circus to catch his 'bus, it chanced that his mind (having glimpsed an advertisement) was full of this particular Play, or rather, of the effect it had produced upon him at the time. For it had thrilled him—inexplicably: with its marvellous speculative hint, its big audacity, its alert and spiritual beauty.... Thought plunged to find something—plunged after this bizarre suggestion of a bigger universe, after this quasi-jocular suggestion that man is not the only—then dashed full-tilt against a sentence that memory thrust beneath his nose: 'Science does *not* exhaust the Universe'—and at the same time dashed full-tilt against destruction of another kind as well...!

How it happened he never exactly knew. He saw a Monster glaring at him with eyes of blazing fire. It was horrible! It rushed upon him. He dodged.... Another Monster met him round the corner. Both came at him simultaneously. He dodged again—a leap that might have cleared a hurdle easily, but was too late. Between the pair of them—his heart literally in his gullet—he was mercilessly caught. Bones crunched.... There was a soft sensation, icy cold and hot as fire. Horns and voices roared. Battering-rams he saw, and a carapace of iron.... Then dazzling light.... 'Always *face* the traffic!' he remembered with a frantic yell—and, by some extraordinary luck, escaped miraculously on to the opposite pavement.

There was no doubt about it. By the skin of his teeth he had dodged a rather ugly death. First... he felt for his Presents

—all were safe. And then, instead of congratulating himself and taking breath, he hurried homewards—on foot, which proved that his mind had lost control a bit!—thinking only how disappointed the wife and children would have been if—well, if anything had happened. Another thing he realised, oddly enough, was that he no longer really loved his wife, but had only great affection for her. What made him think of that, Heaven only knows, but he *did* think of it. He was an honest man without pretence. This came as a discovery some-how. He turned a moment, and saw the crowd gathered about the entangled taxi-cabs, policemen's helmets gleaming in the lights of the shop windows ... then hurried on again, his thoughts full of the joy his Presents would give... of the scampering children... and of his wife—bless her silly heart!—eyeing the mysterious parcels....

And, though he never could explain how, he presently stood at the door of the jail-like building that contained his flat, having walked the whole three miles. His thoughts had been so busy and absorbed that he had hardly noticed the length of weary trudge. 'Besides,' he reflected, thinking of the narrow escape, 'I've had a nasty shock. It was a d——d near thing, now I come to think of it....' He still felt a bit shaky and bewildered. Yet, at the same time, he felt extraordinarily jolly and lighthearted.

He counted his Christmas parcels... hugged himself in anticipatory joy ... and let himself in swiftly with his latchkey. 'I'm late,' he realised, 'but when she sees the brown-paper parcels, she'll forget to say a word. God bless the old faithful soul.' And he softly used the key a second time and entered his flat on tiptoe.... In his mind was the master impulse of that afternoon—the pleasure these Christmas Presents would give his wife and children....

He heard a noise. He hung up hat and coat in the poky vestibule (they never called it 'hall') and moved softly towards the parlour door, holding the packages behind him. Only of them he thought, not of himself—of his family, that is, not of the packages. Pushing the door cunningly ajar, he peeped in slyly. To his amazement the room was full of people. He withdrew quickly, wondering what it meant. A party? And without his knowing about it! Extraordinary!... Keen disappointment came over him. But, as he stepped back, the vestibule, he saw, was full of people too.

He was uncommonly surprised, yet somehow not surprised at all. People were congratulating him. There was a perfect mob of them. Moreover, he knew them all—vaguely remembered them, at least. And they all knew him.

'Isn't it a game?' laughed someone, patting him on the back. '*They* haven't the least idea...!'

And the speaker—it was old John Palmer, the book-keeper at the office—emphasised the 'they'.

'Not the least idea,' he answered with a smile, saying something he didn't understand, yet knew was right.

His face, apparently, showed the utter bewilderment he felt. The shock of the collision had been greater than he realised evidently. His mind was wandering.... Possibly! Only the odd thing was—he had never felt so clear-headed in his life. Ten thousand things grew simple suddenly. But, how thickly these people pressed about him, and how—familiarly!

'My parcels,' he said, joyously pushing his way across the throng. 'These are Chistmas Presents I've bought for them.' He nodded toward the room. 'I've saved for weeks—stopped cigars and billiards and—and several other good things—to buy them.'

'Good man!' said Palmer with a happy laugh. 'It's the heart that counts.'

Mudbury looked at him. Palmer had said an amazing truth, only—people would hardly understand and believe him.... Would they?

'Eh?' he asked, feeling stuffed and stupid, muddled somewhere between two meanings, one of which was gorgeous and the other stupid beyond belief.

'If you *please*, Mr. Mudbury, step inside. They are expecting you,' said a kindly, pompous voice. And, turning sharply, he met the gentle, foolish eyes of Sir James Epiphany, a director of the Bank where he worked.

The effect of the voice was instantaneous from long habit.

'They are,' he smiled from his heart, and advanced as from the custom of many years. Oh, how happy and gay he felt! His affection for his wife was real. Romance, indeed, had gone, but he needed her—and she needed him. And the children—Milly, Bill, and Jean—he deeply loved them. Life was worth living indeed!

In the room was a crowd, but—an astounding silence. John Mudbury looked round him. He advanced towards his wife, who sat in the corner arm-chair with Milly on her knee. A lot of people talked and moved about. Momentarily the crowd increased. He stood in front of them—in front of Milly and his wife. And he spoke—holding out his packages. 'It's Christmas Eve,' he whispered shyly, 'and I've—brought you something—something for everybody. Look!' He held the packages before their eyes.

'Of course, of course,' said a voice behind him, 'but you may hold them out like that for a century. They'll *never* see them!'

'Of course they won't. But I love to do the old, sweet thing,' replied John Mudbury—then wondered with a gasp of stark amazement why he said it.

'*I* think——' whispered Milly, staring round her.

'Well, what do you think?' her mother asked sharply. 'You're always thinking something queer.'

'I think,' the girl continued dreamily, 'that Daddy's already here.' She paused, then added with a child's impossible conviction, 'I'm sure he is. I *feel* him.'

There was an extraordinary laugh. Sir James Epiphany laughed. The others—the whole crowd of them—also turned their heads and smiled. But the mother, thrusting the child away from her, rose up suddenly with a violent start. Her face had turned to chalk. She stretched her arms out—into the air before her. She gasped and shivered. There was anguish in her eyes.

'Look' repeated John, 'these are the Presents that I brought.'

But his voice apparently was soundless. And, with a spasm

349

of icy pain, he remembered that Palmer and Sir James—some years ago—had died.

'It's magic,' he cried, 'but—I love you, Jinny—I love you—and—and I have always been true to you—as true as steel. We need each other—oh, can't you see—we go on together—you and I—for ever and ever——'

'*Think*,' interrupted an exquisitely tender voice, 'don't shout! They can't *hear* you—now.' And, turning, John Mudbury met the eyes of Everard Minturn, their President of the year before. Minturn had gone down with the *Titanic*.

He dropped his parcels then. His heart gave an enormous leap of joy.

He saw her face—the face of his wife—look through him. But the child gazed straight into his eyes. She *saw* him.

The next thing he knew was that he heard something tinkling ... far, far away. It sounded miles below him—inside him—he was sounding himself—all utterly bewildering—like a bell. It *was* a bell.

Milly stooped down and picked the parcels up. Her face shone with happiness and laughter....

But a man came in soon after, a man with a ridiculous, solemn face, a pencil, and a notebook. He wore a dark blue helmet. Behind him came a string of other men. They carried something ... something ... he could not see exactly what it was. But, when he pressed forward through the laughing throng to gaze upon it, he dimly made out two eyes, a nose, a chin, a deep red smear, and a pair of folded hands upon and overcoat. A woman's form fell down upon them then, and he heard soft sounds of children weeping strangely ... and other sounds ... as of familiar voices laughing ... laughing gaily.

'They'll join us presently. It goes like a flash....'

And, turning with great happiness in his heart, he saw that Sir James had said it, holding Palmer by the arm as with some natural yet unexpected love of sympathetic friendship.

'Come on,' said Palmer, smiling like a man who accepts a gift in universal fellowship, 'let's help 'em. They'll never understand.... Still, we can always try.'

The entire throng moved up with laughter and amusement. It was a moment of hearty, genuine life at last. Delight and Joy and Peace were everywhere.

Then John Mudbury realised the truth—that he was dead.

THE OTHER WING

1

It used to puzzle him that, after dark, someone *would* look in round the edge of the bedroom door, and withdraw again too rapidly for him to see the face. When the nurse had gone away with the candle this happened: 'Good night, Master Tim,' she said usually, shading the light with one hand to protect his eyes; 'dream of me and I'll dream of you.' She went out slowly. The sharp-edged shadow of the door ran across the ceiling like a train. There came a whispered colloquy in the corridor outside, about himself, of course, and—he was alone. He heard her steps going deeper and deeper into the bosom of the old country house; they were audible for a moment on the stone flooring of the hall; and sometimes the dull thump of the baize door into the servants' quarters just reached him, too— then silence. But it was only when the last sound as well as the last sign of her had vanished that the face emerged from its hiding-place and flashed in upon him round the corner. As a rule, too, it came just as he was saying, 'Now I'll go to sleep. I won't think any longer. Good night, Master Tim, and happy dreams.' He loved to say this to himself; it brought a sense of companionship, as though there were two persons speaking.

The room was on the top of the old house, a big, high--ceilinged room, and his bed against the wall had an iron railing round it; he felt very safe and protected in it. The curtains at the other end of the room were drawn. He lay watching the firelight dancing on the heavy folds, and their pattern, showing a spaniel chasing a long-tailed bird towards a bushy tree, interested and amused him. It was repeated over and over again. He counted the number of dogs, and the number of birds, and the number of trees, but could never make them agree. There was a plan somewhere in that pattern;

if only he could discover it, the dogs and birds and trees would 'come out right.' Hundreds and hundreds of times he had played this game, for the plan in the pattern made it possible to take sides, and the bird and dog were against him. They always won, however; Tim usually fell asleep just when the advantage was on his own side. The curtains hung steadily enough most of the time, but it seemed to him once or twice that they stirred—hiding a dog or bird on purpose to prevent his winning. For instance, he had eleven birds and eleven trees, and, fixing them in his mind by saying, 'that's eleven birds and eleven trees, but only ten dogs', his eyes darted back to find the eleventh dog, when—the curtain moved and threw all his calculations into confusion again. The eleventh dog was hidden. He did not quite like the movement; it gave him questionable feelings, rather, for the curtain did not move of itself. Yet, usually, he was too intent upon counting the dogs to feel positive alarm.

Opposite to him was the fireplace, full of red and yellow coals; and, lying with his head sideways on the pillow, he could see directly in between the bars. When the coals settled with a soft and powdery crash, he turned his eyes from the curtains to the grate, trying to discover exactly which bits had fallen. So long as the glow was there the sound seemed pleasant enough, but sometimes he awoke later in the night, the room huge with darkness, the fire almost out—and the sound was not so pleasant then. It startled him. The coals did not fall of themselves. It seemed that someone poked them cautiously. The shadows were very thick before the bars. As with the curtains, moreover, the morning aspect of the extinguished fire, the ice-cold cinders that made a clinking sound like tin, caused no emotion whatever in his soul.

And it was usually while he lay waiting for sleep, tired both of the curtain and the coal games, on the point, indeed, of saying, 'I'll go to sleep now,' that the puzzling thing took place. He would be staring drowsily at the dying fire, perhaps counting the stockings and flannel garments that hung along the high fender rail when, suddenly, a person looked in with lightning swiftness through the door and vanished again before he could possibly turn his head to see. The appearance and disappearance were accomplished with amazing rapidity always.

It was a head and shoulders that looked in, and the movement combined the speed, the lightness and the silence of a shadow. Only it was not a shadow. A hand held the edge of the door. The face shot round, saw him, and withdrew like lightning. It was utterly beyond him to imagine anything more quick and clever. It darted. He heard no sound. It went. But—it had seen him, looked him all over, examined him, noted what he was doing with that lightning glance. It wanted to know if he were awake still, or asleep. And though it went off, it still watched him from a distance; it waited somewhere; it knew all about him. *Where* it waited no one could ever guess. It came probably, he felt, from beyond the house, possibly from the roof, but most likely from the garden or the sky. Yet, though strange, it was not terrible. It was a kindly and protective figure, he felt. And when it happened he never called for help, because the occurrence simply took his voice away.

'It comes from the Nightmare Passage,' he decided; 'but it's *not* a nightmare.' It puzzled him.

Sometimes, moreover, it came more than once in a single night. He was pretty sure—not *quite* positive—that it occupied his room as soon as he was properly asleep. It took possession, sitting perhaps before the dying fire, standing upright behind the heavy curtains, or even lying down in the empty bed his brother used when he was home from school. Perhaps it played the curtain game, perhaps it poked the coals; it knew, at any rate, where the eleventh dog had lain concealed. It certainly came in and out; certainly, too, it did not wish to be seen. For, more than once, on waking suddenly in the midnight blackness, Tim knew it was standing close beside his bed and bending over him. He felt, rather than heard, its presence. It glided quietly away. It moved with marvellous softness, yet he was positive it moved. He felt the difference, so to speak: it had been near him, now it was gone. It came back, too—just as he was falling into sleep again. Its midnight coming and going, however, stood out sharply different from its first shy, tentative approach. For in the firelight it came alone; whereas in the black and silent hours, it had with it—others.

And it was then he made up his mind that its swift and quiet movements were due to the fact that it had wings. It flew. And the others that came with it in the darkness were 'its little ones.' He also made up his mind that all were friendly, comforting, protective, and that while positively *not* a Nightmare, it yet came somehow along the Nightmare Passage before it reached him. 'You see, it's like this,' he explained to the nurse: 'The big one comes to visit me alone, but it only brings its little ones when I'm *quite* asleep.'

'Then the quicker you get to sleep the better, isn't it, Master Tim?'

He replied: 'Rather! I always do. Only I wonder where they come *from!*' He spoke, however, as though he had an inkling.

But the nurse was so dull about it that he gave her up and tried his father. 'Of course,' replied this busy but affectionate parent, 'it's either nobody at all, or else it's Sleep coming to carry you away to the land of dreams.' He made the statement kindly but somewhat briskly, for he was worried just then about the extra taxes on his land, and the effort to fix his mind on Tim's fanciful world was beyond him at the moment. He lifted the boy on to his knee, kissed and patted him as though he were a favourite dog, and planted him on the rug again with a flying sweep. 'Run and ask your mother,' he added; 'she knows all that kind of thing. Then come back and tell me all about it—another time.'

Tim found his mother in an arm-chair before the fire of another room; she was knitting and reading at the same time—a wonderful thing the boy could never understand. She raised her head as he came in, pushed her glasses on to her forehead, and held her arms out. He told her everything, ending up with what his father said.

'You see, it's *not* Jackman, or Thompson, or anyone like

that,' he exclaimed. 'It's someone real.'

'But nice,' she assured him, 'someone who comes to take care of you and see that you're all safe and cosy.'

'Oh, yes, I know that. But——'

'I think your father's right,' she added quickly. 'It's Sleep, I'm sure, who pops in round the door like that. Sleep *has* got wings, I've always heard.'

'Then the other thing—the little ones?' he asked. 'Are they just sorts of dozes, you think?'

Mother did not answer for a moment. She turned down the page of her book, closed it slowly, and put it on the table beside her. More slowly still she put her knitting away, arranging the wool and needles with some deliberation.

'Perhaps,' she said, drawing the boy closer to her and looking into his big eyes of wonder, 'they're dreams!'

Tim felt a thrill run through him as she said it. He stepped back a foot or so and clapped his hands softly. 'Dreams!' he whispered with enthusiasm and belief; 'of course! I never thought of that.'

His mother, having proved her sagacity, then made a mistake. She noted her success, but instead of leaving it there, she elaborated and explained. As Tim expressed it she 'went on about it.' Therefore he did not listen. He followed his train of thought alone. And presently, he interrupted her long sentences with a conclusion of his own:

'Then I know where She hides,' he announced with a touch of awe. 'Where She lives, I mean.' And without waiting to be aked, he imparted the information: 'It's in the Other Wing.'

'Ah!' said his mother, taken by surprise. 'How clever of you, Tim!'—and thus confirmed it.

Thenceforward this was established in his life—that Sleep and her attendant Dreams hid during the daytime in that unused portion of the great Elizabethan mansion called the Other Wing. This other wing was unoccupied, its corridors untrodden, its windows shuttered and its rooms all closed. At various places green baize doors led into it, but no one ever opened them. For many years this part had been shut up; and for the

356

children, properly speaking, it was out of bounds. They never mentioned it as a possible place, at any rate; in hide-and-seek it was not considered, even; there was a hint of the inaccessible about the Other Wing. Shadows, dust, and silence had it to themselves.

But Tim, having ideas of his own about everything, possessed special information about the Other Wing. He believed it *was* inhabited. Who occupied the immense series of empty rooms, who trod the spacious corridors, who passed to and fro behind the shuttered windows, he had not known exactly. He had called these occupants, 'they', and the most important among them was 'The Ruler.' The Ruler of the Other Wing was a kind of deity, powerful, far away, ever present yet never seen.

And about this Ruler he had a wonderful conception for a little boy; he connected her, somehow, with deep thoughts of his own, the deepest of all. When he made up adventures to the moon, to the stars, or to the bottom of the sea, adventures that he lived inside himself, as it were—to reach them he must invariably pass through the chambers of the Other Wing. Those corridors and halls, the Nightmare Passage among them, lay along the route; they were the first stage of the journey. Once the green baize doors swung to behind him and the long dim passage stretched ahead, he was well on his way into the adventure of the moment; the Nightmare Passage once passed, he was safe from capture; but once the shutters of a window had been flung open, he was free of the gigantic world that lay beyond. For then light poured in and he could see his way.

The conception, for a child, was curious. It established a correspondence between the mysterious chambers of the Other Wing and the occupied, but unguessed chambers of his Inner Being. Through these chambers, through these darkened corridors, along a passage, sometimes dangerous, or at least of questionable repute, he must pass to find all adventures that were *real*. The light—when he pierced far enough to take the shutters down—was discovery. Tim did not actually think, much less say, all this. He was aware of it,

357

however. He felt it. The Other Wing was inside himself as well as through the green baize doors. His inner map of wonder included both of them.

But now, for the first time in his, life, he knew who lived there and who the Ruler was. A shutter had fallen of its own accord; light poured in; he made a guess, and Mother had confirmed it. Sleep and her Little Ones, the host of dreams, were the daylight occupants. They stole out when the darkness fell. All adventures in life began and ended by a dream —discoverable by first passing through the Other Wing.

2

And, having settled this, his one desire now was to travel over the map upon journeys of exploration and discovery. The map inside himself he knew already, but the map of the Other Wing he had not seen. His imagination knew it, he had a clear mental picture of rooms and halls and passages, but his feet had never trod the silent floors where dust and shadows hid the flock of dreams by day. The mighty chambers where Sleep ruled he longed to stand in, to see the Ruler face to face. He made up his mind to get into the Other Wing.

To accomplish this was difficult; but Tim was a determined youngster, and he meant to try; he meant, also, to succeed. He deliberated. At night he could not possibly manage it; in any case, the Ruler and her host all left it after dark to fly about the world; the Wing would be empty, and the emptiness would frighten him. Therefore he must make a daylight visit; and it was a daylight visit he decided on. He deliberated more. There were rules and risks involved: it meant going out of bounds, the danger of being seen, the certainty of being questioned by some idle and inquisitive grown-up: 'Where in the world have you been all this time?'—and so forth. These things he thought out carefully, and though he arrived at no solution, he felt satisfied that it would be all right. That is, he recognised the risks. To be thus prepared was half the battle, for nothing then could take him by surprise.

The notion that he might slip in from the garden was soon abandoned; the red bricks showed no openings; there was no door; from the courtyard, also, entrance was impracticable: even on tiptoe he could barely reach the broad window-sills of stone. When playing alone, or walking with the French governess, he examined every outside possibility. None offered. The shutters, supposing he could reach them, were thick and solid.

Meanwhile, when opportunity offered, he stood against the tight red bricks; the towers and gables of the Wing rose overhead; he heard the wind go whispering along the eaves; he imagined tiptoe movements and a sound of wings inside. Sleep and her Little Ones were busily preparing for their journeys after dark; they hid, but they did not sleep; in this unused Wing, vaster alone than any other country house he had ever seen, Sleep taught and trained her flock of feathered Dreams. It was very wonderful. They probably supplied the entire County. But more wonderful still was the thought that the Ruler herself should take the trouble to come to his particular room and personally watch over him all night long. That was amazing. And it flashed across his imaginative inquiring mind: 'Perhaps they take me with them! The moment I'm asleep! That's why she comes to see me!'

Yet his chief preoccupation was, how Sleep got out. Through the green baize doors, of course! By a process of elimination he arrived at a conclusion: he, too, must enter through a green baize door and risk detection.

Of late, the lightning visits had ceased. The silent, darting figure had not peeped in and vanished as it used to do. He fell asleep too quickly now, almost before Jackman reached the hall, and long before the fire began to die. Also, the dogs and birds upon the curtains always matched the trees exactly, and he won the curtain game quite easily; there was never a dog or bird too many; the curtain never stirred. It had been thus ever since his talk with Mother and Father. And so he came to make a second discovery: His parents did not really believe in his Figure. She kept away on that account. They doubted her; she hid. Here was still another incentive to go and find her out. He ached for her, she was so kind, she gave herself so much trouble—just for his little self in the big and lonely bedroom. Yet his parents spoke of her as though she were of no account. He longed to see hear, face to face, and tell her that *he* believed in her and loved her. For he was positive she would like to hear it. She cared. Though he had fallen asleep of late too quickly for him to see her flash in at the door, he had known nicer dreams than in his life before— travelling dreams. And it was she who sent them. More—he was sure she took him out with her.

One evening, in the dusk of a March day, his opportunity came; and only just in time, for his brother, Jack, was expected home from school on the morrow, and with Jack in the other bed, no Figure would ever care to show itself. Also it was Easter, and after Easter, though Tim was not aware of it at the time, he was to say good-bye finally to governesses and become a day-boarder at a preparatory school for Wellington. The opportunity offered itself so naturally, moreover, that Tim took it without hesitation. It never occurred to him to question, much less to refuse it. The thing was obviously meant to be. For he found himself unexpectedly in front of a green baize door; and the green baize door was—swinging! Somebody, therefore, had just passed through it.

It had come about in this wise. Father, away in Scotland, at Inglemuir, the shooting place, was expected back next morning; Mother had driven over to the church upon some Easter business or other; and the governess had been allowed her holiday at home in France. Tim, therefore, had the run of the house, and in the hour between tea and bed-time he made good use of it. Fully able to defy such second-rate obstacles as nurses and butlers, he explored all manner of forbidden places with ardent thoroughness, arriving finally in the sacred precincts of his father's study. This wonderful room was the very heart and centre of the whole big house; he had been birched here long ago; here, too, his father had told him with a grave yet smiling face: 'You've got a new companion, Tim, a little sister; you must be very kind to her.' Also, it was the place where all the money was kept. What he called 'father's jolly smell' was strong in it—papers, tobacco, books, flavoured by hunting crops and gunpowder.

At first he felt awed, standing motionless just inside the door; but presently, recovering equilibrium, he moved cautiously on tiptoe towards the gigantic desk where important papers were piled in untidy patches. These he did not touch; but beside them his quick eye noted the jagged piece of iron shell his father brought home from his Crimean campaign and now used as a letter-weight. It was difficult to lift, however. He climbed into the comfortable chair and swung round and round. It was a swivel-chair, and he sank down among the cushions in it, staring at the strange things on the great desk before him, as if fascinated. Next he turned away and saw the stick-rack in the corner—this, he knew, he was allowed to touch. He had played with these sticks before. There were twenty, perhaps, all told, with curious carved handles, brought from every corner of the world; many of them cut by his father's own hand in queer and distant places. And, among them, Tim fixed his eye upon a cane with an ivory handle, a slender, polished cane that he had always coveted tremendously. It was the kind he meant to use when he became a man. It bent, it quivered, and when he swished it through the air it trembled like a riding-whip, and made a whistling noise. Yet it was very strong in spite of its elastic qualities. A family treasure, it was also an old-fashioned relic; it had been his great-grandfather's walking stick. Something of another century clung visibly about it still. It had dignity and grace and leisure in its very aspect. And it suddenly occurred to him. 'How great-grandpapa must miss it! Wouldn't he just love to have it back again!'

How it happened exactly, Tim did not know, but a few minutes later he found himself walking about the deserted halls and passages of the house with the air of an elderly gentleman of a hundred years ago, proud as a courtier, flourishing the stick like an Eighteenth Century dandy in the Mall. That the cane reached to his shoulder made no difference; he held it accordingly, swaggering on his way. He was off upon an adventure. He dived down through the byways of the Other Wing inside himself, as though the stick transported him to the days of the old gentleman who had used it in another century.

It may seem strange to those who dwell in smaller houses, but in this rambling Elizabethan mansion there were whole sections that, even to Tim, were strange and unfamiliar. In his mind the map of the Other Wing was clearer by far than the geography of the part he travelled daily. He came to passages and dim-lit halls, long corridors of stone beyond the Picture Gallery; narrow, wainscoted connecting-channels with four steps down and a little later two steps up; deserted chambers with arches guarding them—all hung with the soft March twilight and all bewilderingly unrecognised. With a sense of adventure born of naughtiness he went carelessly along, farther and farther into the heart of this unfamiliar country, swinging the cane, one thumb stuck into the arm-pit of his blue serge suit, whistling softly to himself, excited yet keenly on the alert —and suddenly found himself opposite a door that checked all further advance. It was a green baize door. And it was swinging.

He stopped abruptly, facing it. He stared, he gripped his cane more tightly, he held his breath. 'The Other Wing!' he gasped in a swallowed whisper.

It was an entrance, but an entrance he had never seen before. He thought he knew every door by heart; but this one was new. He stood motionless for several minutes, watching it; the door had two halves, but one half only was swinging, each swing shorter than the one before; he heard the little puffs of air it made; it settled finally, the last movements very short and rapid; it stopped. And the boy's heart, after similar rapid strokes, stopped also—for a moment.

'Someone's just gone through,' he gulped. And even as he said it he knew who the someone was. The conviction just dropped into him. 'It's great-grandpapa; he knows I've got his stick. He wants it!' On the heels of this flashed instantly another amazing certainty. 'He sleeps in there. He's having dreams. That's what being dead means.'

His first impulse, then, took the form of, 'I must let Father know; it'll make him burst for joy!' but his second was for himself—to finish his adventure. And it was this, naturally enough, that gained the day. He could tell his father later. His first duty was plainly to go through the door into the Other Wing. He must give the stick back to its owner. He must *hand* it back.

The test of will and character came now. Tim had imagination, and so knew the meaning of fear; but there was nothing craven in him. He could howl and scream and stamp like any other person of his age when the occasion called for such behaviour, but such occasions were due to temper roused by a thwarted will, and the histrionics were half 'pretended' to produce a calculated effect. There was no one to thwart his will at present. He also knew how to be afraid of Nothing, to be afraid without ostensible cause that is—which was merely 'nerves'. He could have 'the shudders' with the best of them.

But, when a real thing faced him, Tim's character emerged to meet it. He would clench his hands, brace his muscles, set his teeth—and wish to heaven he was bigger. But he would not flinch. Being imaginative, he lived the worst a dozen times before it happened, yet in the final crash he stood up like a man. He had that highest pluck—the courage of a sensitive temperament. And at this particular juncture, somewhat ticklish for a boy of eight or nine, it did not fail him. He lifted the cane and pushed the swinging door wide open. Then he walked through it—into the Other Wing.

3

THE green baize door swung to behind him; he was even sufficiently master of himself to turn and close it with a steady hand, because he did not care to hear the series of muffled thuds its lessening swings would cause. But he realised clearly his position, knew he was doing a tremendous thing.

Holding the cane between fingers very tightly clenched, he

advanced bravely along the corridor that stretched before him. And all fear left him from that moment, replaced, it seemed, by a mild and exquisite surprise. His footsteps made no sound, he walked on air; instead of darkness, or the twilight he expected, a diffused and gentle light that seemed like the silver on the lawn when a half-moon sails a cloudless sky, lay everywhere. He knew his way, moreover, knew exactly where he was and whither he was going. The corridor was as familiar to him as the floor of his own bedroom; he recognised the shape and length of it; it agreed exactly with the map he had constructed long ago. Though he had never, to the best of his knowledge, entered it before, he knew with intimacy its every detail.

And thus the surprise he felt was mild and far from disconcerting. 'I'm here again!' was the kind of thought he had. It was *how* he got here that caused the faint surprise, apparently. He no longer swaggered, however, but walked carefully, and half on tiptoe, holding the ivory handle of the cane with a kind of affectionate respect. And as he advanced, the light closed softly up behind him, obliterating the way by which he had come. But this he did not know, because he did not look behind him. He only looked in front, where the corridor stretched its silvery length towards the great chamber where he knew the cane must be surrendered. The person who had preceded him down this ancient corridor, passing through the green baize door just before he reached it, this person, his father's grandfather, now stood in that great chamber, waiting to receive his own. Tim knew it as surely as he knew he breathed. At the far end he even made out the larger patch of silvery light which marked its gaping doorway.

There was another thing he knew as well—that this corridor he moved along between rooms with fast-closed doors, was the Nightmare Corridor; often and often he had traversed it; each room was occupied. 'This is the Nightmare Passage,' he whispered to himself, 'but I know the Ruler—it doesn't matter. None of the Nightmares can get out or do anything.' He heard them, none the less, inside, as he passed by; he heard them scratching to get out. The feeling of security made him reckless; he took unnecessary risks; he brushed the panels as he passed. And the love of keen sensation for its own sake, the desire to feel 'an awful thrill', temped him once so sharply that he suddenly raised his stick and poked a fast-shut door with it!

He was not prepared for the result, but he gained the sensation and the thrill. For the door opened with instant swiftness half and inch, a hand emerged, caught the stick and tried to draw it in. Tim sprang back as if he had been struck. He pulled at the ivory handle with all his strength, but his strength was less than nothing. He tried to shout, but his voice had gone. A terror of the moon came over him, for he was unable to loosen his hold of the handle; his fingers had become a part of it. An appalling weakness turned him helpless. He was dragged inch by inch towards the fearful door. The end of the stick was already through the narrow crack. He could not see the hand that pulled, but he knew it was gigantic. He understood now why the world was strange, why horses galloped furiously, and why trains whistled as they raced through stations. All the comedy and terror of nightmare gripped his heart with pincers made of ice. The disproportion was abominable. The final collapse rushed over him when, without a sign of warning, the door slammed silently, and between the jamb and the wall the cane was crushed as flat as if it were a bulrush. So irresistible was the force behind the door that the solid stick just went flat as the stalk of a bulrush.

He looked at it. It *was* a bulrush.

He did not laugh; the absurdity was so distressingly unnatural. The horror of finding a bulrush where he had expected a polished cane—this hideous and appalling detail held the nameless horror of the nightmare. It betrayed him utterly. Why had he not always known really that the stick was not a stick, but a thin and hollow reed...?

Then the cane was safely in his hand, unbroken. He stood looking at it. The Nightmare was in full swing. He heard another door opening behind his back, a door he had not touched. There was just time to see a hand thrusting and

waving dreadfully, horribly, at him through the narrow crack—
just time to realise that this was another Nightmare acting
in atrocious concert with the first, when he saw closely beside
him, towering to the ceiling, the protective, kindly Figure
that visited his bedroom. In the turning movement he made to
meet the attack, he became aware of her. And his terror passed.
It was a nightmare terror merely. The infinite horror vanished.
Only the comedy remained. He smiled.

He saw her dimly only, she was so vast, but he saw her, the
Ruler of the Other Wing at last, and knew that he was safe
again. He gazed with a tremendous love and wonder, trying
to see her clearly; but the face was hidden far aloft and seemed
to melt into the sky beyond the roof. He discerned that she
was larger than the Night, only far, far softer, with wings that
folded above him more tenderly even than his mother's arms;
that there were points of light like stars among the feathers,
and that she was vast enough to cover millions and millions of
people all at once. Moreover, she did not fade or go, so far as
he could see, but spread herself in such a way that he lost sight
of her. She spread over the entire Wing...

And Tim remembered that this was all quite natural really.
He had often and often been down this corridor before; the
Nightmare Corridor was no new experience; it had to be faced
as usual. Once knowing what hid inside the rooms, he was
bound to tempt them out. They drew, enticed, attracted him;
this was their power. It was their special strength that they
could suck him helplessly towards them, and that he was obliged to go. He understood exactly why he was tempted to tap
with the cane upon their awful doors, but, having done so, he
had accepted the challenge and could now continue his journey
quietly and safely. The Ruler of the Other Wing had taken
him in charge.

A delicious sense of carelessness came on him. There was
softness as of water in the solid things about him, nothing that
could hurt or bruise. Holding the cane firmly by its ivory
handle, he went forward along the corridor, walking as on air.

The end was quickly reached: He stood upon the threshold

of the mighty chamber where he knew the owner of the cane was waiting; the long corridor lay behind him, in front he saw the spacious dimensions of a lofty hall that gave him the feeling of being in the Crystal Palace, Euston Station, or St. Paul's. High, narrow windows, cut deeply into the wall, stood in a row upon the other side; an enormous open fireplace of burning logs was on his right; thick tapestries hung from the ceiling to the floor of stone; and in the centre of the chamber was a massive table of dark, shining wood, great chairs with carved stiff backs set here and there beside it. And in the biggest of these thronelike chairs there sat a figure looking at him gravely—the figure of an old, old man.

Yet there was no surprise in the boy's fast-beating heart; there was a thrill of pleasure and excitement only, a feeling of satisfaction. He had known quite well the figure would be there, known also it would look like this exactly. He stepped forward on to the floor of stone without a trace of fear or trembling, holding the precious cane in two hands now before him, as though to present it to its owner. He felt proud and pleased. He had run risks for this.

And the figure rose quietly to meet him, advancing in a stately manner over the hard stone floor. The eyes looked gravely, sweetly down at him, the aquiline nose stood out. Tim knew him perfectly: the knee-breeches of shining satin, the gleaming buckles on the shoes, the neat dark stockings, the lace and ruffles about neck and wrists, the coloured waistcoat opening so widely—all the details of the picture over father's mantelpiece, where it hung between two Crimean bayonets, were reproduced in life before his eyes as last. Only the polished cane with the ivory handle was not there.

Tim went three steps nearer to the advancing figure and held out both his hands with the cane laid crosswise on them.

'I've brought it, great-grandpapa,' he said, in a faint but clear and steady tone; 'here it is.'

And the other stooped a little, put out three fingers half concealed by falling lace, and took it by the ivory handle. He made a courtly bow to Tim. He smiled, but though there was pleasure, it was a grave, sad smile. He spoke then: the voice was slow and very deep. There was a delicate softness in it, the suave politeness of an older day.

'Thank you,' he said; 'I value it. It was given to me by my grandfather. I forgot it when I——' His voice grew indistinct a little.

'Yes?' said Tim.

'When I—left,' the old gentleman repeated.

'Oh,' said Tim, thinking how beautiful and kind the gracious figure was.

The old man ran his slender fingers carefully along the cane, feeling the polished surface with satisfaction. He lingered specially over the smoothness of the ivory handle. He was evidently very pleased.

'I was not quite myself—er—at the moment,' he went on gently; 'my memory failed me somewhat.' He sighed, as though an immense relief was in him.

'*I* forget things, too—sometimes,' Tim mentioned sympathetically. He simply loved his great-grandfather. He hoped—for a moment—he would be lifted up and kissed. 'I'm *awfully* glad I brought it,' he added— 'that you've got it again.'

The other turned his kind grey eyes upon him; the smile on his face was full of gratitude as he looked down.

'Thank you, my boy. I am truly and deeply indebted to you. You courted danger for my sake. Others have tried before, but the Nightmare Passage—er——' He broke off. He tapped the stick firmly on the stone flooring, as thought to test it. Bending a trifle, he put his weight upon it. 'Ah!' he exclaimed with a short sigh of relief, 'I can now——'

His voice again grew indistinct; Tim did not catch the words.

'Yes?' he asked again, aware for the first time that a touch of awe was in his heart.

'—get about again,' the other continued very low. 'Without my cane,' he added, the voice failing with each word the old lips uttered, 'I could not... possibly... allow myself... to be seen. It was indeed... deplorable... unpardonable of me... to forget in such a way. Zounds, sir...! I—I...'

His voice sank away suddenly into a sound of wind. He straightened up, tapping the iron ferrule of his cane on the stones in a series of loud knocks. Tim felt a strange sensation creep into his legs. The queer words frightened him a little.

The old man took a step towards him. He still smiled, but there was a new meaning in the smile. A sudden earnestness had replaced the courtly, leisurely manner. The next words seemed to blow down upon the boy from above, as though a cold wind brought them from the sky outside.

Yet the words, he knew, were kindly meant, and very sensible. It was only the abrupt change that startled him. Great-grandpapa, after all, was but a man! This distant sound recalled something in him to that outside world from which the cold wind blew.

'My eternal thanks to you,' he heard, while the voice and face and figure seemed to withdraw deeper and deeper into the heart of the mighty chamber. 'I shall not forget your kindness and your courage. It is a debt I can, fortunately, one day re-pay.... But now you had best return, and with dispatch. For your head and arm lie heavily on the table, the documents are scattered, there is a cushion fallen... and my son's son is in the house.... Farewell! You had best leave me quickly. See! *She* stands behind you, waiting. Go with her! Go now...!'

The entire scene had vanished even before the final words were uttered. Tim felt empty space about him. A vast, shadowy Figure bore him through it as with mighty wings. He flew, he rushed, he remembered nothing more—until he heard another voice and felt a heavy hand upon his shoulder.

'Tim, you rascal! What are you doing in my study? And in the dark, like this!'

He looked up into his father's face without a word. He felt dazed. The next minute his father had caught him up and kissed him.

'Ragamuffin! How did you guess I was coming back to-night?' He shook him playfully and kissed his tumbling hair. 'And you've been asleep, too, into the bargain. Well—how's everything et home—eh? Jack's coming back from school to-morrow, you know, and...'

4

JACK came home, indeed, the following day, and when the Easter holidays were over, the governess stayed abroad and Tim went off to adventures of another kind in the preparatory school for Wellington. Life slipped rapidly along with him; he grew into a man; his mother and his father died; Jack followed them within a little space; Tim inherited, married, settled down into his great possessions—and opened up the Other Wing. The dreams of imaginative boyhood all had faded; perhaps he had merely put them away, or perhaps he had forgotten them. At any rate, he never spoke of such things now, and when his Irish wife mentioned her belief that the old country house possessed a family ghost, even declaring that she had met an Eighteenth Century figure of a man in the corridors, 'an old, old man who bends down upon a stick'—Tim only laughed and said:

'That's as it ought to be! And if these awful land taxes force us to sell some day, a respectable ghost will increase the market value.'

But one night he woke and heard a tapping on the floor. He sat up in bed and listened. There was a chilly feeling down his back. Belief had long since gone out of him; he felt uncannily afraid. The sound came nearer and nearer; there were light footsteps with it. The door opened—it opened a little wider, that is, for it already stood ajar—and there upon the threshold stood a figure that it seemed he knew. He saw the face as with all the vivid sharpness of reality. There was a smile upon it, but a smile of warning and alarm. The arm was raised. Tim saw the slender hand, lace falling down upon the long, thin fingers, and in them, tightly gripped, a polished cane. Shaking the cane twice to and fro in the air, the face thrust forward, spoke certain words, and—vanished. But the words were inaudible; for, though the lips distinctly moved, no sound, apparently, came from them.

And Tim sprang out of bed. The room was full of darkness. He turned the light on. The door, he saw, was shut as usual.

370

He had, of course, been dreaming. But he noticed a curious odour in the air. He sniffed it once or twice—then grasped the truth. It was a smell of burning!

Fortunately, he awoke just in time....

He was acclaimed a hero for his promptitude. After many days, when the damage was repaired, and nerves had settled down once more into the calm routine of country life, he told the story to his wife—the entire story. He told the adventure of his imaginative boyhood with it. She asked to see the old family cane. And it was this request of hers that brought back to memory a detail Tim had entirely forgotten all these years. He remembered it suddenly again—the loss of the cane, the hubbub his father kicked up about it, the endless, futile search. For the stick had never been found, and Tim, who was questioned very closely concerning it, swore with all his might that he had not the smallest notion where it was. Which was, of course, the truth.

BY WATER

THE night before young Larsen left to take up his new appointment in Egypt he went to the clairvoyante. He neither believed nor disbelieved. He felt no interest, for he already knew his past and did not wish to know his future. 'Just to please me, Jim,' the girl pleaded. 'The woman is wonderful. Before I had been five minutes with her she told me your initials, so there *must* be something in it.' 'She read your thought,' he smiled indulgently. 'Even I can do that!' But the girl was in earnest. He yielded; and that night at his farewell dinner he came to give his report of the interview.

The result was meagre and unconvincing: money was coming to him, he was soon to make a voyage, and—he would never marry. 'So you see how silly it all is,' he laughed, for they were to be married when his first promotion came. He gave the details, however, making a little story of it in the way he knew she loved.

'But was that all, Jim?' The girl asked it, looking rather hard into his face. 'Aren't you hiding something from me?' He hesitated a moment then burst out laughing at her clever discernment. 'There *was* a little more,' he confessed, 'but you take it all so seriously; I——'

He had to tell it then, of course. The woman had told him a lot of gibberish about friendly and unfriendly elements. 'She said water was unfriendly to me; I was to be careful of water, or else I should come to harm by it. Fresh water only,' he hastened to add, seeing that the idea of shipwreck was in her mind.

'Drowning?' came the question quickly.

'Yes,' he admitted with reluctance, but still laughing; 'she did say drowning, though drowning in no ordinary way.'

The girl's face showed uneasiness a moment. 'What does that mean—drowning in no ordinary way?' There was a catch in her breath.

But that he could not tell her, because he did not know himself. He gave, therefore, the woman's exact words: 'You will drown, but will not know you drown.'

It was unwise of him. He wished afterwards he had invented a happier report, or had kept this detail back. 'I'm safe in Egypt, anyhow,' he laughed. 'I shall be a clever man if I can find enouth water in the desert to do me harm!' And all the way from Trieste to Alexandria he remembered the promise she had extracted—that he would never once go on the Nile unless duty made it imperative for him to do so. He kept that promise like the literal, faithful soul he was. His love was equal to the somewhat quixotic sacrifice it occasionally involved. Fresh water in Egypt there was practically none other, and in any case the natron works where his duty lay had their headquarters some distance out into the desert. The river, with its banks of welcome, refreshing verdure, was not even visible.

Months passed quickly, and the time for leave came within measurable distance. In the long interval luck had played the cards kindly for him, vacancies had occurred, early promotion seemed likely, and his letters were full of plans to bring her out to share a little house of their own. His health, however, had not improved; the dryness did not suit him; even in this short period his blood had thinned, his nervous system deterioarated, and contrary to the doctor's prophecy, the waterless air had told upon his sleep. A damp climate liked him best. And once the sun had touched him with its fiery finger.

His letters made no mention of this. He described the life to her, the work, the sport, the pleasant people, and his chances of increased pay and early marriage. And a week before he sailed he rode out upon a final act of duty to inspect the latest diggings his Company were making. His course lay some twenty miles into the desert behind El-Chobak towards the limestone hills of Guebel Haidi, and he went alone, carrying lunch and tea, for it was the weekly holiday of Friday, and the men were not at work.

The accident was ordinary enough. On his way back in the

heat of early afternoon his pony stumbled against a boulder on the treacherous desert film, threw him heavily, broke the girth, bolted before he could seize the reins again, and left him stranded some ten or twelve miles from home. There was a pain in his knee that made walking difficult, a buzzing in his head that troubled sight and made the landscape swim, while, worse than either, his provisions, fastened to the saddle, had vanished with the frightened pony into those blazing leagues of sand. He was alone in the Desert, beneath the pitiless afternoon sun, twelve miles of utterly exhausting country between him and safety.

Under normal conditions he could have covered the distance in four hours, reaching home by dark; but his knee pained him so that a mile an hour proved the best he could possibly do. He reflected a few minutes. The wisest course was to sit down and wait till the pony told its obvious story to the stable, and help should come. And this was what he did, for the scorching heat and glare were dangerous; they were terrible; he was shaken and bewildered by his fall, hungry and weak into the bargain; and an hour's painful scrambling over the baked and burning little gorges must have speedily caused complete prostration. He sat down and rubbed his aching knee. It was quite a little adventure. Yet, though he knew the Desert might not be lightly trifled with, he felt at the moment nothing more than this—and the amusing description of it he would give in his letter, or—intoxicating thought—by word of mouth. In the heat of the sun he began to feel drowsy. He was exhausted. A soft torpor crept over him. He dozed. He fell asleep.

It was a long, a dreamless sleep... for when he woke at length the sun had just gone down, the dusk lay awfully upon the enormous desert, and the air was chilly. The cold had waked him. Quickly, as though on purpose, the red glow faded from the sky; the first stars shone; it was dark; the heavens were deep violet. He looked round and realised that his sense of direction had gone entirely. Great hunger was in him. The cold already was bitter as the wind rose, but the pain in his knee having eased, he got up and walked a little—and in a moment lost sight of the spot where he had been lying. The shadowy desert swallowed it. 'Ah', he realised 'this is not an English field or moor. I'm in the Desert!' The safe thing to do was to remain exactly where he was; only thus could the rescuers find him; once he wandered he was done for. It was strange the search-party had not yet arrived. To keep warm, however, he was compelled to move, so he made a little pile of stones to mark the place, and walked round and round it in a circle of some dozen yards' diameter. He limped badly, and the hunger gnawed dreadfully; but, after all, the adventure was not so terrible. The amusing side of it kept uppermost still. Though fragile in body, his spirit was not unduly timid or imaginative; he *could* last out the night, or, if the worst came to the worst, the next day as well. But when he watched the little group of stones, he saw that there were dozens of them, scores, hundreds, thousands of these little groups of stones. The desert's face, of course, is thickly strewn with them. The original one was lost in the first five minutes. So he sat down again. But the biting cold, and the wind that licked his very skin beneath the light clothing, soon forced him up again. It was ominous; and the night huge and shelter-less. The shaft of green zodiacal light that hung so strangely in the western sky for hours had faded away; the stars were out in their bright thousands; no guide was anywhere; the wind moaned and puffed among the sandy mounds; the vast sheet of desert stretched mockingly upon the world; he heard the jackals cry....

And with the jackals' cry came suddenly the unwelcome realisation that no play was in this adventure any more, but that a bleak reality stared at him through the surrounding darkness. He faced it—at bay. He was genuinely lost. Thought blocked in him. 'I must be calm and think,' he said aloud. His voice woke no echo; it was small and dead; something gigantic ate it instantly. He got up and walked again. Why did no one come? Hours had passed. The pony had long ago found its stable, or—had it run madly in another direction altogether? He worked out possibilities, tightening his belt. The cold was searching; he never had been, never could be warm again; the hot sunshine of a few hours ago seemed the merest dream. Unfamiliar with hardship, he knew not what to do, but he took his coat and shirt off, vigorously rubbed his skin where the dried perspiration of the afternoon still caused clammy shivers, swung his arms furiously like a London cabman, and quickly dressed again. Though the wind upon his bare back was biting, he felt warmer a little. He lay down exhausted, sheltered by an overhanging limestone crag, and took snatches of fitful dog's-sleep, while the wind drove overhead and the dry sand pricked his skin. One face continually was near him; one pair of tender eyes; two dear hands smoothed him; he smelt the perfume of light brown hair. It was all natural enough. His whole thought, in his misery, ran to her in England—England where there was soft fresh grass, big sheltering trees, hemlock and honeysuckle in the hedges—while the hard black Desert guarded him, and consciousness dipped away at little intervals under this dry and pitiless Egyptian sky....

It was perhaps five in the morning when a voice spoke and he started up with a sudden jerk—the voice of that clairvoyante woman. The sentence fled away into the darkness, but one word remained: *Water!* At first he wondered, but at once explanation came. Cause and effect were obvious. The clue was physical. His body needed water, and so the thought came up into his mind. He was thirsty.

This was the moment when fear first really touched him. Hunger was manageable, more or less—for a day or two, certainly. But thirst! Thirst and the Desert were an evil pair that, by cumulative suggestion gathering since childhood days, brought terror in. Once in the mind it could not be dislodged. It spite of his best efforts, the ghastly thing grew passionately—because his thirst grew too. He had smoked much; had eaten spiced things at lunch; had breathed in alkali with the dry, scorched air. He searched for a cool flint pebble to put into his burning mouth, but found only angular scraps of dusty limestone. There were no pebbles here. The cold helped a little to counteract, but already he knew in himself subconsciously the dread of something that was coming. What was it? He tried to hide the thought and bury it out of sight. The utter futility of his tiny strength against the power of the universe appalled him. And then he knew. It was the sun. The merciless sun was on the way, already rising. Its return was like the presage of execution....

It came. With true horror he watched the marvellous swift dawn break across the sandy sea. The eastern sky glowed hurriedly as from crimson fires. Ridges, not noticeable in the starlight turned black in endless series, like flat-topped billows of a frozen ocean. Wide streaks of blue and yellow followed, as the sky dropped sheets of mauve light upon the wind-eaten cliffs and showed their under sides. They did not advance; they waited till the sun was up—and then they moved; they rose and sank; they shifted as the sunshine lifted them and the shadows crept away. But in an hour there would be no shadows any more. There would be no shade.

The little groups of stones began to dance. It was horrible. The unbroken, huge expanse lay round him, warming up, twelve hours of blazing hell to come. Already the monstrous Desert glared, each bit familiar, since each bit was a repetition of the bit before, behind, on either side. It laughed at guidance and direction. He rose and walked; for miles he walked, though how many, north, south, or west, he knew not. The frantic thing was in him now, the fury of the Desert; he took its pace, its endless, tireless stride, the stride of the burning, murderous Desert that is waterless. He felt it alive—a blindly heaving desire in it to reduce him to its conditionless, awful dryness. He felt—yet knowing this was feverish and *not* to be believed—that his own small life lay on its mighty surface, a mere dot in space, a mere heap of little stones. His emotions, his fears, his hopes, his ambition, his love—mere bundled group of little unimportant stones that danced with apparent activity for a moment, then were merged in the undifferentiated surface underneath. He was included in a purpose greater than his own.

The will made a plucky effort then. 'A night and a day,' he laughed, while his lips cracked smartingly with the stretching of the skin, 'what is it? Many a chap has lasted days and days...!' Yes, only he was not of that rare company. He was ordinary, unaccustomed to privation, weak, untrained of spirit, unacquainted with stern resistance. He knew not how to spare himself. The Desert struck him where it pleased—all over. It played with him. His tongue was swollen; the parched throat could not swallow. He sank.... An hour he lay there, just wit enough in him to choose the top of a mound where he could be most easily seen. He lay two hours, three, four hours.... The heat blazed down upon him like a furnace.... The sky, when he opened his eyes once, was empty... then a speck became visible in the blue expanse; and presently another speck. They came from nowhere. They hovered very high, almost out of sight. They appeared, they disappeared, they—reappeared. Nearer and nearer they swung down, in sweeping stealthy circles... little dancing groups of them, miles away but ever drawing closer—the vultures....

He had strained his ears so long for sounds of feet and voices that it seemed he could no longer hear at all. Hearing had ceased within him. Then came the water-dreams, with their agonising torture. He heard *that*... heard it running in silvery streams and rivulets across green English meadows. It rippled with silvery music. He heard it splash. He dipped hands and feet and head in it—in deep, clear pools of generous depth. He drank; with his skin he drank, not with mouth and throat alone. Delicious! Ice clinked in effervescent, sparkling water against a glass. He swam and plunged. Water gushed freely over back and shoulders, gallons and gallons of it, bathfuls and to spare, a flood of gushing, crystal, cool, lifegiving liquid.... And then he stood in a beech wood and felt the streaming deluge of delicious summer rain upon his face; heard it drip luxuriantly upon a million thirsty leaves. The wet trunks shone, the damp moss spread its perfume, ferns waved heavily in the moist atmosphere. He was soaked to the skin in it. A mountain torrent, fresh from fields of snow, dashed foaming past, and the spray fell in a shower upon his cheeks and hair. He dived—head foremost.... Ah, he was up to the neck... and *she* was with him; they were under water together; be saw her eyes gleaming into his own beneath the copious flood.

The voice, however, was not hers.... 'You will drown, yet you will not know you drown....!' His swollen tongue called out a name. But no sound was audible. He closed his eyes. There came sweet unconsciousness....

A sound in that instant *was* audible, though. It was a voice— voices—and the thud of animal hoofs upon the sand. The specks had vanished from the sky as mysteriously as they came. And, as though in answer to the sound, he made a movement— but an automatic, an unconscious movement. He did not know he moved. And the body, uncontrolled, lost its precarious balance. He rolled; but he did not know he rolled. Slowly, over the edge of the sloping mound of sand, he turned sideways. Like a log of wood he slid gradually, turning over and over, nothing to stop him—to the bottom. A few feet only, and not even steep; just steep enough to keep rolling slowly. There was a—splash. But he did not know there was a splash.

They found him in a pool of water—one of these rare pools the Desert Bedouin mark preciously for their own. He had lain within three yards of it for hours. He was drowned... but he did not know he drowned....

A VICTIM OF HIGHER SPACE

'THERE'S a hextraordinary gentleman to see you, sir,' said the new man.

'Why "extraordinary"?' asked Dr. Silence, drawing the tips of his thin fingers through his brown beard. His eyes twinkled pleasantly. 'Why "extraordinary," Barker?' he repeated encouragingly, noticing the perplexed expression in the man's eyes.

'He's so—so thin, sir. I could hardly see 'im at all—at first. He was inside the house before I could ask the name,' he added, remembering strict orders.

'And who brought him here?'

'He come alone, sir, in a closed cab. He pushed by me before I could say a word—making no noise not what I could hear. He seemed to move very soft——'

The man stopped short with obvious embarrassment, as though he had already said enough to jeopardise his new situation, but trying hard to show that he remembered the instructions and warnings he had received with regard to the admission of strangers not properly accredited.

'And where is the gentleman now?' asked Dr. Silence, turning away to conceal his amusement.

'I really couldn't exactly say, sir. I left him standing in the 'all——'

The doctor looked up sharply. 'But why in the hall, Barker? Why not in the waiting-room?' He fixed his piercing though kindly eyes on the man's face. 'Did he frighten you?' he asked quickly.

'I think he did, sir, if I may say so. I seemed to lose sight of him, as it were——' The man stammered, evidently convinced by now that he had earned his dismissal. 'He come in so funny, just like a cold wind,' he added boldly, setting his heels at attention and looking his master full in the face.

The doctor made an internal note of the man's halting

380

description; he was pleased that the slight evidence of intuition which had induced him to engage Barker had not entirely failed at the first trial. Dr. Silence sought for this qualification in all his assistants, from secretary to serving-man, and if it surrounded him with a somewhat singular crew, the drawbacks were more than compensated for on the whole by their occasional flashes of insight.

'So the gentleman made you feel queer, did he?'

'That was it, I think, sir,' repeated the man stolidly.

'And he brings no kind of introduction to me—no letter or anything?' asked the doctor, with feigned surprise, as though he knew what was coming.

The man fumbled, both in mind and pockets, and finally produced an envelope.

'I beg pardon, sir,' he said, greatly flustered; 'the gentleman handed me this for you.'

It was a note from a discerning friend, who had never yet sent him a case that was not vitally interesting from one point or another.

'Please see the bearer of this note,' the brief message ran, 'though I doubt if even you can do much to help him,'

John Silence paused a moment, so as to gather from the mind of the writer all that lay behind the brief words of the letter. Then he looked up at his servant with a graver expression than he had yet worn.

'Go back and find this gentleman,' he said, 'and show him into the green study. Do not reply to his question, or speak more than actually necessary; but think kind, helpful, sympathetic thoughts as strongly as you can, Barker. Your remember what I told you about the importance of thinking, when I engaged you. Put curiosity out of your mind, and think gently, sympathetically, affectionately, if you can.'

He smiled, and Barker, who had recovered his composure in the doctor's presence, bowed silently and went out.

There were two different reception rooms in Dr. Silence's house. One, intended for persons who imagined they needed spiritual assistance when really they were only candidates for the asylum, had padded walls, and was well supplied with various concealed contrivances by means of which sudden violence could be instantly met and overcome. It was, however, rarely used. The other, intended for the reception of genuine cases of spiritual distress and out-fo-the-way afflictions of a psychic nature, was entirely draped and furnished in a soothing deep green, calculated to induce calmness and repose of mind. And this room was the one in which Dr. Silence interviewed the majority of his 'queer' cases, and the one into which he had directed Barker to show his present caller.

To begin with, the arm-chair in which the patient was always directed to sit, was nailed to the floor, since its immovability tended to impart this same excellent characteristic to the occupant. Patients invariably grew excited when talking about themselves, and their excitement tended to confuse their thoughts and to exaggerate their language. The immobility of the chair helped to counteract this. After repeated endeavours to drag it forward, or push it back, they ended by resigning themselves to sitting quietly. And with the futility of fidgeting there followed a calmer state of mind.

Upon the floor, and at intervals in the wall immediately behind, were certain tiny green buttons, practically unnoticeable, which on being pressed permitted a soothing and persuasive narcotic to rise invisibly about the occupant of the chair. The effect upon the excitable patient was rapid, admirable, and harmless. The green study was further provided with a secret spy-hole; for John Silence liked when possible to observe his patient's face before it had assumed that mask the features of the human countenance invariably wear in the presence of another person. A man sitting alone wears a psychic expression; and this expression is the man himself. It disappears the moment another person joins him. And Dr. Silence often learned more from a few moments' secret observation of a face than from hours of conversation with its owner afterwards.

A very light, almost a dancing step followed Barker's heavy tread towards the green room, and a moment afterwards the man came in and announced that the gentleman was waiting. He was still pale and his manner nervous.

'Never mind, Barker,' the doctor said kindly; 'if you were not intuitive the man would have had no effect upon you at all. You only need training and development. And when you have learned to interpret these feelings and sensations better, you will feel no fear, but only a great sympathy.'

'Yes, sir; thank you sir!' And Barker bowed and made his escape, while Dr. Silence, an amused smile lurking about the corners of his mouth, made his way noiselessly down the passage and put his eye to the spy-hole in the door of the green study.

This spy-hole was so placed that it commanded a view of almost the entire room, and, looking through it, the doctor saw a hat, gloves, and umbrella lying on a chair by the table, but searched at first in vain for their owner.

The windows were both closed and a brisk fire burned in the grate. There were various signs—signs intelligible at least to a keenly intuitive soul—that the room was occupied, yet so far as human beings were concerned, it seemed undeniably empty. No one sat in the chairs; no one stood on the mat before the fire; there was no sign even that a patient was anywhere close against the wall, examining the Böcklin reproduction—as patients so often did when they thought they were alone—and therefore rather difficult to see from the spy-hole. Ordinarily speaking, there was no one in the room. It was unoccupied.

Yet Dr. Silence was quite well aware that a human being *was* in the room. His sensitive system never failed to let him know the proximity of an incarnate or discarnate being. Even in the dark he could tall that. And he now knew positively that his patient, the patient who had alarmed Barker, and had then tripped down the corridor with that dancing footstep—was somewhere concealed within the four walls commanded by his spy-hole. He also realised—and this was most unusual—that this individual whom he desired to watch knew that he was being watched. And, further, that the stranger himself was also watching in his turn. In fact, that it was he, the doctor, who was being observed—and by an observer as keen and trained as himself.

An inkling of the true state of the case began to dawn upon him, and he was on the verge of entering—indeed, his hand already touched the door-knob—when his eye, still glued to the spy-hole, detected a slight movement. Directly oppostite, between him and the fireplace, something stirred. He watched very attentively and made certain that he was not mistaken. An object on the mantelpiece—it was a blue vase—disappeared from view. It passed out of sight together with the portion of the marble mantelpiece on which it rested. Next, that part of the fire and grate and brass fender immediately below, it vanished entirely, as though a slice had been taken clean out of them.

Dr. Silence then understood that something between him and these objects was slowly coming into being, something that concealed them and obstructed his vision by inserting itself in the line of sight between them and himself.

He quietly awaited further results before going in.

First he saw a thim perpendicular line tracing itself from just above the height of the clock and continuing downwards till it reached the woolly fire-mat. This line grew wider, broadened, grew solid. It was no shadow; it was something substantial. It defined itself more and more. Then suddenly, at the top of the line, and about on a level with the face of the clock, he saw a small luminous disc gazing steadily at him. It was a human eye, looking straight into his own, pressed there against the spy-hole. And it was bright with intelligence. Dr. Silence held his breath for a moment—and stared back at it.

Then, like someone moving out of deep shadow into light, he saw the figure of a man come sliding sideways into view, a whitish face following the eye, and the perpendicular line he had first observed broadening out and developing into the complete figure of a human being. It was the patient. He had apparently been standing there in front of the fire all the time. A second eye had followed the first, and both of them stared steadily at the spy-hole, sharply concentrated, yet with a sly

384

twinkle of humour and amusement that made it impossible for the doctor to maintain his position any longer.

He opened the door and went in quickly. As he did so he noticed for the first time the sound of a German band coming in noisily through the open ventilators. In some intuitive, unaccountable fashion the music connected itself with the patient he was about to interview. This sort of prevision was not unfamiliar to him. It always explained itself later.

The man, he saw, was of middle age and of very ordinary appearance; so ordinary, in fact, that he was difficult to describe —his only peculiarity being his extreme thinness. Pleasant— that is, good—vibrations issued from his atmosphere and met Dr. Silence as he advanced to greet him, yet vibrations alive with currents and discharges betraying the perturbed and disordered condition of his mind and brain. There was evidently something wholly out of the usual in the state of his thoughts. Yet, though strange, it was not altogether distressing; it was not the impression that the broken and violent atmosphere of the insane produces upon the mind. Dr. Silence realised in a flash that here was a case of absorbing interest that might require all his powers to handle properly.

'I was watching you through my little peep-hole—as you saw,' he began, with a pleasant smile, advancing to shake hands. 'I find it of the graetest assistance sometimes——'

But the patient interrupted him at once. His voice was hurried and had odd, shrill changes in it, breaking from high to low in unexpected fashion. One moment it thundered, the next it almost squeaked.

'I understand without explanation,' he broke in rapidly. 'You get the true note of a man in that way—when he thinks himself unobserved. I quite agree. Only, in my case, I fear, you saw very little. My case, as you of course grasp, Dr. Silence, is extremely peculiar, uncomfortably peculiar. Indeed, unless Sir William had positively assured me——'

'My friend has sent you to me,' the doctor interrupted grave- ly, with a gentle note of authority, 'and that is quite sufficient. Pray, be seated, Mr.——'

'Mudge—Racine Mudge,' returned the other.

'Take this comfortable one, Mr. Mudge,' leading him to
the fixed chair, 'and tell me your condition in your own way
and at your own pace. My whole day is at your service if
you require it.'

Mr. Mudge moved towards the chair in question and then
hesitated.

'You will promise me not to use the narcotic buttons,' he
said, before sitting down. 'I do not need them. Also I ought
to mention that anything you think of vividly will reach my
mind. That is apparently part of my peculiar case.' He sat
down with a sigh and arranged his thin legs and body into
a position of comfort. Evidently he was very sensitive to the
thoughts of others, for the picture of the green buttons had
only entered the doctor's mind for a second, yet the other had
instantly snapped it up. Dr. Silence noticed, too that Mr.
Mudge held on tightly with both hands to the arms of the chair.

'I'm rather glad the chair is nailed to the floor,' he remarked,
as he settled himself more comfortably. 'It suits me admirably.
The fact is—and this is my case in a nutshell—which is all
that a doctor of your marvellous development requires—the
fact is, Dr. Silence, I am a victim of Higher Space. That's
what's the matter with me—Higher Space!'

The two looked at each other for a space in silence, the
little patient holding tightly to the arms of the chair which
'suited him admirably', and looking up with staring eyes,
his atmosphere positively trembling with the waves of some
unknown activity; while the doctor smiled kindly and sympathetically, and put his whole person as far as possible into
the mental condition of the other.

'Higher Space,' repeated Mr. Mudge, 'that's what it is.
Now, do you think you can help me with *that*?'

There was a pause during which the men's eyes steadily
searched down below the surface of their respective personalities.
Then Dr. Silence spoke.

'I am quite sure I can help,' he answered quietly; 'sympathy
must always help, and suffering always claims my sympathy.

I see you have suffered cruelly. You must tell me all about your case, and when I hear the gradual steps by which you reached this strange condition, I have no doubt I can be of assistance to you.'

He drew a chair up beside his interlocutor and laid a hand on his shoulder for a moment. His whole being radiated kindness, intelligence, desire to help.

'For instance,' he went on, 'I feel sure it was the result of no mere chance that you became familiar with the terrors of what you term Higher Space; for higher space is no mere external measurement. It is, of course, a spiritual state, a spiritual condition, an inner development, and one that we must recognise as abnormal, since it is beyond the reach of the senses at the present stage of evolution. Higher Space is a mystical state.'

'Oh!' cried the other, rubbing his birdlike hands with pleasure, 'the relief it is to me to talk to someone who can understand! Of course what you say is the utter truth. And you are right that no mere chance led me to my present condition, but, on the other hand, prolonged and deliberate study. Yet chance in a sense now governs it. I mean, my entering the condition of higher space seems to depend upon the chance of this and that circumstance.' He sighed and paused a moment. 'For instance,' he continued, starting, 'the mere sound of that German band sent me off. Not that all music will do so, but certain sounds, certain vibrations, at once key me up to the requisite pitch, and off I go. Wagner's music always does it, and that band must have been playing a stray bit of Wagner. But I'll come to all that later. Only, first'—he smiled deprecatingly— 'I must ask you to send away your man from the spy-hole.'

John Silence looked up with a start, for Mr. Mudge's back was to the door, and there was no mirror. He saw the brown eye of Barker glued to the little circle of glass, and he crossed the room without a word and snapped down the black shutter provided for the purpose, and then heard Barker shuffle away along the passage.

'Now,' continued the little man in the chair, 'I can go on.

You have managed to put me completely at my ease, and I feel I may tell you my whole case without shame or reserve. You will understand. But you must be patient with me if I go into details that are already familiar to you—details of higher space, I mean—and if I seem stupid when I have to describe things that transcend the power of language and are really therefore indescribable.'

'My dear friend,' put in the other calmly, 'that goes without saying. To know higher space is an experience that defies description, and one is obliged to make use of more or less intelligible symbols. But, pray, proceed. Your vivid thoughts will tell me more than your halting words.'

An immense sigh of relief proceeded from the little figure half lost in the depths of the chair. Such intelligent sympathy meeting him half-way was a new experience, and it touched his heart at once. He leaned back, relaxing his tight hold of the arms, and began in his thin, scale-like voice.

'My mother was a Frenchwoman, and my father an Essex bargeman,' he said abruptly. 'Hence my name—Racine and Mudge. My father died before I ever saw him. My mother inherited money from her Bordeaux relations, and when she died soon after, I was left alone with wealth and a strange freedom. I had no guardian, trustees, sisters, brothers, or any connection in the world to look after me. I grew up, therefore, utterly without education. This much was to my advantage; I learned none of that deceitful rubbish taught in schools, and so had nothing to unlearn when I awakened to my true love—mathematics, higher mathematics and higher geometry. These, however, I seemed to know instinctively. It was like the memory of what I had deeply studied before; the principles were in my blood, and I simply raced through the ordinary stages, and beyond, and then did the same with geometry. Afterwards, when I read the books on these subjects, I understood how swift and undeviating the knowledge had come back to me. It was simply memory. It was simply re-collecting the memories of what I had known before in a previous existence and required no books to teach me.'

In his growing excitement, Mr. Mudge attempted to drag the chair forward a little nearer to his listener, and then smiled faintly as he resigned himself instantly again to its immobility, and plunged anew into the recital of his singular 'disease'.

'The audacious speculations of Bolyai, the amazing theories of Gauss—that through a point more than *one* line could be drawn parallel to a given line; the possibility that the angles of a triangle are together *greater* than two right angles, if drawn upon immense curvatures—the breathless intuitions of Beltrami and Lobatchewsky—all these I hurried through, and emerged, panting but unsatisfied, upon the verge of my—my world, my higher space possibilities—in a word, my disease!

'How I got there,' he resumed after a brief pause, during which he appeared to be listening nervously for an approaching sound, 'is more than I can put intelligibly into words. I can only hope to leave your mind with an intuitive comprehension of the possibility of what I say.

'Here, however, came a change. At this point I was no longer absorbing the fruits of studies I had made before; it was the beginning of new efforts to learn for the first time, and I had to go slowly and laboriously through terrible work.   Here I sought for the theories and speculations of others.   But books were few and far between, and with the exception of one man—a "dreamer," the world called him—whose audacity and piercing intuition amazed and delighted me beyond description, I found no one to guide or help.

'You, of course, Dr. Silence, understand something of what I am driving at with these stammering words, though you cannot perhaps yet guess what depths of pain my new knowledge brought me to, nor why an acquaintance with a new dimension of space should prove a source of misery and terror.'

Mr. Racine Mudge, remembering that the chair would not move, did the next best thing he could in his desire to draw nearer to the attentive man facing him, and sat forward upon the very edge of the cushions, crossing his legs and gesticulating with both hands as though he saw into this region of new space he was attempting to describe, and might any moment tumble into it bodily from the edge of the chair and disappear from view. John Silence, separated from him by three paces, sat with his eyes fixed upon the thin white face opposite, noting every word and every gesture with deep attention.

'This room we now sit in, Dr. Silence, has one side open to space—to higher space. A closed box only *seems* closed. There is a way in and out of a soap bubble without breaking the skin.'

'You tell me no new thing,' the doctor interposed gently.

'Hence, if higher space exists and our world borders upon it and lies partially in it, if follows necessarily that we see only portions of all objects. We never see their true and complete shape. We see three measurements, but not their fourth. The new direction is concealed from us, and when I hold this book and move my hand all round it I have not really made a complete circuit. We only perceive those portions of any object which exist in our three dimensions, the rest escapes us. But, once learn to see in higher space, and objects will appear as they actually are. Only they will thus be hardly recognisable!

'Now you may begin to grasp something of what I am coming to.'

'I am beginning to understand something of what you must have suffered,' observed the doctor soothingly, 'for I have made similar experiments myself, and only stopped just in time——'

'You are the one man in all the world who can understand, *and* sympathise,' exclaimed Mr. Mudge, grasping his hand and holding it tightly while he spoke. The nailed chair prevented further excitability.

'Well,' he resumed, after a moments' pause, 'I procured the implements and the coloured blocks for practical experiment, and I followed the instructions carefully till I had arrived at an imaginative conception of four dimensional space. The tessaract, the figure whose boundaries are cubes, I knew by heart. That is to say, I knew it and saw it mentally, for my eye, of course, could never take in a new measurement, nor my hands and feet handle it.

'So, at least, I thought,' he added, making a wry face. 'I had reached the stage, you see, when I could *imagine* in a new dimension. I was able to conceive the shape of that new figure which is instrinsically different to all we know—the shape of the tessaract. I could perceive in four dimensions. When, therefore, I looked at a cube I could see all its sides at once. Its top was not foreshortened, nor its farther side and base invisible. I saw the whole thing out flat, so to speak. Moreover, I also saw its content—its in-sides.'

'You were not yourself able to enter this new world?' interrupted Dr. Silence.

'Not then. I was only able to conceive intuitively what it was like and how exactly it must look. Later, when I slipped in there and saw objects in their entirety, unlimited by the paucity of our poor three measurements, I very nearly lost my life. For, you see, space does not stop at a single new dimension, a fourth. It extends in all possible new ones, and we must conceive it as containing any number of new dimensions. In other words, there is no space at all, but only a condition. But, meanwhile, I had come to grasp the strange fact that the objects in our normal world appear to us only partially.'

Mr. Mudge moved farther forward till he was balanced dangerously on the very edge of the chair. 'From this starting point,' he resumed, 'I began my studies and experiments, and continued them for years. I had money, and I was without friends. I lived in solitude and experimented. My intellect, of course, had little part in the work, for intellectually it was all unthinkable. Never was the limitation of mere reason more plainly demonstrated. It was mystically, intuitively, spiritually that I began to advance. And what I learnt, and knew, and did is all impossible to put into language, since it describes experiences transcending the experiences of men. It is only some of the results—what you would call the symptoms of my disease—that I can give you, and even these must often appear absurd contradictions and impossible paradoxes.

'I can only tell you, Dr. Silence'—his manner became grave

suddenly—'that I reached sometimes a point of view whence all the great puzzles of the world became plain to me, and I understood what they call in the Yoga books "The Great Heresy of Separateness"; why all great teachers have urged the necessity of man loving his neighbour as himself; how men are all really *one*; and why the utter loss of self is necessary to salvation and the discovery of the true life of the soul.'

He paused a moment and drew breath.

'Your speculations have been my own long ago,' the doctor said quietly. 'I fully realise the force of your words. Men are doubtless not separate at all—in the sense they imagine.'

'All this about the very much higher space I only dimly, very dimly conceived, of course,' the other went on, raising his voice again by jerks; 'but what did happen to me was the humbler accident of—the simpler disaster—oh dear, how shall I put it——?'

He stammered and showed visible signs of distress.

'It was simply this,' he resumed with a sudden rush of words, 'that, accidentally, as the result of my years of experiment, I one day slipped bodily into the next world, the world of four dimensions, yet without knowing precisely how I got there, or how I could get back again. I discovered, that is, that my ordinary three-dimensional body was but an expression—a partial projection—of my higher four-dimensional body!

'Now you understand what I meant much earlier in our talk when I spoke of chance. I cannot control my entrance or exit. Certain people, certain human atmospheres, certain wandering forces, thoughts, desires even—the radiations of certain combinations of colour, and above all, the vibrations of certain kinds of music, will suddenly throw me into a state of what I can only describe as an intense and terrific inner vibration—and behold I am off! Off in the direction at right angles to all our known directions! Off in the direction the cube takes when it begins to trace the outlines of the new figure, the tessaract! Off into my breathless and semi-divine higher space! Off, *inside myself*, into the world of four dimensions!'

He gasped and dropped back into the depths of the immovable chair.

'And there,' he whispered, his voice issuing from among the cushions, 'there I have to stay until these vibrations subside, or until they do something which I cannot find words to describe properly or intelligibly to you —and then, behold, I am back again. First, that is, I disappear. Then I reappear. Only,' — he sighed — 'I cannot control my entrance nor my exit.'

'Just so,' exclaimed Dr. Silence, 'and that is why a few——'

'Why a few moments ago,' interrupted Mr. Mudge, taking the words out of his mouth, 'you found me gone, and then saw me return. The music of that wretched German band sent me off. Your intense thinking about me brought me back—when the band had stopped its Wagner. I saw you approach the peep-hole and I saw Barker's intention of doing so later. For me no interiors are hidden. I see inside. When in that state the content of your mind, as of your body, is open to me as the day. Oh dear, oh dear, oh dear!'

Mr. Mudge stopped and mopped his brow. A light trembling ran over the surface of his small body like wind over grass. He still held tightly to the arms of the chair.

'At first,' he presently resumed, 'my new experiences were so vividly interesting that I felt no alarm. There was no room for it. The alarm came a little later.'

'Then you actually penetrated far enough into that state to experience youself as a normal portion of it?' asked the doctor, leaning forward, deeply interested.

Mr. Mudge nodded a perspiring face in reply.

'I did,' he whispered, 'undoubtedly I did. I am coming to all that. It began first at night, when I realised that sleep brought no loss of consciousness——'

'The spirit, of couse, can never sleep. Only the body becomes unconscious,' interposed John Silence.

'Yes, we know that—theoretically. At night, of course, the spirit is active elsewhere, and we have no memory of where and how, simply because the brain stays behind and receives no record. But I found the, while remaining conscious,

393

I also retained memory. I had attained to the state of continuous consciousness, for at night regularly, with the first approaches of drowsiness, I entered *nolens volens* the four dimensional world.

'For a time this happened frequently, and I could not control it; though later I found a way to regulate it better. Apparently sleep is unnecessary in the higher—the four dimensional—body. Yes, perhaps. But I should infinitely have preferred dull sleep to the knowledge. For, unable to control my movements, I wandered to and fro, attracted owing to my partial development and premature arrival, to parts of this new world that alarmed me more and more. It was the awful waste and drift of a monstrous world, so utterly different to all we know and see that I cannot even hint at the nature of the sights and objects and beings in it. More than that, I cannot even remember them. I cannot now picture them to myself even, but can recall only the *memory of the impression* they made upon me, the horror and devastating terror of it all. To be in several places at once, for instance——'

'Perfectly,' interrupted John Silence, noticing the increase of the other's excitement, 'I understand exactly. But now, please, tell me a little more of this alarm you experienced, and how it affected you.'

'It's not the disappearing and reappearing *per se* that I mind,' continued Mr. Mudge, 'so much as certain other things. It's seeing people and objects in their weird entirety, in their true and complete shapes, that is so distressing. It introduced me to a world of monsters. Horses, dogs, cats, all of which I loved; people, trees, children; all that I have considered beautiful in life—everything, from a human face to a cathedral—appear to me in a different shape and aspect to all I have known before. Instead of seeing their partial expression in three dimensions, I saw them complete—in four. I cannot perhaps convince you why this should be terrible, but I assure you that it is so. To hear the human voice proceeding from this novel appearance which I scarcely recognise as a human body is ghastly, simply ghastly. To see inside everything and everybody is a form of insight peculiarly distressing. To be so confused in geography as to find myself one moment at the North Pole, and the next at Clapham Junction—or possibly at both places simultaneously—is absurdly terrifying. Your imagination will readily furnish other details without my multiplying my experiences now. But you have no idea what it all means, and how I suffer.'

Mr. Mudge paused in his panting account and lay back in his chair. He still held tightly to the arms as though they could keep him in the world of sanity and three measurements, and only now and again released his left hand in order to mop his face. He looked very thin and white and oddly unsubstantial, and he stared about him as though he saw into this other space he had been talking about.

John Silence, too, felt warm. He had listened to every word and had made many notes. The presence of this man had an exhilarating effect upon him. It seemed as if Mr. Racine Mudge still carried about with him something of that breathless higher-space condition he had been describing. At any rate, Dr. Silence had himself advanced sufficiently far to realise that the visions of this extraordinary little person had a basis of truth for their origin.

After a pause that prolonged itself into minutes, he crossed the room and unlocked a drawer in a bookcase, taking out a small book with a red cover. It had a lock to it, and he produced a key out of his pocket and proceeded to open the covers. The bright eyes of Mr. Mudge never left him for a single second.

'It almost seems a pity,' he said at length, 'to cure you, Mr. Mudge. You are on the way to discovery of great things. Though you may lose your life in the process—that is, your life here in the world of three dimensions—you would lose thereby nothing of great value—you will pardon my apparent rudeness, I know—and you might gain what is infinitely greater. Your suffering, of course, lies in the fact that you alternate between the two worlds and are never wholly in one or the other. Also, I rather imagine, though I cannot be certain of this from any personal experiments, that you have here and there penetrated even into space of more than four dimensions, and have hence experienced the terror you speak of.'

The perspiring son of the Essex bargeman and the woman of Normandy bent his head several times in assent, but uttered no word in reply.

'Some strange psychic predisposition, dating no doubt from one of your former lives, has favoured the development of your "disease"; and the fact that you had no normal training at school or college, no leading by the poor intellect into the culs-de-sac falsely called knowledge, has further caused your exceedingly rapid movement along the lines of direct inner experience. None of the knowledge you have foreshadowed has come to you through the senses, of course.'

Mr. Mudge, sitting in his immovable chair, began to tremble slightly. A wind again seemed to pass over his surface and again to set it curiously in motion like a field of grass.

'You are merely talking to gain time,' he said hurriedly, in a shaking voice. 'This thinking aloud delays us. I see ahead what you are coming to, only please be quick, for something is going to happen. A band is again coming down the street, and if it plays—if it plays Wagner—I shall be off in a twinkling.'

'Precisely. I will be quick. I was leading up to the point of how to effect your cure. The way is this: You must simply learn to block the entrances—prevent the *centres* acting.'

'True, true utterly true!' exclaimed the little man, dodging about nervously in the depths of the chair. 'But how, in the name of space, can that be done?'

'By concentration. They are all within you, these centres, although outer causes such as colour, music and other things lead you towards them. These external things you cannot hope to destroy, but once the entrances are blocked, they will lead you only to bricked walls and closed channels. You will no longer be able to find the way.'

'Quick, quick!' cried the bobbing figure in the chair. 'How is this concentration to be effected?'

'This little book,' continued Dr. Silence calmly, 'will explain to you the way.' He tapped the cover. 'Let me now read out to you certain simple instructions, composed, as I see you divine, entirely from my own personal experiences in the same direction. Follow these instructions and you will no longer enter the state of higher space. The entrances will be blocked effectively.'

Mr. Mudge sat bolt upright in his chair to listen, and John Silence cleared his throat and began to read slowly in a very distinct voice.

But before he had uttered a dozen words, something happened. A sound of street music entered the room through the open ventilators, for a band had begun to play in the stable mews at the back of the house—the March from *Tannhäuser*. Odd as it may seem that a German band should twice within the space of an hour enter the same mews and play Wagner, it was nevertheless the fact.

Mr. Racine Mudge heard it. He uttered a sharp, squeaking cry and twisted his arms with nervous energy round the chair. A piteous look that was not far from tears spread over his white face. Grey shadows followed it—the grey of fear. He began to struggle convulsively.

'Hold me fast! Catch me! For God's sake, keep me here! I'm on the rush already. Oh, it's frightful!' he cried in tones of anguish, his voice as thin as a reed.

Dr. Silence made a plunge forward to seize him, but in a flash, before he could cover the space between them, Mr. Racine Mudge, screaming and struggling, seemed to shoot past him into invisibility. He disappeared like an arrow from a bow propelled at infinite speed, and his voice no longer sounded in the external air, but seemed in some curious way to make itself heard somewhere within the depths of the doctor's own being. It was almost like a faint singing cry in his head, like a voice of dream, a voice of vision and unreality.

'Alcohol, alcohol!' it cried faintly, with distance in it, 'give me alcohol! It's the quickest way. Alcohol, before I'm out of reach!'

The doctor, accustomed to rapid decisions and even more rapid action, remembered that a brandy flask stood upon the mantelpiece, and in less than a second he had seized it and was holding it out towards the space above the chair recently occupied by the visible Mudge. But, before his very eyes, and long ere he could unscrew the metal stopper, he saw the contents of the closed glass phial sink and lessen as though someone were drinking violently and greedily of the liquor within.

'Thanks! Enough! It deadens the vibrations!' cried the faint voice in his interior, as he withdrew the flask and set it back upon the mantelpiece. He understood that in Mudge's present condition one side of the flask was open to space and he could drink without removing the stopper. He could hardly have had a more interesting proof of what he had been hearing described at such length.

But the next moment—the very same moment it almost seemed—the German band stopped midway in its tune—and there was Mr. Mudge back in his chair again, gasping and panting!

'Quick!' he shrieked, 'stop that band! Send it away! Catch hold of me! Block the entrances! Block the entrances! Give me the red book! Oh, oh, oh-h-h-h!!!'

The music had begun again. It was merely a temporary interruption. The *Tannhäuser* March started again, this time at a tremendous pace that made it sound like a rapid two-step, as though the instruments played against time

But the brief interruption gave Dr. Silence a moment in which to collect his scattering thoughts, and before the band had got through half a bar, he had flung forward upon the chair and held Mr. Racine Mudge, the struggling little victim of Higher Space, in a grip of iron. His arms went all round his diminutive person, taking in a good part of the chair at the same time. He was not a big man, yet he seemed to smother Mudge completely.

Yet, even as he did so, and felt the wriggling form underneath him, it began to melt and slip away like air or water. The wood of the armchair somehow disentangled itself from between his own arms and those of Mudge. The phenomenon known as the passage of matter through matter took place. The little man seemed actually to be interfused with the other's being. Dr. Silence could just see his face beneath him. It puckered and grew dark as though from some great internal effort. He heard the thin, reedy voice crying his ear to 'Block the entrances, block the entrances!' and then—but how in the world describe what is indescribable?

John Silence half rose up to watch. Racine Mudge, his face distorted beyond all recognition, was making a marvellous inward movement, as though doubling back upon himself. He turned funnel-wise like water in a whirling vortex, and then appeared to break up somewhat as a reflection breaks up and divides in a distorting convex mirror. He went neither forward nor backward, neither to the right nor the left, neither up nor down. But he went. He went utterly. He simply flashed away out of sight like a vanishing projectile.

All but one leg! Dr. Silence just had the time and the presence of mind to seize upon the left ankle and boot as it disappeared, and to this he held on for several seconds like grim death. Yet all the time he knew it was a foolish and useless thing to do.

The foot was in his grasp one moment, and the next it seemed— this was the only way he could describe it—inside his own skin and bones, and at the same time outside his hand and all round it. It seemed mingled in some amazing way with his own flesh and blood. Then it was gone, and he was tightly grasping a mere draught of heated air.

'Gone! gone! gone!' cried a faint, whispering voice somewhere deep within his own consciousness. 'Lost! lost! lost!' it repeated, growing fainter and fainter till at length it vanished into nothing and the last signs of Mr. Racine Mudge vanished with it.

John Silence locked his red book and replaced it in the cabinet, which he fastened with a click, and when Barker answered the bell he inquired if Mr. Mudge had left a card upon the table. It appeared that he had, and when the servant returned with it, Dr. Silence read the address and made a note of it. It was in North London.

'Mr. Mudge has gone,' he said quietly to Barker, noticing his expression of alarm.

'He's not taken his 'at with him, sir.'

'Mr. Mudge requires no hat where he is now,' continued the doctor, stooping to poke the fire. 'But he may return for it——'

'And the humbrella, sir.'

'And the umbrella.'

'He didn't go out *my* way, sir, if you please,' stuttered the amazed servant, his curiosity overcoming his nervousness.

'Mr. Mudge has his own way of coming and going, and prefers it. If he returns by the door at any time remember to bring him instantly to me, and be kind and gentle with him and ask no questions. Also, remember, Barker, to think pleasantly, sympathetically, affectionately of him while he is away. Mr. Mudge is a very suffering gentleman.'

Barker bowed and went out of the room backwards, gasping and feeling round the inside of his collar with three very hot fingers of one hand.

It was two days later when he brought in a telegram to the study. Dr. Silence opened it, and read as follows:

'Bombay. Just slipped out again. All safe. Have blocked entrances. Thousand thanks. Address Cooks, London.—MUDGE.'

Dr. Silence looked up and saw Barker staring at him bewilderingly. It occurred to him that somehow he knew the contents of the telegram.

'Make a parcel of Mr. Mudge's things,' he said briefly, 'and address them Thomas Cook & Sons, Ludgate Circus. And send them there exactly a month from to-day, marked "To be called for." '

'Yes, sir,' said Barker, leaving the room with a deep sigh and a hurried glance at the waste-paper basket where his master had dropped the pink paper.